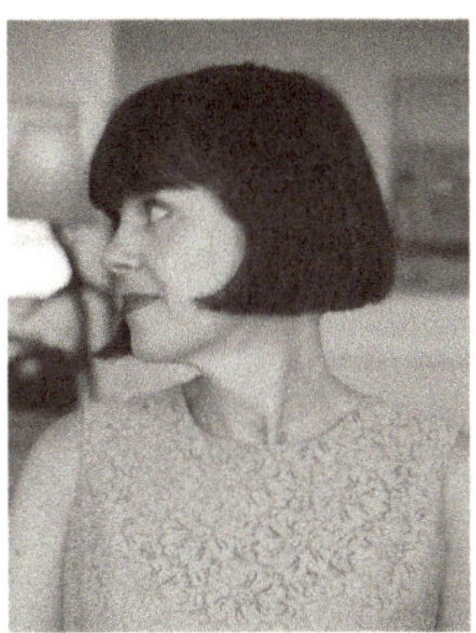

CATHERINE ROBERTSON'S novels have all been #1 New Zealand bestsellers. Her fourth novel, *The Hiding Places*, also won the 2015 Nelson Public Libraries' Award for NZ Fiction. Catherine reviews books for the *New Zealand Listener* and is a regular guest on Radio New Zealand's The Panel and Jesse Mulligan's Book Critic slot. She is married with two grown sons, two Burmese cats, two rescue dogs and a powerful vacuum cleaner. She divides her time between Wellington and Hawke's Bay.

CATHERINE ROBERTSON

Gabriel's Bay

BLACK SWAN

UK | USA | Canada | Ireland | Australia
India | New Zealand | South Africa | China

Black Swan is an imprint of the Penguin Random House group of companies,
whose addresses can be found at global.penguinrandomhouse.com.

First published by Penguin Random House New Zealand, 2018

1 3 5 7 9 10 8 6 4 2

Cover and text design by Rachel Clark © Penguin Random House New Zealand
Cover photograph by LCBallard/iStock
Author photograph © Matt Bialostocki
Prepress by Image Centre Group
Printed and bound in Australia by Griffin Press,
an Accredited ISO AS/NZS 14001 Environmental Management Systems Printer

A catalogue record for this book is available from the National Library of New Zealand.

ISBN 978-0-14-377145-6
eISBN 978-0-14377146-3

penguin.co.nz

To David, Callum and Finn, with love and gratitude.

To Bex, who's been looking forward to this book for ages.

And to Dave Dobbyn's song 'Loyal', because loyalty is what this book is all about.

Gabriel's Bay is an amalgam of several small New Zealand towns, so wherever you think it is, you'll be correct.

Prologue

the dog

The confidence with which the dog circuited the town — it stopped and checked before crossing roads and never hesitated about direction — might have led a casual observer to believe it would make an excellent guide for the blind. And indeed it would have, if the blind person had no other aim but to find food, and wasn't too fussed about quality or freshness.

The blind person would also have to be flexible about their intended destination. Not being stupid, the dog had a standard route for easy pickings — households that preferred flimsy bags to bins with tight lids, the back door of the bakery, where lazy workers took their time to dispose of old stock, and the front door of the takeaway, whose owner liked the dog and often saved snacks for it (yesterday, it had been a saveloy, which wasn't meat by the dog's definition, but was nonetheless delicious). The takeaway owner also liked to fondle the dog's ears and speak to it in a friendly tone. Unlike some other people; for example, those in households without bins, who preferred to yell what sounded like 'Gedardivit!' and hurl the nearest heavy item, usually a boot. The dog had developed an instinct for the wayward trajectory of boots, and had not been hit for months.

No, the dog wasn't stupid, but it was a dog, and as such was easily diverted from its standard route by interesting smells. This morning, the Master had got up early to go fishing and the dog had followed him to the beach, where it had sniffed out a long-dead fish-head and a pile of horse dung and rolled in both. Fortunately, by this time, the Master was already out on the boat, otherwise he might have chucked the dog in the sea. Or worse, marched it back home and blasted it with the hose. The dog hated the hose, but if the Master told it to sit, it sat. This was not just a dog thing; the Master had that effect on people, too. It could be because he was at least a metre taller and wider than anyone else, but then the Master's wife had exactly the same effect and she was only five feet four. However, the dog did not have the same devotion for the Mistress. She was immune to big, brown eyes and ingratiating grins, and thus never slipped it food under the table and told the Master not to, either. The Master obeyed but had been known to throw the dog off-cuts out the kitchen door of the beachfront restaurant that he owned. The Master's best human friend, Gene, called the dog a biological waste-disposal unit. 'Put your foot on its paw and its mouth opens,' he said. The dog was happy to be called anything if it came with scraps. The only name it refused to answer to was 'Comebackhereyoubastard'.

The dog pondered where to go next. The restaurant would be closed up because the Master was out fishing, and home was not an option until the dead fish and horse dung smell had faded, as the Mistress had been known to wield worse than the hose. It was also Sunday, which meant no access to the bakery and more people at home to keep an eye on their rubbish bags. The takeaway would not be open yet, but then again the owner might be cleaning or receiving a delivery. The dog headed off, knowing that the art of being a shameless opportunist was never to assume that any pathways to food were barred.

En route, it checked out the old factory that still smelled faintly of fish, and failed again to find an entrance. It marked its territory wherever it scented another dog, even though everyone knew whose town Gabriel's Bay was. A passing ute beeped at the dog in greeting — Sam, the young man with curly hair who was related to Gene. Sam and his friends often lit fires on the beach and sat around, drinking beer. Occasionally, they would feed the dog corn chips, but tended to keep the sausages and chops to themselves. Young men were unreasonably hungry in the dog's view. Children were much more generous. The Master and Mistress were friends with a lady called Sidney who helped out in the restaurant some nights. She had two boys who loved to play a game where they put a liver treat on the dog's paw and told it to wait for the command to eat. Fortunately, they had the attention span of hopping fleas and so the dog never had to wait long. It hoped the boys did not grow out of the game too soon. It also hoped they did not become more vigilant about where they left their half-eaten sandwiches, biscuits, carrot sticks and apple slices. Their raisins were safe, though. The dog did not like raisins.

Alas, the takeaway was closed and dark, but discarded at the foot of the rubbish bin outside was a box containing greasy chicken bones. The dog was not allowed chicken bones at home, so it ate these bones, and most of the box as well. Further along the footpath, outside the pub, there was a splatter containing mixed food items. It ate those, too.

Down the main street it went, checking bins, the gutter and the spaces between shops. Being a Sunday, not many people were about. Those who were hailed the dog as it passed. 'On a mission, I see,' they said. Or, 'Fat git.' The dog wagged its tail and carried on.

The end of the main street marked the end of the town. If the dog kept going, it would be in the countryside, and if it followed the road all the way, it would be up on the big bush-clad hill that stood between Gabriel's Bay and what his Master called the Big Smoke. The Master often took the dog into the bush when he went hunting deer, pigs and possum. The dog went off alone into the bush, too, though it was looking for animals that were already dead. Personally, it didn't care how dead, but from experience it knew that coming home reeking of rotting corpse was a sure-fire way to bring out the hose. Most times, the dog decided it was worth it.

The faintest scent in the air told the dog that, in fact, a deceased animal was lying further up along the road. The sun was high now and the dog was thirsty. It could turn around and head home. Or it could walk towards the smell and detour down to one of the many creeks that fed mountain water into the sea, or to a horse trough in a paddock that might also contain dung to roll in.

The dog wagged its tail and carried on.

Chapter 1

Kerry

At the airport, Kerry noticed a sign warning visitors to allow more time for their journeys on New Zealand roads. The sign included a picture of said roads, apparently drawn by a person with a partiality for Scalextric tracks made entirely from the curved parts.

'A blatant exaggeration' had been Kerry's thought then. Two days later, on the hill heading over to Gabriel's Bay, his thought was 'What the infernal hell?'

What kind of sadist had decided this was suitable for vehicles? Kerry had motored over mountain passes in Europe with fewer and more manageable bends. The streets of Mumbai had put less demand on his driving skills. He'd felt safer descending into the Grand Canyon on the back of a mule that insisted on walking right near the path's crumbling edge.

He considered pulling over for a breather, but on either side of the road was nothing but a tiny strip of gravel shrouded by forest that looked dense and unsettlingly primeval. Dinosaurs could indeed be dwelling within, happily unaware that they were supposed to have become extinct sixty-five million years ago.

That was probably why New Zealand had no snakes or tigers or, in fact, anything keen to poison and maim you. They'd all been killed off by something worse.

Get a grip, Kerry said to himself. New Zealand has no nasties because when the continents divided, its islands floated away carrying nothing but birds, leaving all the crocodiles, snakes and venomous hairy spiders in Australia, as if the two countries had made a bet and Australia had lost. Besides, it was too late for second thoughts. He was here now, and committed to a new job. He'd had his time to travel the world, put the past behind him, or at least in a place where it wouldn't catch his eye too often and double him over with shame. Eighteen months had passed since the wedding-that-wasn't. Seventeen months and twenty-three days, if you insisted. Seventeen months and twenty-three days trying to reclaim his sense of the man he was, the man he *should* be. Trying to make up for all those years of simply going along, unquestioning, sucked onwards in the slipstream of other people. Being, as Kerry reproached himself on an hourly basis, a twat.

The car's radio yelped back into life, and Kerry yelped right along with it. He'd bought the station wagon at a place called Cheap Cars, which could not be accused of over-promising. It was a Japanese import, a model called a Fielder, which to Kerry had sounded reliable and sporty, despite it being fifteen years old and in a condition that pushed the boundaries of the word 'used'. It was a necessarily no-frills purchase, as Kerry's funds had been reduced by months of travel interspersed with sporadic bouts of poorly paid employment. The car came with air-conditioning that had already stopped working and a dual air-bag that Kerry hoped had not, considering that a crash on this benighted hill had to be inevitable. The radio had first picked up a concert programme and then switched mid-Mahler to a Christian station, on which a father was earnestly explaining blasphemy to his child. Kerry had fiddled but found nothing but static or 'You know, Timmy, "gosh" is really just another way of saying "God" ', and then left it hissing white noise because the hill had begun and he needed two hands on the wheel and all his concentration.

When his nerves stopped jangling, Kerry recognised the radio was now playing 'Child in Time'. Deep Purple. Not the Christian station, then, thank Gosh. The song was a favourite of Kerry's for its anthemic quality and its showcasing of lead singer Ian Gillan's ability to wail. He was a fine wailer at the best of times, was Ian, but this was him at his virtuoso best. Just when you thought he'd hit his peak, he stepped it up a whole other octave.

And, Great Gosh Almighty! Here was the top of the hill! And what a view! As if ordered by Nature's generals to retreat, the forest on both sides thinned and dropped away, revealing a stretch of rolling green dotted with trees and wound through by a glint of river. Kerry could see across the river an old-fashioned bridge, miniature scale at this height, and in the cleft of distant hills a slice of sea, a shifting sparkle of light all that delineated it from the bright blue sky.

Down there, over the bridge and before the sea, was Gabriel's Bay. All the climbing was behind him, and the downward slope looked nowhere near as challenging. It helped that the forest had receded, though Kerry could see that the range continued along to his left, dark green and forbidding. The first settlers must surely have got to Gabriel's Bay by boat, thought Kerry. Where, if they'd been sensible, they'd have stayed until the invention of modern earth-moving machinery made hacking a road over this satanic mound a viable option.

He gave thanks that the Gabriel's Bay website proclaimed it a self-contained town, with a supermarket, two pubs, a petrol station and a doctor's surgery. With luck, he would never need the latter, but nice to know it was there.

The trusty Fielder descended like a champ, positively luge-like on the bends. The Deep Purple song was still going. It was over ten minutes long, Kerry recalled. DJs must love songs like that.

'Ahhh, ahhh, ahhh,' sang Ian, and Kerry sang right along with him.

The road finally began to flatten out, the scrub on either side now making way for fences and the occasional gravel driveway that led to some hardy person's farm. Kerry's Northern Irish ancestors had been landowners, wealthy ones back in the day, with a big house and race horses and undoubtedly their very own bunch of bog-cutting peasants to flog. That was his mother's line, the Irish Protestant Macfarlanes. Not to be confused with his father's line, the Scottish Catholic Macfarlanes, though most people did indeed find this highly confusing. Your parents have the same last name, they'd ask? Kerry would confirm this, and if he didn't know the person well, see if he could get a laugh by adding that it was the only thing his parents had in common. He could only try this with strangers because it was entirely untrue. After thirty-five years of marriage, Kerry's parents were as much in love as ever. Perhaps that's what is wrong with me, thought Kerry. I've been a gooseberry all of my life.

No. He knew his parents loved their only son dearly. That's why it hurt so much that he'd let them down.

He passed a driveway with stone pillars and a sign — Something Wines. A vineyard? That might be nice on a sunny afternoon. Kerry wondered how strict the Gabriel's Bay policepersons were about drink driving. He made a mental note to ask around first before putting it to the test.

Ian was in the final throes. A last series of wails before the jangling guitar and drum finale.

'Ahhh—'

'ARGHH!!!'

The Fielder's brakes juddered, tyres crunching on the loose chip-seal and Kerry held hard on to the steering wheel as the car skewed to a halt.

'What was *that*!' he yelled to the world.

Whatever it was it had gone. He'd seen a movement in the scrub to his left and then a creature had dashed out across the road, right in front of him, and disappeared into the scrub on his right.

He could not identify the creature other than to say it was brown, shaggy and barrel-like. A pig? A short-legged cow? Some kind of squat, round, hairy deer?

'Jaysus, me fecking heart,' as his mother, Bronagh, would have said, even though she'd lived all her life in north-east London. His father, Douglas, being a school science teacher, would have gone online immediately to Google 'hairy brown wild animals of New Zealand' and scrolled through the options until he'd found it.

The radio station was now playing 'Barracuda' by Heart. Its throbbing guitar beat wasn't helping Kerry's own heart adjust to normal, but he decided it was at a safe enough level to put the Fielder into first and drive on.

At least he was nearly there. Five minutes tops, he reckoned. How many other tests could the place possibly throw at him?

He arrived at the bridge. It was, as it had looked from a distance, the old-fashioned span kind. It was also one lane. The road on the other side went up and directly around a bend. You couldn't see what was coming. However, a sign with red and black arrows seemed to indicate that he had the right of way, so on he went, slowly.

Round the bend, at speed, came an ancient bus. As Kerry was now two-thirds of the way across the bridge, who had the right of way seemed irrelevant and he assumed the bus would stop. It didn't. Well, it did, but not until it was right in front of him, a manoeuvre which obviously forced him to stop also. A woman was driving. Mid-fifties, round face, masses of brown curls pulled back in a rough ponytail. She waved at him in a manner that could be taken as friendly but probably wasn't, and then sat there, the bus chugging on idle, wobbling gently. Kerry caught a shadowy glimpse of passengers' heads craning into the aisle, the better to see what was going on.

What was going on, of course, was that he was now reversing, the bus trundling in pursuit, like a circus elephant nudging a ball. He backed up all the way to the start of the bridge and circled onto the gravel shoulder to let the bus pass.

As it did, the woman gave him another wave. Either that or she was swatting away a fly. Kerry saw the passengers' heads turn now towards the bus's rear window, as if intent on memorising the face of the idiot who'd held them up.

Please God, thought Kerry, let that be the bad luck trio over and done with. He knew that he'd made mistakes in his life, but still, this seemed excessive. He'd started this car journey aged thirty-two, and would not be surprised if the rear-vision mirror showed his hair now to be completely white.

God was listening. That, or His attention had been diverted. Kerry only cared that the next ten minutes of driving were bus-, creature- and hill-free. And that having played 'The Ballroom Blitz' by The Sweet, 'Kashmir' by Led Zeppelin and now 'Aqualung' by Jethro Tull, with no ads in between, the radio station was shaping up to be the greatest in the known universe.

Gabriel's Bay. There was the sign. Here *he* was. He'd made it.

He couldn't stop, though. The place of his employment was a house a mile past the outskirts. The job was live-in, and he'd been asked to check in, as it were, the day before he was officially due to start, to give him time to settle into his accommodation. Kerry hoped for something comfortable, but after travels where his beds had included railway station benches, a goat shed filled with goats, and a giant sack of rice, he would be perfectly happy with a wooden board. There was still half an hour before his agreed arrival time, but he should keep moving, just in case. Would not do to be tardy.

He drove through the town slowly, to gain some impression of what would, all going well, be his home for the next six months. He hadn't told his new employer he only intended to give it six months because he might not. He might like it here. He might be able to build a whole new, improved life here around a whole new, improved him.

Gabriel's Bay was small. No doubt about that. The quantity of housing suggested perhaps a few thousand people. There was only one main street, and it was as long as the average pedestrian crossing in London. It was Sunday afternoon, which he hoped explained the emptiness. The number of inhabitants he did spot could have fitted in the Fielder, if they didn't mind a bit of a squash in the back. They seemed ordinary enough, not well-heeled, but not underpass-dwelling scruffy. No one stared at him with the cold eyes of those whose plans for strangers involve banjos and squealing.

Architecturally, the town looked a little like someone had built a set for a Western movie and then, over the years, as parts had fallen down, replaced the wooden buildings with concrete boxes, each with one window and a sliding door. Kerry saw a takeaway, a pharmacy, several shops selling second-hand goods, a clothing store that looked as if it only let in customers aged eighty-five and over, and a lawnmower repair shop. There was a liquor store and what could be the pub, though it could also be condemned; one window was boarded up and the front door looked to have been struck by an axe. He did not see the petrol station or the supermarket, but there could be side streets he had missed. There could, in fact, be a whole other affluent side to Gabriel's Bay. Any town that has a winery close by couldn't be too badly off, surely?

On his right, at the end of the main street, a yellow sign's worn black letters spelled 'Beach'. The town website said the beach campground was so popular in summer that people were advised to book several months in advance. It was mid-October now, so summer was not far off. In London it was autumn, that season of mists and mellow fruitfulness and the ritual purchase of new gloves because you had stuffed your previous pair in the back of the sock drawer and now can only find one. Even though it was weeks off, Kerry's mother would be starting to get excited about Christmas. 'Whut is it with ye and baubles and yon infant in the hay?' said his father every year, to which his mother always replied, 'And this from a man who thinks the Pope fella can do magic.' Kerry hadn't spent last Christmas with his parents, having hightailed it overseas that April, a week after the wedding-that-wasn't. He doubted he'd spend this one with them, either; a nurse and a teacher's salary barely allowed for a weekend camping in The Witterings, let alone a plane trip to the other side of the world. Sometimes, he wondered if he'd ever go back home again.

Woodhall! The sign was so discreet he'd nearly missed it. That was the name of the house owned by his new employer. It sounded grand; *they* sounded grand. Meredith and Jonty Barton. If they were in England, the pair would almost certainly ride to hounds.

The sign was on the left of two white wooden gateposts that marked the start of a driveway covered in gravel. Civilised gravel, though, not the rutted, rough kind Kerry had seen on the farm driveways. This stuff had a hint of limestone, its dust fine and pale.

Kerry drove past English trees — oak, chestnut, sycamore, copper beech. One of those Edwardian-style curved-back wooden benches, painted white. Clumps of those small scented flowery jobs his mother liked — freesias? His father couldn't smell them at all. It was one of those genetic quirks, apparently, like being able to roll your tongue.

Kerry was no gardener, but he could see this one was well tended. Wouldn't win the avant-garde award at Chelsea, to be sure, but it was pleasant and serene.

And here was the house. Nice. Two-storey. Wooden. Painted white (there was a theme emerging here, Kerry thought) with pale blue trim. Bit of ornate fretwork on the upstairs balconies and the wide porch. Old-fashioned style that suggested inside he'd find worn Turkish carpets, Worcester tureens and paintings of dogs and ancestors.

The driveway ended in a wide circle that bordered a stretch of neatly clipped lawn. Kerry parked to one side, checked that he looked presentable in the rear-vision mirror. His hair was always unruly, not much he could do about that; slicking it down with what hairdressers called 'product' only made him look like he was auditioning for a rockabilly band. His shirt was new — bought for less than five quid in Bangkok — and his jeans, as long as he sat carefully, had no obvious holes. His shoes were the pair he'd bought for the wedding. He'd hesitated about bringing them, but they were the best shoes he'd ever owned. He'd abandoned the dove-grey morning suit as being of further use only if he decided to become a magician in Las Vegas.

A lime-chip path curved from the driveway through the lawn, ending at stippled concrete steps that ascended to the porch. The front door had a bronze knocker shaped like a lion's head. Kerry patted its head — 'Are you friendly?' — and brought the ring in its mouth down against the door with a bang that sounded shockingly loud in this quiet place.

Quick footsteps approaching, clunk of a lock, door opening to reveal a dark, wood-panelled entrance. A woman in front of him, in her sixties, neat white buttoned shirt, navy trousers, white curled hair in a layered cut.

'Yes?' Brisk, unfriendly.

'I'm, er, here for the home-help job. I'm Kerry Macfarlane.'

The woman's brown eyes widened. She was good-looking, Kerry thought. A beauty in her day, though, as his mother might remind him were she here, some women definitely improved as they got older.

'Don't be ridiculous,' she said. 'Kerry Macfarlane is a woman.'

'Ah. No. He's a he. He's me, in fact.'

'Kerry-Francis Macfarlane?'

He hoped his smile conveyed charm. 'The very one.'

Meredith Barton, for it must be she, folded her arms. 'In your correspondence, you gave me to believe you were a woman.'

Kerry tried to recall the emails he'd written to her. He'd pretended to have had a few different occupations over the years — usually when drunk and trying to pick up girls in pubs. And, true, he had once dressed in drag for a work party, but—

'I'm pretty sure I did not. Perhaps you—'

'You have a woman's name!' said his accuser.

'Well, no — Kerry is very much a boy's name in Ireland. And my Francis *is* spelled with an "i".'

'You're Irish?'

She made it sound a worse crime than pretending to be a woman. Kerry considered fudging his reply. But this place, this was where he planned to transform into the new, improved him — wasn't it?

'Half,' he said. 'Northern Ireland. Ulster. Though my mother's family moved before she was born to get away from all the sectarian hoo-ha. Which is ironic because she married a Catholic. From Aberdeen.'

'Your father is Catholic?'

'Semi-practising. A man of science, is my dad. He often finds those two things difficult to reconcile.'

'And your mother is, I assume, a Protestant?'

'Not much of one, I'm sure she wouldn't mind me saying. My parents aren't fans of organised religion. Organised anything, really. Having said that, my mother is a Yuletide fanatic and my father can be forcefully evangelical about model railways when you get him going. I myself sang in the school choir for a bit, so I'm reasonably au fait with the biblical ditties.'

Meredith Barton stared at him for an eternity and a half.

'Your father is a model-railway enthusiast?'

There seemed no earthly reason why she should have singled out that fact, but it was better than shutting the door in his face.

'He has a shed out in our back garden. More accurately, our back garden comprises of his shed and a strip of ill-fitting paving stones between it and the house. If I wanted a kick-around, I had to go to the nearest park with my ball and hope the big kids didn't steal it.'

Although her face made the Great Sphinx of Giza look spirited, there was clearly a flurry of activity occurring inside the cranium. Kerry crossed his fingers that the mental dice being thrown would come up double-six on his side.

'I'm sorry,' she said. 'This is not a suitable job for a man.'

And she began to shut the door in his face.

'No, wait!' Kerry prevented her by holding onto the door's edge. 'Please. I've come a very long way for this job. Across oceans, over a huge hill, a one-way bridge and everything.'

'You're not suitable,' she said again. 'I'm sorry.'

The old Kerry might have given up at that point. Accepted defeat and slunk off. But it was not his fault if this woman had hired him without ascertaining his gender. Or, come to think of it, without being too concerned that he had minimal experience . . .

'You had lots of other applicants, then?' he said.

A pause. Had he guessed correctly . . . ?

'I will advertise again.'

Bingo!

'But that may take weeks,' he said. 'And I'm right here, ready to start. I'm also very in touch with my feminine side. My father quite often refers to me as a big Jessie.'

Hesitation, but with a frown. She wasn't sold yet.

'Here's a suggestion,' he said. 'Why don't you try me out — say for a month, and if you think I'm pants, I'll go. No fuss, no bother.'

'Pants?'

'Rubbish. Condensed, I gather, from the original expression "a pile of pants".'

She pressed her lips together. In a manner more thoughtful than disapproving, Kerry was relieved to see.

'A month is quite some time,' she said.

'All right, how about two weeks?'

More hesitation. More frown.

'You can feel free to fire me at any time.'

Her shoulders sagged, which could be a sign that she'd decided it was simply easier to give in. By now, Kerry had no more fingers left to cross.

'Very well,' she said. 'A two-week trial. With the option to sever earlier if it isn't working.'

Yes! OK, so the situation was *entirely* tenuous, but it was better than living in the back of the Fielder until he found something else.

'Thank you.' He offered his hand to his new employer. 'You won't regret it.'

She took his hand. Her own was fine-boned but strong.

'Won't I?' she said. 'Well, that will make a nice change.'

Chapter 2

Bernard

'Meredith's helper arrives today.'

Bernard Weston regarded his wife over the top of *A Laodicean* by Thomas Hardy. Her speech perturbed him on two fronts. One: Sunday after lunch was his time for reading, and Patricia knew that he considered this a time of guaranteed peace. If she did not want to occupy herself in the garden or with some other domestic task, she was welcome to read with him, but there were to be no interruptions until she made a pot of tea for them both at four o'clock. And two: the mere mention of Meredith Barton's name plunged him into a bubbling witch-cauldron of emotion. Eye of regret, toe of shame.

He gave a curt nod, to make it obvious he did not wish to converse. But Patricia persisted.

'A young Englishwoman, apparently,' she said. 'Who's been travelling the world. Probably taking one of those gap years.'

She imbued the phrase with a wary admiration, as if in her mind a gap year were akin to the kind of adventure activity, bungy jumping for example, that required equal parts nerve and foolhardiness and, as such, was only to be attempted by the young.

Bernard and his wife were sixty-three, and their life together had been thus far free of physical exuberance. Unless dementia beset the pair of them, bungy jumps were not likely to feature in their golden years, either.

'I thought I would pop over later in the week,' Patricia continued. 'You see, I know she's been rather anxious about her decision to hire someone. That's why she's kept it so quiet — I suspect she only told *me* because I caught her just after she'd said yes. You know what Meredith's like. Even the Gestapo's finest would struggle to make her confess to being anything less than fully in control.'

Then she added, 'Would you like to come with me?'

An unusual request and not entirely welcome. While Patricia and he could not be said to lead separate lives, they certainly allowed each other space to pursue their own interests. He had his property portfolio, his books and his chairmanship of the Progressive Association, and Patricia had her garden, a book club, and volunteer work of some sort. She seemed also to pay social calls on a variety of female acquaintances, but had never before requested he accompany her. Why now, and why Meredith?

If Bernard had not been married to his wife for well over three decades, he might have suspected an ulterior motive. Once, a long time ago, Patricia had confessed to being jealous of Meredith. 'She's your Galatea,' had been her bitter accusation. 'Your peerless perfect woman.' He had denied it, but perhaps some resentment still lingered, and she felt a need now to test him once again?

But, no, her previous comments proved that while his own emotions might still bubble up, hers had faded to nought in the intervening decades. The two women were quite friendly now.

But not too friendly, fortunately. Despite living within only a few miles from her, Bernard had spent the last forty-six years keeping Meredith at a distance. He had no wish for her and his wife to become such intimates that invitations to dine at the Bartons' would manifest.

'I'm sure you will be all the support she needs,' he replied. And in a tone that was kind but firm, added, 'Now, if you don't mind, my dear, I really *would* like to return to my novel.'

Patricia did not protest, and lifted her own novel from its resting place in her lap. Some dreadful mystery, by the look of the cover: shadowy figure in a foggy setting, out-of-focus title font, dominant colours blue and grey. Bernard gave thanks that his firm had never published such tripe.

She let the book fall in her lap again.

'I wonder what she'll do with her spare time?'

Bernard breathed in to quell his irritation. He had to be fair. Normally, Patricia respected his wish to read in peace. In fact, she was quite protective of his afternoon serenity, and would even refuse to summon him to the phone when his mother called, as Verity Weston often did, preferring those times she knew were inconvenient. Yes, Patricia's urge to speak was out of her usual character, and so he would be patient and indulge her — for a minute or so more.

'I assume you mean Meredith?' he said.

'She's been at Jonty's beck and call for over a year now,' said Patricia. 'She may have forgotten what it's like to have time for herself.'

Bernard employed his kind but firm tone again, with greater emphasis on the firm.

'If anyone knows how to productively spend her days, it's you, my dear,' he said. 'You can remind her of what options are available.'

'Ah, yes,' said Patricia. 'The superfluity of choice that faces me every morning.'

She shut the mystery book with a snap, causing Bernard

further irritation — for the unnecessary noise and for the risk to the book's spine. Even a library mystery deserved to be handled with care. Another woman, after that emphatic gesture, might have leapt up from the armchair, but Patricia was not built for leaping. On her feet now, she smoothed down the front of her skirt and straightened her blouse.

'I think I'll go for a jaunt in the car,' she said.

Bernard had no desire to prevent her. Though he did, with all sincerity, wish her to drive safely, and told her so. Reading had to be paused while the car started up. He could never remember the make — something red and European; cars had never interested him. Patricia loved it, even though it was unnecessarily noisy and went through an inordinate amount of petrol. He'd suggested once trading it in for a Japanese hatchback that had excellent fuel economy, but she refused, claiming that hers had better handling or some such irrelevance.

When the sound of her car had receded, he lifted up his Hardy, and noted, with a silent oath, that his hands were not entirely steady. The Meredith Barton effect. Undiminished for forty-six years.

Bernard had known Meredith all his life — they were both the only children of the area's two largest landowning families. But while his mother considered the Westons to be the equivalent of English gentry, with all the right that entailed to lord it over lesser mortals, Meredith's parents had been more egalitarian, probably because they sensed that the heady days of farm subsidies were drawing to a close, which would put them in the category many English gentry had found themselves earlier that century — asset rich but struggling to pay the bills. However, in those days when farming was still lucrative, the two families had socialised regularly, and Bernard and Meredith had formed an affectionate, close acquaintance that endured through their teenage years, right up until the day Jonty Barton appeared on the scene. On that day the knowledge that he was in love with Meredith had darted through Bernard with the speed of an arrow, though unlike Austen's Emma, he saw also that he had no hope of his love being requited. It was, Bernard reflected, the second-worst day of his life.

Meredith and Bernard were seventeen, and home for the Christmas holidays from their respective private schools. Mr Barton senior had recently moved the family to Hampton, and as a bigwig in the Wool Board he'd attracted the interest of Bernard's mother, who issued an invitation to the Westons' notoriously select Christmas Eve drinks party. When the Bartons arrived, Bernard and Meredith, as was their habit, were huddled in a corner for mutual support, and as a result Bernard had an unimpeded view of Meredith's expression when she caught sight of Jonty. To be fair, she was not the only woman reacting to his entrance, but she was the only one young enough and (Austen again) handsome enough to tempt the tall, muscular and chiselled-featured (more Barbara Cartland, that) Jonty Barton.

To add to his attractions, Jonty was nineteen and excelling at university, where he was studying to become a chartered accountant. On the fast track to become a partner in a major firm, Bernard's mother delighted in telling him. If Verity Weston could have designed her ideal son, he would have been exactly like Jonty Barton: sporting rather than bookish, outgoing rather than shy, robust and attractive rather than slender and bespectacled, ambitious for a proven career rather than wasting time with books. In other words, a single man of guaranteed good fortune, who, judging by the look on Meredith's face that night, would not long be in want of a wife.

Austen to Brontë: Reader, she married him. Jonty did indeed become a partner in a firm of chartered accountants. They had two daughters. They inherited Woodhall when Meredith's parents passed on. Bernard's mother continued to needle him with constant comparisons. How successful Jonty was, how wealthy, how much status he had in the community.

But if Jonty were the hare, Bernard fitted well the role of tortoise. He attained a first-class degree in English Literature, found a job in a mid-sized publishing firm, and met Patricia, who worked in his favourite bookshop. When she asked him out, Bernard was so shocked he couldn't remember saying yes, but as she was the first woman to have shown even a glimmer of interest in him, he would hardly have refused.

He couldn't remember much about the worst day of his life, either, when he and Patricia were informed they could not have children. They must have comforted each other, before they'd quietly re-calibrated their expectations and moved on.

When the publishing firm was acquired in the mid-1980s, Bernard, by that time a shareholder, was suddenly prosperous. Suspecting he'd soon be edged out by the new regime, he quit and, though his affection for publishing tempted him to start a company of his own, his natural caution and sense of duty to Patricia led him instead to buy a commercial building in Hampton.

His mother derided his decision, citing Hampton as a no-hoper's backwater. Which, to be fair, in those days it was. Then it boomed. Bernard bought more property, in Hampton and in Gabriel's Bay. He made a profit on everything he sold. By the mid-1990s, the tortoise was considerably wealthier than Jonty Barton, and had more status, too, having been invited to join numerous civic-minded organisations and boards of local companies. Even Verity Weston had to accept that, though she was not lost for other ways to needle him. And now, of course, the giant had plummeted from his cloud castle and hit the ground hard. Jonty was trapped by a debilitating illness, whereas Bernard was hale and free.

And, aye, there was the rub: even if he had been petty-minded enough to see his ascendancy as a victory, Bernard could never truly relish it. Patricia and he were quite content, and he was grateful for her considerate nature and undemanding companionship. But always in his mind lurked questions about his own actions — or inactions — on that Christmas Eve. Should he have fought for Meredith? Argued that her attraction to Jonty was shallow, purely physical, whereas he, Bernard, had proved for all the years they'd grown up together that he could offer her real, lasting affection? Could he have persuaded her that kindness was preferable to domination and control, humility easier than arrogance? Could he have made her see that she would be so much happier if she chose instead her life-long best friend?

Even the novel in his hands seemed to be a rebuke. Hardy's title — *A Laodicean* — referred to the Bible and the harsh words of the angel of the church in Laodicaea: 'I know your life; I know that you are neither cold nor hot . . . now, because you are lukewarm . . . I am about to spit you out of my mouth.'

On that Christmas Eve, Bernard had been lukewarm, and Meredith had spat him out of her life. But forty-six years had passed. It was foolish to entertain even the faintest hope that there would be any kind of second chance.

Chapter 3

Kerry

Kerry took the turn off the main street to the beach. His new employer — Mrs Barton, until the unlikely event that she indicated a less formal address would be acceptable — had shown him his quarters and asked him to report for duty at eight o'clock tomorrow morning. Now, he had the rest of Sunday afternoon to kill, so he may as well explore what scenic delights Gabriel's Bay had to offer, seeing he'd apparently exhausted what it had to offer in the way of town.

Really, whoever built that website was either deluded or should be prosecuted for false advertising. His father's model-train villages had better amenities and more aesthetic civic design, and they were only a few inches high and made from a kit. Kerry had always enjoyed his father's hobby, but only now did he get a full sense of the pleasure one could gain from creating your own little world. Everything arranged just so — neat, pretty and working without a hitch. Gabriel's Bay was living proof that picture-perfect existed only in pictures, or out in a shed on a base of plywood six feet square.

However, as a bonus his new quarters were miles better than a plank and straw ticking, being a renovated shearer's hut at the rear of the property, five minutes' walk from the house.

'This was a three-thousand-acre sheep farm at one time,' Mrs Barton had told him. 'My family settled this land in eighteen seventy-five, and farmed it successfully, profitably, for over a hundred years. But between the lifting of government subsidies and a generation less willing to do the work, it became unviable. The homestead and gardens, and a few other outbuildings, are now all that's left.'

'Who bought the rest of the land?' said Kerry. 'If that's not a sore point.'

'Various owners,' she replied, 'with varying degrees of competency. With every sale, it seems, the land is broken up into ever-smaller blocks. Our nearest neighbours have been here only six months. They are apparently establishing an organic enterprise.'

'Apparently?'

'I suspect their ambitions may outstretch their ability. They seem a very nice young couple, but rather . . . Let's say, over-optimistic.'

The shearer's hut had been renovated to a taste that Kerry cautiously pegged as feminine. White walls with duck-egg blue trim on the window ledges, a single bed with a patchwork quilt, a chest of drawers and iron-curlicue hooks on the wall for clothing, and a chintz-covered armchair next to a pale green box that served as a side table. The box had round holes in the front, and on the lid the words 'Live birds' shakily handwritten in black pen. Along the back wall there was a tiny kitchen, a fold-up table and two chairs, and a door that Kerry assumed — hoped — led to a bathroom. There was no television, but on the single bookshelf was an old cream-coloured Bakelite radio. The room and everything in it were as clean as a whistle.

'This is very nice,' he said. 'Did you do it up yourself?'

'My daughter did. Nicola.'

Meredith Barton lifted a finger to straighten a watercolour of some purplish flowers in a blue vase.

'This was her haven, before she—'

Kerry noted the catch in her voice, the slight tremor in her hand. Oh, God, he thought, her daughter's died. Then again, there was no knowing what might upset some people. Kerry didn't trust himself to speculate and lacked the courage to ask.

'We lost her eighteen months ago.'

Still a lingering ambiguity, but Kerry felt safe enough to say, 'I'm so sorry.'

'Thank you.'

His employer subjected him to a cool, silent scrutiny, which incited in Kerry an urge to drop to his knees and beg forgiveness for all his manifold sins. Perhaps because she reminded him of an older version of the Madonna in the print in his parents' house, dark-eyed, clear-skinned, not particularly thrilled to be holding up her baby, as if it was the millionth time that day she'd been asked to do so. It was his father's print, of course. His mother only tolerated it because the copper-haired Christ child was, she swore, a dead spit for Kerry as a baby. Kerry grew to have doubts about God being a ginger, but who was he to question a mother's love?

'Nicola's death hit my husband very hard. It brought about the onset of his — condition.'

In her emails to Kerry, Meredith Barton had only said that her husband would not leave his bed, ate very little and shunned the contact of anyone but his wife. No name had been given to this 'condition', but Bronagh Macfarlane, when he called to tell his parents he was off to New Zealand, said, 'If there's nothing physically wrong with him, no heart trouble or low blood pressure or dicky hormones, then it's most likely clinical depression.'

'And is there a cure?'

'He should be getting medical treatment and counselling. Is he?'

'Doesn't sound like it. I got the firm impression the only person who's been looking after him is his wife.'

'But now *she* needs help?'

'I'd say she's needed it from the start, but it's taken her this long to ask.'

'And you'll do what for her?' said Bronagh.

'Cook for the pair of them, do the laundry, run errands. She has a cleaner,' he added. 'And a gardener.'

'Not short of a bob then?'

'Their house has a name.'

'Our caravan has a name!'

'"Adventure before Dementia" doesn't quite have that same posh ring to it.'

'Do they not have family to help out?' asked his mother. 'Children?'

'Don't know,' had been Kerry's answer then. 'If they do, they're not around.'

He'd cursed his poor choice of words as the conversation dropped into a black hole, both of them aware of the distance between them, neither of them willing to raise the subject of when it would be reduced.

'Miss you,' said his mother, finally.

And Kerry had ended the call with 'Miss you, too.'

He'd call his mother again soon, and fill her in on the new, if possibly very temporary, situation. He was already embellishing the story: Jonty Barton, like Dracula during daylight hours. Add in the reserved and stoical Mrs Barton and the ghost of a dead daughter, and the whole set-up was pure *Mysteries of Udolpho*. All it needed was for the gardener to have one eye and a limp, and the cleaner the ability to slide noiselessly up behind you. And at least one room that must never be unlocked.

Oh well, his relationship with anyone at Woodhall would be purely professional. All the more reason to get to know others in the town, make sure he had normal people to talk to. Real people, with whom he could make real connections.

Kerry had never had trouble making friends; he was naturally sociable. But over the past eighteen months, he had come to realise that his idea of friendship was one that required minimal emotional effort. Drinks at the pub, social football followed by drinks at the pub, watching football on the pub's big screen, celebrations — birthdays, getting new jobs, quitting old jobs — at the pub. His group were all good blokes, liked a laugh, ribbed each other mercilessly, shared standard gripes against bosses, people better off than them, and the unfathomable contrariness of women. Kerry had never heard any of them confess to finding life tough, despite evidence to the contrary — redundancy, the break-up of long-term relationships, the death of someone's mum or dad. All that stuff was shrugged off, brushed away with 'Life's a cow', followed by 'Your round?' No friend had ever phoned Kerry for a heart-to-heart. No one had ever confided in him, or asked for his help. Was that a reflection on him, or just typical of the kind of men he used to befriend? Could he be a different kind of man here? Did he have it in him?

But before he put it to the test, he needed food. It was three o'clock and he was famished. If he found nothing at the beach but sand, he'd head on back to the all-purpose takeaway he'd spotted.

He passed a couple more shops — a dowdy video store, fishing supplies — and an old printing firm that seemed to have been shut for some time. Across the road, there was a sign that said, with admirable brevity, 'Plumbing', next to a repairer of small electrical appliances. The commercial buildings, such as they were, petered out into scrubland, some areas fenced with chain link, though there seemed to be nothing but derelict sheds to protect. Then the road swung round and suddenly Kerry had sea to his left, bordered by tussocky dunes and a low fence half-submerged by sand. On his right was a collection of small houses, all showing signs that seaside living here was not always as tranquil as today. Rusty roofs, cracked and pitted corrugated plastic, stripped paint, wind-burned leaves on sparse plants. Halfway along, beachside, was a track to drive down if you wanted to launch a boat; Kerry spotted a wooden jetty. Just past that was a small parking lot, room for ten cars at most, and a series of four wooden boat sheds, raised up on short piles, Kerry assumed to avoid being washed out by unusually high tides or buried by massive sand drifts, or both.

The first three boat sheds looked to be exactly that, with padlocked doors and ramps for access. The last shed had no ramp — just a set of narrow wooden steps, and its door was not padlocked, but wide open, held fast by a hook on the side. Above the door was tacked a sign painted on a slab of driftwood: 'The Boat Shed'. Kerry could see tables and chairs inside. A seaside café? Or someone's private lounge? He swung into the parking lot, slotting the Fielder in next to an aging flat-deck utility, once red, a Honda motorcycle and, to his surprise and slight alarm, a police car.

As he got out of his own car, a young policewoman appeared in the shed's doorway, in one hand a plastic refillable coffee cup and in the other a brown paper bag. She was in her mid-twenties, dark-skinned, dark hair pulled back in a short ponytail, attractive and slim with an athletic, no-nonsense gait. She spotted him, stopped for a moment to assess him, swiftly and unsmiling, then gave him a single nod.

Kerry decided against 'Afternoon, officer', and instead gave a nod of his own.

And that, it seemed, was their interaction complete. The policewoman hopped in her car, secured her lunch, slotted on a pair of dark glasses and drove off.

So much for making new friends. On the plus side, unless the owner was being strong-armed into paying for protection in kind, it seemed that coffee and food were indeed on offer inside.

Kerry took the steps to the front door and peered in. He was greeted by a tantalising aroma of roasting meat, but not by a person. Right at the back was a lean-to kitchen, and, through its open door, Kerry glimpsed the beach, heard male voices and smelled cigarette smoke. The interior walls of the shed were painted a pale yellow, and on them hung all manner of art and object — a carved wooden rifle, a photographic portrait of a white-haired woman with a tattooed chin (Māori, he assumed), an early advertising poster of a farmer herding sheep at the foot of snowy mountains. At the back was a short bar, with a coffee machine at one end and a lampshade with a stand made from deer antlers at the other. On a shelf were a blue ukulele, a pair of cowboy boots and a stuffed weasel. Six bleached-wood tables were matched with bright painted folding chairs, and four stools allowed for sitting up at the bar. The whole place could fit, at a guess, twenty-five people, though Kerry doubted that anyone around here paid much heed to fire safety regulations.

He reached the bar, hoping his footsteps would have alerted the men beyond, but either they hadn't heard him or they'd chosen not to.

'Hello?' he called.

'Fuck off,' called a voice in return.

It wasn't the first time Kerry had been told that. And his hunger was such that he was not about to be deterred.

'I have a wad of ready cash and I'm willing to spend the bulk of it right now.'

Silence. A scraping of chair legs. A heavy tread. And then the back doorway was entirely filled. Kerry's palms began to sweat.

The man was easily six-foot-seven, blond and blue-eyed like an advertisement for the ideal Aryan. His outdoorsy perma-tan meant he could be anywhere from mid-fifties to a one-hundred-and-five. He wore a lumberjack plaid shirt, sleeves rolled up to reveal forearms the size of sheep and hands that could crack coconuts without aid. If Kerry lay on his side, he suspected his entire length would fall short of the breadth of this man's shoulders. The only thing that slightly detracted from the effect was that he was wearing a red-and-white frilled apron.

The giant placed two hands on the bar and leaned forward. Kerry did his best not to lean back.

'We're closed,' said the giant.

'You served the policewoman,' Kerry protested.

'Special case.'

'What if I beg?'

The giant blinked twice, surprised.

'Seriously,' Kerry continued. 'I am so ridiculously starving, I have no shame.'

A chuckle from the back doorway. The giant's companion. Rounder and much shorter — but then, who wasn't? — of Polynesian descent, Kerry guessed, neat salt-and-pepper beard. Short-sleeved brown shirt with a swirly pattern that Kerry assumed was also Polynesian.

The companion rested his crossed arms on the bar.

'Not from round here, are you?'

'Positively Sherlockian,' said Kerry. 'Was it the fact you've never seen me before that tipped you off?'

Swirly-shirt man sucked in his bottom lip, and treated Kerry to a look that was both amused and challenging.

'I should warn you,' he said, 'that we treat banter seriously in these parts. I should also let you know that I am the current holder of the title Archbishop of Banterbury, and I don't intend to relinquish a hold on it anytime soon.'

'Noted,' said Kerry. 'But just so *you* know, if starvation wasn't making me light-headed, I would consider rising to that challenge.'

The giant gave a despairing shake of his head, a movement that could precede him either going back outside, or punching one of them in the face. Not the companion, Kerry guessed. He had the look of a long-time offsider, a Sancho Panza to the giant's Don Quixote, had the latter been a World Wrestling SmackDown champion instead of a delusional barmpot on a knackered nag.

'We done here?' the giant enquired.

'No!' said Kerry. 'Can I buy some food? Please.'

'Fine,' the giant said. 'What're you after?'

Kerry checked around for a menu. None was evident.

'Er, what have you got?'

The giant frowned, as if this was a tricky question. 'Bit of crayfish?'

'What's that I smell cooking?'

'Slow cooked pork. Not ready. Another two hours.'

'Anything else?'

The giant gave him a look. 'Bit of crayfish?'

'Just the thing,' said Kerry.

When the giant was safely in the kitchen, Kerry asked the companion, 'Er, are your crayfish the same as those little American snappers some idiot released in our British waterways?'

'Nup. Ours are big, like lobster.'

'Lobster? Look, when I said I had cash, I—'

The giant shoved a plate in front of him. 'Crayfish roll: ten bucks.'

Kerry looked down at a soft white bread roll that smelled home-baked, stuffed to overflowing with lobster meat, iceberg lettuce and mayonnaise.

'I have died and gone to heaven,' he said.

'Great,' said the giant. 'Gate fee is ten bucks.'

Kerry handed it over.

'Want a beer?' said the companion.

It was now three-fifteen in the afternoon, but then, he didn't have to start work until the morning. 'Is there more than one kind?'

The companion bent to the fridge behind him and retrieved a bottle. It was plain brown, with no label except a white sticker with the word 'Beer' written on it.

'I'll take that as a "No", then,' said Kerry. 'How many bucks is that?'

'For you, five.'

'For everyone else?'

The companion chuckled.

'What are you doing here?' he asked. 'Passing through?'

Kerry had taken a bite of his roll, and was seriously tempted just to shove the entire thing in his mouth, so delicious it was. But he chewed properly, slowly, like his mother had drilled into him — 'Don't bolt your food, you'll get a torsion of the bowel' — and swallowed politely before answering.

'I've taken a job at Woodhall,' he said, 'helping Mrs Barton. Cooking, errands, laundry, general all-purpose domestic aid.'

Raised eyebrows, at two different levels.

'Meredith kept that quiet,' the companion said.

'Why shouldn't she?' said the giant. 'It's certainly not *your* bloody business.'

'Didn't say it was.'

'You're pissed off you didn't know, though.'

The companion, Kerry noted, was indeed somewhat irked.

'And why you?' he demanded of Kerry. 'What are *your* qualifications?'

Be bold and honest. Ish . . .

'Well, my mother did insist I keep my bedroom tidy,' said Kerry. 'But I suspect my major recommendations were that I was available and happy to accept a certain level of pay. A low one, in other words.'

'You here legally?' said the companion.

'Not your business, either,' said the giant. 'Nosy bastard.'

The companion rolled his eyes. 'So have you met the not-so-patient patient?'

'Not yet,' said Kerry. 'I mean I know about him — that he took to his bed after the death of his daughter. And that he seems to be against medical intervention. And that Mrs Barton is possibly a saint.'

'He was always a bit of an arsehole, old Jonty,' said the giant. 'And a pompous git.'

'Yeah,' the companion agreed. 'But he was a good advocate for the Bay. Knew how to kick the Council's butt. Unlike the current bunch of Progressive Association dickwads.'

Kerry finished his roll and desperately wanted to lick his fingers to get the very last traces of tastiness, but he settled for a paper napkin.

'Good?' said the giant.

'Now, normally, I'd be tempted to lie because I find you highly intimidating, but in this case I don't need to. That was truly, hands down, the best thing I've eaten in months.'

He finished wiping his fingers, stuck out his hand.

'I'm Kerry,' he said. 'Kerry-Francis Macfarlane.'

He braced himself for the return shake, but the compliment seemed to have softened the giant.

'Jacko Reid.'

'Gene Collins.'

By contrast, the companion's grip made bones crunch, and he held Kerry's hand just that fraction too long. Kerry did not flinch.

Gene grinned, released his hand.

'Welcome to Gabriel's Bay.'

Too many hours and plain-packaged beers later, Kerry found himself sitting on sun-warmed dunes, watching gulls squabble over mussels adhering to a great copper-black tangle of seaweed.

Along the beach at water's edge, lifting a spray of surf bright as tossed diamonds, galloped a gleaming bay horse, ridden bareback by a young woman with long, blonde hair and a face of such surpassing gorgeousness that Kerry caught his breath. She glanced across at him, lifted a hand in greeting, then bent her head over the horse's mane and dug a heel into its flank, and the pair sped down the sand like the wild, free creatures they were.

Saints be praised, thought Kerry, with a quick apology to his father.

This might turn out OK after all.

Chapter 4

Sidney

'Sid.'

Jacko Reid handed Sidney Gillespie a jar of bread-and-butter pickles. She removed the lid with one swift twist and handed it back.

'Ta.'

'No problem.'

'That's a real talent,' said Gene from his seat on the Boat Shed's back doorstep. 'What's your secret?'

'I trained with Lego,' she told him. 'Could never find the little brick separator thingy and didn't want to bugger my knives.'

'Lamb shoulder and six bread rolls OK?' Jacko asked.

'Whole shoulder? You sure?'

Jacko totted up the items Sidney had brought him in a cardboard box. 'Four jars of honey, two lettuces, two heads of broccoli, bunch of spinach, three lemons, spring onions and a cabbage. Yep, that's more than fair. You seen the price of broccoli right now?'

'Luckily, I don't have to look.'

'People make their own luck,' said Gene.

'Fuck off,' said Jacko. 'People work hard and take responsibility.'

'That's what I meant.'

'Say what you mean better then.'

'Now, now,' said Sidney. 'Don't make me reach for the wooden spoon.'

'Your boys fight a lot?' Gene said.

'They're boys. They're less than a year apart. What do you think?'

'There were six of us in my family,' said Jacko.

'Let me guess,' said Sidney. 'You were the runt?'

'My oldest brother's six-nine. Weighed twelve pounds at birth.'

'Jesus,' said Gene. 'Your poor mother. We're all runts in my family. Short, round and brown, like a set of lawn bowls. Samoan genes got smashed by the potato Irish.'

Sidney could see her reflection in the kitchen stove's stainless-steel splashback. It was blurry and, she knew, about as accurate as a funhouse mirror, but it still made her glum. Her boys seemed to be taking after their long-absent father, who'd remained as slender as a fishing pole no matter what he ate. Metabolism, he put it down to, but despite agreeing with Jacko about luck, Sidney knew that the shape you were born with had little to do with hard work or merit or anything under your control. If you were born with the whippet gene like Fergal, or the chubster DNA like her, that's just how it was. Eating and exercise habits could affect your weight but not your overall look. Sidney could eat lettuce all day and she would still have broad hips and no waist. And she'd be starving to boot.

Why couldn't she have been born with a figure like — pick one — Casey Marshall's? Lean and athletic, Casey made a shapeless, square police uniform look good. Or Olivia Jensen's? No, scratch that. Olivia looked like she was made of garden twine, all taut and stringy. Sidney didn't want prominent veins and sinews. Just a little less . . . width. She could also cultivate the attitude that you should love your body no matter what shape it was. But let's face it, that wasn't going to happen in her lifetime.

Reminder: Olivia's daughter, Madison, was coming around after school today. Sidney would have to set her and the boys up with some activity that didn't require too much supervision — French cricket in the back garden, perhaps? — so Sidney could have an undisturbed hour to tutor her student. It wouldn't be a problem. Madison was an easy kid, polite, obliging, fair-minded, but just competitive enough to want to keep playing games with Aidan and Rory, who, let's face it, viewed school, eating and sleeping as dull, worthless intervals between the real point of life — sport. Fortunately, they were smart and loathed losing, so they were both doing fine at school. Not so brilliantly at sleeping or keeping their voices down to anything under a bellow, but you couldn't have everything.

Clearly, thought Sidney, if that were possible, she would have an income that didn't make her hyperventilate every time she opened a bill, a house that wasn't quietly and determinedly rotting, a figure like Casey's, and a reliable, thoughtful, caring and *present* male lover.

'Don't suppose you can work Saturday, Sid?'

Jacko blew cigarette smoke out the kitchen door. Sidney had long since discovered there was no point in tut-tutting. Jacko's father had dropped dead at fifty-nine from a massive heart attack, and Jacko had no doubt he was in for the same fate.

'Reaper's coming,' he'd say. 'Good behaviour won't delay him.'

Jacko's wife, Mac, worked for Dr Love, the town's long-standing GP. Sidney knew Mac did not share her husband's opinion of his imminent and unavoidable demise, and would be elated if he packed in the smokes.

'But he won't be told, by me or anyone,' Mac had said to her. 'The voice of God could come out of a burning bush and all he'd do is bend down and light a fag off it.'

'This Saturday?' Sidney said.

'Devon's at some family hui. Mac can mind the boys.'

Devon, Jacko's extra help Thursday to Sunday, was one of a huge family. Over the past century the originally all-Māori bloodline had become more of a braided river, merging with the DNA of Scottish whalers, Dutch cheesemakers, Polish refugees and, legend had it, a Cheyenne chief from Wyoming. Devon was generally dependable, but family came first.

'Sure,' said Sidney.

It was a bit of extra income. And the boys wouldn't care. They loved Mac, and they especially loved King, the Reids' enormous chocolate Labrador, who would play any game with them as long as they rewarded him with food.

'That new bloke might come in,' said Gene. 'I think he liked it here.'

Sidney refused to bite. This was a regular ploy.

'He's about your age. OK-looking, if you like them ginger.'

'Talks a lot,' was Jacko's contribution.

'Got a job helping out Meredith,' said Gene.

Now that *was* interesting.

'Is she paying him to hold a pillow over Jonty's face?' Sidney said.

'That remark displays a sad lack of Christian compassion,' said Gene. 'The man is ill.'

'The man is an intelligent human being who has decided to opt out of life, thus making his wife a virtual slave.'

'Who's now getting help. From a ginger bloke who, as Jacko says, talks a lot.'

'It's Jonty who needs help,' said Sidney. 'But, oh, no — he insists on continuing to make his wife's life a misery. Selfish git.'

'Mac says Doc Love goes up to the house every month,' said Jacko. 'Sits and reads to him.'

'Reads him what? The riot act?'

'A biography of Field Marshal Erwin Rommel.'

'That would drive *me* out of bed,' said Sidney.

'Doc uses it as an opportunity to assess him, seeing Jonty won't come to the surgery.'

'And his professional opinion is . . . ?'

'Can't help anyone who doesn't want to be helped.'

'Next time, Doc Love should bring all six volumes of Churchill's Second World War history,' said Sidney. 'And smack Jonty around the head with each one in turn.'

'You know, Meredith could leave if she wanted to,' said Gene.

Sidney turned on him.

'*Could* she? You *think*? It's *her* house — her *family's* house — and *her* garden. That place was old, sad and tired when they moved in — it was *her* effort that brought it back, while Jonty was off playing bloody golf with his accounting cronies. It's mostly *her* money, too. Jonty obviously thought himself a big cheese, but he was a partner in an accounting firm in bloody Hampton, for Pete's sake! Hardly Goldman Sachs in New York! The bulk of their wealth is *her* inheritance, nothing to do with him. But if she *left* him, he'd get half of *everything* that's hers: house, garden, dosh, the lot. If she wanted to stay in Woodhall, she'd have to buy him out, and you *know* he wouldn't go cheap. But, sure, she could leave if she wanted to. Easy!'

As if carried on the reverberation, Jacko's cigarette smoke floated out the door. Gene sucked in his bottom lip, nodded.

'You've been giving it some thought, then?' he said.

'Ohh . . .' Sidney dragged her palms down her face. 'Yep,' she said. 'I'm brilliant at identifying the problem. I know exactly what's *not* working. For me, for Meredith, for this town — I could give you a comprehensive list right now of everything that's buggered. But I can't give you any solutions, can't work out how to fix even *one* thing. Useless . . .'

Gene was still nodding, eyes off in the middle distance. Jacko stubbed out his cigarette, reached to the top shelf, handed Sidney a jar of sauerkraut.

She twisted off its lid, handed it back.

Jacko said, 'Lamb'll be ready at five o'clock.'

Olivia wasn't due to pick Madison up until six — at the earliest; punctuality wasn't her strong suit — so Sidney bundled the three children into the back of her car, promising them a kick around on the field after they'd swung by the Boat Shed. The boys in particular had been really good this afternoon, playing cricket out the back and doing their best to keep the noise down while she guided a fifteen-year-old boy through the Macbeths' relationship dynamic ('Yes, he could have stood up to his wife, but that would have made it a very short play.'). Sidney's student, Franz, was the son of Filipino immigrants who'd come for seasonal orchard work out of Hampton, then found full-time jobs on a dairy farm and stayed. Franz was bright, excelled at maths and science, but, as his parents spoke little to no English around the house, found subjects that required written fluency a struggle. Sidney coached him as best she could, for the little his parents could afford to pay.

She'd asked the kids to stay in the car while she fetched the lamb from Jacko, but may as well have asked the ocean to stop being salty. By the time she returned, they were all out, kicking the soccer ball around the car park, and with them was a man about her age. With ginger hair. Sidney cursed, and not all that quietly.

He didn't hear. Was too busy blocking Rory, who had the ball and was trying to kick it around him. It wasn't a serious attempt to block, Sidney saw, but he was making it look like one. The ginger-haired man set his legs a little too wide apart, and Rory took the opportunity to shoot the ball straight between them.

'Nutmeg!' cheered the man. 'Perfectly executed. High-five, my friend.'

Rory, delighted, gave the man a slapping high-five.

'Next stop, White Hart Lane,' said the man.

'Ergh.' Aidan screwed up his face.

'Now, come on. How can you not be a Spurs fan?'

'Arsenal!' Aidan and Rory both punched their fists in the air.

'But their mid-field is so lightweight. And there's simply not enough aerial supremacy at the back.'

Aidan and Rory paused for a microsecond.

'Arsenal!'

The man turned to Madison. 'Are you my last hope?'

'I liked Gareth Bale,' she said. 'But he's gone now, isn't he?'

'Alas, yes. Sold for a million-squillion, possibly even a bajillion, euros to the Spaniards. It's like they've been waiting this long to take revenge for the Armada.'

He spotted Sidney.

'Hello! Are these yours? I found them running wild, like mustangs.'

'They were told to stay in the car. Weren't you?'

The boys squirmed.

'It was ho-ot.'

'Well, put the windows down when you get back in. Hurry up, or we won't have time for a kick around. Madison's mum's coming to pick her up soon.'

Soon-ish, anyway.

'Kick around?'

The man looked as if she'd said they were about to go to

Disneyland, or a place where they were giving away free ice cream.

'Don't suppose I could join you?' he added.

'Yes!' Aidan and Rory punched the sky yet again.

Sidney wavered. He was a complete stranger, but Jacko and Gene had met him, and, should anything dodgy occur, they knew where he lived. Besides, Meredith had hired him, and while her judgement when it came to Jonty might be completely skew-whiff, in all other respects it was as sound as a bell.

'Why not?' she said. 'We're heading to the field. By the rugby clubrooms. Do you need a lift?'

'I will follow in the trusty Fielder.'

He indicated a dusty grey station wagon, of a similar vintage to her own car, a battle-scarred maroon hatchback.

'I'm Kerry,' he added. 'Kerry-Francis Macfarlane.'

'Sidney.'

She turned to face the direction the children had sped off in.

'*Achtung!*' she yelled. '*Schnell!* In the car! Now!'

Honestly, she'd have more chance of being heard if she beamed signals into the Horsehead Nebula.

Kerry shaped his hands into a megaphone. 'Last one in's Bobby Zamora!'

And all three children came running.

'Whoof. Let me rest my weary bones like the old, arthritic man I am.'

Kerry collapsed down beside her on the bleachers, still catching his breath from a solid half-hour of running. His hair wasn't really ginger, Sidney had already observed, more the russet-bronze of autumn leaves. A touch of sweaty dampness made it almost brown, the same colour as his eyes. It was an attractive combination, and Sidney felt a nip of envy. All through her teens, she'd craved to have curly auburn hair like Anne of Green Gables, but every morning, she'd woken to the same straight, shoulder-length bob, a hairstyle her mother considered neat and becoming (as opposed to fashionable and slutty), in a colour that refused to be firmly brown but which wasn't light enough to be properly blonde. She'd shaved her head once, when she met Fergal, and started growing it back immediately — 'Whose head has *corners*?' she had demanded of her reflection. She henna-dyed it when they moved to Gabriel's Bay, but when the boys came, eleven months apart, and Fergal buggered off, she'd had no money or time to faff with dye, and so reverted to the neat bob and her natural colour, which a generous person might call fawn. At least she could trim it herself.

'Is this the only playing field in town?'

Kerry was taking in the extent of the Gabriel's Bay rugby club headquarters — changing room, storage shed, scoreboard and the tiered seats beneath them, all wooden, all needing a new coat of paint. The field was end-of-season rough, grubbed up by spiked boots and scuffling men. The three children, and Kerry, Sidney saw, had mud splatters to mid-shin. She hoped the boys would leave their shoes outside without being reminded. Ever-thoughtful Madison she didn't have to worry about.

He'd been great with the kids, Sidney had to acknowledge, had none of that competitiveness that seems to possess grown men when playing with children. She'd seen one father at the primary-school sports day jostle his own son during the egg-and-spoon race, and then do a shimmy dance of triumph as he crossed the line first, while his eight-year-old followed, sobbing and trailing bits of smashed boiled egg. And that didn't even come close to the displays of aggression on the sideline of kids' rugby and netball matches, from both dads *and* mothers. The latter, Sidney conceded, being the loudest and most foul-mouthed of all.

'The only other proper field is at the high school in Hampton,' Sidney replied. 'The primary school here has a concrete netball court, and some grass that's used for school sports. But nothing this big. And, as you've experienced, the boys do need a bit of space around them. Ideally, something the size of the Nullarbor Plain.'

'So does this field double for football and rugby?'

Sidney laughed. 'The only football in these parts is rugby. Try to pollute this hallowed ground with a poofter's round-ball game and the club members would come after you brandishing full bottles of Lion Brown.'

'Is that a beer?'

'Stretches the definition.'

'But your boys?' said Kerry. 'They love football. I can tell.'

Rory and Aidan were taking turns attempting a round-the-world move with the ball, which Kerry had made look easy. To their credit, they weren't giving up.

'They're happy enough to play with each other,' said Sidney. 'And Madison, when she's around.'

Madison, having quietly observed Kerry's technique, was giving the boys advice. 'You need to hold it on your foot for longer.'

'She's not yours?'

'No, no, no. Daughter of—'

Olivia wasn't exactly a friend, was she?

'—a neighbour. Who—'

Nor could it be truthfully said that Olivia could not mind her daughter because of work commitments.

Sidney decided to change the subject.

'I hear you've taken a job helping Meredith Barton.'

'Small-town grapevine? Mind you,' Kerry added, 'it wasn't

much different at home in Dalston. If you'd had a rough night and suspected you'd done something regretful, you just knocked on Mrs McKegg's door and she'd confirm it in all its gory detail.'

'And with glee, I imagine.'

'Well, it would have been churlish to deprive an old lady of her last pleasures in life.'

'So — have you met Jonty?' Sidney said.

'I have.'

'Did he acknowledge your presence?'

'He did. In the sense that he turned over in his bed and faced the wall.'

'God, that man.' Sidney fanned her face. 'I get all het up and furious at the mere *mention* of him.'

'You think he's faking it?'

'Oh, what do *you* think?'

Kerry looked out over the field to where Madison was patiently throwing the ball up into the air so the boys could practise their headers.

'Personally? I'm so constantly at sea about what makes *me* tick, I wouldn't presume to understand the first thing about anyone else.'

Chapter 5

Mac

On the whiteboard in Dr Love's surgery was what looked to Mac like a drawing of a uterus. As the last patient had been a seventy-five-year-old man, it seemed unlikely, but, as always with Doc Love, it would be a waste of time trying to guess.

'Explaining how insides work?' Mac pointed to the drawing.

'The military tactics of German tank commander Heinz Guderian.'

'Never heard of him.'

'Possibly the single greatest tactician of World War Two. Created the concept of *Blitzkrieg*.'

'Much good it did them,' said Mac.

'Well, for a while there—'

'You've got ten minutes before Mrs Swanson turns up with her menopause—'

'It and I are old friends.'

'—so get this down you.'

Mac placed a cup of tea and two pieces of shortbread on the desk, next to the large piece of metal shrapnel that acted as a paperweight and which Doc Love's father, while fighting in Burma, had apparently extracted from the skull of a dead Japanese soldier.

'Jacko says Meredith Barton has finally hired some help,' she told him.

'Welcome news.'

'My opinion is it gives Jonty even more of an excuse not to make an effort. Can't you prescribe some antidepressants for her to crush into his tea?'

'That would be unethical.'

'Not much point striking you off, is there?' said Mac. 'Not when you're just about to retire?'

Doc Love gazed at her through his black-rimmed specs, smiled faintly. 'Am I?'

Curse the man, thought Mac, and his Gandhi-like dedication to passive resistance.

'Finish your shortbread,' she ordered, as she headed back to reception. 'And don't drop crumbs.'

Sheila Swanson was already in the waiting room. She was sixty-one and had been experiencing menopausal symptoms for twelve years. Doc Love had told a disbelieving Mac that it was perfectly possible, but she remained sceptical. Sheila Swanson was single and Mac suspected her monthly appointments with the gentle doctor were as close to intimacy as the woman would get beyond the pages of the *Outlander* novels. Probably unfair, but still, Doc Love had too many patients as it was with genuine ailments and injuries. He didn't need his schedule clogged with time-wasters who couldn't cope with the odd hot flash.

'Is he in?' Sheila asked, as soon as Mac sat down behind the reception desk.

'No, he's dead. I'm just about to call the mortuary.'

Sheila recoiled, stricken.

'Oh, for God's sake, of course he's in,' said Mac.

'That was horrible of you,' said Sheila. 'More so than usual.'

‘I’m in an unusually bad mood.’

‘I mean, he’s not as young as he used to be.’

‘Yes, that’s how aging works.’

Sheila was getting all misty-eyed, Mac saw. She might have to be horrible again, snap her out of it.

The front door opened. In came the ten-forty and eleven o’clock appointments, Evan Olsen (fifty-three, obese, badly controlled Type 2 diabetes) and Ngaire Bourke (sixty-eight, emphysema, still smoking like a chimney). Normally, neither of them would turn up early for appointments because they were scared of Mac, who tended to reinforce what Doc Love told them, minus the tact.

‘Ngaire’s neighbour was dropping her off,’ said Evan. ‘Gave me a lift.’

Mac didn’t need to say, ‘The walk would have done you good’. Her expression did it for her. Evan snatched up a magazine, buried his head in it. *Brides,* Mac was amused to note.

Doc Love’s door opened and he stood there blinking, as if he’d been beamed down unexpectedly from another planet. If Mac hadn’t worked for him for twenty years, she’d swear the man was in the first stages of dementia. What he was doing, in fact, was swiftly and unobtrusively assessing his patients, noting their demeanour, posture, skin colour, any new visible spots or scars — small differences that could signify something much larger. His memory seemed inexhaustible; he could retrieve decades-old information about patients with no apparent effort. His capacity for compassion was likewise enormous. How the hell would they cope without him?

Doc Love smiled and beckoned. ‘Sheila.’

The woman practically levitated across the room, sailing on a pink cloud of pure devotion. Mac ripped open the first envelope of the day’s mail. If it contained junk, it would be sorry.

Information leaflets, from the Ministry of Health. Topics — heart disease and cancer, the two biggest reducers of the country’s already small population. Main causes — smoking, bad diet, alcohol, inactivity. Being a lazy, beer-guzzling, fagging fatso, in other words. Or her husband, Jacko, who was neither fat nor lazy, but who ticked too many risk-factor boxes for comfort. He was fifty-five but refused to get a check-up. What was the point of knowing? was his rationale. He'd rather be like Lemmy from Motörhead, who only found out he had cancer two days before he died of it. 'Now, that's my kind of hard bastard' was how Jacko had put an end to that and any subsequent conversations.

Mac caught sight of Evan's eyes peering anxiously above '537 Ideas for an Epic Wedding'. She must be emitting a sonic boom of irritability. Thinking about Jacko did that, not to mention Doc Love's refusal to set a deadline for his retirement.

Truth was, the stress was no one's fault but her own. She was taking on burdens that were not hers to carry. Jacko might be her husband, but his health was his responsibility, his choice. She had the right to express an opinion, but that was it. And it wasn't her responsibility to find a successor for Doc Love. It wasn't his, either — it was the town's. If they didn't want everyone to have to drive over to Hampton, then the so-called Gabriel's Bay Progressive Association should get off their arses and advertise for a replacement.

Damn it. Jacko would assume the position for Doc Love before that happened. No, if Mac didn't take action, no one would.

'You been—'

Ngaire's question was put on hold as she coughed up her own lungs and possibly those of two other people. She flapped her hand, indicating she'd be as right as rain in just a sec. Mac sighed, pushed the health information leaflets to one side. Might as well hand the present patients a guide to conversing in Swahili.

Eight minutes later, Ngaire said, 'You been down the shops yet?'

Mac knew what she meant. Every week, Doc Love gave her

a morning off to drive a busload of old people over the hill to Hampton so they could go to the supermarket, visit the library and get their pension money out of the bank, none of them trusting to such new-fangled technology as an EFTPOS card. Once a month she also took a group to the Hampton community hall for Rummikub, dominoes and euchre. The second-hand coach had been bought by Doc Love, and given to the town. Naturally, it had been dubbed the Love Bus.

'You know we go every Monday,' she said.

'I was laid up. Back trouble. 'S why I'm here.'

Back trouble was the least of her worries, thought Mac. As well as emphysema, she had brittle bones and cirrhosis. The worst day of Ngaire's life was when they banned smoking inside the Bay's one remaining pub, the Crown. She could still be found there most evenings, in the so-called garden bar — a concrete square out back with a bit of bare trellis and sand-filled plastic buckets for the butts — cadging ciggies off any other smokers desperate enough to sit there.

'Next Monday, then,' said Mac. 'Eight-thirty sharp.'

'I've run out of cash, see.'

'Uh huh.'

Mac opened a piece of direct mail from a drug company. It had been beautifully designed, had its own special box that held information leaflets and a stylish and probably quite expensive promotional item meant to stand on the reception desk so that patients would see the name of the drug and feel inspired to ask for it. Mac chucked the whole lot in the bin. She did not like clutter.

'I've run out, see.'

'I can lend you twenty,' said Evan.

'You can't lend it to her,' said Mac.

'Well, I—'

'Lending it implies she will pay you back.'

'I will,' said Ngaire. 'Next Monday, see.'

'She won't,' said Mac. 'Not next Monday nor any Monday after.'

'Well . . .'

Mac could see Evan's male pride battling with his natural caution.

Male pride won. 'I could give it to her.'

'Awww.'

Ngaire clasped her bony hands, thrilled. Evan couldn't back down now. He tugged his wallet from his trouser pocket — not an easy manoeuvre for a five-foot-ten man who weighed one-hundred-and-thirty kilos — and handed a twenty-dollar note to Ngaire, who kissed it with a wet smack. Evan moved his head to one side, in case she planned to do the same to him. Caught Mac looking at him.

'It's neighbourly,' he said, with a hint of a pout.

'Don't have to justify it to me,' she replied. 'Your money. Your choice.'

'I can put this appointment on my account, right?'

'Again, your choice. I'll be in touch about your balance at the end of the month.'

Sweat began to bead on Evan's forehead. He reached for the tissues on the magazine table. Mac waited for them to disintegrate into damp shreds in his hand. She didn't have to wait long.

Doc Love's door opened. Sheila Swanson emerged, flushed and smiling. Mac tried to rid her mind of the images that had leapt in there.

'Ngaire.'

The good doctor's tone implied he had been counting the hours of her absence. Mac had no idea how he always managed to sound so sincere. Strike that — she knew perfectly well why. He sounded sincere because he was.

'Forty dollars,' she said to the pink-faced Sheila. 'But getting closer to your senior citizens' discount card every visit.'

'You won't stay long, will you, Mac?'

Doc Love stood by the front door, in his hand the Gladstone bag that had been his father's, and on his person a military-grey trench coat that dated from the 1970s which, along with his square, black-rimmed specs, was now the height of hipster fashion. All he needed was a trilby hat and a gelled moustache.

'No, no,' said Mac, busy at the computer. 'Last bit of admin. Ten minutes max.'

'I will lock this door,' he told her. 'For my personal reassurance only. I'm sure you'd handle yourself admirably in any crisis.'

'Good night,' said Mac, to encourage him out the door. 'See you in the morning.'

'Yes, indeed.' He made it sound as if it were a treat he was looking forward to.

The door lock clunked into place. Mac leaned back in her chair and breathed out.

She could be about to open a super-sized can of worms, but damn it, no one else had a hand up to take this on. No one else was even thinking about how they'd all cope if Doc Love retired. *When* he retired. No 'if' about it; the only question was when, but Mac couldn't see him lasting more than another year. He was seventy-two, for Pete's sake, should have been pottering in his garden and painting miniature soldiers for the past seven years. Should have written that history of tank warfare he'd been talking about since she started working with him two decades ago, when she was a thirty-three-year-old mother of two who'd finally gone off to school, which left her craving some productive employment. Doc Love had taken her on part-time, let her job-share with another receptionist, even though that wasn't the most convenient option for him. Those two kids were grown up now, left home both of them, and Mac had worked full-time for the past five years, except for Monday mornings, when she drove the Love Bus and Doc Love went out on house calls.

For all that many of his patients tried her patience, she knew that they would suffer, not just health-wise but emotionally, if they had no choice but to drive to Hampton. Some of them, especially those in her group of oldies, might find the prospect so intimidating that they would simply refuse. Might put up with whatever affliction they had until the only vehicle taking them over that hill was an ambulance. Or a hearse.

Doc Love listened. He cared. He treated patients as whole human beings, not just a set of symptoms or a problem to be solved as quickly as possible, fobbed off with a scribbled prescription.

Healthy communities needed empathetic health practitioners. And while empathy might not have been Mac's strong point — someone had to give the tough love — she had no doubt about its value. Or the price of its loss.

On her computer was a website where you could place advertisements for GPs that would be seen by doctors all over the country. Mac had no one's permission to do this but that didn't seem important. Small, remote towns were finding it increasingly difficult to attract doctors, locums and nurses, and Gabriel's Bay was as small and remote as they came. It would take time, Mac reckoned, to find someone — the right someone.

Permission was irrelevant. What mattered most was to start now.

Chapter 6

Madison

Madison ate her breakfast, and made her lunch with what she could find in the fridge. She was going to Aidan and Rory's after school again today, so she'd better pack her book in her bag, too. It was about a girl whose mother had abandoned her in a religious group who refused to let her use her real name. She'd bought the book in the second-hand shop with half of the twenty-dollar note her dad had mailed her for her ninth birthday. She'd spent five dollars more on sweets for Aidan and Rory, making sure to ask Sidney first if it was all right. Madison's own mum said sugar was poison.

'If you want to blow your hard-earned cash on these two jokers, that's up to you,' Sidney had said. But she'd looked pleased.

After packing her schoolbag, Madison tidied up her bedroom because Oksana the cleaner was coming today. It didn't seem fair that Oksana should do all the work when Madison was perfectly capable of picking up after herself.

Her mum didn't share that view, and left stuff everywhere: plates, wine glasses, used tissues, even her undies.

'That's what a cleaner's for,' she told Madison. 'And I intend to get the full benefit from the Ox's well-muscled Russian forearms.'

If Oksana minded, she never said. She'd pick up the cash Madison's mum left on the kitchen table, stuff it in her purse, and go about cleaning the house in a fierce way that made the floors and surfaces sparkle, but which had already broken the spiky green-glass bowl that her mum said cost a fortune even though it was ugly, a limited-edition Tracy Emin paperweight, her dad's Tivoli iPod dock, every roller-blind cord but one, four Riedel wine glasses and two heads off the Dyson vacuum cleaner.

Oksana told Madison she was descended from Genghis Khan. 'I am Tatar,' she said, making it sound like she was saying goodbye. 'Strong. Not afraid. I have seen tigers in Siberia, war in the Afghan mountains. Not afraid.'

Madison's dad wasn't happy about the broken stuff, but they needed to keep Oksana because she was OK being paid in cash. He thought it was funny that he and Oksana had the same opinion of the tax department.

Before they came to Stonelands, they used to live in Auckland. Madison was only seven when they moved, but she remembered there were lots of arguments. Her mum didn't want to leave the city and her friends, but the house had to be sold, according to her dad, and so did the beach house on Waiheke Island, because the buildings he'd bought in Wellington needed earthquake strengthening or the tenants 'would walk'. And the resort development in Samoa wasn't happening as fast as it should — 'bloody island time' — and the banks were getting 'a bit toey'.

He promised Madison's mum that they'd only need to live at Stonelands for a year, 'Eighteen months max, until things have eased up. It'll be great,' he said. 'Like a country retreat. Plus, it's a properly good investment — the wine sales are a bit sluggish, but the land's worth a fortune. We'll flick it when the market's on the up. Money for jam.'

Aidan and Rory's mum, Sidney, made jam but she sold it at the market for only three dollars a jar.

Madison liked a lot about her new home. The teachers at her school were nice, and she didn't have to wear a uniform like at her old school. She made friends — well, Aidan and Rory — and the other kids were a bit loud and rough, but they weren't too mean. She liked being free to run around outside. Before, she'd had nannies who didn't really want to take her anywhere because of getting stuck in traffic, and her mum didn't like her making noise inside, and the house only had a small courtyard with spiky plants. There was a pool, but she wasn't allowed to go in alone, and the nannies got bored watching her, and her mum preferred just to sunbathe, and her dad was too busy. At Stonelands, she could walk through the vines, if there weren't any workers or machinery, and on the surrounding land as long as she didn't go too far from the house. She liked not having a nanny anymore, too, but she knew it wasn't all that convenient for her mum to drive her places, like school.

What Madison didn't like was that, not long after they moved, her mum and dad started arguing. Once, they were shouting in the kitchen so loud that Madison heard. Her mum called her dad a liar, and he said he was getting it all sorted but could she just rein it in until he did, and her mum said no way because he owed her for what she'd given up, and then went to her room and slammed the door.

And then her dad started being away heaps more than usual, and when Madison got up the courage to ask about it, her mum said he had to spend lots of time in Auckland now because he was 'up to his eyeballs in alligators'. 'Seriously,' she added, 'your bloody father is like a reverse King Midas. If he dived into Scrooge McDuck's gold pile, it would evaporate in an instant, leaving nothing but the stench of empty promises.'

Madison wasn't sure what any of that meant. But she'd been happy to know her dad wasn't gone for good. He came down every few weeks, and she'd always ask if perhaps he could take her to the movies in Hampton. Or to the beach? He'd give her a quick hug and say, 'Sweetie, sure, but not this time. Next time, OK?'

He never said when the next time would be, but Madison didn't mind. It gave her something to look forward to every day.

Bedroom tidied, she went back to the kitchen to check the clock. It was time to leave for school, but her mum wasn't up yet. Madison knew her mum didn't really like getting up early to drive her, but there wasn't a school bus, so she had to.

That's why she went to Aidan and Rory's house after school most days, because it meant her mum's afternoon didn't get cut short. Plus, her mum didn't want to feel obliged to give the Booth sisters or Reuben Coates a lift home. Lots of kids like Aidan and Rory walked to school because they lived in town. But others lived in the country, and if their own parents couldn't drive them, other parents usually helped out.

On the road to Stonelands, there was Tanya and Shari Booth, who lived on a farm. They were one year younger and one year older than Madison, and wore old clothes and gumboots. They never had sneakers for PE, just bare feet. They didn't seem to ever wash their hair and they smelled like sheep's wool and roast meat, which wasn't that bad. Occasionally, their gumboots would have sheep poo on them, but that didn't smell too bad, either. Sort of sweet, like grass.

The Coates family didn't have a farm, just an old house with a rusty roof and no paint left on the outside and an overgrown garden with rubbish in it. Reuben Coates was at her school, and no one knew how many brothers or sisters he had, but everyone knew that an older brother was in jail. Some of the bigger kids used to tease Reuben about it. He was only eight, but he swore at everyone and tried to punch them all the time. He got into trouble a lot. Madison heard her mum and one of the other mothers saying he should be expelled or, preferably, put down.

When she told Sidney that, Sidney gave a little high laugh and said, 'Of course. I mean, what's the difference between a frightened, possibly abused small boy and a rabid dog?' And she'd banged the cordial glasses down on the bench in a way that made Madison not want to ask her what she meant.

The Booth sisters and Reuben made her mum shudder, and she'd sometimes driven past pretending not to see that they didn't have a ride.

Madison checked the clock again. It was way past time to leave. She didn't like waking up her mum, but she'd be late for school if she didn't.

'Mum?'

She tapped on the bedroom door. No answer. She knocked louder, and pushed open the door.

'Mum?'

Her mother's bed was empty. Madison checked the ensuite bathroom. Empty, too.

She went back out into the hallway. 'Mum!'

A crash. The back doorknob hitting the kitchen wall. Oksana was here.

'You are not gone to school?' Oksana said when Madison ran into the kitchen.

'Can't find Mum.'

'She asleep?'

'No, I looked in her room.' Madison knew there must be a good reason why she wasn't here. 'Maybe a friend needed her help and she had to go out?'

'Car here.' Oksana made a 'tsk' sound. 'She up at cottage. With Germans.' She pulled her phone out of her bag. 'I call her . . .'

Of course! Her mum must have had a sleepover at Rainer and Elke's! Rainer was the vineyard manager, and Elke was his partner. They lived in a little cottage next to the big building with the huge metal vats where they made wine. Yesterday before dinner, Madison's mum had been calling her dad and getting no answer, so she'd left a message with lots of rude words, and then she'd walked out of the house and up the driveway. She went up to Rainer and Elke's quite often 'for a drink and a mutual bitch about your father', she said. Madison was glad she was never invited — Rainer was always so grumpy.

Madison heard her mother's voicemail, tinny through Oksana's phone. Oksana tsked again and hung up without leaving a message. Her pink-lipsticked mouth was pursed tight, which made it wrinkle around the edges so that it looked a bit like a spiky flower. Madison's mum hated her own wrinkles, even though they didn't seem very obvious. She blamed Madison's dad for giving them to her, and for the fact she couldn't fly to the city to get them fixed. 'This backwater's idea of a beauty treatment is a blue rinse,' she'd said.

'You need ride to school,' said Oksana. 'Already late.'

Madison nodded. She should have left five minutes ago.

'I could ring Ms Gillespie?' she suggested.

Sidney let Madison call her by her first name, but most other people preferred it when she was more polite.

'Too late,' said Oksana. 'Beside, she not taxi service. Come all this way. Use up her petrol. I take you.'

'But — that would use your petrol.'

'Your mother pay. I tell her.'

Madison wasn't sure her mother would agree, but she definitely did not want to be late for school. She had a bit of birthday money left over. She could pay Oksana and pretend it came from her mum.

'Quick. Fast, fast.'

Oksana swept her along in front, out to her car, an ancient Peugeot the colour of hot mustard. Madison liked that a small spider had built a shimmery web over the passenger side-mirror. She would never tell Oksana, who would dust it off, find the spider and squish it dead. The web would be her secret. She watched it sparkle and quiver like a fairy's wing all the way to school.

'The boys said Oksana dropped you off this morning,' said Sidney. 'Where was your mum, sweetheart?'

It was after school now, and Madison was sitting with Sidney at the kitchen table. Aidan and Rory were outside kicking a soccer ball against the side of the house. Madison calculated they had ten minutes left until Sidney told them to stop, and threatened to sell them to the CIA for use in practice interrogations.

'She had a sleepover at Rainer and Elke's.'

Sidney's eyebrows rose. 'A sleepover? OK . . .'

'She went up before dinner, and I guess they invited her to stay.'

'Wait. You didn't have *dinner* together?'

Sidney was frowning, and her voice was suddenly sharp. Madison started to feel all prickly and squirmy, as if she and her mum had done something wrong. But she knew her mum trusted her to look after herself. 'You're a big girl now,' she said. 'Nine. A proper tweenie. We should buy you some makeup.' And her mum hadn't been that far, had she? Madison had her mum's mobile number, and Rainer and Elke's, too. They were only a phone call away if she had a problem.

'I ate Oksana's soup. She brings us food every week, and last night there was still some soup left, so I microwaved it. It had meat bits and cabbage in it — and it was really delicious,' she felt compelled to add.

'Cabbage soup. Right . . .'

Sidney sort of sighed the last word through her teeth.

But all she said next was, 'How's your book?'

Madison was grateful Sidney didn't want to talk about her mum anymore.

'*Really* good. The mother nearly died having a baby, but the kids saved her!'

Sidney poked the book up with a finger so she could read the back cover.

'Huh. And I thought Laura Ingalls was pushing the boundaries of young fiction when she began stepping out with Almanzo Wilder.'

Sidney held up her drawing. 'What do you think?'

It was meant to be a new label for her jam and the other stuff, like chutneys and pickles, that Sidney sold at the farmers' market. It was supposed to be some fruit and vegetables and a bumblebee, Madison guessed. The bee was big and furry and black, and looked more like an angry spider that had sprouted tennis racquets.

'I know,' said Sidney. 'Rubbish. Why do I bother? I'll tell you why,' she added, although Madison hadn't spoken. 'Because I crave to be one of those women who can overcome the fundamentally antagonistic properties of glitter and glue and soggy paper and create things of beauty and joy forever. I want to enrich this crappy house with colour-dipped candles, stencilled wall patterns, *ombré* light shades, pastel picture frames, découpaged trays and appliquéd wotnots. I want to master felting, and crochet, and paint effects with a sponge. I want to whip up whimsical labels with pen and ink. And you know, I could. I could achieve *all* of that if it weren't for one fundamental issue. I have no artistic talent whatsoever.'

She screwed up the paper and tossed it with her left hand all the way across the kitchen towards the bin. It hit the flap square-on and went in.

'I could draw you something?' offered Madison.

'Why not? Why not add humiliation to my sense of failure?'

Madison was about to apologise, but Sidney beat her to it.

'Sorry, Maddie. Ignore me. I'm old and crotchety. I would *love* it if you drew me a label. But finish your book first.'

A knock on the front door. Sidney checked her watch.

'Well, this'd be a first,' she muttered and then gave Madison a quick guilty glance, as if she hadn't wanted her to hear.

'Feel free to tell those boys to stop recreating the finale of the Edinburgh Military Tattoo,' she said as she went to answer the door.

But Madison didn't mind the kicking. She couldn't even really hear it once she got back into her book. The main character had decided to run away from the religious family, and it looked like some of the other children might go with her — if they could figure out how to get away. They were all super brave. Madison would feel very alone if she was apart from her mum.

'Hello there.'

The voice made her jump. She looked up wide-eyed at the young man who was smiling at her.

'Sorry,' he said. 'Good book, is it? Love it when they grab you like that.'

'Barrett, you know Madison, don't you? Rick and Olivia Jensen's daughter?'

'Sure. Saw you up at Stonelands when I came to install the GFCI.'

Madison remembered. He was an electrician. The GFCI was a circuit-breaker, which Rainer wanted because one of the workers had got a shock from some of the equipment. Her dad had said the accident was just a one-off, but Rainer had got super grumpy, said it was a major health and safety issue, and it was lucky the worker hadn't died. Rainer asked her dad if he'd prefer to be prosecuted, which would cost him a lot more, so her dad okayed the electricians.

'I thought you were called something different?' Madison said.

'Brownie? That's my nickname.'

'What? Because Darkie was taken?' said Sidney.

Madison couldn't tell if she was joking or not.

Barrett/Brownie didn't look embarrassed.

'No, it was because I was a bit of a teacher's pet at school. They started calling me Brown Nose, and then . . .'

'And you're still letting them, now you're actual adults?'

He shrugged. 'Could be worse. Down the club we've got Donkey, Thumper, Rooter, Nutsack—'

'OK, yep, fair point, well made.'

'If you like, you could pretend it was because of Elizabeth Barrett Browning,' he said, with a smile that made Sidney give him a funny, sort of wriggly smile of her own.

'So what's the problem with the power?' he asked.

'If I switch the light on in the laundry, every other light in the house goes off,' said Sidney. 'Boomph! Black-out.'

'Sounds like a wiring fault. Overloading.'

'Expensive?'

'Not *necessarily* . . .'

'I love the way that almost sounded not like a lie.'

'We'll work something out,' said Brownie.

'Thanks,' said Sidney. 'Again. As usual. Barrett.'

'My mother blesses you from heaven.'

A brr, brr noise. Sidney's phone jiggled along the table like it was trying to run away. She grabbed it, checked the screen.

'Speaking of mums.'

But then she took Brownie through into the laundry, so

Madison couldn't hear if it was her mum or someone else's.

When she came back Sidney said, 'You're staying for tea and then I'll run you home.'

Where Madison's mum would be waiting. They could have cocoa together — well, her mum would have a glass of wine — and watch *Project Runway*.

Aidan and Rory's ball beat against the house like the ticks of a big clock, counting down until it was time to go home.

Chapter 7

Sam

'Did you give her one?'

Sam watched Brownie's face, interested in his reaction to Tubs's question. His mate was nodding, as if giving his reply serious consideration. Wasted effort. Anything more than 'Give her one, yeah' would go straight over Tubs's head.

'Give her one, yeah!'

That was Deano. Their foursome's ever-reliable stooge. He was the only one not sitting on the sand dunes, but was up on his feet, chucking stones at the gulls bobbing on the water. They didn't even twitch a feather.

'Tubs, mate,' said Brownie. 'There are *multiple* reasons why that would never happen, but let me start with one you might have a chance of understanding. It was mid-afternoon and there were three children in the house.'

'So?'

'So little kids can only be left alone for so long before they want to know where you are. And, unlike you, I'm not done in twenty seconds.'

'Woo!' said Deano, acknowledging the burn.

'And the main reason why congress with Ms Gillespie would never occur,' said Brownie, 'is that, to her, I'm a boy. I'm barely a decade older than her youngest. Sidney Gillespie is a grown woman with a healthy self-respect. If I came onto her, she'd laugh, pat me on the head and send me on my way.'

'Are we still boys?' said Sam. 'We're nineteen.'

'We're boys in most people's eyes,' said Brownie. 'Most people here, that is. That's the trouble when everyone's known you since you were born, and are probably also familiar with the details of your conception.'

Sam nudged a shell with his sneaker.

'Time to leave then, eh?'

'Aw, come on,' said Tubs. 'Whaddya want to go to Christchurch for? There's nothing there. It all fell down.'

'Well, duh,' said Sam, 'that's why they need builders. No end of work still. Tradies are making serious money.'

He poked Brownie in the arm.

'Yeah, yeah,' said his mate. 'You know I can't.'

'Uncle Gene said you could get your dad assessed. Y'know, for a care home? They don't just take old people.'

'Mate, no. I mean, great that old Gene-o wants to help, but no. OK, yeah, Dad's health is completely buggered, but his mind is fine. If I even *casually* brought up the idea of a home, he'd crawl into the bush and end it. I'm not exaggerating. Not one iota.'

'My dad's fit as he ever was.'

If you listened hard, you could hear the wariness behind Tubs's boast. Sam had seen Mr Hanrahan in a rage many times. Seen the after-effects, too. But Tubs admired his dad, looked up to him — had to, the man was almost as tall as Jacko Reid — and desperately wanted to be like him.

'His hands are strong-as.' Tubs crushed the empty beer can.

'Dad grip,' said Brownie. 'It's a recognised phenomenon.'

'Eh?'

'It's a thing.'

Sam thought about his own dad. Wyatt Kirby was a big, broad-chested man, with curly blond hair and beard like a Viking, but he'd never had a fight in his life.

'Violence proves nothing,' he said, 'except that you have no self-control.'

Having run out of stones, Deano tossed his empty beer can instead, which fell well short of the water. He jogged back to flop down on the dune next to Tubs.

'You're not going to leave that there, are you?' said Brownie.

'Leave what?'

'Your can, man. Defiling my ancestral ground.'

'Who says it's yours?'

'Generations of dead forebears.' Brownie pointed at the sky. 'They're watching you right now, and they're *angry*. Take care on your way home.'

'Bullshit,' said Deano, but he couldn't help a quick glance upwards.

Déjà vu, thought Sam. That was a thing, too, wasn't it? But not real, just your mind tricking itself into believing it had seen something before.

So what would you call what was he experiencing now? Looking at his three friends, he could see them at every age, right from when they all first got together at the Gabriel's Bay Playcentre, aged three. He could see Tubs small and round, and then big and round, and briefly lean, when he got that summer job as a shearing hand. Now, round again, he worked at his dad's car dealership in Hampton, washing cars, fetching lunch and coffee for the sales guys, talking for the past two years about training as a mechanic or a junior sales rep.

Sam could see Deano, small and wiry always, not much taller than he had been when they'd started high school. Deano lived with Loretta, his fiancée, though no wedding date was ever mentioned. He did seasonal work on orchards and odd jobs up at Stonelands winery. Sam also strongly suspected that he dealt in weed. Loretta's job in the bakery wouldn't account for the big-screen all-bells-and-whistles TV that turned up in their place two months ago. He hoped Deano wasn't being stupid. The weed market around here belonged to a local branch of a big gang, who also distributed P and E and bath salts and whatever the latest crap was that idiots wanted a buzz from.

And Brownie, his best mate. The handsomest of all of them, though that wasn't hard, with Tubs so round and Deano so scrawny and he, Sam, with his mad blond-brown Afro curls. Smartest, too — Brownie was top of the class; they teased him about it. Sam had always wanted to be a builder, so leaving school in year twelve didn't bother him. But Brownie might have gone to university, if his mum hadn't suddenly died.

Millie Tahana had been a social worker, in charge of a whole team working with families and children at risk. 'That woman is a rock,' Sam's mum, Talia, once said. 'And I wouldn't want to be between her and a hard place.' Yep, Brownie's mum was tough as — Sam had dreaded her catching him doing something wrong. She'd had no patience with excuses or justifications or blaming someone else. 'Don't complain, don't explain,' she used to say. 'Step up and sort it out.'

Millie had collapsed working late one night at the Hampton office. Heart failure, no warning. Nothing anyone could have done.

Brownie was gutted, as you would be, but he'd mourned and come out the other side, quieter but still recognisably Brownie. But Brownie's dad, Ed — it was like some kind of internal warrant of fitness had run out, like Millie had been propping up his immune system. Three weeks after her tangi, he got diagnosed with chronic obstructive lung disease, even though he didn't smoke, and neither did Millie. Second-hand smoke, Doc Love had said, or dust and chemicals from Ed's early days working in the paper mills. It could even be genetic, but that was rare. There was no cure.

Ed went downhill fast. His breathing got worse and worse, and he got more and more tired. He had to quit his job, couldn't play sport and, after a few months, couldn't even walk to the clubrooms.

Sam's dad, Wyatt, said, 'It's like watching a bloody kauri tree with dieback. Slow death from the inside.'

Doc Love came round every Monday morning with the oxygen machine, but it was Brownie who had to do everything else for his dad — help him dress, make his meals, make sure he was OK during the night.

'Thank God for Barrett,' Sam's mum said, but his dad hadn't been so sure.

'Pretty bleak situation for the lad, don't you think?' he said. 'Smart, handsome, with all his life in front of him, and now what? What's his future look like? Doc Love says Ed could go on like this for years yet.'

That's why Brownie couldn't go with Sam to Christchurch. Which meant this was the last full summer they'd spend together. Come January, this group of mates would be no more. Even if Sam came home next Christmas, it wouldn't be the same. His old life would soon be nothing but a memory.

Maybe that's why he was getting these flashbacks? Seeing the four of them as they had been, mates through school. To be honest, he and Brownie had bugger all in common now with the other two. Tubs and Deano still acted like they were fourteen, like time had stopped five years ago, giving them no reason to grow up.

But when Sam looked at them now, all he could see was the four of them as kids, playing peewee rugby, building a fort in the bush, shooting BB guns, running wild and shouting with that loud, pure joy that makes every adult within five miles yell at you to shut up. Is that what happened when you became an adult? You forgot about joy? You forgot how to fizz with the simple pleasure of being alive?

'You boys OK here?'

Standing in the gap of the dunes, thumbs hooked in her belt. Constable Casey Marshall. All four of them stood up to face her.

'Just enjoying a few beverages, officer,' said Brownie. 'We'll be off soon.'

'Who's driving?'

'I am,' said Sam. 'I've only had one.'

'Good to hear. Where you headed?'

'Aw, what's this?' Tubs protested. 'Twenty questions?'

'Twenty questions is a parlour game that rewards deductive reasoning,' said Casey. 'I think you mean — is this the third degree?'

Tubs blushed. 'Yeah, whatever.'

Sam heard him mutter an extra word under his breath.

'And that's a violation of public order,' said Casey. 'Summary Offences Act 1981. Though in your defence, you can say that you didn't intend for it to be overheard.'

Tubs couldn't look at her. Concentrated on digging the toe of one boot into the sand.

'I'm dropping Tubs and Deano off at the clubrooms, and Brownie at home,' said Sam. 'I've got a family meal at Uncle Gene and Aunt Liz's.'

Casey laughed. 'Sing Star for after-dinner entertainment?'

Sam cringed, but there was no point avoiding the question. Everyone in town knew the Kirby-Collins clan had more than its fair share of double-X chromosomes. Sam had two younger sisters, and Uncle Gene and Auntie Liz had three daughters.

'Adele song pack,' said Sam.

He knew his mates wouldn't snigger out loud because of Casey.

But he was definitely going to get shit later.

'Could be worse,' said Casey. 'My niece has the soundtrack to *Frozen* on high rotation. Thank God for noise-cancelling headphones.'

She snapped back into official mode. 'Right. Time to head off. Twilight's about to descend and you know what comes into force then.'

'Vampires?' said Deano.

'Worse,' said Casey. 'The liquor ban.'

She scanned the beach, spotted the empty can.

'The litter laws, however, are in force twenty-four seven, so make sure you take that with you.'

'How d'you know it's ours?' said Deano.

'Deano.'

Brownie pointed to the box at their feet, one dozen, same brand. Between the empties and the ones still in the box, even Deano could count only eleven cans.

'Even if it weren't, you'll do your bit as good citizens,' said Casey. 'Won't you?'

Like they were little kids back in school, all four of them shuffled and muttered, 'Yeah.'

'Good answer. Have a safe evening, boys.'

'Fucken bitch,' said Tubs, when Casey was safely out of range. 'Deserves a good seeing to.'

'Deserves a good seeing to?' said Brownie. 'Jesus, Tubs. Do you actually think about what comes out your mouth?'

'She was a fucken bitch to us!'

'No, Tubs, she wasn't. She simply called you out for being insulting and Deano for being a retard.'

'Hey!'

'She's a lesbian,' said Tubs. 'Everyone knows that.'

'Nah, actually, she's dating a dude from Hampton who teaches mixed martial arts,' said Sam. 'Mum told me.'

'Thinks she's too good for Bay men, then?'

'Jesus.' Brownie snatched up the box, stuffed the empties back in. 'It really *is* time to go. Fetch that can, Deano. And *don't* argue. I've got a hotline to my ancestors, and I won't hesitate to use it.'

On the way back to the car, Deano said, 'Are you OK about going to Christchurch, Sammo? Aren't you worried about the skinheads?'

'*Skin*heads? No, why?'

'Because you're — you know . . .'

'Part nigger?' said Brownie.

'Yeah. Nah. Um . . .'

'Deano, I'm, like, a quarter Samoan,' said Sam. '*You* look browner than I do.'

'I work outdoors!'

In the back seat of the car (Sam's dad's ute, which is why he never trusted anyone else to drive), Tubs said, 'So — this is kind of it, isn't it?'

'What? The end of all our youthful hopes and dreams?' said Brownie.

'Jeez, you're full of shit sometimes,' said Tubs. 'Nah, the last time we'll all hang out together over summer. Unless Sam boards his mobile up again and they fire him.'

'Once. I left my phone behind a wall *once*!'

'Well, fair dues,' said Brownie. 'You'd have to be as retarded as Deano to do it twice.'

'Hey!'

'We should do something,' said Tubs. 'Over summer. Make it one to remember.'

Sam knew Brownie's expression exactly mirrored his own.

'Hello? Tubs? Is that you?' said Brownie. 'Or have you swapped bodies with Bryan Adams?'

'So poetic!' said Sam.

'Fuck off,' said Tubs. 'I mean it. Let's have a really shit-hot last summer.'

'Doing what?' said Deano.

'Dunno. Have a few parties?'

'That's every summer,' said Brownie.

'Well, how about we go on a hunting trip?' said Tubs. 'We've always talked about hunting together. Dad'd lend us the gear.'

Mr Hanrahan was a keen hunter. Went up the bush in a big four-wheel-drive with spotlights. Or paid a fortune to get choppered in with his rich mates. He'd been to Africa twice. Shot a lion. And an elephant. Had the framed photos to prove it.

'Hunting what? Possums?' said Brownie.

'Deer, dickhead. Plenty of red deer in the hills.'

'You won't get stags with really big antlers till the roar,' said Deano. 'Not until March.'

Brownie swivelled in the front seat to stare at him. 'When did you become an expert?'

'My dad used to hunt . . .'

'That's right,' said Brownie, softly. 'I remember now.'

'Taught me how to shoot.'

Sam remembered, too. Deano's dad was a full-blown alkie now, but when they were kids, he'd been a pretty capable bushman. That's why Deano had always been the best shot with a BB gun. Brownie and Sam hit the targets about even. Tubs was useless. No patience.

'What do you think?' Brownie said to Sam.

If he were to be completely honest, Sam would rather spend the time with his family, even if that meant being surrounded by girls who never, *ever* stopped talking.

But there was a symbolism in the idea that attracted him, and which seemed a way to relieve some of the guilt he felt more and more when around Tubs and Deano. He and Brownie were best mates, and they always would be. Sam knew that even if they were apart for months, once they met again, they'd pick up right where they left off, no strain, no effort. But Tubs and Deano — the gap between them and him and Brownie had opened years back and it would only keep widening. Eventually — or perhaps rapidly now that Sam was leaving — there'd be a separation that childhood bonds wouldn't be strong enough to prevent. Separate lives, separate ambitions — if the word 'ambition' could be applied to Deano. Separate ideas about the world.

One last summer. A full stop. A farewell. They'd part forever, but on good terms, and with good memories.

'Let's do it,' said Sam.

Chapter 8

Kerry

'Broken.'

Oksana held up the vacuum-cleaner cord. It was frayed at the end where the plug should have been.

'I tell you. Vacuum no good. Electrolux is good. Strong. You buy Electrolux.'

'Oksana.'

Kerry saw Meredith regulate her breathing. He'd had only two conversations with Oksana, and both had made his head spin.

'You need to remove the plug by holding onto it and easing it gently but firmly from the wall socket,' said Meredith. 'You cannot remove it by tugging hard on the cord.'

'Should not break. I tell you.'

'It *won't* break,' persisted Meredith, 'if you are more careful.'

'I'll take it in to the electricians this afternoon,' said Kerry. 'Should be a simple repair.'

'Is bad vacuum,' said Oksana. 'You buy Electrolux.'

'I will consider it,' said Meredith. 'Thank you.'

Oksana lifted her coat from the kitchen chair where she always left it, despite Meredith's requests for her to hang it in the coat cupboard. The coat was long and quilted and a tinselly purple-pink. Oksana was a big fan of the pink colour-wheel. Today, she had on a pair of pastel pink Ugg boots, a rose-patterned jumper over purple leggings, and was carrying a fuchsia tote bag with 'Juicy' stamped on it in big black letters. Kerry had no idea how old Oksana was — sixty? — but it was obvious that in her youth she'd been a beauty, all high cheekbones and huge brown eyes. Today, she was still a handsome woman, with arms more muscular than those he'd seen on body builders. Male body builders.

'Next week, I do windows,' she informed Meredith.

'Shall I buy more glass cleaner for you?'

'Pshhh!' Oksana waved her hand as if dispelling bad air. 'Vinegar! Newspaper! Other is waste of money.'

'Very well. If you're sure.'

Oksana shoved her tote bag onto her arm and yanked open the back door.

'Next week — windows.'

'That sounded like a threat,' said Kerry, as Oksana's Peugeot revved down the drive.

'The glass will gleam like diamonds,' said Meredith. 'But woe betide any loose panes.'

'I can see now why dusting is included in my job description.'

Meredith's expression was severe.

'She must never find out that it's you and not me. I had the devil's own job convincing her to hand back the dusting cloths. Manufactured some falsehood about insurance, for which I'm rather ashamed. But she had managed to lift the silver wire from my grandmother's cloisonné vase, and snap the leg off a nineteenth-century French bronze tiger.'

'How does one snap a bronze?'

'Oksana locked herself in the hall cupboard once; there's

no door handle on the inside, which I *did* warn her about. She punched her way out. With her bare fists.'

'She told me she was descended from Genghis Khan,' said Kerry. 'A direct line, it seems.'

He trucked the kettle to the sink. Oksana's visits generally required a restorative, and it was too early in the day for straight Scotch. Meredith had already sat down in a chair. If she'd been a less genteel lady, he guessed, and more like, say, his mother, she would have let out a whoosh of air and an earthy expression of relief.

'How did she end up in Gabriel's Bay?' He placed the tea things on the table. 'Shall I pour?'

'Thank you,' said Meredith. 'And as to Oksana, I have not asked and she has not divulged. There are two persistent rumours. One is that she was a concierge on a Russian merchant vessel, jumped ship and was granted refugee status — her first job was at the Bay's now-defunct fish-processing plant. The other is that she was a mail-order bride, and the man she lives with is her husband.'

'And the man she lives with is—?'

'A recluse. His surname is, I believe, Torvaldsen. As to his first, and how he came to the area, no one knows.'

'A mysterious recluse,' said Kerry. 'Intriguing.' He sipped his tea. 'They never caught Lord Lucan, did they?'

Meredith raised a faint smile. 'Torvaldsen is in his sixties, according to those few who have glimpsed him. If he were alive, Lord Lucan would be well into his eighties.'

'Shame,' said Kerry. 'Could be just the ticket to bring the visitors flocking. "Roll up, roll up! See the nanny-murdering, noose-evading former British peer! BYO rotten fruit!"'

'Are we in need of flocks of visitors?'

'Well, feel free to strike me for impertinence — though not *too* hard — but Gabriel's Bay isn't exactly awash with tourist dollars. Or dollars of any kind, for that matter.'

'Not unexpected. It's a very small town.'

'Used to be bigger, though?'

Meredith hesitated, as if she were about to unlock a door that might swing open to reveal not one skeleton but a whole grinning row.

'The nineteen-eighties were a difficult decade for us,' she said. 'Farming subsidies were lifted. Government businesses — post, telephone, railways, banks — were privatised. The fish factory, cheese factory *and* the tobacco packing plant closed down. By the mid-nineties, the area had lost, at a rough estimate, twelve hundred jobs. For a town with a population of only five thousand at its height, the impact was — substantial.'

'And no more employers came to fill the gaps?'

'Some, yes. But no large ones, and few that offer more than seasonal or part-time work, or that pay above minimum wage. Most jobs are now either in Hampton or further out still. Hence the reduction of the Gabriel's Bay population by at least a third, and many of those remaining are elderly, or unemployable.' A wry smile. 'And some of us who fit into both those categories. Soon, we may be all that's left.'

Outside the kitchen window, Kerry heard the snip of hedge shears. Mr Phipps, the gardener, a man who spoke less than Jonty Barton but who kept Woodhall's garden looking fresh and blooming despite using tools that Noah would have called old-fashioned even while measuring up in cubits.

'I must tell him I intend to pot the hanging baskets,' said Meredith. 'I didn't bother last year, but I feel I'd now like to see some colour on the verandah.'

'Do you need me to stop by the nursery?'

Gabriel's Bay didn't have a garden centre — Kerry had quite a list now of what the town didn't have — but a group had formed a sort of plant collective, selling seedlings beneath the awning of the Legion of Frontiersmen's headquarters, empty since the death in 1992 of its last patriot and adventurer, former sapper Gordon C. Micklethwaite.

'Thank you, no,' said Meredith. 'I'm not sure yet what I want.'

Her way of saying she'd like to potter amongst plants. Kerry had assumed responsibility for most of the errands, and was glad to see that Meredith had taken the opportunity to make time — even if only half an hour — for herself. He liked his employer, liked being at Woodhall. He hoped she would keep him on.

Kerry had not been admitted again into Jonty's room, which, quite frankly, suited him fine. But Sidney's conviction that the man was a shameless faker niggled away, and among today's errands was one he would omit mentioning to Meredith, namely a visit to Dr Love, to find out if he could proffer any advice.

Another piece of information Kerry chose not to mention was that he'd answered the telephone yesterday morning, when Meredith was upstairs.

'Who are you?' the young-sounding woman on the other end had demanded.

'Kerry Macfarlane, new all-round provider of help to Mrs Barton. And you?'

'Help? What kind of help?'

She would never get a job in customer service with *that* manner.

'Preparing meals, running errands, light housework. Tasks of that ilk.'

'Wiping my dad's arse?'

Her dad?

'Not yet. But I won't shirk if that's required.'

'Are you live-in?'

'I have my own lamp. When your mother needs me, she simply gives it a rub.'

'Jesus,' she said. 'Mum must have been fucking desperate if she picked you.'

'May I take a message?' said Kerry. 'Your mother is busy with your father.'

'Wanker.'

'Is that the message?'

There was a slight pause. 'Fuck it, I'll call back,' she'd said. And hung up in Kerry's ear.

Given the tenor of the conversation and the fact Meredith had not told him about a second, living daughter, it wasn't much of a leap for Kerry to deduce relations were strained. Knowing her angry daughter was about to call might cause Meredith anxiety, so he decided not to forewarn her.

It bothered him, though. Concealment of one piece of information might be reasonably overlooked. Two and the scales tipped towards untrustworthy. The new, improved Kerry Macfarlane was supposed to be sincere and scrupulously honest. Even old Kerry hadn't been sneaky, only shallow.

He hoped whoever judged would see he meant well by it.

'I'll wash these dishes,' he told Meredith, as he gathered the tea things. 'And then I'll be off to town. Any last requests?'

There were none. Kerry washed and dried the tea set — Royal Worcester, his mother would approve — and headed out to the Fielder. Mr Phipps was bent over the roses, inspecting, Kerry assumed, for insects. The gardener was in his usual uniform of steel-cap boots and thick socks, a ribbed jumper apparently knitted from old porridge and the shortest shorts Kerry had seen outside a Rihanna video.

The best legs, too. Mr Phipps must be pushing seventy but he had the slender, toned legs of a young female ballet dancer, with skin that was tanned, unblemished and without discernible hair. Possibly because all the hair Mr Phipps possessed was concentrated in his ears and nose. From those two features, grey hair sprouted, as frilled and tightly whorled as ornamental kale. It should have been repulsive, but somehow it seemed natural, organic. Mr Phipps when at rest, for instance taking a cup of tea, blended into the garden setting like a moss-covered tree stump. It might explain why he didn't talk, only nodded. He was some kind of vegetative deity.

Kerry greeted him. 'Mr Phipps.'

A nod. And almost a smile! Well, it *was* spring. The season of snowdrops and hope and new beginnings. When he started the car, the radio began to play ZZ Top's 'La Grange'. No one could listen to that song and not feel perked up by several degrees.

Finding a park in the exact location he needed, Kerry once more saw the upside of living in a small town. Easy parking. *Free* parking. Unlike London, where the city took a lien on your vital organs in return for allowing you to park outside your own house.

Walking past the video store — who still owned a video player? — Kerry saw the female police officer standing in the alley next to a teenage boy with the figure of a marrow — bulbous head and body, no neck.

'Bit of advice, Wade,' she was saying. 'If you want to tag a wall, don't use your own name.'

Kerry walked on. He'd decided to get his surreptitious errand over and done with first. Dr Love's surgery was in a stand-alone bungalow painted white-stucco with blue trim. The waiting room was empty, and sported the kind of nineteen-seventies-style furniture pieces that hipsters snapped up as junk-shop bargains only to find they were still ugly when repainted and reupholstered. But it was as neat as a pin, and somehow homely, welcoming.

The short, round-faced woman with masses of curly brown hair eyeing him from the reception desk looked distinctly unwelcoming. She also looked familiar. Kerry tried, but couldn't place her.

'Yes?' she said.

'I've taken a job up at Woodhall.' He assumed this would no longer be news. 'I'd like to talk to Doctor Love about Jonty Barton.

I don't want him to breach patient confidentiality or anything,' he added. 'I just need a steer on how best to manage the situation. Any tips or advice that might be of benefit.'

'Of benefit to Jonty?'

For a small woman with fluffy hair, she was surprisingly fierce.

'Er, no,' said Kerry. 'To Mered— er, Mrs Barton. I mean, I *am* helping her with my job and all, but I feel — I don't *know*, it's just an instinct — there might be more ways I could be of use.'

'You mean like secretly crushing antidepressants into his gruel?'

Was she joking?

'Although, of course,' she continued, 'that would violate all kinds of ethics. And possibly laws.'

If she was, she had a masterful poker face.

'Which I could happily ignore if it weren't for the extraordinary level of respect I have for my employer.'

'That's the end of that idea, then?' said Kerry.

'It is,' she said. 'More's the pity. And I doubt Doctor Love has any better ones. If he had, he'd have put them in place by now.'

'So I'm wasting my time?'

She stared at him. It was like being critically assessed by an ancient powerful god that had assumed the form of a koala — confusing and terrifying in equal measure.

'Why do you want to help Meredith?'

'Because, er, I like her. I admire her. I—'

'I'll rephrase. What's in it for you?'

Kerry decided to fight back.

'She's leaving me thousands in her will. Many thousands. We haven't nailed down the exact figure as yet.'

Was that a smile?

'I'll tell Doctor Love you called in,' she said, 'and that you're interested in what can be done to improve Mr Barton's — condition. And you can pass on my regards to Mrs Barton and tell her that, without her sanity and clarity at meetings, the Progressive Association has regressed into a pack of fools who couldn't find their arses with both hands. Couldn't find an arse, full stop, if it were sitting on their face.'

'The Progressive Association?'

'Self-appointed guardians of the Bay's future. Who have not a clue how to reverse our town's decline. See my previous comment about finding arses.'

'It *is* in decline, is it?' said Kerry. 'How badly?'

'Are you a professional do-gooder?'

Again, Kerry decided attack was the best form of defence. Show a woman like this an ounce of fear and her teeth would be in your throat before you could say 'Shih Tzu'.

'Card-carrying and internationally endorsed. Problem with that?'

'You had a kick around with Sidney's boys.'

A feint to catch him off-guard. She was dangerously good.

'Are you looking for a reason to arrest me?'

The woman actually chuckled. Kerry relished the victory, but felt it safer to celebrate on the inside.

'I'm Mac,' she said. 'Mac Reid. You've met my husband, Jacko.'

That made *so* much sense.

'Kerry Macfarlane.'

'How long will you be staying here?' said Mac.

'Er, how long *should* I stay?'

'Sidney's boys love soccer.'

'Football.'

'If you say so.'

'Ninety-nine-point-nine per cent of the world says so.'

'They could do with a coach.'

'Happy to oblige,' said Kerry. 'Anything else?'

'Know anyone with a medical degree?'

'Er, my mother's a trained nurse.'

'Father?'

'Science teacher.'

'Useless.'

'Not at all,' said Kerry. 'He's quite the whiz with a sliding bevel.'

Mac folded her arms.

'Does your mother have connections within the British medical profession?'

'You mean — "connections"?' Kerry mimed the inverted commas.

'Is she in touch with doctors looking for jobs overseas?'

'Would you like me to ask her?'

Mac ripped the top sheet off a memo pad, scribbled on it.

'My email,' she said.

Kerry put the note in his pocket.

'Was there something else?' said Mac. 'Next appointment's due.'

Why not? Be courageous. Be direct. Be purposeful!

'I don't suppose you can tell me the identity of the very attractive young woman with blonde hair who rides a horse on the beach?' said Kerry.

Mac's eyebrows rose, and she began to laugh. It wasn't the gosh-how-funny-aren't-you-a-stitch kind of laugh. It was the mocking, belittling kind. And it went on and on.

Kerry left, dragging his dignity behind him by one leg.

Someone had keyed the door of the Fielder. Etched their name. Wade.

Kerry lifted the vacuum cleaner from the boot. On the way to the electricians, because he knew he'd never win a fight with Mac Reid, he fantasised instead about beating marrow-boy to a pulpy ooze.

Chapter 9

Sidney

Kerry's blush extended from his collarbone to his hairline, Sidney observed with amusement. Even the backs of his hands had gone pink. And he was shifting around on the Boat Shed bar stool like someone was poking him from below.

To be fair, few people kept their composure when they first met Devon. It wasn't every day you saw someone that good-looking — like a milk-coffee-tinted Rossetti portrait, tall and graceful, classical features and that extraordinary curtain of thick blond hair. The genetic dice had rolled only once to create Devon — the rest of his extended family were thickset and cheerfully plain. Two of his older sisters formed the front row of the Hampton women's rugby team. In the family's regular gatherings, Devon stood out like a swan surrounded by starlings. To their credit, the family didn't value beauty over character and never treated him any differently, which had allowed Devon to grow up gloriously uncaring about his looks. He couldn't help but be aware of their effect, but other people's reactions were their problem, not his.

When he was sixteen, Devon had been offered a modelling contract by a New York agency, who'd seen a photo of him and his horse, Tiu, on Instagram. The money had reportedly been significant, but Devon had turned it down without hesitating. 'Too much time away from family,' was his reason. 'Too much time indoors.' He worked evenings Thursday to Saturday at the Boat Shed, and weekdays at a horse rescue centre and training stables south of Hampton, where he was building a reputation for getting results with animals ruled too mad or wild to save from the knacker's yard. In between, he was studying for a degree. Sidney would be happy if her boys grew up with half Devon's work ethic.

'I, er, I saw you riding your horse on the beach the other day,' said Kerry. 'Beautiful creature.'

Kerry's voice sounded a little high and strangled. Sidney knew he'd have to get over his awkwardness pronto. Devon refused to have anything to do with people who went weird around him.

'You a horseman?'

Devon put a beer down in front of him. Kerry took four large swallows in quick succession.

'My mother's family used to train racehorses.' Kerry sounded more like himself now. 'In Northern Ireland. Won several derbies, I gather. But that was early last century, before we lost all our money. I'm named after my ancestor, who was known in Gaelic as *Kerry na Kopple*, or Kerry of the Horses. Which all might suggest I'm leading up to answering your question with a resounding "yes" but, sadly, the truth is I've never been on a horse in my life.'

'Never too late,' said Devon. 'I could start you on Tiu. He's fast but he's safe.'

'What does "Tiu" mean, Dev?' said Sidney.

'A few things, depending on where you're from. If you're Ngāi Tahu, it's north wind.'

'Blow bonnie breeze my lover to me,' said Kerry.

'What?'

'Old song. About hopeless love.'

Jacko stepped in from the kitchen. Devon was tall, but with Jacko behind him, the pair looked like the largest and smallest in a set of Russian dolls.

'You eating?' Jacko said to Kerry.

'Yes, please. What am I having?'

'Pāua fritters.'

'As in — "I got the power"?'

'As in abalone,' said Sidney. 'It's a shellfish. Tastes amazing if you know how to cook it. Like burned rubber if you don't.'

'Yes or no?' said Jacko, impatient.

'I'm game,' said Kerry. 'Bring on the power.'

He told Sidney, 'I ate a fertilised duck embryo in the Philippines. Boiled in its own shell.'

'Ergh,' she said. 'Was that as disgusting as it sounds?'

'If it sounds more disgusting than re-eating your own vomit, then yes.'

'Saw Tubs Hanrahan do that,' said Devon. 'Chucked up into a beer glass then drank it again.'

'Did he *mean* to?' said Sidney.

'Kinda had to. Club initiation.'

'Which club? League of Morons?'

'Kinda.' Devon made a quick face. 'Rugby club.'

'Of course. Silly me.'

Sidney knew why Devon had no fondness for the club. He'd been an athletic boy at school, still was, and a good rugby player, fast and strong in the backline. But as he grew from a typical skinny, mop-haired kid into his current looks, the rugby gang couldn't handle it, found it threatening. They might dress up in drag at the Christmas parties, but actual androgyny was a step too far. A bloke who could be mistaken for a girl? One more beautiful than their own girlfriends? That fried their tiny brains, that did,

Sidney decided, made them uncertain, anxious. So they did what fearful, threatened men always do — got nasty.

The men of Devon's family had always been club members. His great-great-granddad captained the first Gabriel's Bay team. His great-uncle had played at county level and was once selected for an All Blacks team. He spent the match on the bench, but that was enough for lasting glory and a framed photo on the clubroom walls. Devon's dad, uncles, brothers and cousins had all played, and most would still come down on a Saturday night for a drink. Sidney had heard that when the abuse started, subtle at first, soon not subtle at all, Devon knew his family would quit in protest — or more likely bash someone and get in trouble — so he quit first. Told his family he had a job on Saturday nights and then asked Jacko to employ him. Which Jacko did, even though back then the business could barely afford to pay Jacko. As it turned out, Devon brought in customers. People drove over the hill to eat at the Boat Shed, coming the first time to look at the boy who could have been a supermodel, and returning because Jacko's food was so good. Many also enjoyed the frisson of terror they experienced whenever Jacko spoke to them, or simply stuck his head around the kitchen door. People, Sidney had long since concluded, were weird.

'I met his wife today.' Kerry nodded towards the kitchen.

'And survived, I see,' said Sidney, with a smile.

'I'm still checking whether parts of me are missing.' Kerry leaned closer, so as not to be overheard. 'What is Mac short for? Mack the Knife?'

'Why don't you ask her?'

'Ah, ha ha.' Kerry sat up again. 'I may be a fool, but I'm not stupid.'

'Did you talk to Mac about Jonty?'

'She's even less of a fan than you are.'

'That's because Mac has the best bullshit detector in the land,' said Sidney.

'Ain't that the truth,' said Devon.

The front door opened, and Devon went to greet a young couple who'd come in with a baby. The Boat Shed had steady custom tonight, both dine-in and takeaway, which was good to see. Sidney knew the café wasn't a real indication of the town's fortunes, or her own, but when it was busy, life didn't feel *quite* such a grind. It helped, too, that Gene was absent. Sidney enjoyed Gene's quick wit and trenchant humour, but knew that if he were here, he'd be ribbing her mercilessly about sitting up at the bar with Kerry, which would dilute how much she was enjoying his company. This was quite a surprise. Gabriel's Bay people with the vocabulary and intellectual horsepower for proper to-and-fro banter she could count on one hand, Gene being the middle finger. Kerry was witty in a less confrontational style, plus he gave off a straight-up vibe that Sidney responded to. Fergal had possessed a way with words and an easy charm, but that was a shiny veneer disguising rottenness beneath. Sidney remembered his apology when he finally rang to say he'd left her. 'I'm so, *so* sorry, but I'm just that kind of guy. We need our freedom. You're better off, believe me.' She'd been too shocked at the outrageous clichés to yell at him, though she'd done a lot of yelling in her mind since. Committed occasional violence, too.

But enough of that. She was here, having a rare evening out, with people who were fun to talk to. She lifted her wine and found she'd finished it. Devon was taking water to the couple with the baby. They seemed very happy with each other, with their little family. She hoped that would continue.

'It's sensible to pace ourselves,' said Kerry, who also had an empty glass. 'One every hour is what they say.'

'It's one every month for me,' said Sidney. 'Maybe two. I can't afford to go out more often. Certainly can't afford to drink wine at home. I could set up a still, I suppose, use my potato peelings. I do enjoy having an intact stomach lining, so perhaps not.'

'Speaking of home,' Kerry said, 'where are the boys?'

'I gave them matches for a fire and told them not to answer the door,' said Sidney. 'No, they're at a birthday party sleepover.'

'Madison's?'

'Definitely not.'

'Her parents not the sleepover type?'

'Her parents aren't even the parents type,' said Sidney. 'Her dad's in Auckland most of the time — in financial strife, so the rumour mill has it. And her mum—'

Sidney hesitated. On the one hand, she could have empathy for Olivia. She knew what it was like to be forced into the role of solo mother, with little support and bugger-all financial certainty. But on the other, Olivia was a grown woman, with a brain and all limbs intact. If she didn't like how her life was, she could take responsibility and change it — move away, get a job, give lovely Madison a stable home. Instead, Olivia was acting up like a spoiled teenager, all sulky and rebellious, giving her gorgeous daughter the bare minimum care.

'Madison's mum is struggling a bit, to put it mildly,' she told Kerry. 'But Madison never, ever complains, so I have to accept that she's happy enough.'

'Only children can often be very loyal to their parents.'

'You speak from experience?'

'I do,' said Kerry. 'Mind you, my parents adore each other, and have always been quite nice to me, too, which helps.'

Devon was back behind the bar. He offered another beer to Kerry, who refused — 'Driving' — then pointed an enquiry at Sidney's wine glass.

'Why not?' She held it out for a refill. 'I'm walking home.'

'Er,' Kerry began, 'please don't think me presumptuous—'

'No, you can't come home with me.'

His startled face caused her to be the one to blush. Stupid, making a crack like that. Now he'd think she thought there might be a possibility he'd fancy her. Sidney knew she wasn't the type of woman men fancied. Fergal did, but that was years ago, when she was as pretty as she'd ever get — before children and worry and lack of money widened her hips and dulled her bloom.

Fortunately, Devon had popped into the kitchen to give Jacko the new orders, so Sidney only had to be embarrassed in front of one person. She should make light of it, but no brilliantly self-deprecating words came to mind. She took a big swig of wine instead.

'Sorry,' said Kerry. 'I started off cack-footed there. What I *meant* to say was — would you consider letting me coach your boys in football? And any other children you know might be keen? If what you said earlier about the town's preference for the oval ball is true, then who knows how many young fans of the beautiful game have been driven underground?'

He looked and sounded sincere. Seemed convinced that he, not she, had made the blunder. Seemed genuine in his offer.

Sidney wanted to believe him, because Aidan and Rory would *love* having a football coach. On the other hand, the keener the expectation, the greater the disappointment. She would not put her boys at risk.

'Why do you want to do that?' she said. 'Have you got the time to commit to it? How do you see it working — where would they play, how would they get there, what—?'

'Jeez, Sid.' Devon set two plates in front of them. 'Take your foot off the poor bloke's neck.'

'No, no,' said Kerry, quickly. 'They're all fair questions. If they were my children, I wouldn't shove them into the care of any old person with shorts and a whistle, either.'

He squinted down at his plate. 'What colour is pāua in the wild?'

'Mollusc colour,' said Sidney. 'In this case, perfectly caramelised on the outside by excellent cooking. The green specks are coriander, I'd say.' She took a bite. 'A hint of garlic, too. Delicious,' she told Devon.

'My kuia, my grannies, would call it too bloody fancy,' he said, with a grin. 'They'd say all you need's flour, milk and egg, pinch of baking soda. Mince the pewa, too. That's the soft part,' he explained to Kerry. 'And mind you take the teeth out.'

'*Teeth*?' Kerry's fork halted mid-way. 'What kind of mutant mollusc has *teeth*?'

'All of them,' said Devon. 'Except the bivalves.'

'Devon's studying for a Bachelor's in Biological Science,' said Kerry. 'Distance learning.'

'Yeah, only another million years to go,' said Devon.

'I am full of admiration,' said Kerry. 'I did the easiest degree I could, in the shortest possible time, and I regret it.'

'Order up!' came from the kitchen, and Devon hopped to it.

'What did you study?' Sidney said.

'IT. Worked for ten years as a database administrator. Company that made software for the healthcare industry.'

'Sounds—'

'Dull,' said Kerry. 'Deathly, stupefyingly dull. And so it was. But it was secure, and it paid OK, and we had a weekly fish supper and cocktails night.'

'Don't feel bad,' said Sidney. 'I did an Art History degree. I have out-of-date supermarket coupons that are more valuable.'

'How did you come to Gabriel's Bay? Were you brought up here?'

'No. Brought up in a well-off, middle-class, urban home. Very tidy and tasteful. Everything matched, including my parents.'

'I'm picturing an abundance of ecru,' said Kerry. 'And tiny guest soaps that are never used but regularly dusted.'

'Uncanny,' said Sidney. 'I ended up here because I followed a man with a vision.'

'Jesus?'

'Well, he did have a beard.' She jabbed her fork into a fritter. 'And a dream of a simpler, community-based lifestyle. He wanted to grow vegetables, and keep chickens and bees, and barter with neighbours, and carve wood, and have loads of children who would all run naked around the garden.'

'Sounds idyllic.'

'Then he discovered that even a simple life requires you to haul arse and actually work.'

Sidney bit into her fritter.

'We used my savings as a deposit on a falling-down house,' she said. 'Had two babies less than a year apart. And when Rory was two months old, he left.'

'Ouch,' said Kerry. 'I'm sorry.'

'It was nine years ago,' said Sidney. 'I'm still here, still standing.' She swigged the last of her wine.

'Still furious, too,' she said. 'How about you? Why are you here?'

'Oh. Well . . .'

Jacko loomed over them. Held out to Sidney a jar of preserved plums. She twisted off the lid. Jacko went back to the kitchen.

'Wait,' said Kerry. 'What was that?'

'Plums,' said Sidney. 'Black Doris variety. Meredith's, I'm pretty sure.'

'No, that routine with the jar!'

Sidney shrugged. 'I'm good at getting lids off.'

'Better than a man with hands that could crush *cars*?'

'Seems so.'

Devon came to clear their plates.

'Pudding?' he said. 'It's homemade vanilla ice cream and warmed plums with chocolate sauce. Also homemade, and with a kick.'

'Shouldn't,' said Sidney.

'Oh, come on,' said Kerry. 'Without you, there'd *be* no pudding.'

'*And* you're walking home,' said Devon.

'Very well,' she said. 'But if I can't button my jeans tomorrow, I'll punch you both in the head.'

'A threat I take seriously,' said Kerry. 'Now that I've seen what you can do with lids.'

'Were *you* serious?' said Sidney. 'About the coaching?'

'Entirely. It'll be mainly skill work, so I've already asked, and the primary school's given me permission to use their grounds. And if we ever have enough children for a match, I'll beard the rugby club in their lair and beg a go on their field.'

'What about kit?'

'The school has some balls they'll let us use,' said Kerry. 'Flat as hedgehogs on the M1 but I've bought a pump, and a whistle. And a first-aid kit that I hope will be redundant.'

Sidney was impressed. He really *had* given it some thought. Hadn't proved his ability to stick at it, of course, but it was a good start.

'Do you want me to put a notice up at school? How many kids can you handle?'

'Fourteen's probably the limit. If we did end up finding another team to play, we'd have eleven plus substitutes.'

'Girls, too?'

'Absolutely.'

'Ages?'

'Preferably no younger than nine and no older than twelve.'

'When?'

'How about Wednesdays after school? I have some flexibility with my hours.'

Sidney nodded, mulling it over.

'We could make that work,' she said.

'We?' said Kerry.

'You'll need help wrangling,' said Sidney. 'And I'm an expert wrangler.'

'Thank you.'

'You're welcome. And thank *you* for taking this on.'

Devon placed two bowls down on the bar. The aroma of real vanilla, boozy chocolate and sweet-tart fruit, creaminess marbled with ruby juice and glossy dark swirls. Sidney might still regret her decision tomorrow, but right now, she would only enjoy.

'However, if you let my boys down,' she added. 'I'll wreak such almighty vengeance upon you that you'll wish you'd never been born.'

She smiled at him.

'Just so we're clear.'

Chapter 10

Madison

Madison leapt out of Sidney's car and ran into the kitchen to tell her mum the exciting news. She was in a soccer team! No — *football.* She *had* to remember to call it football, because when anyone called it soccer, Kerry clutched his heart and pretended to be mortally wounded. He said if anyone called it soccer during training, they'd forfeit their chocolate fish at the end.

'Mum! Mum!'

She banged the door open, even though she knew her mum hated rushing and noise. Didn't mean to, she was just so *excited.*

'Mum—?'

No one was in the kitchen, or in the room off it that she wasn't allowed to call the sunroom because that was tacky. Madison's house was only one level, but there were lots of rooms all linked by hallways that went off in different directions. She headed off towards what her mum called her reading room, though she didn't read many books, mainly the shiny magazines that got sent through the mail.

She could hear voices. Two people. Her mum. And her dad!

Madison sped up. Her dad had said he wouldn't be here

until next weekend. He'd said he was going to come down *last* weekend and take her to the bookshops in Hampton, but some work stuff came up. He must have dealt with it quicker than he'd expected.

The door to the reading room was partly closed, and the tone of the voices coming through the gap made Madison wonder whether she shouldn't go in. She was used to her mum sounding a bit cross when she talked to her dad — 'snippy' is what Sidney called it — or really cross, which usually meant she was about to slam a door. Her dad never raised his voice, but sort of laughed and protested at what her mum said, like he was trying to convince her she had it all wrong. Sometimes his voice went like Aidan and Rory's did when Sidney accused them of what she called 'wheedling', sort of sing-songy and high.

But her mum and dad weren't snippy right now, or wheedling. Their words were all breathy, coming out hard and quick, piling on top of each other. They sounded *scared*.

'Rick, are you hearing yourself?' said her mum. 'You're like the Black Knight in Monty bloody Python, still thinking you can fight with all your limbs hacked off.'

'I *can*,' said Madison's dad. 'We'll find a buyer for the vineyard, no problem. Then that'll clear the IRD debt and give me some leverage to tell the bank to shove it, the lying arseholes. No way I signed finance deals that weren't interest-only.'

'So everything hinges on selling this place? Even though it hasn't made a profit since you bought it? Or ever?'

'We'll find a buyer, Liv,' said her dad. 'Land's still worth a shitload.'

Madison's mum gave a short, sharp laugh. 'What's this "we" business, white man? You *owe* me, Rick, you seriously do. *You* made me come to this hick hellhole. *You're* the one who's created this financial cesspit. All *I* did was be naïve enough to trust you.'

'You *can* trust me,' said her dad. 'It's a temporary hitch. It happens all the time to the best of us — parameters shift and you have to adjust. We — *I'm* adjusting. And I'll get us back on track, I promise.'

They stopped talking, and Madison wondered if her dad was giving her mum a hug.

But then her mum said, 'I can't even divorce you, can I? Unless I want an IOU written on a Post-It as settlement, right?'

Her dad said nothing, and Madison heard her mum give that short laugh again, softer this time, and murmur something that sounded like 'Sumvabish'.

Then her mum spoke up again. 'OK, but I'm not living on bloody dry bread and country air. I want a *decent* bloody allowance — and I don't really give a shit how you manage it. Understood? It's the *least* you can do.'

'Liv, there's only so much—'

'You *owe* me,' said Madison's mum, quite fiercely.

Her dad was quiet for a moment.

When he spoke, his voice was flat. 'Sure. OK. I'll sort it out.'

'Great,' said her mum, though she didn't sound like she meant it. 'Can you piss off now? Don't worry about leaving me alone. I've given up trying to escape.'

Footsteps towards the door. Suddenly, Madison didn't want them to know she was there. She turned and ran, back to the kitchen. Where she found a surprised-looking Sidney.

'Hey!' said Sidney. 'I popped back because you left your book in the car. And I know how much—'

She bent down to peer in Madison's face.

'You OK?'

Before Madison could say anything, her dad walked in. Yanked open the fridge and grabbed a beer without noticing either of them. When he did, he almost dropped the bottle.

'Christ.'

His face was all red and cross-looking, and his hair stuck up on top. Her dad's hair used to be blond, but now it was mostly grey, though he still got the hairdresser to put highlights in it. 'The famous Rick Jensen frosted tips,' her mum had said once.

'Hi,' said Sidney. 'Sorry to startle you. I'm returning Maddie's book.'

And just like that her dad stopped looking all annoyed. He straightened up, set the beer down on the counter, and stuck out a hand.

'Hello,' he said, with a bright smile. 'I'm Rick Jensen. And you must be—?'

'Sidney Gillespie. Mother of Madison's friends, Aidan and Rory. We *have* met before.'

Sidney's own smile was polite but thin, like the one she'd put on when a religious person had come to her house with two children, selling magazines.

'Of course!' said Madison's dad. 'Apologies. It's been a long day.'

And then all *three* of them leapt, as they heard a big smash in another part of the house. Oksana wasn't around, so Madison's mum must have accidentally dropped something.

'Mm,' said Madison's dad. 'Perhaps I should go and check on that?'

Another big smash. Her dad winced, but kept smiling.

'That, too.'

'How about I have Madison tonight?' said Sidney.

'Madison?'

Her dad blinked, like she'd been invisible before and had only just appeared. His smile widened, and his eyes went all crinkly, so she knew he was glad to see her.

'Hey, sweetheart,' he said.

Madison ran over and hugged him around the waist. Her dad patted her shoulder, but his head kept turning towards the other part of the house, where her mum was, as if expecting something else to go smash any minute.

'I could have Maddie sleep over at my place,' said Sidney. 'While things here are . . .'

Her dad's phone beeped and he snatched it out of his pocket with one hand, while his other kind of scooped Madison off his middle.

'One moment,' he said, and walked off into the living room, where he could talk in private.

Madison heard Sidney suck in a long breath and blow it quietly out.

'OK, Maddie,' she said. 'Go and fetch a change of clothes, and your toothbrush.'

Madison hesitated. Her dad was home for the first time in ages, and both her parents had sounded really upset and worried before, like they needed a hug.

She could hear her dad talking, but couldn't make out what he was saying. He didn't like to be interrupted when he was on the phone.

'Go on,' Sidney's voice was kind. 'We'll call your mum and dad before you go to bed.'

Madison went to her bedroom and gathered up a set of clothes, making sure to put in two pairs of underpants, just in case, and a jersey because you never knew what the weather would do. She got her toothbrush and some toothpaste, and placed everything carefully in the small brown bag with the pattern that sort of looked like stars and flowers along with the letters LV that her mum said stood for Louis someone. Her dad had bought the bag in New York, but her mum said it was a knock-off, so she gave it to Madison.

As she walked out her bedroom door, Madison remembered

that she'd been excited when she first came home, about tomorrow after school being their first football training session. The excitement had all gone now — it was like a big fist was pushing her feelings down, and taking up space inside her, making it hard to breathe. She got a pair of shorts, anyway, and a spare t-shirt and her old sneakers, so she wouldn't dirty her special new ones that her mum had ordered all the way from France.

Then she realised that if her dad was home, then maybe he could watch her train? A tiny new bubble of excitement managed to escape past the big fist, and Madison ran back to the kitchen to tell her dad, ask if he could come.

But the only person waiting was Sidney, who took her bag and said, briskly, 'Come on. We'll go back and make pikelets. With your favourite jam — blackberry.'

Outside, Aidan and Rory were kicking a ball at the drystone wall that a man had taken a whole two months to build out of yellowish rocks that looked like old cheese. Each time the ball hit, there was a little cloud of yellow dust and bits of rock crumbled onto the ground.

Sidney didn't tell Aidan and Rory off like she normally would. She didn't say anything at all, and Madison saw the boys look at each other with round eyes. They got straight in the car and didn't even make a fuss about who had to sit in the middle.

Madison felt bad that she hadn't said goodbye to her mum and dad. But Sidney had promised she could phone them tonight, before she went to bed, so she'd look forward to that. Her mum *and* dad — she could say goodnight to both of them *and* tell them about football training.

The big fist felt lighter, and Madison closed her eyes and imagined how pleased her mum and dad would be when she told them all about Kerry and football and the fun she was going to have tomorrow.

'Kerry's a girl's name.'

Madison knew Tanya Booth was being mean because she didn't like Kerry telling her she couldn't train in gumboots.

'Yeah,' said her older sister, Shari. 'Are you gay?'

Madison felt suddenly worried that they might ruin the first football training. But, to her relief, Kerry didn't seem bothered at all.

'Thank you both,' he said, 'for that perfect introduction to our training session's rules. Listen up, team, and learn by heart because I will give no second chances . . .'

He held up his hand, pointed a finger at the sky.

'Rule One: you're a team and a team has eleven players of equal standing, so don't hog the ball and don't be a prima donna. Rule Two—'

'What's a prima donna?' said Shari.

'Someone who throws tantrums when they can't get their way,' said Kerry. 'Or who sulks, or blames others when they make a mistake.'

'Like Madonna did 'cos her son didn't want to live with her?' said Shari.

'A fine example, Shari. Thank you.'

Kerry put up his second finger. 'Rule Two—'

'Is prima donna named after Madonna?'

'Just a happy coincidence. Two—'

'Have you seen Madonna in concert?'

'Shari,' said Kerry. 'This is football training not *Pop Idol*. Be quiet now, and we can discuss the oeuvre of the Material Girl over our chocolate fish. Two—'

'Is oovra like another word for—?'

'*Two*: show respect at all times — to each other, the opposing team, the referee, the spectators, and any and all random passers-by. That means: no name-calling, no swearing, no arguing and, as per Rule One, no sulking or tantrums.'

'*Ow*!'

Rory clutched his arm, pointed at Lincoln Turvey.

'He stuck me with his compass!'

'Lincoln.' Kerry held out a hand.

Lincoln shook his head and kept on shaking it until he must have been dizzy. He did that a lot in class. Madison had heard one of the mothers say he had a disorder, but she wasn't sure what that meant.

'Rule Two also means no hurting, Lincoln,' said Kerry. 'No hitting, biting or kicking, or assault with any kind of weapon, including those of maths instruction. If you can't manage it, I'll have to send you home. If you *can* manage it, I'll let you blow my whistle after the session. Loud as you like.'

Madison could tell that Rory really wanted Lincoln to go home. But Lincoln nodded, passed the compass to Kerry, and then spun in circles on the spot.

'Rule Three,' said Kerry. 'No cheating. I'll be lenient while we're learning how to play, but after that — straight to the sidelines. Right.' He clapped his hands together. 'Are we all clear on the rules? Are we all willing to play by them?'

He stared around at the group, making sure everyone looked him in the eye. All the kids nodded. Lincoln kept on nodding after everyone else had stopped.

'OK. Champion. Let's get to it. Who's played before? Apart from Rory and Aidan?'

Madison put up her hand. So did Dylan Weir. And Reuben Coates.

'You have *not*,' Tanya Booth to him. 'You're *such* a liar.'

Reuben tried to punch her on the arm and missed. For a bigger girl, Tanya moved pretty quickly. She skipped away, laughing at him, and he chased her, head down and bellowing like a small charging bull.

Kerry stepped in front, caught Reuben by the shoulders and held him gently until he stopped trying to run.

'Whoa there, partner,' said Kerry. 'Tanya, stop smirking or you're going home.'

'He isn't nine, either,' said Shari. 'He's only eight. The notice said you had to be nine.'

Reuben began to bellow and wriggle again.

'Whoa-oh, listen up,' said Kerry. 'Being eight is no problem. You're fast, aren't you? You'll get around the bigger kids easy, I'll bet.'

Reuben wouldn't look at Kerry, but he stayed still, and you could tell he was listening.

'Oh, man,' said Aidan. 'Are we *ever* going to play? It's been like *ten minutes*.'

'You cool?' Kerry asked Reuben.

He nodded, so Kerry let him go.

'OK, said Kerry. 'Ball skills. It's all about control — making that ball go exactly where you want it to.'

'Back of the net!' Rory punched his fist in the air.

'Indeed, Rory. But before that, you need to move it along the ground, fast and efficiently, and you need to pass it accurately, so . . .'

Kerry showed them a few moves, and then divided them into two groups. Madison went into the 'played before' group with Rory, Aidan, Reuben and Dylan. The other group had Tanya and Shari, Lincoln and Peter Gilbert, whose mum worked in the library in Hampton. Peter had super-thick glasses and was very good at maths, and spoke like he was English even though Madison knew he'd been born and brought up in Gabriel's Bay.

Madison's group did an exercise called Gladiator, where they had to try to stop Aidan kicking their balls away from them and out of the playing area. Aidan was the best player by miles, so it was easy for him to get the ball off everyone. Everyone except Reuben, who *was* really fast, like Kerry had said.

Madison saw Aidan getting frustrated. When he got frustrated, sometimes he lashed out. She looked away to see if Kerry was watching, but he was busy with the others, who were playing a game where their balls were dogs they had to take for a walk. 'Your dog wants to sniff a tree!' said Kerry, and they had to dribble the ball over to a cone. Everyone was giggling and it *did* look like fun, but Madison wished Kerry would turn his head her way, because she really needed him to make sure Aidan didn't get too cross and start—

Smack! Right in the face, hard enough to knock her over onto the concrete.

Madison sat up, holding her face and gulping for air, trying not to cry. It *stung*!

Kerry slid onto his knees next to her. 'Let me see.'

She moved her hand from her cheek, which was all hot and still stinging.

'Ouch,' said Kerry. 'Sit tight and I'll get the ice pack.'

'It was Reuben!' shouted Aidan. '*He* did it!'

'*Oo*-oo.' The Booth sisters sang together. '*Reu*-ben's gonna *get* it.'

'Quiet!' Madison had never seen Kerry angry before. 'Reuben is *not*—'

But Reuben was already sprinting across the courtyard.

'Reuben!' Kerry yelled after him.

Too late. He'd disappeared behind the prefabs.

'All well?'

Sidney walked up, jingling her car keys. Saw Madison on the ground.

'Maddie!'

Sidney crouched down, but had to move back when Kerry came with the ice pack.

'Hold that on your cheek,' he told Madison. 'Long as you can stand it.'

All the other kids were standing around now, mouths open — 'catching flies' as her mum would say. Madison felt embarrassed, and worried that she might get whoever kicked the ball into trouble. She was sure it must have been an accident.

'How on earth did *this* happen?' said Sidney.

'Reuben Coates kicked a ball right in Madison's face!' Aidan spoke in a gasping rush.

'Yeah, but you *made* him,' said Dylan.

'Did *not*, you—!'

'Enough!' said Kerry. 'Dylan, what do you mean?'

'*Mum*, he—' Aidan sounded even more gaspy.

'Your turn next,' said Sidney, firmly. 'Dylan?'

Dylan had a pale, round, freckly face that reminded Madison of brown sugar sprinkled on a bowl of milky porridge. But he was nice — shared his stuff, liked things to be fair.

'Aidan couldn't get the ball off Reuben,' said Dylan. 'So he took Madison's ball while she wasn't looking and kicked it at him real hard, and Reuben kicked it back real hard but it went all wonky and hit Madison right in the face.'

'OK,' said Kerry. 'I think I'm clear. Aidan, is that what happened?'

Aidan hung his head, scuffed his toe on the ground, mumbled.

'Speak up, Aidan,' said Sidney. 'We all need to hear.'

'Yes-that's-what-happened,' said Aidan, not much louder.

'And yet you blamed it all on Reuben?' said Kerry.

'Yesssss . . .' Aidan sighed it out.

'Well, you owe that young man an apology,' said Sidney.

She stared out at the prefabs where Reuben was last seen. 'Poor little duck.'

And the fist that had been pressing down inside Madison seemed to expand like a big hard balloon, and her throat got tight and the gulping sobs she'd managed to keep at bay burst right out of her, and the tears that ran over the ice pack felt cold when they dripped onto her hand.

Sidney gathered her up in a hug.

'Dear, oh, dear,' she murmured. 'You're such a brave girl, but sometimes it's all too much, isn't it?'

Madison wasn't sure what she meant, but she was glad to be comforted by Sidney, who was the only grown-up she knew who wouldn't let her go until she'd stopped crying, and who didn't mind tears and snot all over her top.

'And that,' Kerry said, 'concludes our training for today. Dylan, Tanya — go and pick up the balls, Rory and Aidan, the cones. That will give me time to figure out how to get you all home.'

Chapter 11

Mac

Mac read through the list of '11 Heart Symptoms You Can't Ignore!' and tried to ignore how many could apply to Jacko.

Of course, they could all equally be nothing to do with heart disease. Snoring — that was common. Even *she* snored when she slept on her back. Breaking out into the sweats — Jacko worked in a hot kitchen, worked *hard*. And he wasn't a small man — took a lot of energy to manoeuvre a six-foot-seven, hundred-plus-kilo frame. Coughing — well, he smoked and he liked it. Tiredness — again, he worked hard, worked long days.

Mac smacked her finger on the mouse, despatched the site to oblivion. Pointless. If Jacko dropped dead tomorrow, his epitaph would still read 'No regrets'. And there was much to be admired about that attitude. Because what was the alternative? Worry, anxiety, shrinking your life to the point where you'd never take a risk because you'd never do *any*thing. You'd stay boxed up in the tiny space you'd created and live a diminished, fear- and excuse-filled life. Might as well move into a coffin. Save everyone time and effort.

Yes, Jacko's philosophy beat wimping-out hands down. His 'less talk, more action' approach was what had attracted Mac in the first place, back when he was seventeen and she barely fifteen. While other young men puffed hot air about their plans to conquer, Jacko was already halfway up the mountain. If he didn't know how to do something, he'd find out — read a book, recruit an expert. If he got stuck, found it hard, he'd push through. The rare times he gave up were when he knew something wasn't for him; he didn't feel like he could truly commit.

Those dead ends were few, because he had a sound awareness of what he *didn't* want to do. He didn't want to be employed, disliked the restrictions of set hours and narrow job descriptions. He didn't want to sit at a desk, or exercise his brain but not his body. He didn't care how much he earned. He *did* care that he was paid a fair price, and built a reputation for holding a hard line in negotiations. He'd worked as a deer culler, top-dressing pilot, hunting guide, deck-hand on a deep-sea trawler, fitter and turner for mussel barges, arborist, pest-control officer and, briefly, vehicle wrangler for a film shoot.

Most of his jobs evolved naturally from the ones before. Which is why the Boat Shed had been such a surprise to onlookers. It seemed wrong for Jacko to tie himself to one location, indoors at that. It also disproved their long-held belief that he ripped meat raw from the bone and seasoned it with glass. There were some who'd still not recovered from their first sight of Jacko in an apron.

But those close to him knew Jacko had always been interested in food. He had taught himself to cook in his teens, when he first started hunting. Mac chuckled whenever she read about the new trend of nose-to-tail cooking or young chefs who used phrases like 'connecting with our food' or 'meat morality'. There was a certain level of respect for the animal in Jacko's no-waste policy, sure, but in the main he used everything because everything tasted good — if you knew how to cook it. Customers of the Boat Shed accepted there was no set menu and that Jacko served whatever was most readily available, which might be lamb shoulder, crayfish and venison, but might also be brains, liver and glands. The interval before your meal arrived was often accompanied by the adrenaline surge sought by Russian-roulette players and Japanese businessmen staring down a plate of *fugu*. As it happened, most customers had the palate of an igneous rock formation, and went away happily unaware that they'd eaten bovine stomach lining and not a delicious crumbed schnitzel.

Mac fingered the pendant she wore always, but kept tucked inside her top, private. It was a piece of greenstone, pounamu, given to Jacko by a Māori friend from whose land it came. Jacko had taught himself how to stone-carve, had made a simple love-heart, polished it so it shone like a mermaid's tail, and given it to Mac on their first wedding anniversary. Since then, it had been yanked by grabbing babies, left once on the beach (found, never taken off again) and re-threaded five times. It was hard, but it felt soft. If she lost it, she'd be bereft.

The waiting room's sole patient, Agatha Robotham, gave a small, polite cough, and Mac shot daggers at her, which she instantly regretted. Fortunately, Agatha was bent over her needlepoint. A cushion cover, she'd explained, in a William Morris pattern that looked to Mac like boiled seaweed. Everyone knew Agatha loved everything Victorian, and could occasionally be seen around town in a leg o'mutton-sleeved basque with double bust darts, a five-gored skirt and a feather-trimmed Alpine felt hat. What only a few knew was that in between embroidering domestic accoutrements, Agatha created steel-boned corsets out of lace, satin and raw silk, and sold them over the internet to dominatrices and burlesque dancers worldwide. For a pretty penny, Mac might add.

The email icon started to bounce. Two new messages. One from a Bronagh Macfarlane — who? Oh, right, the chatty bloke's mother. And the other from Harry, her and Jacko's son, currently on a cattle ranch in Ontario. Mac opened that one first.

Ontario, wrote Harry, was already colder than a witch's tit in a brass bra. He had seen moose, black bear and grey wolf, and was thinking about applying for a job in a wolf sanctuary. Or maybe he'd come home and do a proper search for those moose rumoured to still be living in the hills. He ended by telling her not to worry, his dad was like an old farm tractor — simple mechanics, strong enough to push over trees, took anything you threw at it and kept going.

Ah, the robust confidence of the young — you had to love it, despite it being of no earthly practical use. And it was only right. Lessons from Greek myths notwithstanding, what son wants to see his dad as fallible, mortal? Mac wrote a reply, wished him good luck with the wolves. Ended with 'love, Mum'. She wouldn't bother him again with her concerns.

On to Mrs Macfarlane. Whose email was short and breezy — she was a nurse, after all. She included a link to a site that advertised international placements. 'A lot of applicants will be rubbish,' Bronagh warned. 'Google-translated English, dubious qualifications. But if you're willing to sift, give it a go.'

A foreign doctor. Now *there* was an idea. Intriguing and, let's face it, amusing. Mac could gain hours of entertainment watching Gabriel's Bay folk react to a Dr Wei, Babatunde or Zubizaretta. She could be female, too. Even better.

Two weeks had passed since Mac had covertly advertised the position. She'd received one application, from a city GP who wanted a quieter pace of life. He said he was sixty-two and keen for an early retirement. Mac wished him an early death for wasting her time.

What was wrong with people? The salary was — pretty good. The location — OK, the location had some accessibility issues, but when you got here, you were by the sea, close to all kinds of Nature, in fact. Where were the medically trained Greenies, the alternative lifestylers, the Coast-to-Coasters? Doctors were all about wellness these days, removing stress, getting back to the land and community. Surely this was the perfect place to achieve all that and more?

Oh, hell. Who was she kidding?

Doc Love's door opened. He'd been with Shania Birtwell, a fifteen-year-old dropout who was seven months pregnant, which didn't stop her smoking and drinking and shagging a bloke who had the instincts of a rodent but half the mental capacity. The baby would almost certainly have fetal alcohol syndrome. As would the others that would inevitably come later. Mac knew Shania and her feral boyfriend were about as likely to practise birth control as they were to take up ikebana.

Shania waddled out without paying. Mac didn't bother to call after her.

Doc Love appeared, as usual, unperturbed. He cared, but he knew the limits of his powers. He'd do his duty by Shania, offer sensible, simple advice, spell out the consequences of her actions in his non-judgemental manner. But he could not force her to change, and he would not try. What happened next was over to her.

'Agatha, please do come in.'

And off trotted grey-bunned, bespectacled Mrs Robotham, corsetier to stiletto-toed mistresses and titillating dancers across the globe.

Four-thirty. Agatha was that day's last patient. Once she'd shut up the surgery, Mac had intended to go home, eat the dinner Jacko always left for her, pour a large glass of pinot and watch whatever mindless pabulum was on television. With luck, *Project Runway*.

However, it was no ordinary Thursday. It was the night the Progressive Association met. Mac was still of the view that they'd be more handbrake than help with finding a replacement for Doc Love, but the imp inside her was rubbing its hands. How much fun to lob the foreign-doctor grenade into their comfortable laps and watch them blow steam and shriek like boiled kettles.

Tim Gunn could survive without her additional commentary. At seven o'clock, she'd be at the Gabriel's Bay community hall, in the front row of the world's most uncomfortable seats. Smiling. Ready.

'Were these designed as instruments of penance?'

To Mac's surprise, Mrs Macfarlane's little boy, Kerry, had sat down right next to her in the hall. She was less surprised when, after a minute, he began shifting about on the folding wooden chair.

'Possibly,' said Mac. 'The folk who built the hall were Methodists.'

Kerry craned to inspect his chair and hers more closely.

'I can see how it works,' he said. 'The seat is a fraction too short, so the edge digs into mid-thigh, and then the back slopes a fraction too much, so you can't rest your full weight on it for fear of tipping over, so you have to sit upright, thus ensuring your mid-thigh area presses all its weight onto the edge. Really, it's genius.'

'Why are you here?' said Mac.

'Curiosity,' said Kerry. 'And you?'

'Stirring,' said Mac.

'For a cause? Or just for fun?'

'Shh. Committee's assembling. Feast your eyes. Or shut them in horror. Up to you.'

Eight people walked up onto the stage, and took their seats at the long table. Mac could describe the arrangement without looking. In the middle: Bernard Weston, chair for the last too many years. On either side: his favourite acolytes, Nicholas Sharp and Elaine 'I *beg* your pardon' Pardew. Next to Nicholas — Derek Beale ('Bealer the Squealer'), Maureen Ropable (real name, Roper) and Tinker 'Wanders off' Wadsworth; and next to Elaine — Geoffrey Naylor ('Prince Joffrey') and Wendy Bevin, who insisted on taking the minutes, despite not knowing shorthand or being able to write fast enough to keep up.

Bernard cleared his throat, and made a meal of finding the right page in his leather-bound jotter, smoothing it down, and then removing his Parker pen from the jotter's special loop and holding it up so that everyone could see that it was (a) gold and (b) activated by a twisting motion vastly superior to the click of those plastic disposables.

'Get on with it, you pompous twat,' Mac muttered. 'You're not opening Parliament.'

Besides Mac and Kerry, there were four people in the hall, including Patricia Weston, who must surely only come to these meetings out of some misplaced sense of matrimonial duty. Mac liked Patricia, despite her choice of spouse. She was what everyone called 'a good sort', which was true but also a compliment along the lines of 'lovely personality' or 'kind eyes' — the type you give to women who are large and frumpy. Patricia Weston's wardrobe consisted entirely of A-line skirts, buttoned blouses and sensible shoes, plus she wore flesh coloured pantyhose all year round, and, Mac adjudged, a panty girdle. Her hair was set in neat grey curls à la Her Majesty, and on formal occasions, she brought out her string of pearls. Mac had long since stopped caring about the aging process — Oil of Olay could shove its seven signs up its arse — but she was surprised every time she recalled that Patricia was only ten years older than her, a mere sixty-three. The Queen Mother had looked younger at 101, though all that gin might have had a preserving effect.

Patricia caught Mac looking at her and smiled. Mac smiled back, while resenting the fact she now felt like a terrible, mean-minded person. If Patricia didn't care how old she looked, then no one else should give a tinker's cuss.

Of the other people in the hall, Mac recognised the crunchy organic bloke who'd bought the lifestyle block next to Meredith, a dreadlocked blonde woman from the plant co-operative, and Corinna Marshall, Casey's older sister. Corinna also caught Mac looking at her, but instead of smiling, she winked. *That* boded well.

'Good evening, everyone, and welcome.' Bernard spoke loudly, as if the hall was full. 'I call this meeting of the Gabriel's Bay Progressive Association to order.'

Mac quelled an urge to heckle, and then a more serious urge to fall asleep as the minutes of the previous meeting were reviewed, with Wendy's factual errors, omissions and solecisms noted in detail and corrected before acceptance was moved and seconded. The financial report was mercifully short, the association having few funds to transact, but no less dull.

Kerry, she observed, remained bright-eyed throughout.

'You find this interesting?' she said.

'I once sat through a two-hour meeting where the main topic was whether or not we should reformat our Excel spreadsheets with pastel colour-coding.'

Bernard cleared his throat again, pointedly this time. Mac resisted giving him the finger. Bad behaviour was temporarily satisfying, but wouldn't help her cause.

'Now, to items of general business,' said Bernard. 'We have six on the agenda. The first of which being a noted increase in graffiti on signage, walls and sundry other surfaces. Elaine, this is your item. Would you care to elaborate?'

Elaine would and she did, at length. Seemed the form of vandalism known as tagging was experiencing a renaissance, and

Elaine demanded more thorough and active police enforcement and *much* stricter penalties.

'Bring back the stocks?' whispered Kerry.

Mac shook her head. 'No less than public flogging.'

'I have written a letter on the association's behalf to the Police Area Commander in Hampton,' said Elaine. 'I trust my colleagues have no objections?'

If they did, they wisely kept schtum. Otherwise, they'd be next under the lash.

'Thank you, Elaine,' said Bernard. 'Item two . . .'

And as the committee got het up about household refuse in the town's recycling bins, recidivist violators of bylaws regarding dogs, skateboarders (a general, free-flowing rant), and whether bicycles could safely be leaned up against shop windows, Mac stayed sane by playing Angry Birds on her phone, accompanied by Kerry's occasional 'Nice shot'.

'Now to item six.' Bernard paused and gave a little smile. 'A point we have debated before, on many occasions, but to no conclusive end. However, this time, evidence has been found that would seem to strongly support a certain point of view.'

'Better brace ourselves,' said Kerry. 'He's working up to something big.'

'Item six,' said Bernard again, for those who had lost track or died. 'The usage of the apostrophe in Gabriel's Bay. Is it or is it not correct?'

'Oh, for the love of God,' said Mac.

A rustle and scrape behind. Mac turned to see Corinna Marshall on her feet. But she wasn't leaving. She wanted to speak.

'Yes?' Bernard said, obviously wishing he could vaporise her.

'Tēnā koutou.' Corinna nodded to the committee, and to the others in the hall. 'Tēnā koutou katoa. Apologies, I should wait until General Business, but I have two small children at home and need to get back. But I won't take up too much of your time.'

In good lawyer fashion, she did not wait for any objections.

'This is a courtesy,' she said, 'to let you all know a proposal has been submitted to the New Zealand Geographic Board to change the name of Gabriel's Bay back to its original name of Onemanawa. The consultation process runs from now until the end of January, so there will be plenty of time to make submissions.'

Corinna bestowed a warm smile on the speechless committee, picked up her bag.

'Thank you,' she said. 'I'll let you get back to your apostrophe. E noho rā.'

Mac wanted *very* badly to whoop, but settled for grinning from ear to ear. Those Marshalls — she'd known them since they were toddlers, watched them grow into strong, independent women who took no shit from anyone.

Bernard — Mac had to give him credit — acted decisively. As the committee began to splutter and squawk, he raised his voice and shut them down.

'In the light of that — revelation,' he said, 'we will defer discussion on item six until such time as we have more information.'

He closed and up-ended his leather-bound jotter, tapped it firmly on the table. 'I hereby bring this meeting to a close.'

'Were you in on that?'

Mac only just heard Kerry above the hubbub erupting at the top table.

'Nope. News to me.'

'Are you piqued that she stole your stirring thunder?'

Mac sat back, defying the folding chair to tip, and watched the body language of affront and accusation — jabbing fingers, huffing cheeks, protruding neck veins.

'Not at all,' she replied. 'I think that's *more* than enough fun for one evening.'

Chapter 12

Kerry

Meredith hadn't mentioned it again, but Kerry knew that didn't mean she'd forgotten. And if the answer was bad news, better not to delay discovery. Though, it had to be said, putting it off did have its attractions . . .

No, no, no. Bravery, integrity were the watchwords. Stiffen the sinews. Gird the loins.

'Mrs Barton?'

Meredith was replacing a book on the shelves of the library-cum-study, a room that had been, she said, Jonty's favourite. It was certainly the manliest in the house, its décor reminiscent of a Victorian gentleman's club with high-backed leather chairs, dark wood panelling, stuffed game birds in glass domes and a lingering whiff of cigar smoke and misogyny.

'Yes, Kerry?'

She had been upstairs reading to her husband, and sounded polite but weary. In other words, entirely as usual.

'Er, on Monday, it will have been two weeks,' he began. 'My trial period will have come to an end and I thought we should discuss — well . . .'

Her expression became marginally more weary, though it was hard to tell in the gloom.

'What are your thoughts on the matter?' she said.

'Mine?' said Kerry, surprised.

'How have you found this past fortnight?'

An urge to keep the job at all costs vied with his previous pledge to integrity. If there was a seam of sentiment beneath that cool exterior, now was the time to mine it shamelessly.

'I've very much enjoyed living here,' he said. 'I enjoy the flexibility and autonomy you have given me. I don't find any of the tasks dull or onerous. And I'm, er, becoming very fond of Gabriel's Bay. I'm making some friends, and also I've—'

Anxiety stalled him. To say he'd already set up as a children's football coach sounded presumptuous, as if he'd taken for granted that his trial period would be a success. Plus, he'd not told Sidney about the trial, nor that he might not be able to stick around if Meredith let him go. He liked Sidney, would like to get to know her better. And from what he *had* gleaned of her character, he was sure she wouldn't allow dissemblers a second chance.

But he should have known that while Meredith chose to remain mostly within her house, it did not mean she was out of the loop. Oksana brought a weekly bulletin — heavily seasoned with the paprika of judgement — and there was the telephone, of course. Given proper thought, it was obvious she'd know exactly what he was up to.

Even so, he felt somewhat pinned to the spot when Meredith said, 'I gather you acquitted yourself well coaching the children. Sidney was full of praise.'

How to open up the wound of ambivalence . . .

'That's, er, very generous of her,' he said.

'She doesn't praise lightly.'

. . . and rub the salt well in.

'I'm sure she doesn't.'

And Meredith hadn't answered his initial question. Oh well. Now that he was already stinging, he may as well seize that nettle.

'Mrs Barton, have you made a decision? About whether or not I can stay on?'

Curse it, she seemed hesitant. His brain scrambled. What could he say, what could he offer that might convince her?

Glancing hastily around the library for inspiration . . .

Yes! That was it! Maybe. No . . .

Yes! Or at least — why not?

'I'd be willing for you to expand my job description,' he said.

Now she was the one taken by surprise.

'Expand? How?'

'I, er, could take over some of your care duties with your husband? Take him his lunch. Read to him. Perhaps a couple of days a week?'

Hesitant, still. But wavering . . . ?

'I'm not sure that would work. My husband is very . . . particular.'

'If it doesn't, then I'll cease forthwith. We'll go back to the way we were. No problem.'

Now, *that* was a new look she gave him. Knowing, almost amused, as if they both now shared a secret. Or was she merely entertained by his transparent desperation?

'What do you think?' he prompted. 'Shall we give it a try?'

'I'm unable to pay you any extra,' she said.

'No need.'

'And you're prepared for my husband to be . . . difficult?'

Particular. Difficult. Euphemisms for what, Kerry wondered? Selfish, tyrannical, faking old bastard?

That amused look again. And before he could answer, Meredith said, 'I am aware of the prevailing opinion about my husband's condition.'

No comment seemed wise. And a mental note to do better keeping his thoughts off his face.

'But no one knows him as I do,' Meredith went on. 'And if we are, in your words, to give this a try, then I will need to impart some of that knowledge to you.'

Ok . . .

'My question then becomes — are you a man of discretion? And by that, I mean not only one who can keep confidences, but also one who can judge how best to act. Are you such a man?'

By asking that question, Meredith Barton had just given him the benefit of the doubt. Now, it was up to him to confirm or deny.

'I can't promise to be a pure and absolute success,' he told her. 'But I *can* swear to do my utmost to reward your trust.'

Cool? She was Narnia's White Queen!

'Very well,' she said.

Kerry braced for the 'However . . .'

But all Meredith said was, 'Come with me. I have something to show you.'

Kerry followed, and hoped it wasn't a sign of weak character that he really did not want it to be a body.

Meredith led him to the wooden outbuilding behind the garage, and next to the shed in which Mr Phipps stored mysterious substances. His tools he kept at home, and brought with him each time in a green canvas bag. In the shed, Kerry had glimpsed metal containers with rusted screw-tops and jars filled with a brown liquid that could be animal, vegetable, mineral or a category new to science. Kerry assumed Mr Phipps used it on the garden, as insect control or plant food, but would advise anyone who smoked not to stand too close to the open shed door.

The adjacent building was the width of a triple garage, and you entered at the far end through double doors fastened with a large bolt and padlock. The padlock was hanging open. Meredith removed it and, with some effort, though she did not ask for help, slid back the bolt. A string hung down in the doorway. A tug and the place was illuminated.

'Good Lord,' said Kerry.

He was Gulliver, in the portal to a tiny world. Around two sides of the room ran a wide raised platform, and on it, snow-capped mountains soared, tiny waterfalls ran down to streams and then to a river that flowed past forests, through farm meadows dotted with stock and crops, and wound on around villages, with greens, cottages and churches. Kerry spotted a fairground complete with Ferris wheel, a windmill, a lighthouse on a cliff, barges on the river and, of course, railway signals, water stops and stations.

'How does it compare to your father's?' Meredith said.

'His would fit in that small corner there,' said Kerry. He moved in for a closer inspection. 'But in terms of the quality of workmanship and over-arching technical and aesthetic principles, I'd say my father and Mr Barton would nod to each other in mutual acknowledgement.'

He stood up. 'That is, if it *is* Mr Barton's work?'

'It is,' said Meredith. 'Yes, it is very much his.'

'Does it still go?'

'It does. Every month, Mr Phipps checks the connections, keeps the tracks and trains free of dust.'

It was all Kerry could do not to jump up and down, begging her to switch it on.

'But, as you can see,' she added, 'it is still only part-finished.'

He had been so bedazzled by his first impression that he'd not seen, until now, that half the raised platform along the shed's rear wall was empty.

'What was he going to put there?'

'I couldn't say,' Meredith replied. 'But he always drew plans before he started work; he was quite meticulous about it. I don't know, myself, if any exist.'

Kerry understood. He was not to go fossicking in private drawers or cupboards, but if he *did* manage to connect with Jonty, the whereabouts of any such plans was a topic that could be raised.

'My husband began building this over twenty-five years ago,' said Meredith. 'He gained enormous pleasure from it. It suited his careful nature, his attention to detail. And when the girls were small, he would let them build their own train set — a simple wooden one — on the floor, and they would make trees from iceblock sticks, and rivers from cellophane, bring in their plastic farm animals, their Matchbox cars . . .'

'Not into dolls, were they?'

'Neither of them. Lego, trains, cars, Meccano. I think the closest they ever had to anything "girly" was Fuzzy Felt.'

'When I was four, I had a teddy bear I named Mabel,' said Kerry. 'Until another child laughed at me and I re-christened it Ron.'

Meredith wasn't listening. She was lost in another time, when this room was filled with activity, when her husband and daughters worked away on their creations side by side, productively, happily.

'The girls spent less time in here, of course, as they grew up,' said Meredith. 'But even after she'd left home, Nicola always kept an eye out for items that might suit. She had creative flair, could see the potential in objects, see what they might become with a bit of paint, a few additions and alterations. That continued shared interest made for a strong bond between her and her father . . .'

When she turned back to face him, Kerry could see her discomfort.

'I gather that the other day you spoke to my youngest, Sophie?'

So she *had* called back.

'Briefly.'

'No doubt.'

Meredith twisted the ring she wore on her middle finger, a diamond and sapphire job that looked old and valuable, and may have been her engagement ring, as on that finger was only a plain gold hoop. Had she lost weight, and not bothered to get the ring re-sized?

Kerry had a sudden, unwelcome vision of a solitaire diamond that he'd once placed on another finger. Ages ago now, miles away. Which meant no reduction in the shame whatsoever.

'Sophie lives as an artist, in Whanganui,' said Meredith. 'Until recently with a boyfriend, from whom she has now separated. The reason for her call was a request for money to use as a deposit on another flat. I did not give it to her.'

This day was certainly turning into one of true confessions. Kerry felt torn between wanting to know more, and wanting to avoid seeing dignified Meredith rip open her chest and offer him her still-beating heart. Her question earlier — was he a man she could trust? Was he a man who could equably absorb another's hopes and fears and respond with compassion, wisdom? Or was he the same glib surface-slider who deflected real emotions with a joke, bounced them up into the ether where they burst, quickly, harmlessly, like party balloons?

'How old is Sophie?' he asked.

'Thirty-one.'

Older than he'd expected. Old enough to be independent. Kerry's parents hadn't exactly sold his bed when he started university, but they'd made their expectations clear. They couldn't afford his fees, so he must take a loan and, ideally, a part-time job. He could stay at home until he found a flat, but find a flat he would. Kerry accepted this at the time as he accepted most other influences on his life — without question. He couldn't truthfully say that it had steered him down a *wrong* path, but it was a path he'd followed blindly nonetheless.

That said, he'd never rung home asking for money. Forgiveness, yes, but not hard cash. He had *some* pride.

'It's a difficult balance,' said Meredith. 'Loyalty and love versus principles. Difficult to decide whether, indeed, balance is required. Or whether one should put love first, no matter what.'

'You can't hug a principle,' said Kerry.

'No,' Meredith agreed. 'But you can't hug a tyrant, either. That's not the kind of relationship they desire.'

Who was the tyrant? Daughter or husband . . . ?

But show-and-tell time was over. Meredith's face closed up, cooled smooth.

'If you wish to continue working here,' she said, 'then the job is yours. Your first reading session will be tomorrow — may as well throw you in.'

'Thank you!' Kerry began, resisting again the urge to drop to his knees. 'I'm really *very*—'

'My husband tolerates only one author,' she went on. 'And that is Nietzsche. We are currently halfway through *Twilight of the Idols*. You'll find it in the library.'

Under 'N', which also stood for, at a wild guess, 'No fun'. Though, to be fair, all Kerry knew of Nietzsche was that he'd sported a moustache like a sorghum broom. That and some saying about looking into the abyss.

'I'll tell Mr Barton to expect you tomorrow afternoon at one-thirty. I've been reading to him for an hour,' said Meredith. 'You may set your own schedule.'

As she walked towards the shed door, expecting him to follow, Kerry took a last look at the perfect miniature world created by Jonty Barton (with a bit of help from one daughter, at least). He *must* ask if he could take photos of it to send to his father. Who knows, it might encourage his parents to hit up a loan shark for money to come over. Not that his mother would be *quite* so thrilled about the contents of an even bigger shed, but she could always tour the Hampton wineries by bicycle.

A thought occurred to him.

'Forgive me if this sounds impertinent,' he said, 'but what did you do while the rest of your family were building railways? Did *you* have a hobby?'

Meredith paused, one hand on the doorframe. The sun behind lit her grey hair gold.

'I suppose it would be irrational not to show you. Now that you've seen this.'

Goodness. She seemed embarrassed!

'However, I'd request you keep in mind,' she added, as she shut the shed door, 'that you once had a teddy bear named Mabel.'

Chapter 13

Sidney

'Did you see inside the little books?' Sidney asked.

'I didn't dare even *ask* to touch,' said Kerry. 'Each one has a tiny story, handwritten. And the *carpets*. All that miniature cross-stitching. Would have driven me blind. And bats.'

Sidney watched Kerry shake his head, in disbelief, amazement. He was generally at a high pitch of enthusiasm, she'd come to realise, but this subject had geed him up to a whole new level of bright-eyed and bushy-tailed. He radiated the glee of a child who's spotted the hiding place of the biggest Easter egg.

'The last time my mind was this boggled,' he said, 'was when I learned that fire doesn't cast a shadow. Oh, and when I read that I'd been eating chocolate digestives wrong side up all my life. Chocolate on top — who knew?'

He sipped on a beer that was already empty, his mind still roaming the rooms of a tiny house. Behind the bar, Sidney polished another glass and set it on the shelf. She'd agreed to stand in again for Devon, who'd driven off that morning to a horse stud to assess a newly acquired colt that was proving harder than expected to manage. The owner had heard of Devon's reputation, and had hired him for the whole weekend, all expenses paid. Sidney was pleased for him — thoroughbred studs were where the big money was in the horse world.

'The house was made originally as a toy for the girls, did she tell you?' Sidney asked.

'She did,' said Kerry. 'But they preferred the model railway, and so Meredith took over. Evicted the lumbering doll family who could never stay upright, binned all their ugly plastic furniture and started again from scratch. Made all the furnishings, ornaments and carpets. Even handpainted the wallpaper.' He shook his head again. 'Astonishing.'

'What's astonishing?'

Gene pulled out a stool, sat up beside Kerry at the bar.

'Your ability to work approximately one hour a day and yet still run a profitable business,' said Sidney.

'The art of leadership is delegation,' said Gene. 'And training underlings to know exactly what you want.'

Sidney handed him a beer.

'QED,' said Gene, smugly.

'I have a list of horrible things I can do to your food,' said Sidney. 'A long one.'

'You're out of luck. I'm eating at home tonight. The girls are cooking.' Gene winced. 'They've discovered the Disney food blog. Apparently, we're having Lady and the Tramp Spaghetti, followed by Matterhorn Macaroons.'

'Sounds pretty good.'

'They scrap over how many yoghurt-covered raisins they get in their cereal bowls,' said Gene. 'I'm not sure they're ready for a sustained collaborative effort, but we'll see. Anyway — here's to hiding until it's all over.'

He and Kerry clinked beer bottles.

'And what have you both been astonished by?' Gene said again.

'Remember, the town that gossips together—'

'Is like every other town,' said Sidney. 'If you insist: Kerry saw Meredith's doll's house today.'

'Oh, *man*,' said Gene. 'Did you see the little books? And the fruit bowl with those teensy grapes? And the freaking *cutlery*. Man, I have fingernail clippings bigger than those teaspoons.'

Sidney saw Kerry's eyes widen at Gene's sudden animation.

'Has everyone seen the doll's house?' he asked.

'Before Jonty packed a sad,' said Gene, 'Meredith used to let people tour her house and garden. Once a year, as part of a fundraiser for some charity — children, or cancer, or maybe children *with* cancer.'

'I see,' said Kerry. 'And was this event popular?'

'Sure,' said Gene. 'She'd get a couple of hundred people through, easy.'

Sidney had been watching Kerry. 'What are you scheming?' she said to him. 'You have a scheming look about you.'

'It's my face,' he said. 'It has a naturally inquisitive cast.'

His smile was meant to charm. Sidney was annoyed to find that it did. She busied herself polishing glasses she'd already polished. It was five o'clock. The Boat Shed had just opened and Jacko had popped back to his house to fetch some fresh parsley. No problem — the diners wouldn't start to trickle in for another half-hour, so, as always, she spent this time ensuring everything was spotless. Jacko hated even a hint of mess, had once bawled out Devon for not removing a dead fly from a high shelf. When Devon pointed out that no one but Jacko would have been able to see it, Jacko said that didn't matter. What mattered was being arsed enough to ensure every aspect was perfect, even if the only judge was you. That's how you slept straight at night. Knowing you'd done all you could.

'Er, did the visitors also see the model railway?' Kerry asked.

Gene snorted. 'Jonty let the *hoi polloi* near his precious tracks? Hell, no.'

'Have either of you seen it?'

'Nope,' said Gene. 'Rumours only.'

'Me neither,' said Sidney. 'But I know Mr Phipps thinks it's amazing.'

'*How* do you know?' said Kerry. 'Did he spell it out in semaphore?'

A stomping up the back steps announced Jacko's return.

'Jacko!' called Gene. 'You seen Jonty Barton's model railway?'

Jacko ducked under the kitchen doorframe. In front of his chest, he held a bunch of parsley, like a bouquet. Silently, Sidney dared Gene to make a comparison with bridesmaids.

'Nup,' said Jacko. 'But Doc Love reckons it's better than his war-game dioramas.'

'Game? You mean — toy soldiers?' said Kerry.

'And tanks,' said Jacko. 'He's got dioramas of the Second Battle of El Alamein, the Battle of Prokhorovka — Russkis versus Jerries — and Operation Goodwood.'

'You sound very informed,' said Kerry.

Jacko cleared his throat, straightened his shoulders.

'Might have been up to have a little play.'

'A *play*?' said Gene.

'Yeah, you know,' said Jacko. 'You roll the dice, make your move.'

'Wait, wait, wait.' Gene held up a hand. 'Are you saying your manoeuvres are dictated by chance, not by how the battle actually went?'

'How it works.'

'So — you can alter the course of history? Like a time lord?'

'It's a game, you berk,' said Jacko.

'Yes, I think damage to the fabric of the universe is minimal.'

Kerry leaned forward. 'Are you and Doctor Love the only ones in on this?' he asked Jacko.

'Nah, there's a bit of a crew. Old Phippsy's a regular. Agatha Robotham. Tinker Wadsworth. Chester from the video store and Peg, his fiancée. Few others.'

Gene stared at him. 'You never asked *me*.'

''Cause you're a sceptical git and a fucking joker!' said Jacko. 'You gotta take it seriously or it's no fun.'

'I'm surprised you let girls play,' said Sidney.

'Bloody brutal,' said Jacko. 'That Aggie Robotham'd bayonet you without blinking.' He glanced down, seemed surprised to see the parsley. 'Enough yakking,' he said. 'Some of us have to work.' And he ducked back into the kitchen.

Kerry was nodding, with a faint smile, as if a theory he'd long held had finally been proven.

'Tell me,' he said, 'am I right in thinking that if Gabriel's Bay had always been a tourist destination, then the impact of losing its major employers might not have been so dramatic?'

Sidney and Gene exchanged a glance.

'Economics isn't my field of expertise,' said Gene, 'but I'd say that would depend on whether tourism could expand to fill the gap. The town would have to be committed to doing more than before. Few extra postcards won't create new jobs.'

'Other towns have built up their tourism,' said Sidney. 'Kaikōura, with the whales. Ōāmaru, with the Victorian heritage. Hampton's made a huge effort to capitalise on its wine and food producers.'

'True,' Gene nodded. 'You get smaller businesses lined up around a theme, like crafts or food, and then you have a bigger proposition than they could provide individually. Place gets known as — I don't know — Macramé Town or whatever.'

'Sock Town,' said Sidney. 'Norsewood. Or Pottery Town — Temuka!'

'Bra Town,' Jacko called out. 'Cardrona.'

'Bras?' said Kerry.

'There's a bra fence,' said Gene. 'A fence to which people, not necessarily women, have attached bras.'

'It's now used to raise money for breast cancer,' said Sidney. 'There's a donation box.'

'And people travel specially to see it?' said Kerry.

'It's bras on a fence,' said Gene. 'What's not to like?'

'We love eccentricity here,' said Sidney. 'And the hokier the better. Like the house decorated entirely with pāua shells, or the one built from glass bottles. The replica Stonehenge. The big carrot—'

'The giant jersey,' added Gene.

'As in cow?' said Kerry.

'As in knitted jumper. It's about five metres wide if you stretch the sleeves out, and two metres high.'

'Too small for Jacko, then,' said Sidney, with a grin.

'Maybe that's how we bring visitors to Gabriel's Bay?' said Gene. 'Jacko at the top of a massive beanstalk, chanting "fee, fi, fo, fum".'

'Put you under a bloody bridge,' came from the kitchen. 'Like the troll you are.'

'Now, now,' said Sidney. 'Don't make me get out my wand.'

'As the bishop said to the actress.' Gene swivelled on the bar stool to face Kerry. 'So is there a point to all this tourism talk, besides using up oxygen?'

Kerry had his elbows propped on the bar, hands around but not quite touching the beer bottle at which he stared, as if it were a devotional object he was contemplating.

'What if,' he began, 'Gabriel's Bay united around its own tourist attraction? One that existed, but which would evolve, as townspeople contributed to it?'

'Such as?' said Gene.

'Oh my God,' said Sidney. 'The miniatures! The model railway, the doll's house, the toy soldiers! We can be Tiny Town!'

'With Jacko as our mayor?' Gene laughed. 'Come on,' he added, as Sidney gave him a look. 'New Zealanders *love* irony.'

Quietly, Kerry said, 'I'm serious about this, you know.'

'Why?' Gene's smile vanished. 'Why this sudden need to crusade for a place you've lived in for all of two minutes?'

Fair question, Sidney had to admit. She saw Kerry frown, deliberate over his answer.

'Because the opportunity has presented itself,' he said. 'And I'd like to take it.'

Gene sucked in his bottom lip. 'You want to be the big man?'

'That's not fair,' Sidney protested.

'Yeah?' said Gene. 'This isn't *New Zealand's Got Talent*. We're not talking about one person's shot at their fifteen minutes of fame. We're talking about people's lives and livelihoods and, more importantly, their hopes and bloody dreams.'

He jabbed a finger at Kerry. 'You come in, spouting promises, saying sure, sure, I can make it rain, the drought will be over, trust me — you do that, and you don't come through and you'll have been crueller than if you'd told them right from the start that they were all fucked. You get me?'

Movement behind Sidney. Jacko in the doorway, silent, listening.

Kerry's face had lost colour everywhere except for two bright spots on his cheekbones. Sidney felt a stab of pity; he'd had this great idea, but that was nowhere near as important as having trust. Gene was right — Kerry had been here two minutes. Not long enough to earn him the right to speak, and to be heard by open, willing ears.

'I get you,' Kerry said.

He got off the bar stool, drew out his wallet and handed Sidney a five-dollar note. And then, with a quick, terse 'Good night', he left.

'You know, it *isn't* a bad idea,' said Sidney, after the door had swung shut.

'If he hasn't got the balls for a fight,' said Gene, 'he hasn't got a shit show of making even the greatest idea fly.'

'For once, mate,' said Jacko in the doorway, 'I agree with everything you say.'

Sidney liked to walk for a bit on the beach before heading down the streets that led to home. The boys slept over at Mac and Jacko's whenever she worked. Tomorrow was Saturday, and Mac said she'd drop them back about ten. A peaceful morning should be a treat, but somehow, to her irritation, Sidney knew she wouldn't enjoy it. Doing nothing made her feel lazy, unproductive, and on top of that she missed the boys.

Without them, who *was* she? The thought made Sidney anxious every time. What had she done with her life apart from be mother to them? She had no professional qualifications and minimal work experience — the odd jobs she did didn't count. She had no talent for anything creative, so the life of an artist was out. When the boys left home — a few years away yet, but it *would* happen — she'd be there in an empty house, where she could fill her day watching either the mould spread in the bathroom or the borer beetles eat the last floorboard in the hallway.

There was the garden, she supposed. But that was a hobby, not a job. Sure, she could make a few bucks here and there from jam and pickles, but that was hardly showing entrepreneurial flair. Maybe she could sell stuff over the internet? Sidney rolled her eyes at her own stupidity. Might as well set up a phone-sex line.

The moon was out, and Sidney stopped to watch it glimmer on the water, a silver-gilt path on velvety black sea, the sky above more of a steely grey. It was a scene that cried out to be drawn by someone with skill. When Sidney was twelve, she'd been given a set of drawing pencils, all different thicknesses so you could make bold lines or soft shading. She'd been given a sketchbook, too, with beautiful textured paper. She'd tried to draw a leaf — a simple shape that didn't move; how hard could it be? — but realised after a couple of pencil strokes that she would never be able to render it with even passing accuracy. She gave up both the drawing, and any hope of being competent at art. She put the pencils and sketchbook away in a drawer in her bedroom.

Even though Sidney had not thought of those pencils in years, their loss felt briefly acute. Another regret. Another path not taken because she'd given up too easily.

Not having any faith in herself — that was the core of the problem. She had no faith in her ability to overcome obstacles. No faith in her ability to make good decisions — she always believed someone else knew better. That was why she'd followed Fergal so readily. He seemed so sure, so gleamingly, flawlessly positive—

'Shit!'

'It's OK,' said the figure that emerged from the dark dunes. 'It's me.'

'What are you doing?' Sidney said, crossly. 'Have you been there all night?'

'What time is it?'

'Just after nine.'

'Not all night, then,' said Kerry. 'Only four hours.'

Oh, for God's sake, *really*? Was he that pitiful? She'd thought

Gene unnecessarily cruel, but he could well have underplayed it.

It occurred to her that her irritation was out of proportion. Should she cut him a bit more slack? Or was that asking to be disappointed?

'In my defence,' said Kerry, as if she'd spoken aloud, 'I wasn't sulking. I was thinking.'

'For four hours?'

'Well, no, I went and got a Chinese takeaway and ate that first.'

'You missed out on Jacko's once-a-year cassoulet — homemade sausage and confit duck leg from ducks he shot himself,' said Sidney. 'Slow-cooked, with home-grown new season's green beans.'

'My kung pao chicken was perfectly adequate.'

A soft night wind carried to Sidney the scents of seaweed and ozone, and smoke from someone's chimney.

'I'm heading home,' said Sidney. 'Too cold to hang around here.'

'May I walk with you?' said Kerry.

Sidney wanted to say no. He might want to rehash his spat with Gene, and she wasn't in the mood to listen to justifications and complaints, especially ones that had been brewing for four hours.

Then again, she enjoyed his company. He made her laugh, and she was a die-hard sucker for people who made her laugh.

A less welcome thought bobbed up: she found him attractive. Sidney shoved it back down. That was her loneliness talking, and as usual it sounded delusional. He'd shown *no* signs of being attracted to her, plus, more importantly, he hadn't yet fully proven himself. The best idea was night air unless you had the gumption to see it through to the end.

But he did make her laugh . . .

'Sure,' she said. 'If you want.'

They walked in silence as Sidney led them off the beach, across the beachfront road and down the first side street.

'I don't know where you live,' said Kerry.

'Not far. I'm one of the old bungalows with the big back gardens.'

'Do you own or rent?'

'Bank owns most of it.'

'Er, look, feel free to tell me to sod off,' said Kerry, 'but how do you keep your head above water financially?'

'I don't really,' said Sidney. 'I breathe through a straw called the sole parent benefit, and because the boys are at school I have to find a required number of paid hours of work a week, but I can't earn more than a certain amount because then our compassionate government starts deducting from my benefit. So I tutor high-school students, work once or twice a week at the Boat Shed, and help Mr Phipps with his bees. And then I barter with neighbours, as my feckless ex intended but never got around to, and I make a few bucks selling sticky stuff in jars.'

'Wait. Did you say — *bees*?'

'Mr Phipps has hives — not the medical kind. I help with maintenance, bee feeding, disease prevention, honey harvesting — routine tasks like that; he manages swarm control. The hives hunker down for winter between April and August, so there's not much to do then, but Mr Phipps pays me the same amount anyway, bless him, and in return I cook him meals and do a bit of cleaning, and keep him well stocked with sticky stuff in jars. We're starting to be busy again now, though — well, the bees are. Come the end of December, we'll have the first of the honey.'

'Why do I feel I should have known this before?' said Kerry.

'We haven't exactly shared our life's stories, have we?'

'I suppose not, no . . .'

The tone of his voice made Sidney wish Gabriel's Bay had decent street lighting, so she could see the expression on Kerry's face.

'Something to hide?'

She kept her voice light, but she really did want to know.

He drew in a long breath.

'I was going to be married,' he said. 'Wedding was aborted. On the day.'

'Oh, God.'

Jilted. Now, that *was* bad luck. At least she'd been dumped the ordinary way, and not in front of an audience.

'I'm still ashamed of how clueless I was,' he said. 'Of how happy I was to skate over the surface, when I should have been paying proper attention — to the direction my life was heading and to the person I'd committed to spend it with. I hadn't bothered to really get to know her — it was as simple and as stupid as that.'

'I didn't know Fergal was going to leave me until he had,' said Sidney. 'That's clueless squared.'

'Your ex's name was Fergal?'

'Born in Enniscorthy. County Wexford.'

'Can't trust those Southern Irish,' said Kerry. 'Us half-northerners, now . . .'

An attempt at a joke, but he didn't sound happy. Well, it wasn't her job to cheer him up. In fact, having felt sorry for him only seconds ago, now she felt a perverse need to grill him more about the tourism idea, test his mettle. Test his worthiness, said a small voice. She told the small voice to shut its trap.

'You know, Gene's right,' said Sidney. 'To make your Tiny Town idea work, you'll have to be committed. So can I ask — what *is* your motivation?'

'I'm not sure I can give you a definitive answer,' he replied. 'I'd say there are a whole slew of reasons sloshing around in the front-loader of my psyche. There's my dad, who started building his own model railway set before I was born, so I've known it all my life. When I was young, it was a real world to me and I gave all the tiny people names and made up stories about them. When I got a bit older, I could appreciate the technical side, the mechanics, the skill involved. And then the historical aspect began to appeal — why this locomotive, this span bridge, this old building? Ultimately, I think the greatest appeal was the romance, the nostalgia, the way my dad and I could retreat to a better place and time. The fact that *this* Britain never existed was irrelevant — it came to life every time we closed the door to our shed.'

'Is your dad still alive?'

'Still alive, still teaching science to secondary school students who think H_2O and CO_2 are the symbols for hot and cold water.'

'And your mum?'

'Nurse. The old-school kind who carries a cold spoon about her person.'

'Why on earth?'

'Instant detumescing device.'

'Huh,' said Sidney. 'I must remember that.'

'And my other reasons?' Kerry went on. 'Run-of-the-mill wanting to prove myself sort. Desire to do something worthwhile, serve a wider purpose — you know, be a force of Nature rather than a feverish, selfish little clod of ailments. Your basic drive not to be scrabbling around at the bottom of Maslow's hierarchy of needs.'

My God, Sidney thought. Shaw and psychology. Words longer than one syllable. How attractive was that?

'What do *you* think of it?' said Kerry. 'The idea?'

Good question. Despite her reservations about Kerry, or at least her need to gain further evidence of his character, she judged him so far to be honest.

'I think it has real merit,' she said. 'I'm happy to offer my support.'

'Thanks. I appreciate that.'

He sounded surprised. Fair enough, she hadn't been exactly gushing.

'And if you give it your all, Gene will come around,' she added. 'He won't stop giving you shit, but as soon as he can see you've made real headway, he'll back you, too.'

'Gene's support is a mixed blessing, I suspect,' Kerry said. 'But I'll take it.'

'What's the next step?'

'Talk to Meredith. If I can win *her* over, everyone else will be a breeze.'

'Don't forget the Progressive Association. Or the Bunch of Ass as Mac calls them.'

'I have them in my sights.'

They'd reached Sidney's gate. Which she'd had to re-attach yet again last weekend. It didn't help that the boys wrenched it open and slammed it shut. Every. Single. Time.

'Your house is sweet,' said Kerry. 'Most appealing.'

'Look again in the harsh light of day,' said Sidney, with a sigh. 'It's like the bit from the movie *Psycho* where what they think is a sweet little old lady in a chair turns out to be a rotting skeleton.'

Kerry put his hand on her upper arm, and for one alarming moment Sidney thought he was about to pull her to him. But all he did was give her arm a quick squeeze.

'Thank you,' he said.

And then his eyes widened at something behind her. 'What the hell is *that*?'

Sidney turned, saw a large, barrel-like shape saunter across the road.

'King,' she said. 'Foraging.'

'And a king is — what type of animal?'

Sidney laughed. 'He's Jacko and Mac's dog! Chocolate Labrador. On the big side, definitely, mainly because he's a typical Lab — if it's food, he'll eat it. If it isn't, he'll eat it anyway. Cardboard, plastic, furniture — all edible as far as King's concerned.'

'And he roams loose?'

'All the time. And all over, even out into the country. I suppose all that exercise helps keep his weight down.'

'I see . . .'

He stared down the road, frowning, as if unconvinced.

'Well, best get in.' Sidney slipped quickly through the gate. 'I'll see you next week at training?'

'Right! Yes!' Kerry's attention snapped into focus. 'I'll make sure young Reuben knows he's welcome back.'

Sidney's urge to grill him about that, too, was overridden by a stronger urge not to prolong their conversation. The arm touch had thrown her — and not because she *hadn't* liked it.

Delusional. He considered her a friend, that's all. A pal, a mate.

She grabbed her keys from her pocket, unlocked her front door.

'Good night,' she called, as she began to shut it.

'Good night!' she heard Kerry respond. 'See you soon!'

Yes, see you soon. Old pal, old buddy . . .

Sidney flopped down on her sofa, dislodging more foam from the gap that she *must* get around to patching up. She should ask Agatha to help her; that woman knew how to wield a needle.

And maybe she should ask Doc Love to give her some hormone-suppressants — or whatever drug might prevent hopeless, delusional attractions to men she didn't even really know. Though after tonight, to be fair, she now knew more about him than before.

Left at the altar. How awful would *that* be?

No! She couldn't think about it — she'd only feel sorry for him, and that was the slippery slope that tipped you headfirst into the quagmire of affection. Best to keep it polite, amicable, nothing more. Just having a laugh. Like mates.

Silence all around her, except for the ticking of the old mantel clock her grandmother had left her. It was made of dark wood, quite ugly, but it had cost her nothing and it still kept good time.

Tick. Tick. Tick.

Sod symbolism. Sod hormones and delusion. Sod being alone in an empty house.

Despite it not being even ten o'clock, Sidney went to bed. And lay there in the dark until sleep finally sodding came.

Chapter 14

Sam

'What does Ohnee-what-the-fuck mean anyway?'

Tubs fished another beer out of the lake, cracked it open.

'Onemanawa?' Brownie pursed his mouth. 'I suppose the closest translation is "sands of my heart".'

'Sand up my arse, more like it,' said Tubs. 'Fucken stupid.'

'Why?' Deano said. 'If that was what it was called before?'

Tubs's lip curled. 'Who says it was called that before? It's been Gabriel's Bay for like a hundred fucken years, so why say that's wrong now? Just stirring, if you ask me. Local "ee-wee" creating a stink so they can bribe more dosh out of the government.'

Mr Hanrahan's words, Sam knew. Tubs's own grasp of politics and history was less firm than the grip he had on the wet beer can, which had already slipped once out of his hand.

'Because, of course,' said Brownie, 'the government owes us nothing.'

'Your lot are getting fucken *millions* from them!' said Tubs. 'Whereas what have us white folks got?'

'Autonomy over your own culture and language,' said Brownie. 'The lion's share of land and property ownership. Majority representation in business, politics and the judiciary. Easier access to higher education. A society focused around your traditions and customs—'

'Aqueducts,' said Deano.

'*What?*' said Tubs.

'Monty Python,' said Deano. 'What have the Romans ever done for us?'

'You're a fucken weirdo.'

Tubs drained his beer, chucked the can on the stones beside him and fetched another.

His third, though Sam knew he shouldn't be counting. They were Tubs's beers, as was the brand-new tent they'd put up — plenty of arguing until Deano started reading out the instructions, which meant they had to completely dismantle everything and start again. Mr Hanrahan had provided the tent, plus rifles and ammo, backpacks, sleeping bags, binoculars, Tilley lamps, camp stove and pots, chillers filled with cans of beer and a ton of food, and then he'd lent them a new double-cab ute — a black one with leather seats and a fat chrome sports bar sticking out the back. All Sam and the others had to supply were spare clothes.

'And our souls,' Brownie had whispered to Sam as they loaded up.

Sam, voted most sensible behind the wheel, drove them into the ranges, up a steep, rutted dirt road, hemmed in by thorny bush that seemed intent on scratching the shit out of the ute's paintwork, and slowly down the other side, bumping and rolling over boulders and potholes, to a campsite beside a small lake. There was a Department of Conservation hut there, but it was closed for maintenance — some joker had left a frying pan on the stove, according to Tubs, and the inside was black with smoke damage and smelled acrid and toxic, like burned plastic. So they'd set up the tent on a grassy patch under some trees, unloaded the gear and, at Tubs's insistence, were now sitting on the stony lakeshore, rewarding themselves with a few bevies.

'We should start cooking soon,' said Sam. 'Otherwise it'll be too dark to see.'

'Chill,' said Tubs. 'We've got the lamps.'

Deano hopped up. 'I'm onto it.'

He was perkier than Sam had seen him for ages. At primary school, Deano was like a terrier dog, never still, always nagging at them to play a game, run around. About halfway through high school, he discovered weed and that slowed him down. He could still pull out a turn of speed on the rugby field, but after school Deano quit playing. Tubs didn't play much anymore either, preferring to socialise in the clubrooms than train. Brownie — he made the team for most matches, but since his mum died he played with a quiet intensity that somehow created a distance between him and his team-mates. He wasn't aloof, exactly — he joked and laughed with the others. But there were times when he'd stand apart, beer untouched, staring off at nothing. If he caught Sam looking at him, he'd wink and Sam would feel relieved, though he wasn't sure why.

Sam was nagged every so often by the thought he should ask Brownie if he was OK. But he figured that if there *was* something wrong, Brownie would say. Until that happened, Sam felt it was pretty safe to assume Brownie was all right. Even though, like Sam's dad had said, he had more to handle than perhaps he should at his age.

Maybe that was why Brownie stuck with their group? For the same reasons Sam did — part habit, part need to hang onto a connection that had been part of his life since he could remember. Sam had family, a few other mates he'd met building, and no doubt he'd make new friends in Christchurch. But if Brownie stopped being friends with the three of them, who would he have in his life except his sick father?

Still, he seemed happy enough right now, amused by Deano bustling around like a mother hen. Sam stood up. Better go do his duty.

'Do you want to help us with the kai, bro?' he asked Brownie.

Brownie smiled, shook his head. 'Too many cooks,' he said. 'But I'm happy to fetch the fire extinguisher from the truck. Just in case.'

As it turned out, all Sam had to do was unpack the plates and cutlery. Deano sorted through the food and with swift decisiveness arranged it all into piles — one for each of their weekend's meals, and the rest for taking with them in their packs. Deano then lit the stove, and in fifteen minutes had made a meal of vegetable fried rice and canned tuna with a dash of chilli sauce. Hardly cordon bleu, but hot, tasty and filling.

They ate sitting around a fire that Brownie had built on the stones. The night was clear and the stars starting to appear above. When he was ten, Sam had learned to recognise all the constellations. Orion's Belt, Canis Major, Scorpius, the Southern Cross, the Pleiades or Seven Sisters — the Māori Matariki. He'd forgotten them all now except the Southern Cross. Fortunately, being nameless didn't make them any less beautiful.

Tubs clattered his empty plate onto the stones, belched.

'You'll make someone a great wife, Deano,' he said. 'How are you at blow jobs?'

'Less competent than you,' said Brownie. 'From what I hear.'

'Fucker.'

Tubs was six beers down now, but he was happy enough, grinning instead of scowling. Drinking could make Tubs go either way. Last weekend, he'd got into a scrap at the clubrooms. He'd given one of the older guys an angry lecture about mistakes he'd made in the day's game, and if he hadn't been Rob Hanrahan's son, the club lads would have taken him outside and kicked the shit out of him. Sam knew this because he'd heard Uncle Gene telling his dad. Not because the lads were afraid of Mr Hanrahan, his uncle said, but because Tubs's dad hated being made to look bad, and if he found out his son had breached club etiquette, been an embarrassment, he'd find the shit the lads had kicked out of Tubs, stuff it back in and kick it out of him all over again. General consensus was that even Tubs didn't deserve that. But, said Uncle Gene, the fat kid was *seriously* testing the limits of the club's compassion.

'What's the plan for tomorrow?'

Sam directed the question to the group but really he was only asking Deano.

And Deano answered. 'Have breakfast, get packed, walk up into the hills. There are some clearings further up that deer often hang out in. Who knows? We might spot the odd chamois, too.'

'Chamois?' Tubs said. 'I clean cars with a fucken chamois, dickhead.'

'Which were originally made from the skin of the chamois mountain goat,' said Brownie. 'The chamois here *and* the deer are non-native European imports. Like you lot.'

'Yeah, yeah.'

Tubs got up, swayed then recovered, headed to the trees. The sound of peeing carried clearly and went on for so long, the others looked at each other and laughed.

'He'll return a shrivelled husk,' said Brownie. 'A raisin of his former self.'

Tubs didn't return, but instead wavered towards the tent, took five goes to open the flap. They heard the thud of his body landing on, hopefully, his sleeping bag.

'Shit,' said Brownie. 'Welcome to Snoresville. No sleep for the sober.'

Deano was collecting the dirty dishes.

'I'll boil up some washing water,' he said. 'Get these clean for tomorrow.'

'Need a hand?' said Brownie.

'Nah, she's right. I like doing it.'

'Will you wake us up in the morning, Deano?' said Sam.

'Sure.'

'Will you tuck us in and read us a story?' said Brownie.

'Fuck off,' said Deano.

But he sounded happy, and all the while he cleaned up, he hummed.

His mood should have made Sam happy, too, but instead, it filled him with a sudden dread. This should be Deano's life, not sifting between odd jobs, smoking weed and sitting on the couch watching shit TV with Loretta, who looked like one of the lumpy bread rolls she sold and could barely string two words together. He should be using his skills, alongside people who valued him. Not flogging dope for evil bastards who couldn't give a rat's arse about anyone, and with whom there was no such thing as a second chance.

Sparks, rising glowing motes, caught his eye. Brownie was poking the fire with a stick, to revive the dying flames. The light shining from below made his face look hollowed out, ghostly, and Sam remembered them all one Halloween at his house, torches propped under their chins, jumping out at Sam's little sisters and cousins, who went shrieking down the hallway, spurting pee. Nowadays, the girls wouldn't turn a hair, would sneer and say 'Whatever, losers'.

'Ready to bag some stags?' Sam said to Brownie.

'If I end the day without being shot by Tubs, I'll call it a success.'

'We could remove his bullets while he's not looking.'

Brownie's smile went up in one corner only.

'That's our Sam,' he said. 'Always watching out for us.'

Sam couldn't tell if his friend meant it as compliment or criticism. He didn't ask, kept quiet, lay back on the stones and stared into the swirls of stars that had died eons before anyone he knew had even been thought of.

The tent came down quicker than it went up, was slung in the back of the ute, along with the empty chiller, Tilley lamps and cooking gear. Rifles were stuffed into bags, and the backpacks, sleeping bags and a pile of soaked clothing chucked on top of everything. It was a shit packing job, but everyone was too pissed-off to take more care. Which, Sam thought but didn't say, was the whole reason they were pissed-off in the first place.

He drove from the campsite, everyone silent and sulking. Then the recriminations began. Tubs. Couldn't help himself.

'I had the fucken shot,' he said. 'I called it.'

'*I* called it,' said Deano. 'You were just standing there, like a stunned mullet.'

'Does it matter?' said Brownie. 'You both missed. Doe all of thirty metres away, in open country, and you both missed.'

'I *missed*,' said Tubs, 'because Deano fucken fired when *I'd* called it!'

'*I* called it!

'What, in fucken sign language? Sorry, I wasn't looking at you. I was looking at the deer I was all ready to shoot!'

'Wonder you could see anything!' said Deano. 'You were still fucken half-pissed!'

'Peace, lads, peace,' said Brownie. 'At least you found a deer. Sam and I found squat.'

Sam shot him a quick look. That wasn't true. Deano had split the group up, sent Sam and Brownie off the track and through the bush, promising a clearing on the other side. The bushwhacking seemed to go on forever, and they kept getting smacked in the face by branches or tangled in bloody supplejack vines.

'Jesus,' Brownie had puffed. 'What's the point? All our swearing and noise will have scared off every animal for miles.'

As he spoke, they popped out into the promised clearing, and at its far edge was a young stag, a spiker, antlers only part-grown. Sam froze, expecting the stag to bound away, but though its head went up and its nose twitched, it stayed where it was. Side on. A perfect target.

Sam hesitated. He knew, in theory, where to place the shot, and he was a decent enough marksman. But the biggest animal he'd ever shot was a possum. What if he messed up? What if it ran away, injured, and bled to death over days?

Brownie hadn't moved either. His friend's rifle stayed slung over his shoulder, his head cocked to one side as he gazed at the stag. Brownie pointed two fingers.

'*Bang*, *bang*, young buck,' he whispered. 'You're dead.'

The stag heard him, darted away into the bush, vanished. Turned out to be their only opportunity all day. Whatever, losers.

From the passenger seat, Brownie gave Sam a quick wink. No need to share, it said.

'And then you bloody fell in the river!' Deano's outrage hadn't lessened. 'At the easiest bloody crossing spot ever!'

'It was a loose stone!' said Tubs. 'You'd have fallen, too!'

'But I didn't.' Deano jabbed a finger into his own chest. 'Because *I* wasn't half-pissed!'

'Fuck off.' Tubs folded his arms, mutinously. 'I was fine.'

'Hunting's no place for alcohol! Guns and booze *don't* mix!'

Deano was seriously worked-up. Brownie turned around.

'You're right, mate,' he said. 'But leave it now, eh? You've made your point.'

Sam doubted that — Tubs would barely take advice from someone he respected, let alone Deano. But Brownie was right. Leave it.

'Yeah, s'pose,' Deano muttered.

Sam hadn't meant to hit the large pothole, but was glad of the distraction as they rattled around the cab like dice in a cup.

'Jeez, Sammo,' said Brownie. 'It's incredible we've got this far still alive. Don't end it now.'

Sam lifted his foot off the gas. 'Sorry.'

For the next few minutes, there was silence in the cab. Tubs and Deano sulking, Sam concentrating on the road. Brownie was the only one who seemed relaxed. He watched the scenery out the window.

Then he said, 'You know, Tubs, even you and I are related. In fact, we all share a common ancestor.'

'Bullshit,' said Tubs. 'How's that possible?'

'One in every two hundred men alive today is descended from Genghis Khan.'

'It's true!' said Deano, suddenly perky again. 'I read it on—'

He stopped. Blushed.

Brownie flashed a grin at Sam, and in a coaxing tone said, 'Read it on what, Dean, my friend? You can't slide out of this one.'

Deano mumbled, but Brownie had sharp ears.

'A female sanitary item, you say? Well, well.'

'What the fuck are you doing with — no, never mind,' said Tubs. 'Don't wanna know.'

'They have these facts on the wrappers,' said Deano. 'Like Leonardo da Vinci could play tennis with one hand and draw with the other, and rats can understand two different human languages.'

'Can they understand that you're a *retard*?'

'Hey!'

Bicker, bicker, back and forth it went. But the atmosphere had lightened, was almost back to normal.

The end of the rutted shingle road came into view, and Sam drove a little faster, feeling buoyed, lifted up, the way he might if he'd just had a lucky escape.

Chapter 15

Mac

'Give it here.'

Mac held out a hand, beckoned with her fingers.

Ngaire kept hold of the plastic soft-drink bottle.

'You're not getting on the bus if you don't,' said Mac.

'Could she not anyway?' said Emil Olsen. 'Her bloody coughing drives me barmy.'

'Aw-aw,' Ngaire protested. 'Can't help it, can I?'

'Bloody can,' said Emil. 'You can quit the bloody fags!'

'That's enough from you,' Mac warned him. 'Ngaire. Bottle.'

She plucked it from Ngaire's grip, unscrewed the top, took a sniff.

'Wow,' she said. 'I think the Americans burned jungles with this in Vietnam.'

'It's lemonade!' said Ngaire. 'Mostly.'

'I should tip it out on the ground,' said Mac. 'Except that I care more about the land than about you. I'll give it back when I drop you home.'

She stashed the bottle in her canvas bag, a freebie from another drug company that sported the words 'Don't let diarrhoea wreck your day' in large purple letters.

'Listen up,' she said to the waiting old folk. 'Any concealed booze, knives or Word Search puzzles, and you're banned from the Love Bus. Got it?'

'What's wrong with Word Search?' said little Ena Lester.

'Anyone who doesn't know the answer to that,' said Mac, 'will be taken to the Hampton dementia ward and left there.'

Silence.

'Right. All aboard. Chop-chop.'

Mac stood beside the steps to help up the less steady, counted everyone off — a necessary routine after Doris Te Puhi was left behind. Doris was found again in Paper Plus, engrossed in the latest issue of *Grazia*, unaware she'd been abandoned. Mac was relieved and resentful in equal measure, and vowed no one else would get lost on her watch. She might be forced to strangle them and toss their corpse off the hill, but they wouldn't get lost.

Twelve, thirteen, fourteen . . .

Numbers had been dwindling steadily since the first Love Bus run two years ago. And they were down another since last week. Albert Chapman. Massive stroke on Saturday morning. Quick, said Dr Love. Mercifully so.

Mac stood by the driver's seat, checked her passengers were seated. Took a while, so best to be sure. Be a waste of a morning if she had to spend it in A&E.

'Listen up,' she said. 'Albert's not with us today because he's dead.'

Sharp intakes of breath, cries of surprise. Seriously, what kind of small town was it if news took more than a day to get around?

'Don't worry, he didn't suffer,' said Mac. 'Big stroke. Dropped him like a stone.'

Little Ena sniffled into her hankie. Ngaire emitted a series of 'Aws'.

'We'll have a cup of tea in his memory at the Kozy Kettle,' said Mac. 'And one of his favourite buns. All right?'

Nods. Fewer sniffles.

Tea and a bun. Taking the place of expensive therapy since the invention of the mug.

Mac started up the bus, which shuddered and coughed like Ngaire, before firing into life. On its last legs, too, perhaps? This lot would be stranded without it. The only other bus service was the school bus that delivered Gabriel's Bay teens to and from Hampton High. Mac couldn't see the two lots of passengers being thrilled with each other's company. Though Ngaire would have plenty of new marks to cadge ciggies and booze off.

But who else in town showed a speck of interest? Who else cared about these oldies? It was hardly a hot item on the Progressive Association's agenda. To be fair, Mac had started up the Love Bus run without consulting a single person apart from Dr Love, so if her service was now taken for granted, she had no one but herself to blame. If anyone needed to add it to the Bunch of Ass's agenda, she did. Which meant she now had two issues to speak to them about. Double the time forced to watch self-righteous pomposity ooze from their pores like mucous from a hagfish.

Seemed her life was full of issues she was being forced to address alone. Having decided not to share her concerns about their father with her children, she had tentatively raised the subject with Gene. He and Jacko might scrap like toddlers, but their friendship was limpet tight, had been since primary school, where seven-year-old Gene had discovered that bullies could be encouraged onto a more virtuous path through the simple expedient of pointing out Jacko and leaving the rest to their imagination. He also ensured they knew he was Jacko's best mate, and, even if that hadn't been true at the start, Gene made it so in short order. His sharp wit and Jacko's physical presence equalled a team no one messed with.

They looked out for each other, and any kid being unfairly picked on, he'd told Mac. Unfairly, Mac questioned? Some knucklebrains deserve all they get, Gene replied. Mac couldn't disagree.

Was denial a knucklebrain characteristic? Did Jacko deserve what he might get? On the internet, Mac had seen an image of a billboard advising men to get checked for prostate cancer. The headline read 'One in three men will die from stubbornness'. Below it, someone had scrawled 'No, we won't!'

Hardy ha ha.

Man-pride solidarity meant Mac couldn't ask Gene outright if he had any concerns. It was like fly fishing — she had to cast the line gently upstream and wait for the bite. In five attempts, all she got was a nibble, an offhand mention that he'd caught Jacko having to rest between loads, while carrying groceries from his car to the Boat Shed kitchen. Gene joked that he'd have to recruit another partner to shift the murdered bodies, and then moved on to another subject, leaving Mac wondering if she could pay someone to spy on Jacko during the day. Not likely. Cover around the Boat Shed was minimal, and Jacko's eagle eye for detail would spot a camera inside pronto.

She *could* ask Sidney to keep an eye on him on the evenings she worked, but Mac knew the small income was important to her, and the truth was that the end of Jacko would mean the end of the Boat Shed. Mac didn't want Sidney to worry without cause.

So it seemed her best option was to trust in Gene's frankness, trust he'd speak out if he were worried, tell his mate. Of course, he could well meet with exactly the same resistance that she had, and quite possibly — wonderful thought — already had.

Mac punished the Love Bus's gearbox with a vigorous change.

'Gently, Bentley,' said Emil Olsen.

He'd chosen to sit up front, away from Ngaire, who didn't like to be too near to Mac. Unlike his son, Evan, Emil was as spare and gnarled as an old fence post. The late Mrs Olsen, neé Pugh, had provided the chubby DNA, and had died of a blocked artery — the obstruction, Mac was convinced, being pure whipped cream.

'Emil,' said Mac, 'how do you feel about foreigners?'

Emil had strong opinions on the tobacco industry, the International Monetary Fund and the Catholic Church. It only followed.

'What kind?' he said.

'The human kind.'

'Doing what?'

At this early stage, Mac felt it wise to be vague.

'Taking positions of responsibility within your community.'

'What kind?'

'The responsible kind. Teachers, JPs, dentists, that sort of thing.'

Mac recalled another internet gem her daughter, Emma, had sent her. Small town hashtags. Number one:

#TheLocalsAren'tQuirkyThey'reRacist.

'Can they speak English?' said Emil.

'They can. They may have an accent.'

'Do they eat strange food?'

This coming from a man of Norwegian descent, who ate fish that had been steeped in lye, and had the consistency of the underside of a bar of damp soap.

'No stranger than anything you can order at the Chinese takeaway.'

Emil thought for a minute.

'What was the question again?'

'Never mind.'

Silence while Mac navigated the hill bend known as The Crunch, which could have been named after the V-shaped position people attained doing abdominal exercise, but was, in fact, a reference to the last sound you'd hear if you messed it up.

‘There’s an African lady in the library,’ said Emil. ‘From Burkina Faso.’

‘And how do you feel about her?’

‘She knows her onions.’

Emil could mean this literally. He had a vast vegetable garden, made vaster after Mrs Olsen’s death when he was able to rip up her dahlias and replace them with scarlet runners.

‘How would you feel if she was — let’s say — your nurse? If you met her in hospital?’

‘Not likely,’ said Emil. ‘She’s a trained librarian.’

‘OK, how about a *different* African woman? How would you feel being nursed by her?’

‘By who?’

‘Never mind.’

She might slip the subject into conversation after they’d paid tribute to Albert with tea and buns. Better still, she’d search out the African librarian and ask if she had any medically trained relatives back home. Don’t ask, don’t get was Mac’s motto.

Though what you got, she had to admit, wasn’t necessarily what you wanted.

Dr Love opened his door, smiled briefly to acknowledge Mac’s return, and beckoned in his next patient, a truck driver with sleep apnoea.

‘I’ll see you in two weeks,’ he said to the patient exiting.

Olivia Jensen. Fleshless as beef jerky, forehead smooth as a marble chopping board. Touch of redness in the eyes and a few broken capillaries around the nose, though, Mac noted, as Olivia reached the reception desk. That's because fighting the course of Nature was like carrying live squid in a string bag. Always something slips through.

'Forty dollars,' she said. Held out her hand for Olivia's well-thrashed credit card.

'I'll put it on account.'

'On *account?*'

Mac let her eyes travel to Olivia's perfectly French-manicured nails. Odds were low that she'd had them done for ten bucks by Peg in Gabriel's Bay, who went house-to-house flogging franchise cosmetics. Peg wasn't bad at makeup and nails, but she did like to embellish. Her latest hairstyle was a rainbow-hued bob with a green cat's head shaved just above the nape of her neck, and her own nails were currently adorned with Disney princesses. Peg wore fifties-style dresses in cartoon-print fabrics, a fashion choice that would no doubt make Olivia dry-heave.

'Will that be a problem?'

Oh ho. Olivia's tone was all smooth-silk above, but beneath Mac heard the ding-dong of the boxing-ring bell.

No need to step right in now, however. For one thing, the next patient had arrived. Patricia Weston, early as always, and radiating her usual propriety. Patricia would be upset if Mac went for the TKO on Olivia. No, she'd have to settle for a quick jab to the kidney.

'No problem at all,' Mac replied. 'Plenty of our patients find it more convenient to pay their bills at the end of the month. You know, when the bank account's filled up again.'

'Thank you,' said Olivia's mouth. Her eyes said, 'Cow.'

Mac held her gaze, unblinking, until Olivia had to pretend she always intended to look for her keys in her handbag. Said keys in an iron grip, she stalked out to where her car was no doubt parked in a handicap space.

Patricia lowered *Condé Nast Traveller*, the 'Intimate Caribbean' issue.

'An unhappy woman,' she said, to Mac's great astonishment. 'Entirely of her own making, don't you think?'

'Is it? I had the impression her husband was the one managing their finances.'

'You mean mismanaging?' said Mac. 'Got himself in four flavours of strife by the sound of it. The IRD's after him; ACC, too, for unpaid levies. The bank's calling in some massive loan, and wants everything he secured it by sold, including Stonelands. The Samoan resort development's ground to a halt with all kinds of planning issues, so no buyer with an ounce of sanity would take that on. And his Wellington properties are buggered, so ditto. It's a mess, and Rick made it.'

'And entangled his poor wife and daughter in the process,' said Patricia.

'OK, poor daughter, I'll give you,' said Mac. 'Madison is a complete innocent. But Olivia? Hell no. Her sole motivation for saying "I do" was an express ticket to Easy Street, and she's spitting tacks that it's all crashed down. "For poorer" was not part of *her* matrimonial vows.'

'That's a little harsh, if I may say so,' said Patricia. 'Isn't it possible she may have fallen in love?'

'No,' said Mac. 'It isn't. Anyway, why are you feeling a need to defend her? You barely know her. Are you involved in some charity that rescues miserable wives?'

What answer Patricia might have given was lost, as Doc Love showed the truck driver out, and invited Patricia to enter. Mac peered after her, trying to glean a clue from her expression, but the truck driver blocked the way, and the door closed.

'Doc said I could put this on account,' said the truck driver, a large, bearded man in a flannel shirt, who clearly rated Paul Bunyan as a style icon.

‘Of course he did,’ said Mac.

‘Um, is that OK?’ the big man asked.

Mac wasn’t inclined to adopt her reassuring voice, but then he looked so pitiful. Luckily, being that large, he probably wasn’t picked on by bar fighters. He was a creature that relied on its deceptive appearance to stay safe, like one of those butterflies with wings patterned like an owl’s eyes.

‘It’s perfectly fine,’ she said, and even mustered a smile. ‘I’ll mail the statement at the end of the month.’

He left, and there were no more patients waiting. She may as well use the next twenty minutes productively, if that word could be applied to filtering through yet another mountain of rubbish applications from overseas ‘doctors’ who had all the credibility of Mrs Joyce Zuma, who worked in the packaging and courier department of the Central Bank of Nigeria and needed Mac’s help to shift a consignment of twenty million American dollars, all in used hundred-dollar bills.

Bronagh Macfarlane had warned her, true, but it was hard not to be dispirited that the frontrunner for the job was currently Mrs Joyce Zuma herself, by dint of the fact she correctly spelled ‘consignment’.

Mac hadn’t raised the subject with her Love Bus group. The tea-and-bun session for Albert had threatened to turn maudlin, so she’d cut it short. Her patience was thin anyway, after two incontinence incidents, one lot of groceries forgotten in the public loo, three close calls crossing streets, and, despite the librarian producing photographic evidence, Bob Thatcher remaining convinced that his favourite historical romance author, Jude Deveraux, was a man.

‘Jude *can* be a man’s name,’ the librarian had whispered to Mac, thereby capturing the entirety of Bob’s argument in a nutshell.

On the other hand — Mac glanced at Doc Love's closed door — it was some comfort that nobody knew what she was up to, so she needn't feel embarrassed at producing no result. But as reinforced by the plastic waiting-room clock, time was a-ticking on.

Well, you knew what they said. No rest for the wicked.

Chapter 16

Kerry

'"O my brothers. Why so soft, so pliant and yielding? Why is there so much denial, self-denial, in your hearts? So little destiny in your eyes?"'

An excellent question.

'"This new tablet, O my brothers, I place over you: Become hard!"'

Paired with an answer that surely must have sounded less dodgy at the time. Although earnest intellectuals, in Kerry's experience, tended not to be aware of the double-entendre. Unlike shallow people such as himself.

And, by God, that was the end! Kerry had made it all the way through *Twilight of the Idols* with only minor headaches. Being shallow, he had not a clue what the broom-moustached one was on about, but then he wasn't reading it for himself. He was reading it for the man in the bed, who didn't seem to care one way or another whether morality was an idiosyncrasy of degenerates or that Christianity was the metaphysics of the hangman. His demeanour *suggested* a hangman, one weary after a long day of suspending people from the hempen noose. But while Nietzsche punched at his shibboleths with unflagging zeal, Jonty Barton had all the vigour of old celery. Why he wanted to hear Nietzsche's writing was a mystery.

Could the clue have been at the beginning, where the moustached one asserted: 'What does not destroy me, makes me stronger.' Seemed Nietzsche was a fan of what he called 'life's school of war', was adamant that wounds had the power to re-invigorate. Perhaps old Jonty found some comfort in that?

Or perhaps the point was that there was no comfort, only the hair-shirt penance of being bored witless, leavened only by the pleasure of knowing his reader was suffering right along with him.

Oh, look, they still had twenty minutes left.

'What next, Mr Barton?' said Kerry. '*Ecce Homo*, or *The Gay Science*? Or are they the same book with different titles?'

It was a terrible joke and in worse taste, but this was Kerry's third day of reading to a man who did nothing but lie on his back and stare at the ceiling, and he was starting to feel the kind of relentless desperation that Sisyphus must have experienced every time he watched the boulder wend its merry way once more to the bottom of the hill. Kerry had tried a spot of casual conversation, but it turned into an amateur ventriloquism skit — he both asking and answering the questions — so he gave up.

No response this time, either. As Kerry flipped through both books, he began to hum Monty Python's drunken philosophers song.

'Stop that.'

JesusMaryMotherofGod — *speech!*

'Apologies,' said Kerry. 'Just making my selection. Eeny-meeny — oh, why not? *Ecce Homo* it is.'

'His last work. Published post-humously.'

Kerry might be reading it post-humously, too, after dying from boredom mid-sentence. But now that Jonty was showing interest in actual verbal communication, it might be better to encourage him. With luck, he could keep a conversation going for the remaining eighteen minutes and twenty-two seconds of their session.

'What did he die of?'

'Insanity.'

That would have been Kerry's second guess. After being clubbed to death by someone forced to read his entire oeuvre in one sitting.

'He ordered the German emperor to go to Rome and be shot.'

'I can see how that might have raised the odd eyebrow,' said Kerry.

'They committed him to the clinic of renowned psychiatrist, Otto Binswanger.'

Kerry snorted. Couldn't help it.

Jonty Barton shifted his gaze from the ceiling. He had a drift of white hair around a bald patch, an aquiline nose and a straight, stern mouth. Kerry had mentally pegged him as the love child of Statler and Waldorf from *The Muppet Show*, but under Jonty's stare, he revised that image to Edward the First in *Braveheart*, as played by Patrick McGoohan. There was a hint of the same ice-eyed cruelty, though Kerry felt somewhat sure Jonty Barton wouldn't chuck him to his death out of a castle window.

'You're a frivolous young man, aren't you?' he said.

'In my defence,' said Kerry, 'Binswanger is a very funny name.'

Jonty's resemblance to Edward Longshanks was now quite uncanny.

'Only to those with the intellectual capacity of a flatworm.'

Insults! Was that a good sign? Should he retort — perhaps that's what Jonty needed, to be gingered up? Or should he back off, be conciliatory?

The man's mental state was fragile, so no doubt backing off would be the prudent option. But then there was the matter of the subject that everyone — well, Gene — at the Boat Shed had insinuated that he'd never dare raise. Now that the door of conversation had been opened a crack, shouldn't he seize the chance and fling it wide?

Kerry had never wished more fervently for Bronagh Macfarlane to appear by his side and gee him up the way she used to at the children's playground when he was small. 'If you want to go for a slide, you'll need to climb the ladder. If you don't, we can go home. Up to you.' His mother excelled in setting firm parameters.

Up the ladder, or go home? What would new, improved Kerry choose?

'Mr Barton,' he said, 'now that we're chatting, may I run an idea past you?'

'What sort of idea?' said Jonty, testily.

Kerry surreptitiously checked the window latches.

'How would you feel about letting people come and look at your trains?'

'People? What people?'

'Anyone who wants to see them. And, er, who's prepared to pay a small entrance fee. Which, of course, would be used to benefit Gabriel's Bay, and—'

Kerry swore Jonty's white fringe of hair stood suddenly on end, like a human Van de Graaff generator.

'What, what—?' he began to splutter.

'The town needs a boost, a tourist attraction.' Kerry spoke faster, while feeling like a bomb-disposal expert searching frantically for the blue wire. 'And your trains have such great appeal, even more so if we combine them with the other miniature displays that—'

'Out,' said Jonty quietly. Which was, of course, more unnerving than if he'd shouted.

Kerry knew when to quit. Well, he didn't really, but now seemed as good a time as any.

'Of course.'

He stood, placed *Ecce Homo* gently on the bedside table, for whoever was to read next. Odds were high that it would not be he.

At the bedroom door, Kerry decided on one last, no doubt fruitless and ill-judged, appeal.

'Will you at least think about it?' he said. 'It will cost you nothing, but the wider benefits could be truly significant.'

Then he scarpered downstairs, his mind working now how to explain this to Meredith. On the plus side, he'd got Jonty talking. On the downside — well, he'd cross that bridge when he came to it, and if he ran across it really fast, he might get over before it collapsed.

He took the last stairs at a jump, landing in the hallway just as the phone rang. Meredith was out, gone to the plant nursery to pick up her order for the hanging baskets.

'Barton residence,' he said.

'Not you again,' said the voice he now knew belonged to Sophie Barton, younger daughter and, putting two and two together, unsuccessful artist.

'No, I'm his evil twin,' said Kerry. 'We job-share. How can I help?'

'Is the old bat out?'

'If you mean Mrs Barton, then, yes, she is not at home.'

'"Mrs Barton". God.'

'I call my own mother Ma,' said Kerry. 'And she calls me collect. Being a poorly paid nurse and all.'

He could practically hear the rattle of eyeballs rolling back in a skull.

'When's she back?'

'Later on.'

Kerry felt disinclined to be more helpful.

Instead of the click of her hanging up in his ear again, Kerry could hear breathing.

'I've got a show,' she said.

A show of what? Hands? Oh, right. Of her art.

Kerry was struck with sudden pity. She was so desperate to tell someone, she'd called a mother she didn't really get on with, and now had to resort to sharing her news with a person she'd never met. He wondered who else there was in her life.

'Congratulations,' he said. 'Where?'

'You wouldn't have heard of it.'

'I'm foreign,' said Kerry. 'Ninety-nine per cent of this country is unknown to me.'

She named a place that, after further questioning, turned out to be a town fifty kilometres on the other side of Hampton. It was even smaller than Gabriel's Bay, but had established a reputation as an artists' enclave. Two of the country's leading painters had their studios there, and a medley of arts and crafts practitioners had gathered around them, so that a visitor could now buy anything from an abstract landscape worth many thousands to chunky ceramic mugs featuring cartoon kiwis giving a thumbs up. Sophie's work fell somewhere in between, though when she talked about fellow artists' work being 'the sort of leaves and hearts shite that's always called "Aotearoa Flax Dreaming" or some bollocks' it wasn't a stretch to infer that she wished to be nearer the top end.

Her exhibition was scheduled for the three weeks leading up to Christmas. It came with a residency on-site, which was a neat solution to the issue of her having no fixed abode.

'Will you spend Christmas at home?' Kerry asked.

Sophie, who'd been softening to the point where she could almost be called chatty, snapped back into hostile mode.

'Home? That's a laugh.'

'Do you not feel welcome here?'

Kerry knew full well that he was trundling into a minefield, but it was turning out to be that sort of day.

'My mother's a critical control freak who thinks I'm a complete loser, and my father is lord of the arseholes,' said Sophie. 'What do you think?'

The sound of a car. Meredith. He could always tell — even the way she drove was courteous and restrained.

'Your mother's home,' said Kerry. 'If you'd like to hold, I'll tell her you're on the line.'

'Don't bother,' said Sophie. 'Just tell her about the bloody show. Actually, don't bother about that, either. It's not like she'll come.'

And, once more, she hung up in his ear.

If I ever have children, thought Kerry — and he certainly would like to one day — I hope we will stay friends. Then again, if they're born with the personality of a medieval siege weapon, perhaps, even with top-flight, textbook parenting, there's nothing you can do.

He went outside to help Meredith unload the car.

'Are these what my mother calls Busy Lizzies?' he said, ferrying pink-blossomed plants to the verandah.

'No, those are petunias. Busy Lizzie is a common name for impatiens.'

'That's my darling mother,' said Kerry, cheerfully. 'Common as muck.'

Meredith gave him a reproving look. 'That's not what I meant.'

'She wouldn't care. Once, her family lived grandly, but those days are long gone. Now, she ribs my father for posh pretentions when he orders his fish crumbed instead of battered.'

He didn't see if she smiled or not, being engaged in lugging a bag of potting mix that insisted on arching its middle, much like a toddler unwilling to sit in its pushchair. With relief and a hint of revenge, he dropped it hard onto the gravel by the verandah.

'How was your morning?' said Meredith.

He could prevaricate now, put off the full confession until later. Or never. Never sounded good. But that felt like a backward step, a letdown after he'd taken a great leap forward in bravery. Up the ladder, or go home.

'He spoke to me. Mr Barton.'

Meredith paused, a frizz of sphagnum moss in her hand.

'What did he say?'

'He told me Nietzsche ended up in the loony bin. The bin of Binswanger, which I found amusing,' said Kerry. 'Then he called me frivolous. Then I asked if we could open up the model train to the public. And then we mutually agreed that our reading session was at an end.'

'I see.'

No doubt she did — right through his best casual delivery.

The sphagnum moss was being picked at, tendrils floating down like curls at the barber.

'The model train to the public . . .'

Her voice had a ruminating quality to it that could go either way but probably wouldn't. Kerry braced himself to be summarily fired.

'Where on earth did that idea spring from?'

'Er, it was more of a collation of ideas,' said Kerry. 'The train, your dollhouse, and Doctor Love's battle-game sets. Which I haven't seen but gather are—'

'Very detailed,' said Meredith. 'Doctor Love is quite the craftsman.'

'And I've been thinking about how small towns boost tourism.'

'Rather limited appeal, don't you think? Terribly old-fashioned?'

'I disagree,' said Kerry. 'The appeal is timeless. Takes us to a perfect world, where everything works, and everyone's tiny but happy.'

'You have been thinking.'

That sounded very nearly positive.

'We needn't do it at Woodhall,' said Kerry. 'We could find a space in town, an empty shop, or warehouse. Display everything so that people can see but they can't touch, unless supervised. Staff it with volunteers on a roster. And—'

Too far? No — up, up!

'—I also wondered if we could rope in locals to contribute. Finish the model train set, make new objects for the dollhouse, paint new soldiers. The more people we involve, the greater the commitment. It won't work half as well if the town doesn't get behind it.'

Meredith glanced down at the pile of moss fronds at her feet, ceased picking.

'Am I the first you've told? Apart from my husband, of course.'

'Erm, I may have floated the idea past Sidney,' Kerry admitted. 'And possibly Jacko Reid and Gene Collins . . .'

'Gene?' Meredith's eyebrows rose. 'Was Gene supportive?'

'In principle' seemed a safe and not entirely mendacious answer.

'But my husband was not?'

'To be fair,' said Kerry, 'I rather sprung it on him. I mean, one minute, Nietzsche, and then — whammo — his beloved trains being goggled at by the great unwashed. Though we could always place those little bottles of hand-sanitiser by the door.'

Was that the *tiniest* of smiles?

'Frivolous may have been an understatement,' she said.

Prompted by a sense that it was now or never, Kerry stepped closer.

'Look,' he said. 'I know I joke about, I *know* I play Mr Quippy far too often, but I'm very serious about this. *I* believe it could work. I believe it could be *fun*.'

Meredith arched an eyebrow. 'Mr Quippy?'

'I've never laid claim to *good* jokes.'

'The project would require funding. For promotion at the very least.'

'Maybe. Maybe all we need is good free publicity.' He shrugged. 'I *am* half Scottish.'

The petunias on the verandah were rosy pink and pale yellow. Tasteful. Not garish. Meredith Barton did not take risks with her colour schemes.

'Let me also think about it,' she said to him.

Good enough. A lot better, in fact, than being fired.

There was the small matter of her husband possibly not wanting Kerry to darken his bedroom door again, but that could wait. Never hurt to quit while you were ahead.

'Thank you,' he said. 'I appreciate it.'

A nod. Then a frown.

'Aren't you due at the school, for coaching?'

Yikes, the time!

His watch showed five to three. He'd have to motor.

'Go on,' said Meredith, as he hovered. 'You mustn't let the children down.'

The list of those he mustn't let down, Kerry mused as he drove at a speed just shy of illegal, was growing all the time. And it was always possible he'd taken on more than he could manage. Letting people down might be inevitable.

The radio, as if it knew, began to play 'Radar Love'. The Fielder's tyres protested on a corner, but he did not lift off.

He'd made the top of the ladder. Now to muster the courage to slide.

Chapter 17

Sidney

Seven minutes late. Not that bad, Sidney supposed, but late was late. And when it was children waiting, to them even one minute seemed like forever.

It was lucky she'd decided to come — the group had already turned feral. The Booth sisters winding up Lincoln; Dylan and Aidan hacking each other's ankles under the guise of going for the tackle. Rory bossing Madison and Peter. And Reuben, now that Kerry had arrived, struggling to release his hand from hers.

He was the reason she'd arrived after school. Sidney knew Kerry had not talked to Reuben or his teacher, which meant a snowball's chance of the boy returning to practice today. She'd grabbed the teacher before school, asked her permission to talk to Reuben, gained his reluctant agreement to let Sidney meet him after the bell and escort him to practice. He'd probably thought she wouldn't turn up — not a lot of adult reliability in Reuben's life, she guessed — but she had, and now she tightened her grip on his hand, bent to put her face level with his.

'You're really good at football, Reuben,' she said. 'And we all want you here.'

His expression was a heartbreaking mix of adult 'Yeah, right' and eight-year-old 'Really, truly?'

'We want you here,' Sidney assured him. 'Go on.' She let go of his hand. 'Go and meet Kerry at the car.'

He ran off. Kerry greeted him with a high-five, and Sidney held her breath until it was returned. Arm around the boy's shoulder, Kerry led Reuben over to the group, and began, not a minute too soon in Sidney's opinion, to take charge, call order. Good thing he had a knack with children, or his lateness might have put him at too much of a disadvantage. With children, an authority vacuum usually means anarchy. And why not? If the grown-up can't be bothered turning up on time, then why should *they* bother following rules?

Sidney's crabbiness at Kerry began to ebb when he turned to look at her, mouthed 'Thank you'. And it eased away entirely as she watched how he brought Reuben back into the fold, let him choose the first training exercise, used him as an example of how to kick a ball correctly.

She wasn't needed now, should be getting on home. She had a new student starting tomorrow, who wanted help with both Art History and English, and Sidney could use some quiet time with her ancient copy of E.H. Gombrich's *The Story of Art*.

But she lingered, her eye now on Madison, who, for once, was not coming to Sidney's house, but being picked up after training by Rick, who was now spending more time at Stonelands, 'to tidy it up for sale,' according to Mac, 'which is a euphemism for finding a giant rug to sweep all the crap under.'

Sidney hated that her first reaction to this information from Madison had been scepticism. Hated the sinking feeling, the worry about Maddie being let down. It was little comfort that she'd be back to run the Booth sisters and Reuben home, and so could ensure that Madison walked to the Boat Shed with Aidan and

Rory if — inner cynic corrected to 'when' — Rick failed to appear.

Lately, Olivia and Rick had been upping their use of Sidney's home as free after-school care for their daughter, and it was starting to grate. Today was the first afternoon in a week that Madison wouldn't be eating dinner at Sidney's. The first she'd see either of her parents before seven, sometimes even eight at night. For so many reasons, that simply wasn't right.

OK, so scrabbling around for money and keeping creditors at bay must be a full-time job for Rick. But Olivia, from what Sidney could tell, had diddly squat to occupy her. All she did was lounge around at home, or treat Rainer and Elke's place like her local bar. She'd even stopped driving to Hampton, and God knows how food got in the house because the only stop she ever made in Gabriel's Bay was Dr Love's surgery. Patient confidentiality prevented Mac spilling the beans about why, but Madison had once mentioned 'Mummy's pills', so odds were Olivia was on Prozac or some such modern-day nerve tonic.

A small part of Sidney felt a twinge of guilt. If Olivia actually *was* depressed, then that was rough, and could explain why she rarely went out any more. But the rest of Sidney wasn't prepared to be sympathetic. The rest of Sidney, quite frankly, believed both Rick and Olivia were taking the piss. They took flagrant advantage of her good nature because they *knew* that Sidney would never do anything to hurt Madison. How could she tell that sweet, darling child that she wasn't allowed to come over anymore? That she couldn't play with Aidan and Rory, who, while not being the most compatible playmates, were Madison's only real friends. How could Sidney banish Madison to a life of absent parents, both physically and emotionally, where the only person to look after her was a fierce Russian in her sixties, who, by all accounts, was a gnat's chuff away from quitting her job.

But it cost her money to feed another mouth, and though Rick and Olivia might be in a financial hole, they were hardly paupers. And yet neither of them had offered to contribute a brass razoo for petrol or food, or even to say thanks for Sidney's time. Not only that, but they mucked her around by changing plans last minute, were *never* on time, and never, ever properly apologised!

Damn it. Sidney couldn't tell whom she was most angry at: Rick and Olivia for their chancing, rude slackness, or herself, for not putting her foot down and insisting enough was enough.

Oh, well, at least she could take comfort that Madison *did* have her support. Not that she ever complained about her home life, the angel. Look at her there, dribbling balls between cones with such concentration. She always did her best, always gave wholeheartedly, even when the recipients might not deserve such generosity.

'Penny for them?'

Kerry beside her, faintly sweaty, which — Sidney cursed the primitive power of pheromones — smelled better than she would like it to. The kids were now taking turns to kick balls into the 'goal' (a breeze-block wall with unevenly drawn chalk lines).

'Sorry I was late,' he added. 'Thanks for holding the fort. And Reuben.'

'I thought you were going to make sure he came?'

His mouth twisted, guilt at being caught out.

'I was,' he said. 'I didn't get onto it. I should have.'

'They need to be able to rely on you.' Sidney fought an urge to become shrill. 'This is important to them.'

He rubbed his face. 'I know. I'm sorry. Again . . .'

Sidney's urge this time was to slap him about the head, slap some reliability into him. But that segued straight into a mental montage of every male cinema hero in history subduing protesting females with a kiss. Honestly, what was with her brain? Was it lying on a sofa watching soaps and scarfing marshmallows?

'I need to go,' she said, briskly. 'But I'll be back to do the up-country run. You'll take Lincoln home, won't you?'

Peter and Dylan were within walking distance, too, but Lincoln lived out Woodhall way, with parents who didn't really know what to do with him, but who fortunately had a large back garden in which he could zoom around for hours and not bother anyone.

'I will,' said Kerry, adding, 'I *will!*' when she gave him a look.

Then he said, 'I don't suppose I can entice you out for a drink tonight?'

What kind of drink? Friendly? Date-y? Not that it mattered.

'No babysitter.'

'Right. Er, what if I brought the drink to you?'

Friendly. No doubt now. Men on dates didn't want to be within a mile of children with inconveniently sharp hearing.

'Sure. Why not? If you want a quieter house, come around at eight.'

His smile flashed broad and — she should stop using this word — charming. But watching him head back to the children, she allowed herself a frisson of anticipation. How long had it been since she'd spent an evening with a man, even if he only wanted to talk about himself? Men liked to tell Sidney their problems, despite the fact she usually told them to buck up and get it together. Being a bit round and averagely pleasant-looking, she gave out motherly vibes. Certainly didn't give out sexual ones. Kerry was the first bloke who'd asked her out for — 'a while' was the only unit of time she could bear to admit.

Sidney walked home, picked up E.H. Gombrich, and over the next forty-five minutes retained not one word.

'I'm still seething,' she said, as Kerry opened the wine.

'I'll fill it to the top,' he said. 'Throw this standard drink nonsense to the wind.'

'Thank you.' Sidney took the glass, carefully, because it was indeed brimming. 'But don't let me quaff in anger. It's not pretty.'

'He did apologise.'

'Really?' said Sidney. 'You mistook those insincere platitudes for an apology?'

'He acknowledged that we'd been put out.'

'His first reaction was *irritation* that he had to drive to the Boat Shed to fetch Madison. Only then did he realise we'd been waiting for him for fifteen bloody minutes at the school, sweating like bomb-disposal experts over the unstable gelignite that is the Booths, Lincoln and Reuben. And then he spouted weasel words, before slinking off.'

Kerry had taken a seat in the old armchair across from Sidney, who'd commandeered the sofa and was tempted to stretch right out on it. It wasn't a date, she had no one to impress, and Rick Jensen's rudeness plus a car ride with both Reuben and the Booth sisters had left her as frayed as Mr Phipps's garden twine, which looked to have been recycled year on year since the sixteenth century.

'Not wanting to put a gloss on his behaviour,' said Kerry, 'but he did pick her up. Fifteen minutes late, I grant you, but at least he didn't disappoint Madison.'

'Yes, there's that,' said Sidney. 'Though, to be honest—' She lowered her voice; the boys were in bed, but that did not mean they were asleep. 'I wonder if Madison is better off spending as little time as possible in that environment. Rattling around in that big house, with only occasional company from a dodgy, unreliable father, and a mother who seems to have checked out completely. How can that be good for her?'

'And what will happen when the vineyard is sold?' Kerry also spoke quietly. 'Will they go their separate ways?'

'Oh, God, I can't bear to think of it,' said Sidney. 'In my darkest moments, I have this vision of them fighting each other *not* to get custody of Madison.'

'If you're that concerned,' said Kerry, 'can you not have a word?'

'Non-stick Rick would only fob me off,' said Sidney. 'And I'm not even sure Olivia sees me as a fellow woman, but more as a helpful child-minding dog, like Nana in *Peter Pan*.'

Kerry laughed, and Sidney felt the surge of satisfaction that comes with pulling off a funny line. Instantly, the feeling u-turned and sank downwards as gloom. He probably thought the comparison was apt rather than ridiculous. The comparison *was* apt, the only difference being she'd not yet had to prevent her children being abducted by fairies.

'How are the bees?' said Kerry.

OK, jam jars and beehives. In the absence of cats, perhaps she could become a crazy bee lady.

'The queen is laying eggs with a speed and efficiency Japanese factories would envy,' said Sidney. 'So we've added a queen excluder and placed honey supers on the top deep, plus we're checking the varroa mite treatments, and the pollen stores to see if we need to feed supplements. Checking for wax moth, too. Stuff like that.'

Kerry's mouth hung slightly open. 'I have to confess I lost you at "queen is laying eggs". I had a vision of Her Majesty roosting and that was that.'

'You could come with me one time, if you like?'

That didn't sound like flirting, did it? It was bees, for heaven's sake, not etchings.

'I *would* like,' said Kerry. 'Though I'm probably more interested in witnessing Mr Phipps utter an actual word. I'm still not convinced he can, despite your assurances.'

'He's no chatterbox, that's for sure,' said Sidney. 'Even when his wife was alive, he never talked much. Mary didn't, either. I suspect they communicated by telepathy.'

'When did she die?'

'Oh, gosh — five years ago now. In sad circumstances, too. She went for a hike in the bush and didn't come back. They found her body in a stream. Seemed she'd slipped while crossing, knocked herself out and drowned. Poor Mr Phipps was bereft. She was only sixty-seven.'

'That *is* sad,' said Kerry. 'I'm sorry for the old boy. Any children?'

Sidney shook her head. 'He and Mary married late, in their forties. She was a local girl. He'd been a train driver. Drove the last of the steam trains and shifted to diesels, as they all had to. Quit when the railway was privatised in the eighties, moved here, met Mary, who I *think* had been divorced or widowed, and took up as handyman, gardener and beekeeper.'

'And enthusiastic war-gamer by all accounts,' said Kerry. 'By the way, does he have a first name? Not that I intend to call him anything but "Mr Phipps".'

'Titus.' Sidney smiled at Kerry's wide eyes. 'I know. Like something out of Dickens.'

Kerry raised his glass. 'To Titus Phipps! Whose middle name is, with luck, Montague or Uriah.'

'Or Ebenezer, or Smike.'

'Or — who's that joker in *Great Expectations*?' Kerry snapped his fingers. 'Pumblechook!'

'Or Wackford,' said Sidney.

'Wackford! God, yes, I'd forgotten about old Wackford.'

When was the last time she'd had a conversation like this? With Gene and Jacko, she was only a bit part, a stooge for their double act, never an equal. Mac? Perhaps, but when did they ever have time to sit down for a proper chat? And besides, Mac thought novels were for the weak-minded who couldn't deal with the real world. Even *Crime and Punishment* had been too airy-fairy for her liking.

Had she even talked like this with Fergal? She remembered listening, rapt, as he painted idyllic pictures of their life to be, his accent soft and beguiling. She remembered him being romantic, wooing with wildflowers and poetry. But had he been funny? Looking back, laughter was not what she could recall.

And now here was Kerry, putting his serious face on.

'I wanted to ask your advice,' he said.

Of course he did.

'Both Jonty and Meredith have promised to think about showing their miniatures to the public, and I hope to enlist Doctor Love this week—'

'Wait — *Jonty* promised?'

'Well, he didn't say no.'

'That he said anything at all is my point.'

'What do you know about Sophie, their daughter?' said Kerry.

'Is this a diversion?' said Sidney. 'To steer me away from a Jonty hate-rant?'

'Just curiosity. And cowardice — I daren't ask Meredith.'

Sidney sighed. 'From what Mac has told me, seems that Nicola was always seen as "the good daughter", and Sophie the stroppy tearaway. Jonty, in particular, actively favoured Nicola. Went to her graduation from law school, but not Sophie's from art school, even though she achieved a First Class Honours degree.'

'Really? I got the impression she wasn't making a living as an artist, so I assumed she was, er—'

'A bit shit?' said Sidney. 'I've only seen her early stuff, but she's very talented. She just also happens to be intractable and demanding, which was OK for a couple of years when she could claim to be an *enfant terrible*. But the act — and she — quickly got old, and now none of the top galleries will touch her. And without that kind of patronage, it's nigh-on impossible to reach buyers with serious money.'

'Influence,' said Kerry, nodding. 'That's the key.'

'And that's what *you* need,' said Sidney. 'If you want your miniatures idea to take off. You need the right people on your side.'

'Which brings us back to the start — me asking your advice,' said Kerry. 'Do I need to woo the Progressive Association? Or is Mac's opinion of them universal?'

Good question. Sidney sipped her wine, deliberated.

'If you *don't* have them on your side, it won't be a disaster,' she said, 'but it will definitely limit your options. For example, Bernard Weston owns enormous amounts of commercial property in town, so if you needed a venue . . . Elaine Pardew is on the Hampton District Council, and it would be loads easier if they were behind it, at least in name. Geoffrey Naylor comes from money, and gets a big woody from being the one everybody comes begging to. And every single committee member, apart from Tinker, is a fixture in the Hampton Rotary Club or the Soroptimists — all those organisations that are magnets for well-off, late-middle-aged white people. Which means they know absolutely *every*one.'

'In other words, get wooing,' said Kerry, glumly.

Sidney fetched the wine bottle, topped up both glasses. As she poured his, Kerry gave her a look she recognised. Her sons were not usually subtle about their demands, but every so often they'd play the appealing, big-eyed urchin card.

'Ha, not likely,' she said, as she resumed her seat. 'I've ruled myself out of contention for wooing. Had a set-to with Maureen Roper about her wish to remove Judy Blume and Captain Underpants from the school library — didn't quite call her a Nazi cow, but, you know. And when Prince Joffrey — that's Geoffrey Naylor — groped me at Doctor Love's Christmas drinks, I grabbed his fingers and bent them right back.'

'With your lid-conquering hands of strength,' said Kerry.

'Too right. Horrible perv.'

'Anyone else you've made an enemy of?'

'Not directly,' said Sidney. 'But they all know I'm mates with Mac.'

Kerry screwed up his mouth. 'Another I need to woo, don't I?'

'Oh, without Mac's support you are *definitely* toast,' said Sidney. 'My gosh, isn't this lobbying business a thorny thicket? Are you sure you're up for it?'

This time his expression surprised her — ambition she read in it loud and clear, and more than a hint of mischief. He was Reynard the Fox — red-haired trickster, schemer, adventurer — and suddenly, urgently, she wanted to be part of whatever he had planned.

Damn it to hell, she had a crush on him. But — she took a breath — no one knew. *He* certainly had no clue, and that's how it would stay, as her secret. And with willpower, the crush should quickly fade. No one need *ever* know.

Good. All sorted. No harm done.

'Want to watch *Project Runway*?' she said.

Chapter 18

Madison

The day was cloudy and cold. Too cold, really, to be outside, but Madison had found a blanket to sit on (she hoped it was old), and she wore the pink quilted coat Mum had bought her online from Burberry. In her lunchbox, she had some of Oksana's dumplings, microwaved and wrapped in foil to keep them warm, an apple and the last of Sidney's chocolate chip biscuits. Aidan and Rory said it wasn't fair how many Sidney let her have, but she hadn't been greedy, had eaten only one a day, which sort of made her feel better about hiding them from her mum, who would never put biscuits on the shopping list she gave to Oksana.

Oksana had told Madison's dad that there was never any food, and said she would go to the supermarket if he gave her more cash. Madison's mum said Oksana would rip them off, but when Oksana dumped the shopping on the kitchen floor she placed the receipt and the change on the table so no one could miss it. Madison's mum complained once that Oksana didn't always follow the list she was given, but Oksana said, 'I buy for growing child, not *alkash*.' Madison guessed that word meant 'adults'.

Blanket, lunchbox and book wouldn't all fit in her schoolbag, so Madison had hung the blanket over her arm, and trudged with it all the way up the hill to the copse of trees beside the top vines. From the house, the trees looked soft and light, a friendly green hideaway, but close up, they were a tangle she had to push through, branches catching on her coat and leaving marks. Underneath, the ground was bumpy, and muddy, too, after last night's rain, and the light through the leaves was only bright in patches, so it took Madison a good five minutes to find a place where she could sit and read that wasn't too uncomfortable and wouldn't make the blanket too dirty.

She thought about going back to her room, but that morning, when she was getting dressed, she'd heard her mum and dad yelling. Well, her mum was yelling but her dad sounded quite angry, too, saying something about buying things on Trade Me. Madison had crept out to go make herself breakfast, but even in the kitchen she could still hear her parents yelling, so she'd gone out onto the back verandah and seen the friendly looking trees, and decided to go there instead. It would be a kind of adventure, like the *Famous Five* children had, though without ginger beer and buns, and potted meat, which didn't sound all that nice anyway.

Madison's book was one Sidney had lent her, an old one about a boy who was picked to go to wizard school. Written decades before Harry Potter, Sidney told her, and by a way-better author, though J.K. Rowling was good, too. The book didn't have jokes in it like Harry Potter — the boy was very serious, and quite cross a lot of the time, which was fair enough because the other boys were bullying him about the fact he'd been a lowly farmhand, a goat-herder. There was one other student who was his big rival, and they were competing with magic, and the boy was just, maybe, about to make a really big mistake with a spell—

'Woah!'

The voice made Madison jump a mile. Clutching her book, heart thumping, she scrambled up onto her feet, started backing away.

'Hey, hey, don't be scared.'

The man put his hands up in front of his chest like he was surrendering. 'Didn't mean to startle you. Just surprised to see you is all.'

She knew him, sort of. Knew his face. He came and did work around the vineyard for Rainer, mowing and maintenance and stuff. Rainer had other contractors at the moment, too, mainly from overseas, which was OK because he spoke French and Spanish as well as German and English. The workers were shoot-thinning and wire-lifting at the moment — Madison knew the right words. They started early, even on weekends.

She saw the cigarette between the man's fingers, the messy roll-your-own sort. That's why he was here. It was break time.

The man saw her notice the cigarette, made a face and tucked it into his jeans pocket. Pointed at her book. 'What're you reading?'

He had the kind of unwashed look that would make her mum shudder — black jeans and a t-shirt with stains, yellowish-brown skin and greasy, long hair. Plus he had a *huge* bruise around his eye, and two of his fingernails were all black, like they were dead. But his face was kind, and his smile was nice, open, not creepy. He was a lot younger than she'd first thought, too. Looked more like a skinny kid than a grown-up.

Madison held out her book. He took it, kept his thumb inside to mark her page.

'Oh, yeah!' he said. 'Ged! And the dragons!'

'Are there dragons?'

'Yep. And three more books after this one.'

Really? Madison hoped Sidney had those, too.

He handed it back, gestured to her blanket and schoolbag. 'Picnic?'

'Um . . .'

She could share the dumplings with him, she supposed. And half the biscuit.

He mistook her hesitation. 'Private. I get it.' He smiled to show he wasn't offended. 'No worries. I'll find another spot.'

'Is this *your* spot?'

'Well, I don't *own* it,' he said. 'But I come here most days I'm working.'

Madison thought about all the branches she'd had to break on her way in.

'I didn't hear you walk up,' she said. 'You didn't make much noise.'

He gestured behind him. 'There's sort of a path. You have to go right round the back.'

She'd remember that for next time.

He was rocking back on his heels, thumbs hooked in the front pockets of his grubby jeans. Didn't seem in a hurry to find his other spot. Perhaps he didn't get to talk to people much?

'How did you hurt your eye?' was all Madison could think to ask.

'Ah . . .' He squinted upwards, as if trying to remember. 'You know. Kind of a fight.' Shrugged his shoulders. 'Dumb stuff.'

When he wasn't smiling, his face got all pinched, and his eyes got big, like one of those skinny rescue dogs they showed on TV ads. Madison felt sorry for him.

'Do you want a biscuit?' she said. 'Chocolate chip.'

'Sure!' Shrugged again. 'Don't have anything to offer you, though.'

'That's OK.'

Madison handed him the last biscuit, watched him wolf it in two bites.

'Are you wire-lifting?' she asked.

'Mowing.'

The word came out soggy, crumby. He swallowed, then his face brightened. 'Want a ride? I could give you a ride on the tractor?'

That sounded like fun! But . . .

'I'm not allowed,' said Madison. 'Can't go near any of the machinery, or get in the way of the workers. Health and safety.'

'Health and safety, eh?'

He ducked his head, mumbled at his feet. 'Yeah, well you don't wanna mess with health and safety.'

She'd upset him. 'I'm sorry.'

'Nah!' His head came up, eyes wide. 'Not your fault! It was a dumb idea.'

He bent his neck again, nudged a root with the toe of his boot.

A shout, faint, from a distance, but she recognised the voice.

'Rainer,' she said. 'He sounds like he's cross.'

'Yeah, well, who isn't?'

The man spoke more to himself than to Madison. Then he shivered, like a wet dog or, as Sidney said, like someone was walking over his grave. Madison didn't like it when she said that. Didn't like thinking of Sidney having a grave.

'Better head off,' he said. 'Get back to making an honest living.'

Suddenly, she realised they hadn't been introduced.

'I'm Madison,' she said. 'Madison Jensen.'

He nodded. 'Everyone calls me Deano.'

'I'll make sure I'm not in your spot next time.'

'Nah, you're welcome to it. I'll find another. Know the bush round here real well. See ya,' he said, and added, 'Thanks for the biscuit.'

Madison watched him walk away. With his colouring and black clothes, he kind of blended in to the bush. 'Yallery-brown', like the fairy in the book Sidney had but which Aidan and Rory thought was too girly.

'We'll look at it together, then,' Sidney had said to her. 'Just you and me.'

Madison couldn't hear Deano anymore. She was alone. The light was even greyer now, and she felt hemmed in by shadows and spikes.

She stuffed the book and lunchbox back in her bag, grabbed the blanket and folded it up over her arm without shaking it out, and then she followed where Deano had gone, doing her best not to run. Luckily, he'd been right about the sort of path, and she popped out of the bush into the fields that edged the vineyard. Rainer and Elke's cottage was just over the fence, so she climbed it, and ran all the way down the driveway to home, where she found her dad's car gone and no one — she double-checked — inside the house. Maybe her mum and dad made up and went for a drive together? Madison felt sad that she hadn't been there to go with them.

But her room was dry and warm, and her bed comfortable, and after she'd put the blanket in the laundry and hung up her coat, she lay on her bed, eating dumplings and apple, reading all about Ged, and the terrible shadow creature he summoned by mistake, and which would follow him forever, intent on his destruction.

Chapter 19

Bernard

'Come into the parlour.'

Bernard mentally added 'said the spider to the fly', and followed Elaine into what his mother would have called a sitting room. 'Parlour is vulgar,' she'd told him, 'though not as vulgar as lounge.'

His mother would also have disapproved of the furnishings, for which the words 'pink' and 'fussy' seemed exclusively to have been invented. Verity Weston might even have hissed audibly at the tissues concealed within a dainty floral-painted wooden box with a slit in the top. The room had a strong antiseptic lavender smell about it, and when he took the over-stuffed chair Elaine offered him before bustling out to fetch the tea things, Bernard was startled by what sounded like a cat sneezing. Surreptitious investigation revealed that the noise, in fact, emanated from an air-freshening device perched amongst the Lladró figurines on one of the many side tables. He should have known it wouldn't be a cat. Cat hair and claws would not be permitted within a mile of this immaculate and no doubt highly flammable furniture.

A chinking of china announced Elaine's imminent reappearance. Bernard did not usually take sugar, but today he'd make an exception. If Elaine had summoned only him and none of the others, then he expected to be on the receiving end of a prolonged hectoring disguised as a rational and morally unassailable request for him to do his duty as chairman and accede to her wishes. Today would not be the first time. No indeed.

Elaine set down the tray — more dainty floral wood — and arranged herself, pantyhose-clad knees demurely inclined, on the adjacent chair. The tea set resembled the kind of wedding cake that always turns out to be inedible. Bernard received his cup of tea and braced himself.

'And how is your dear mother?' said Elaine.

As a destabilising opening salvo, this could not be bettered. Bernard had hoped by this time in his life to have his mother's criticisms restricted to those dark, wakeful imaginings that inevitably occur at four in the morning. As it happened, at ninety-five, Verity was physically diminished and mentally anything but. She ruled the Iris Murdoch Rest Home in Hampton in the manner of seventh-century Empress Wu Zetian, who had her enemies kept alive as long as possible while they were dismembered piece by piece. Bernard had witnessed a retired army major, recipient of several medals for valour, cringe like a beaten dog when Verity passed him in the hallway.

'My mother is very well, thank you.' Bernard hoped his reply did not convey how fervently he wished the answer could be otherwise.

'An example to us all,' said Elaine.

'Indeed.'

She offered a plate. 'Lemon slice?'

'No, thank you.' There was already enough acid in his stomach.

Elaine took a slice, nibbled on one corner while Bernard once more reviewed the list of possible reasons he'd been summoned. He had his suspicions about the most likely, but Elaine was quite capable of surprising him. Patricia had owned a cat like that once.

It would hide in the shrubbery, a different place each time, and leap out to sink its claws into his shins.

'Now, Bernard, I'm sure you're aware of this silly model town idea?'

It was clear she expected him not to be, and Bernard gave silent thanks to Dr Love. During a routine appointment last week, Charles had let slip the idea for the miniature tourist attraction. Mac Reid had intuited the situation the moment Bernard stepped out of the doctor's room.

'You blabbed, didn't you?' she accused her employer.

'*Mea culpa*,' he replied. 'Perhaps you'd like to make Mr Weston a cup of tea and fill him in on the details?'

And he'd beckoned in the next patient, apparently oblivious to the daggers being directed at him from the reception desk.

Mac Reid said, 'Do you want one lump or two, Bernard? I'm referring to the tea, of course.'

He'd made an exception to his no-sugar rule that day as well.

But that surprise initiation meant he was now well prepared to converse on the subject with Elaine. He even held a secret trump card, to be played if required, possibly with a flourish.

'I am indeed aware of the model town idea,' Bernard told Elaine. 'I will reserve judgement on its "silliness" until I have more information.'

Ever resourceful, Elaine tried another tack.

'But you surely can't support the pressure that it puts on poor Meredith?'

'Is she feeling pressured?'

'Of course she is,' said Elaine. 'She has an infirm husband and a large house that requires considerable upkeep. How can she devote time to this nonsense?'

'But she also has help now,' said Bernard. 'From that young British chap — what's his name? Macfarlane.'

His wife, Patricia, had been true to her word and visited Woodhall. She reported back that Meredith had introduced her to the new employee, while narrating her mistake regarding his gender with her usual self-deprecation.

'He has a hint of the travelling snake-oil salesman about him, and could talk the hind legs off a chesterfield sofa' had been Patricia's impression. 'But he's a charming young man, and I believe Meredith is quite happy to let herself be charmed.'

Bernard had been perturbed by how much his hackles rose at that last comment. Charmed indeed! Surely Meredith had the perspicacity and good sense to see through *that* veneer?

However, he could only agree with Patricia's view that, 'Even if he proves impractical as a helper, it will be good for Meredith to have some spark and humour around the place. Jonty's illness, Nicola's death, Sophie's — well, whatever you want to call that behaviour — all that blackness must weigh on her terribly.'

But the hackles rose again, when his wife added, 'To be honest, I'm amazed at her fortitude. If I was in her place, I'd be tempted to pack it all in and hightail it to Marrakech.'

'Meredith would not even *contemplate* abdicating her responsibilities,' he protested. 'She is a woman of *character*.'

'Of course she is, dear.'

Patricia's voice, he thought, held a suggestion of weariness, but her expression was, as usual, mild and affectionate.

'She's never been anything less.'

Yes, indeed. Patricia had that entirely right. Meredith was a woman of character and fortitude. She was not the weak, incapable creature Elaine was attempting to paint her as. She was her own woman, who made decisions on her own terms. And he would say so.

'I sincerely doubt Meredith would agree to anything she didn't care for,' he said. 'Nor would Charles Love.'

'But it isn't up to either Meredith or Charles, is it now?' Elaine responded, smoothly. 'This is a proposal that needs to go through the proper channels.'

The moment had arrived. Time to play the trump card.

'Well, in fact,' said Bernard, 'I have received a submission to include it as an agenda item for our upcoming meeting. Which I am bringing forward a week, by the way, due to work commitments.'

That was not entirely true. He had brought the meeting forward because Mac Reid had told him to.

Fortunately, Elaine cared more about the agenda item than the meeting itself.

'A request from whom?'

'As it happens, from young Macfarlane himself. And Sidney Gillespie and Mac Reid.'

'Oh, *well.*' Elaine exhaled the last word in a derisive puff. 'A foreigner who probably doesn't even have legal residency status, a solo mother on the benefit, and—'

Bernard understood the hesitation. Mac Reid defied simple categorisation. Plus there was always the lurking suspicion that she might somehow be listening in.

'And what *nonsense*, anyway. A display of miniatures. How childish.'

Bernard forbore from pointing out that (a) children were often the main target for tourist attractions, and (b) model towns and railways, not to mention Queen Mary's dollhouse, were still drawing crowds worldwide. There was an extraordinary model railway display in Hamburg that he was dying to visit, and no trip to England would be complete without several hours ambling around the Bekonscot model village. He wouldn't even *begin* to mention Legoland.

To be fair, it was not what he personally had pictured for Gabriel's Bay, but he could admit that his vision of becoming a

UNESCO centre of literature or, at the least, twin to some bookish overseas town like Hay-on-Wye was almost certainly unobtainable. His own library was, in his eyes, magnificent, but his eyes were the only ones he'd allow to view it. The *state* of the books Patricia brought home from the Hampton library — notes penned in margins, jam and crumbs and who knows what else adhering to pages. And the folded corners! Bernard shared the opinion that there were only two types of reader — those who used bookmarks, and monsters.

Elaine was going on now about — he wasn't sure — dust, possibly? The displays would gather dust; that was a fact. However, there were volunteers who'd relish dusting — Sheila Swanson, Chester in the video store, who had one of those obsessive-compulsive disorders . . .

But enough. Elaine had one reason and one reason only for objecting to the idea — it was not hers.

'I, for one, feel the concept has merit,' he said. 'I appreciate that we will have much to work through before it becomes a reality, but it's different, it appeals to a wide range of ages, and it's something with which the entire town can be involved. Young Macfarlane has already spoken to some of our local artisans, and they are keen to contribute. Even if it fails to boost the town's coffers, it will, at the very least, boost town morale.'

He reached for a piece of lemon slice, ate it while Elaine gaped.

'And since you are so concerned about Meredith,' he said, wiping his hands on a lacy napkin, 'I will talk to her myself before the meeting. If she *is* being pressured, then, rest assured, I will act accordingly. If not, then I intend to receive the proposal with an open mind. And that is all I have to say on the matter.'

'Bernard,' said Elaine, after a short but resonant silence, 'you surprise me.'

If she'd been on form, decided Bernard as he drove home, she would have added, 'What would your mother say?' For the first time in their twenty-plus-year acquaintance, he had put her at a disadvantage.

But she would regroup. She would recruit allies. That bloody awful Geoffrey Naylor for one. Maureen, probably. Tinker was confused at the best of times, so he'd be easily led, as would Wendy. Nicholas and Derek could go either way, but even if he gained their support, they'd be grievously outnumbered.

More dangerously, she might agitate amongst her colleagues at the Hampton District Council. Bernard made a note to tell young Macfarlane to approach the influencers quickly, before she had a chance to poison the well.

Gaining wide support from within Gabriel's Bay would also be crucial. If the whole town rallied behind the idea, surely even Elaine would not try to prevent it?

Bernard observed the speed limit on the eighty-kilometres-an-hour stretch that led towards his home, where Patricia would be waiting, eager to find out how he had fared with the woman she insisted on calling 'Elated', 'because she is always so very pleased with herself'.

But in his mind, it was not Patricia to whom he recounted his, albeit temporary, triumph. It was Meredith, her brown eyes sparkling, as she sat amused and, yes, charmed, by his tale of besting the manipulative she-beast in her own lacy, pink lair.

Chapter 20

Mac

Ashwin Ghadavi. Twenty-eight. Born and brought up in Ahmedabad, Gujurat province of India. Received primary medical qualification from University College of London. Foundation training at — yada, yada. Considered paediatrics, decided on general practice — obviously. Reason for applying — it's a big, beautiful world out there, time to break free from the shackles of filial duty and stride like Ulysses into a new adventure!

Not his exact words, but that was the gist. A good boy, an obedient son, who'd probably wanted to be a writer instead of a doctor, and who now wanted to live life on his own terms, and as far away as possible from his family.

Mac read the application through again. He might be a bit a soft, bit of a Mataji's boy. Ngaire would run rings around him. And how the heck would he cope with Shania Birtwell and the fetal tragedy she was about to unleash? Doc Love might be compassionate, generous, thoughtful and all those good things, but he did not shirk from telling it straight. More importantly, he detached himself from the outcome — if his patients chose to ignore his advice, then he'd keep giving it, but he wouldn't let their idiocy keep him awake at night. Dr Ghadavi — young, earnest, by the book — might fret more, might try cajoling, begging and, if he were bold enough, demanding. None of it would work, and then he'd fall into despair. His virtuous, teetotal, vegetarian habits would fall by the wayside, and he'd end up hanging out with Ngaire, swigging cheap vodka from a lemonade bottle and staining his lovely white teeth with cadged smokes.

Or he might be totally fine. Impossible to tell without a proper interview. Skype, preferably, so she could stare him down. And that interview couldn't happen until Mac knew she had a job to offer him. Well, it couldn't happen *ethically*.

Nope. Time for a sit-down with Dr Love.

His last patient for the day had departed, but he had not. No time like the present.

Mac rapped on his door and opened it up. It was ajar, so she knew she didn't have to wait for him to permit her entrance. He was at his desk, thumbing through a war-gamers' magazine. On its cover was a painted figure of Queen Victoria holding what appeared to be a brass-trimmed bazooka.

'Looks like Aggie Robotham,' said Mac. 'Only less corseted.'

'I suspect Victoria in her later years had a figure that resisted corseting.'

'What's with the weaponry? Did Prince Albert come back as a zombie?'

'Steampunk,' said Doc Love. 'A science-fiction subset inspired by the costuming and technology of the Victorian era.'

'Oh, right,' said Mac. 'In other words, an excuse for moustaches, monocles and misogyny. I can see how that might appeal.'

'An absence of tanks is the barrier for me.'

'Are you still coming with us to the Progressive Association meeting?'

Doc Love blinked at her over the top of his magazine.

'Why wouldn't I?'

Mac sucked her teeth. 'I could think of fifty reasons why anyone, including me, would want to back out.'

'I've said I'll be there, so be there I shall.'

His eyes returned to the page.

Mac stood there, strangely unable to speak the words queuing in her head. Why? She knew she wouldn't offend him — couldn't offend him. Was it that the prospect of his retirement bothered her more than she wanted to admit? The prospect of watching patients, people she knew and mostly liked, receiving substandard care. Not that his replacement would be incompetent, but who could reach the bar that he'd set? And how would *she* get on with a new person? Would she have the patience to learn a whole new set of habits and quirks? Would they cope with *her* quirks, or whatever term more accurately described her personality? After twenty-two years she might be out of a job, and no one else, not even Jacko, would take her on. The Love Bus — even that might have to stop, because who'd pay for the petrol if she wasn't earning?

She'd been so focused on finding a replacement that she'd failed to put any thought into what life with that replacement might be like. How irksome.

'Was there something else?' said Doc Love.

'Yes,' said Mac. 'Do you have any tips for getting a man to come in for a check-up?'

'Do you have a specific concern about his health?'

He knew exactly which man she meant.

'More a free-floating anxiety,' said Mac. 'He's fifty-five. He smokes. He works too hard. His father died youngish of a massive heart attack.'

'How about I call in one morning? Pass the time? Observe?'

Mac shook her head. 'No, he'd spot that ruse a mile off.'

'Then why not invite us all to your place after the Progressive Association meeting?'

'Good call,' she nodded. 'Even if all you do is quietly put the fear of God into him.'

'It isn't God we fear,' he replied. 'It's loss. Diminishment. Being less than we were.'

'We don't want to go gently, you mean? Yes, well, that's Jacko — rage, rage.'

Doc Love smiled. 'It's past six, Mac. What else can I help you with?'

How did he know? Decades of seeing people, she assumed. Seeing *them*, not just their illnesses and complaints.

'I think we — the town — need to plan for your retirement. And to do that—'

'You need a date.'

'Bingo.'

He laid the magazine to one side. Queen Victoria aimed her bazooka at the window. Doc Love's Skoda would take a direct hit if she let fly.

'How many candidates have you short-listed?' he asked.

'None!' Oh, what was the point? 'All right, one. Seems the only people who want to work in a small town are charlatans and imbeciles.'

'Thank you.'

She ignored him. 'The only halfway decent one turned up in my inbox last night. Do you want to have a look?'

'Now there's a question,' he said. 'If I stare into the abyss, will it stare back?'

'You're retiring, not checking into a room at Dignitas.'

He reached out, ran his finger over the piece of shrapnel on his desk, the one that might have been plucked from a dead man's shattered skull.

'Rage, rage, Mac,' he said, quietly.

Hell. How *stupid* of her not to realise. She wasn't the only one dreading the prospect of his last day as Gabriel's Bay's GP. How stupid, and how blind had she been?

'Look,' she began, 'we don't have to—'

'We do,' he said. '*I* do.'

'Yes, but—'

'It's time. You've known it for — how long?'

Mac never blushed, but she did now. 'I like to plan ahead, that's all!'

'Very wise.'

'You are OK — aren't you?' she ventured.

'I'm in fine fettle, Mac,' he said. 'I've simply resisted adjusting to the inevitable.'

'Join the club.'

Tapped his finger on the shrapnel, once, a gesture of resolution.

'Show me your candidate,' he said. 'The one person you deem worthy of the people of Gabriel's Bay.'

'I thought Elaine was going to burst,' said Kerry. 'Literally burst like a boiled tomato.'

'It's true,' Sidney told Jacko and Gene. 'She swelled up like a puffer fish. The buttons on her cardigan barely held.'

'Puffer fish can die from inflating too much,' offered Devon. 'Dickheads who bash on aquariums should be forced to eat the poisonous ones. No filleting.'

'I'd like to feed Prince Joffrey toxic puffer fish,' said Sidney. 'He's such a Creepy McCreepface.'

'Probably his online name,' said Kerry. 'And he wonders how people can tell it's him.'

He and Sidney were next to each other at the table they'd all crammed into at the Boat Shed. Quite close, Mac noted; almost shoulder to shoulder. Were they an item?

Or, now that she'd begun to look harder, was the affection more on Sidney's side? Young Mr Macfarlane could turn on the charm, but was he actually interested in her, as more than a willing audience for his jokes?

Mac knew Sidney cited the dearth of local men who were available and/or had IQs above mollusc level as her reason for steering clear of new relationships. She didn't *want* to be forever single, but she was picky about who she took up with, who she allowed into her and her children's lives. Mac respected that — had never believed any man was better than none, and was eternally grateful that life had put Jacko her way. Sidney, too, deserved an equal match, and if she saw one in the ginger joker, then all power to her. With luck, her budding affection would either be requited or she'd be let down gently, kindly. If not — well, there was always tar and feathers, and rolling him down the hill to Hampton wearing nothing but a barrel.

'What about old Bernardo the Bore?' asked Gene. 'How did he react?'

'Surprisingly well,' said Mac. 'Did his usual "We need more evidence of viability" spiel, as if we can conjure up some magic data that will eliminate every last skerrick of risk. But apart from that, he was on our side, I'd say. Which is surprising given he was all carrot-up-the-jaxie when I talked to him at the surgery. What do *you* think?'

She directed the question to Doc Love, who had taken a seat that allowed him to observe Jacko behind the bar, where he occupied four-fifths of the space, forcing Gene and Devon to squash into the corner. At Jacko's feet lay King, who'd hoovered up the floor scraps in the wake of the night's last customers.

'I believe Bernard has a great fondness for model trains,' said Doc Love. 'And has visited the miniature world displays at the Windsor Legoland more than once.'

'Has he now?' said Gene. 'Bear Grylls will be coming to him for tips on how to live more dangerously.'

'But Elaine wasn't buying it?' said Jacko.

'Elaine would sooner buy used dog faeces,' said Mac. 'And she's got Joffrey right behind her — sorry for the mental image there — and Fraulein Ropable. Wendy will leap to obey whoever shouts loudest and Tinker, bless him, wouldn't know if he was voting for a miniature display or for turning Gabriel's Bay into an alien-worshipping cult.'

'Don't underestimate Tinker,' said Doc Love.

'Too right,' said Jacko. 'Last time we met on the battlefield, he kicked my arse. Like Attila the Hun he was. A one-man horde.'

'And the Squealer and Sharp were keeping their powder dry,' Mac continued. 'Waiting to see which way the wind blows.'

'Carrying either a smell of musty books or too much Yardley eau de toilette,' said Gene.

'But then we had us lot and Patricia Weston, and Aggie Robotham, Chester and Peg cheering from the sidelines,' said Mac.

'To the crazies.' Gene lifted his beer. 'A bit of nutso always improves the flavour.'

'Casey and Corinna are on board if we support the name change to Onemanawa.'

'Bribery,' said Jacko.

'Politics,' said Mac. 'They'll support us anyway. I know all the embarrassing things they did when they were young.'

'And Meredith?' said Gene. 'Her support's pretty key, isn't it?'

'Mrs Barton has agreed, on the promise that we keep her

dollhouse absolutely safe,' said Kerry. 'But I, er, still need to get permission from Mr Barton to move the trains.'

'Plus we need a venue,' said Sidney. 'Little things like that.'

'What about the old fish plant?' Devon said. 'Been empty for years.'

'Still smells of fish,' said Mac. 'And it's too big.'

'Don't need all of it,' said Devon.

'Suppose not . . .'

'Where is it?' asked Kerry.

Everyone pointed to the north-east.

'You've seen that scrubby area on the corner?' said Devon. 'That was the side entrance. Plant faces the wharf.'

'There's a wharf?' said Kerry.

'Kind of,' said Devon. 'Still standing, but hasn't been maintained. Neither has the jetty. No point. No vessels. Only recreational fishers here now, and they launch next door, off the beach.'

'So is the area dangerous?'

'A few hazards,' said Jacko. 'Nothing a working bee and some electric fencing couldn't sort out.'

'Who owns it?' said Kerry. 'I could get in touch.'

Everyone looked at everyone else.

'Good question,' said Gene. 'Used to be the Caraccis, didn't it? Old Italian fishing family? But who knows if they've flogged it since. Suppose District Council will have records . . .'

'Can't we think of another venue?' said Mac. 'This is getting awfully complicated.'

'Have you considered the Legion of Frontiersmen's headquarters?' said Doc Love. 'It's a good size, and centrally located.'

'We did,' said Sidney. 'But it's been nabbed by the plant collective. They've got an arrangement with the Legion's national body — somebody's granddad was a member. They'll only lend it out to community projects that fit with their ethos of — I quote

— "peaceful, inclusive and non-binary collaboration". Plus, you have to make room for the world cinema club every Thursday night, and the Tuesday-morning toddler music group. So all told, not that practical.'

'Peaceful collaboration in a space previously occupied by war veterans,' said Gene. 'I guess that's progress for you.'

'What about some of Bernard's empty shops?' Mac said. 'If he *is* on our side, he should come to the party and help out.'

'I suspect he'd prefer to benefit from a Gabriel's Bay resurgence by filling those shops with new paying tenants,' said Doc Love.

Mac folded her arms crossly. 'Avaricious git.'

'Probably not an epithet that will encourage him to *stay* on our side,' Doc Love admonished mildly.

'Fish factory, then?' Kerry said.

'Looking good,' said Devon. 'And with a bit of elbow grease, it'll smell that way, too.'

'Right,' said Kerry. 'I'll pursue it.'

'Sorted,' said Jacko. 'Time for a smoke.'

He had the cigarette already in his mouth, spoke out the corner. 'Come on, boy.'

And King followed his beloved master out the back door.

Mac couldn't help a glance at Doc Love, but as usual his expression was serene, unreadable. Oh, well, he was an excellent observer. If he'd seen anything of concern, he'd let her know.

Sidney yawned, covered her mouth with her hand.

'Sure you've got the stamina for this, Sid?' Gene needled.

'Not all of us live life at your sedate pace,' she retorted. 'But I'd better be off home. Your nephew will be bored senseless by now. He was aghast when I said I didn't have Sky.'

'Sam's a good lad,' said Gene. 'We'll miss him when he goes.'

'Best thing for him,' said Mac. 'Sooner he ditches those loser friends of his the better. Well, Barrett's all right, but the other two?'

'They've been mates since primary school,' said Gene. 'But, yeah, I'm with you on it being a good move. Pity Barrett won't go with him.'

'Oh, I dunno about that,' said Devon.

'What do you mean, Dev?' said Sidney.

Devon shifted, uncomfortable. 'Dunno. Just — something not right about him.'

'Dev, the lad's mum died only last year, and now his dad's an invalid,' said Gene. 'Who *would* be quite right in those circumstances?'

'Yeah, but I still say there's something off about him.' Devon scowled, trying to pin the feeling down. 'It's like he *seems* ordinary, jokes around, one of the blokes and all that, but there's like this *shadow* part to him. He hides it, but it's there.'

'Dev, your woo-wah is off the charts,' said Gene. 'Barrett's an ordinary lad who's had a rough time. End of.'

'Whatever.' Devon began to clear away the glasses. 'But for the record, my woo-wah has so far proved one hundred per cent correct.'

'Yeah, you and the Justified Ancients of Mumu.'

'All *righty* then.' Sidney stood. 'Time to go. Time to save Sam from the horrors of poor people's TV.'

Kerry hopped up also. With alacrity, Mac observed. Perhaps it wasn't one-sided after all?

'Want a lift?' he asked her.

Sidney hesitated, then smiled. 'Why not?'

Kerry saluted the others in farewell. 'Thank you for your efforts tonight, everyone. Stellar work.'

'Job's only just begun!' Gene threw after him.

'We know!' was lobbed back by Sidney at the door.

'And I, too, must away,' said Doc Love.

Mac caught his eye. He understood, smiled.

'Sleep tight, Mac,' he said, which meant he'd seen nothing to concern him unduly, but it would indeed be good if she could persuade Jacko in for a quick check-up. Oh well. It had been worth a shot.

'See you in the morning,' he added.

'Without fail,' she replied.

The crosswind as the front door swung shut brought a waft of cigarette smoke in from outside.

'Night, Gene,' said Mac. 'Shut the door on your way out.'

She pushed past Devon in the kitchen, loading the dishwasher, and sat beside her husband on the back steps. King had gone, off on one of his foraging trips that took him far and wide. Mac had asked Jacko if they should keep King at the house for his own safety. No need, said Jacko. He'd always come back.

Jacko put his hand on her knee. He was the kind of man who didn't believe in the need to say 'I love you' more than once. Once you'd said it, it stood until you said otherwise.

Mac put her own hand over his, and sat with him until it was time to go home.

Chapter 21

Kerry

Sidney would have no patience with Nietzsche. If Sidney read a line like "For it is man who creates for himself the image of woman, and woman forms herself according to this image" she'd want to reach down the ages and yank hard on his moustaches. Then again, Sidney might agree wholeheartedly that it was bonkers to bring up women to feel ashamed of erotic thoughts. Nietzsche could almost redeem himself in Sidney's eyes with that idea. And undo it in an instant by advising women not to talk too much in the presence of potential lovers, because "Men are most surely seduced by a certain secret and phlegmatic tenderness." Phlegmatic tenderness, my bum, Sidney would say. All it means is that smart women who speak their minds make men's willies droop.

At that moment, Kerry realised Sidney's name had popped into his mind no less than thirty times in as many minutes. Her face, too, arose to blot out the real face in front of him because he preferred to see her smiling mouth, her blue eyes and her apple-like cheeks. (He suspected Sidney wouldn't like her cheeks being compared with round apples, but to him that fruit was the epitome of natural rosy-hued perfection.) He wanted to hear her quips, and her full, unfettered laugh in response to his own. He wanted to curl up beside her on the battered old sofa and force her to dissect for him the secret of Tim Gunn's mild, bespectacled appeal.

If he had a magic wand, he'd be on that sofa with her right now instead of ploughing through — God, how many? — three hundred-and-eighty-three philosophical aphorisms. And all the while waiting for a chance to act on his mother's advice. Not that he had a clue yet exactly what that might entail.

Kerry had been in Jonty's dog box for close to a fortnight, banned from coming anywhere near the bedroom or even speaking too loudly downstairs (he had a carrying voice, apparently). Meredith had taken over the reading again, and Kerry had done his best to make it up to her by doing extra chores, and preparing meals he knew to be special favourites of hers.

Then, yesterday morning, out of the blue, Meredith announced that Mr Barton had requested Kerry's presence once more. For what reason, she could not say, and Jonty didn't seem inclined to explain, greeting Kerry with a curt nod and then, as had been usual, proceeding to ignore him. Meredith had spurned *Ecce Homo* for *The Gay Science*, so Kerry took up where she'd left off, at aphorism twenty-four, *Different forms of dissatisfaction*, passed the hour without incident, and so he was here again today.

An absence from Nietzsche hadn't made his heart grow fonder of florid philosophy, but at least it gave him a chance to relieve Meredith, and to gird himself up for action. If he were to follow his mother's advice, he'd need nerve, opportunity and smart thinking. So far, Kerry had drawn a blank on all three . . .

The night after Jonty banished him, a worried Kerry had phoned Bronagh.

'Did I push it too far?' he asked her. 'Have I kicked a man when he was down?'

‘Thing is, we all sink below the line at some point,’ Bronagh said. ‘Grief, trauma, just ordinary old hard life can send us down. Most of us come up again naturally, or with a bit of help from medication, after about three months. However, some don’t, and that’s when we’d diagnose the depression as clinical. But there are recognised symptoms for clinical depression, so let’s see how many your fella is ticking. He eats three squares?’

‘He does. And tea and biccies in the afternoon.’

‘Aches and pains?’

‘None complained of.’

‘Feelings of suicide? Attempts?’

‘Nope. Small-town grapevine’s pretty reliable on that front.’

‘Mind sharp?’

‘As a sharp thing. Tongue, too.’

‘So that’s a tick for irritability. Low self-esteem?’ said Bronagh.

‘If so, he hides it well.’

‘So we’re left with fatigue, possibly, and social withdrawal definitely, refusing to leave his bed. Any shagging? Is he getting his hole?’

‘God, Ma!’ Kerry protested. ‘How would I know?’

‘Old people do it, too.’

‘Yes. Thank you. Move on.’

His mother went quiet, weighing up the evidence. In the background, he heard his father shouting imprecations in Scottish, as was his routine when reading the morning newspaper, and Kerry felt pole-axed by homesickness. But home would have to wait a while longer. Until he’d proved himself worthy of it.

‘His wife’s been letting this go on, hasn’t she?’ said Bronagh.

‘Well . . .’

‘She’s not put her foot down, said enough of these shenanigans?’

‘Small-town grapevine says she hasn’t,’ said Kerry.

‘Then, maybe— OK, no. Forget it.’

'What?'

'I'm not qualified to diagnose, especially not from afar.'

'But you have a hunch, I can tell. Go on, spit it out.'

'You promise not to blame me if it's rubbish?'

'You never blame *me*.'

'OK, then,' said his mother. 'My unqualified *hunch* is that he's come out of his depression but is too afraid and ashamed to face the world again. Many people see mental illness as weakness, particularly men, and even *more* particularly men who pride themselves on their mastery, their control. Before all this, was he a fella who liked things just so?'

'He was an accountant who built model trains. Favoured the daughter who behaved.'

'There you go. So now he's convinced that the outside world sees him as weak because that's how he sees himself. Won't risk that humiliation, can't bear it. But he craves to feel a sense of self-worth again, so how does he regain it? By being dominant and controlling in the one place he can — his home. Make sense?'

'So he's not *quite* faking it,' said Kerry. 'But he *is* being a bit of a bastard.'

'You could look at it through that uncompassionate lens, yes.'

'He's not a man who inspires compassion. But I can cope because I'm being paid to,' he said. 'The one I feel sorry for is his wife.'

'I could throw in another term I'm unqualified to use,' said his mother. 'And that's "enabling".'

'Or she's simply hit a brick wall too many times,' said Kerry. 'I'd really like to help her, but I'm afraid of making another, even bigger mess. Any unqualified suggestions on a way forward?'

'You say he responded to being provoked?'

'Well — much in the way Mr Tiddles responded to me poking him off the sofa.'

'Always amazed me how fast that old cat could move,' said Bronagh. 'All right, if your man's gig is all about dominance and control, albeit in a limited domestic sphere, then you need to interrupt that dynamic. Or rather, you need his wife to interrupt it.'

'Go on.'

'No, that's all I have. Over to you now.'

'Ma, come on! Help me out here!'

'Jaysus, if you're going to be this much of a sap, you've got no chance of liberating the poor woman from her oppressive yoke.'

Up the ladder, or go home.

'OK, OK . . . So, what you're saying is that I need to get Mrs Barton to put her foot down?'

'And preferably keep it down.'

'Then it's *both* of them I need to provoke into action, isn't it? I need to force them into an ultimatum situation, high noon at the Not-OK Corral.'

'Now you're getting it.'

'That sounds so risky as to be potentially catastrophic,' said Kerry. 'And I've still no idea how to go about it.'

'You'll think of something,' said his mother.

'Glad someone has faith in me,' said Kerry. 'Though you know I'll come crying to you if it all goes horribly wrong?'

'Course you will,' said Bronagh, happily. 'I'm your ma.'

Kerry knew the flaws in his own personality were down to him; he'd fed and fostered his own weaknesses. One of those was his inability to deal with conflict. Whenever anger threatened — particularly from within — he leapt in front of it and performed like a circus clown, in effect beating it into submission with a rubber chicken and a nose that went honk. It was his signature move — the sidestep, the diversion. It was how he avoided *any* feeling that made him even slightly uncomfortable. Anger, shame, romantic commitment . . .

Kerry flipped to the back of *The Gay Science* and found it contained an appendix of thirty poems entitled *Songs of Prince Vogelfrei*. If that wasn't a sign to act now, nothing was.

'Have you finished?'

God, he'd been quiet too long.

'No, just losing the will to live,' said Kerry. 'Friedrich may be one of the great thinkers of our age, but overall he's a crashing bore.'

'I'm not surprised you've found it above your intellectual capacity,' said Jonty. 'I can't imagine you have it in you to reach even the end of a Wilbur Smith.'

His mouth formed a tiny smile — supercilious but also triumphant. He was enjoying the opportunity to let the insults fly.

That's why Jonty had asked Kerry back: so he could knock him down again. Having got a taste for it in their previous encounter, he wanted more. He'd got bored with Meredith being unassailable and wanted the return of a target he could lay into, for fun and without guilt.

And, more importantly, without risk that the target would fight back. *I own you*, was the other message of that smile. If you want to keep your job, you'll take the blows while tugging your forelock in servile gratitude.

Thing is, Kerry *did* have a choice, and that was to tell Meredith he was giving up. That, despite assurances, he'd failed to stick it out, and now she would have to take over again. Which, Kerry knew, she would accept with good grace but a heavy heart. He'd seen her mood over the past two weeks and it had not been a happy one. His guess was that Meredith liked reading to Jonty even less than he did.

A little bell in his head went 'ding', like an oven-timer telling him an idea was ready. To roll with the simile, the idea might also be half-baked. But it was the only one he had. Pretend Jonty is Mr Tiddles, it said. And poke away.

'Oh, I meant to say — Mrs Barton's all in favour of including your model train in our miniature tourist attraction,' said Kerry.

Jonty's smile vanished. 'Don't be ridiculous. She's said nothing to me.'

'*Hasn't* she?' Kerry was all wide-eyed innocence. 'It must have slipped her mind.'

Watch those claws, now.

'My wife will accede to *my* wishes on the matter,' said Jonty. 'You have been misinformed.'

'There *does* seem to be some sort of misunderstanding, doesn't there? Shall we call Mrs Barton in to clarify?'

'Of course not!' Jonty sat up. His dressing gown gaped to reveal flannel pyjamas, in a red tartan that Kerry was delighted to see belonged to Clan Macfarlane.

'There is *no* misunderstanding,' Jonty raged. 'It's perfectly clear. The train is *not* to be touched!'

The bedroom door swung open.

'What's wrong?' said Meredith, her brown eyes anxious. 'I heard raised voices.'

'Take him away,' Jonty ordered.

'Why?' Meredith frowned at Kerry. 'What have you done?'

And thus the (in hindsight obvious) defects in the plan were laid bare. Kerry now had to admit that he'd been baiting Jonty with lies.

'I told Mr Barton you'd no objection to the model trains being included in our project.'

'Which is nonsense, of course,' said Jonty, huffily. He wasn't even looking at her, concentrating instead on refastening his dressing gown.

Meredith's expression became as smooth as an icy pond. Kerry braced himself.

'Not at all,' she said. 'I'm happy to give my — our — full support.'

Ka-boom! Pow! Two jaws hit the floor!

Kerry risked a glance at Jonty. It was like a cartoon, where a person's head became a shrieking red whistle. Jonty was so discombobulated that all he could do was puff air.

'But, but — those are *my* trains,' he managed to say.

'And Gabriel's Bay needs them,' said his wife. 'I'm lending my doll's house, and Charles Love is lending his battle scenes. I think the whole effect will be quite splendid.'

Then she said, 'And if you don't mind, I have some errands for Kerry to run. I'll return at four to bring you your tea.'

'But—'

'Come along, Kerry.'

And Kerry trotted off obediently in her wake.

Meredith led them to the kitchen, and gestured for Kerry to take a chair. She, however, stayed standing and fixed him with a stern look. He was taken back to primary school, and Mrs Chorley asking for the culprit who'd thrown the paper dart to put their hand up, while staring, with accurate instincts, only at him.

'I'm sorry,' he said. 'I backed myself into a corner.'

'And had to lie your way out?'

'Again, I'm very sorry.'

Meredith, much like Mrs Chorley when he was nine, did not look mollified.

'Thank you,' he said. 'For rescuing me.'

Was that a hint of a smile?

'I didn't do it for you,' she said. 'I did it for my own sanity.'

Kerry had no idea what to say to that.

'It's astonishing what you can put up with because you've become used to it,' she said.

Nor that.

'It wasn't until you took over that I realised the full extent of my loathing for the man.'

Right! He'd caught her drift! Probably . . .

'Nietzsche?' he said.

'Of course.'

'Just checking.'

'If I'd told the truth back there, it would have been impossible for you to continue reading. And I couldn't — I simply *could* not face it.'

Kerry decided not to mention that Jonty might actually prefer him to stay, owing to him being a wonderful target for scathing insults. This conversation was going much better than expected.

'Well, thank you anyway,' he said. 'It was more than I deserve.'

'Oh, I wouldn't say that . . .'

Meredith finally pulled out a chair, sat opposite him.

'You put me on the spot and forced me into action,' she said. 'And that action has been long overdue.'

She briefly clasped her hands, as if in prayer.

'I love my husband,' she said, 'but it's time. Time to get him some *proper* help. I should have sought it long ago. I'm ashamed to realise *how* long I've let it go on.'

He couldn't think of any words of comfort that didn't sound false, so he kept quiet. Until a thought struck him.

'Er, I suppose I should ask whether you *do* support the project?' said Kerry. 'Or whether that was just—'

'A handy fib?'

She decided to put him out of his misery.

'The train is by rights mine as well,' she replied. 'And, yes, I would like to see it part of this whole venture.'

'That's terrific,' said Kerry. 'Er, thank you yet again.'

'When do you need it? Moving it will take some preparation.'

'Oh, no rush,' said Kerry. 'The factory's a way off being de-fished.' He leapt up. 'Let me make tea.'

It wasn't a grand gesture of thanks, but it would have to do. This had been, thanks to her, a better day than most. Full of achievement and good news to tell his mother. And Sidney. He'd enjoy telling Sidney everything about today.

Sidney, Sidney, Sidney . . .

Meredith wasn't necessarily the best person to ask, but she was right here. And, as his mother would say, better out than in.

'Do you think Sidney likes me?'

Meredith's eyes widened. 'Likes you?'

'You know — like *that* . . .'

'Ah.' Meredith nodded. 'That.'

'I'm not sure,' said Kerry. 'Can't tell.'

'Why don't you ask *her*?' Meredith suggested.

Sound advice. *Obvious* advice. But when? He'd used up his quota of courage for today, wrung it dry like a rag. Tomorrow, then. Or after football? Or maybe on Friday . . . ?

His employer wore a faint smile, as if she'd gleaned the machinations of his cowardly mind. Which might explain Kerry's strong impression that she wasn't entirely laughing with him.

Chapter 22

Sidney

My God, Kerry could talk! Sidney had already pegged him as chatty, but this was chatty dialled up to eleven. Was he nervous or something?

All she'd done for the past hour was hand him tea and biscuits, and interject with the odd pertinent question. Mainly she nodded and smiled while he told her — everything . . .

Football training had gone well, no tantrums or casualties, and now nearly fifty per cent of them grasped the concept of how to kick a ball. Did she know there was a new indoor sports centre in Hampton? Maybe, one week, they could drive over and play five-a-side? Yes, there were only nine children, but they could play four-a-side with rolling subs. Yes, there was a fee. Not much, but — sure, only an idea, put it in the pending basket.

Lincoln's mother came to pick the boy up as he had an orthodontist appointment, so that's why he'd got to Sidney's a bit earlier than arranged — sorry to have interrupted the tutoring. Nice girl that Ines, what was she, Spanish? Oh, Portuguese! Lovely country. Shame about all those British tourists. What was she studying? Renaissance art, eh? Had either of them noticed that the Botticelli Venus lacked shoulders? Seriously, her neck flowed right into her arms.

Yes, the Booths and Reuben were picked up by Mr Booth in a utility vehicle that looked like it had done a tour in Iraq. Genetics are strong in that family, aren't they? Reuben seemed fine — Mr Booth put him up front in the passenger seat, girls in the back. Those dogs were a bit fierce. Pig dogs? Was that a breed? Right! That explained the scars.

Tea? Yes, lovely. Madison and the boys doing homework in their rooms, were they? Oksana was tut-tutting about her that very morning. Madison a bee-ootiful girl but only so much Oksana could do, not being a slave and all that. Dretful atmosphere in the Jensen house. Rick never home, and when he was, he slithered about like rat snake. Olivia like *shishiga* — Google says it's a female goblin creature that harasses people. Accused Oksana of spending too much on rubbish bags. She'd better watch herself, or she'd find her Lindauer laced with Drano.

And in breaking news, Dr Love spent the whole of yesterday evening at the Barton house. Not clinical depression but extreme social anxiety, bordering on paranoia, was his diagnosis. Mental illness was a tough nut to crack, if she'd pardon the pun. His mother — his own, not Dr Love's — said that even with medication and skilled psychotherapy, getting people back into the social swing was a slow business, and they should be prepared for setbacks. And Jonty wasn't exactly Colin in *The Secret Garden*, now, was he? He wasn't gagging to leap out of bed, frolic in the flowers with Mary and Dickon and the forest creatures. His legs must be wasted in a similar way, come to think of it, given all that lying around. Unless he was secretly doing calisthenics in between meals and Nietzsche? Now there was an image.

Shortbread! Wonderful. He *would* take two, ta muchly. Did she want a tour of the fish factory? Yes, it *had* been rather miraculous, hadn't it? Maybe there was something in this petitioning the universe business? Beaming positive requests to the stars and letting the law of attraction reward you in kind? Right you are, yes, all bollocks, but that Australian woman made *so* much money from the idea, it boggled the mind. Yes, people *were* stupid and gullible, but there was something terribly seductive about the promise of free riches, wasn't there? Ha, ha, yes, as all Nigerian scammers well knew.

Where was he? Oh, yes, fish factory and the generous old Italian owner. Sad, really, he was the last of a fishing dynasty, who'd given up on trying to sell. Had moved with his sons to Wellington, where the boys had set up a restaurant, doing well. Sons didn't care what he did with the old factory, which was a relief — getting embroiled in an Italian family spat could be fatal. No, not from Sicily, Amalfi Coast. But the Mafia were everywhere, weren't they? Yes, could possibly be influenced by those movies. Although *The Godfather 3* was an abomination. One viewing was one too many.

Not *bad* inside the factory. OK, pretty bad. Would need *quite* a few willing hands to get it shipshape. What did she think of asking the rugby club to help out? Would she come with him to ask this Saturday night? OK, fair enough. He'd been in enough changing rooms to know that it wasn't entirely a woman-friendly culture. But, you know, if they went together? No, he was not afraid! It was simply that they might respond better to a local. Yes, he had asked others. Gene was taking the girls to the movies in Hampton. Jacko was working. Devon was also working, and besides wouldn't go near the place if you paid him. Mac laughed. A lot. And then she said no.

Please . . . ?

She was a star!

Yes, he owed her. Yes, agreed, big time.

Could he start to repay her by cooking dinner? He had time to shoot out and buy the ingredients from the Four Square. Yes, for them all, him included. If that was OK?

Great! He'd buy a bottle of wine, too. For later.

If staying later was OK?

Great!

He'd be off to the shop then.

Was that a shouted request for Magnums from the bedroom? Were they allowed Magnums? Did she want a Magnum? A Trumpet. Was that like a Cornetto?

Mint choc-chip, got it.

It was the *least* he could do. She was a star. Really. She was wonderful . . .

OK, then! Car keys? Ah, in his pocket.

Back in a tick!

Sidney closed the door behind him. Touched her cheeks, found them to be toasty warm. Had she imagined? He'd leaned in and for a second there, she thought he might—?

She shook her head, which only made her dizzier than she'd been while listening to Kerry in full flight.

'Mum!' came from the bedroom. 'Mum, Rory's kicking the wall and he won't *stop*!'

'Ow! *You* stop!'

Thank God, a distraction. Sidney marched off, praying both boys would put her red face down to irritation and not — whatever it was. Nothing. It *had* to be nothing.

Didn't it?

Saturday night at the rugby clubrooms. Sidney had expected the worst and it was worse than that. God, what was it with men in packs? Men singly were generally OK. Apart from Rick Jensen. And Fergal at the end. And creepy Geoffrey Naylor. But then there was Jacko, and Gene, and Doc Love, Devon and Mr Phipps — all terrific human beings. Kerry, too, she allowed, though she still didn't feel she knew him well. Even after Wednesday night. *Especially* after Wednesday night.

He'd cooked dinner — a simple pasta and tomato sauce, because the Four Square was, to put it mildly, a bit limited in its range. But the food was tasty, and the kids ate everything on their plates. And then instead of TV, he checked their homework, read to them from *The Jungle Book*, supervised their 'ablutions' as he called it, and got them off to bed after one last Mowgli story.

Then he and Sidney had sat, drank wine, talked some more — he paused for breath this time, proved to be actually quite a good listener. Around ten, he said he should go, and at the front door, he kissed her. And she kissed him back, and they stayed pressed together in the doorway for she wasn't sure how long. She broke it off, not prepared to go further. He wasn't put out, seemed hugely chuffed that she'd allowed him to go that far. They'd agreed he'd drive to her place tonight, walk together to the clubrooms, and they had made no plans beyond that, which had left Sidney in a tizz for the rest of the week.

What did he expect tonight, apart from moral support? Did he expect to come home with her afterwards and—

She didn't know him. She didn't know *herself* — had no clue what she wanted. Her body had responded as bodies do to the kiss (which was very good, yes it was), but her mind had begun right then to flip and ping about like a pinball machine, and hadn't stopped. So many doubts, so many questions. Most of which, she knew, could only be answered over time, as you got to know a person, got to see them unguarded, under stress, making choices — all those occasions when the real them, their real values, came out. When the cracks appeared.

He *seemed* like a genuine guy. And he fancied her — how often had *that* happened in the past nine years? The stirring of lust in her front doorway had been a revelation, which she couldn't help being thrilled by. He wanted her — *her*! Plump, pleasantly average Sidney, not some svelte young beauty! Brilliant! Thank you, Kerry Macfarlane, for having excellent if anomalous taste.

But then — flip! ping! — she didn't *want* to be grateful! More than that, she didn't want to become used to what he offered, didn't want to be seduced by him not only physically but also emotionally. He could buy her wine, he could cook, mind children. He could take the load off, practically and financially — they could share. *Such* a seductive promise. Such a dangerous one. Sidney hated that she felt always on the knife-edge of financial disaster, but she managed, she coped — and she did that all on her own. Yes, her neighbours and friends helped, but she helped them in return — she wasn't *dependent* on them. She couldn't afford to become dependent. Couldn't afford to be let down.

A mind raging with doubts and insecurities wasn't the best to bring into a stuffy, beer-fumed room packed with leering men. Were there *any* other women here? Oh, yep, that girl from the bakery, wearing a skirt inadvisably short for bar-stool seating. And a smattering of others Sidney recognised by sight, most the type of women who, by about age fourteen, had surrendered any possibility of being self-determined and submitted to a life that was done *to* them and not usually in a good way, or by good men. Yes, all right, she should check her privilege, acknowledge her comfortable, well-educated start in life. But even so, why didn't they want more for themselves? Why couldn't they see that there was more to *have*?

'Even the dead beasts on the walls are staring at us,' Kerry whispered.

'Didn't you see the "No Gingers" sign on the door?' she replied. 'It was right above "No Homos", "No Feminists" and "No Shandy-sipping Woofters".'

'Ha, ha,' said Kerry, without conviction.

'OK, there's Sam, Gene's nephew,' said Sidney. 'And Barrett. Let's put them at risk of total ostracism and head their way.'

Such nice-looking boys, said the DNA within her that, if she weren't vigilant, would make her a cheek-pincher in her golden years. Sam with that hint of coffee in his skin, green-speckled eyes, and those brown-blond corkscrew ringlets that Sidney always wanted to call 'boing-boing curls' after Milly Molly Mandy's Little Friend Susan. Barrett, darker, and with the classic pugilistic handsomeness of early-years Brando or Elvis. And that smile, my God. The kind that made part of your brain start trying to play down a thirteen-year age gap.

Devon's warning came to mind, but Sidney could not give it credence. Barrett was courteous, thoughtful, a dutiful son, and Sam's best friend. Sam was far too gentle to stick by someone who had a bad side.

'Howdy, gents,' she said. 'How's your evening so far?'

Sam resembled a dog wondering why it was being punished. 'OK . . . ?'

'Sam, Barrett, this is Kerry. He's working for Mrs Barton.'

Barrett extended a hand. 'Think I've seen you around?'

'I came into your premises,' said Kerry. 'With a broken vacuum cleaner.'

'Oh, yeah.' Barrett grinned. 'Cause of damage: Russian vigour.'

'Yes, they broke the mould when they made Oksana,' said Kerry. 'Or, more likely, she did.'

'Dad told me she put a filleting knife to a guy's throat when she worked at the fish factory,' said Sam. 'All the guy did was pat her, um — backside.'

'Oh, I seriously doubt that's all he did,' said Sidney. 'But nice segue, Sam, into the exact subject we've come here to raise. Kerry?'

'Could I buy you both a beer?' he said. 'Bribe you to listen for ten minutes?'

'Oh, nah, it's OK,' said Sam. 'Our mate's just gone to—'

'Here ya are, girls.'

The mate was back, jug in hand. Sidney's heart sank a little. Not that she knew Tubs Hanrahan particularly well. But his father, Rob, was a self-important, big-noting a-hole, who wore alligator-hide cowboy boots, for Pete's sake, and threw his weight around at the Boat Shed, acting like he was doing them a huge favour by giving them his custom. Devon *hated* serving him, gritted his teeth at the endless insinuations, though he knew it would be worse if he actually *were* a girl. Rob was a finger-snapper, demanding instant attention, and if he wasn't shit-scared of Jacko he'd be a faultfinder, too, the kind that sends back meals just because they can.

Sidney assessed Rob's son. Lardy, shifty, nowhere near as attractive as his two friends. He made a feeble attempt to give her the once-over, but when he met her gaze she raised one eyebrow and he instantly blushed. As she suspected: bravado on top, jelly underneath.

'Tubs, you know Ms Gillespie,' said Barrett. 'May I introduce Kerry, who has requested that we lend him our ears for a speech he prepared earlier.'

'Yeah?'

Tubs tried to give Kerry the once-over, too, the sizing-up macho version. Met only a smile and an extended hand, which he accepted, ever so reluctantly, like he'd catch foreign, unmanly cooties.

'A short speech, I promise,' said Kerry. 'And the next round's on me.'

Sidney watched while he talked, compared him to the men around them. The key difference was that Kerry seemed entirely at ease with himself, whereas these guys were about as comfortable as cats adrift on a rubber raft. Sure, they *seemed* relaxed — they bantered with each other, teased and mocked in that dry, laconic way. But their interactions followed a proscribed routine, a tight script that must not be deviated from. This was a tribe and its members would rather die than not belong. It defined who they were; without it, they were nothing.

Sidney's tolerance for male bullshit was normally nonexistent, but at that moment, she experienced a brief surge of empathy. How hard must it be to always conform to such rigid rules? To never say what you really feel? To have to live by 'it's all good, bro', that most perfect suppressor of uncomfortable discussion?

Not as hard as conforming to expected female standards, of course. At least the blokes got beer. Whereas women got waxing kits that stripped the hair from their pudendas, and yoghurt that prevented bloating. Good one.

'What do you think?' Kerry had reached the end of his sales pitch. 'Would the club be willing to send out a message to its members, calling for volunteers?'

'Um,' said Sam. 'I guess . . .'

'Can but ask,' said Barrett. He pointed at an older man leaning against the bar. 'Earl over there's club captain. I'd advise you to get him now while he's only five pints down.'

Sidney said, 'What about you lot? Will *you* help?'

'Clean up the fish factory?' Tubs snorted. 'Not likely!'

'Sam?'

He wouldn't look at her. 'Um . . .'

'That means yes,' said Barrett. 'Yes, we'll be glad to help. Tubs, too.'

'Yeah, right!'

Barrett put his arm around Tubs's shoulders, squeezed in a way that must have felt harder than it looked, because Tubs instantly deflated.

'It's your civic duty, mate,' said Barrett. 'The dues you owe this ol' town.'

'Well, fucken Deano's coming, too,' muttered Tubs. 'No way he's getting out of it.'

'Where *is* Deano?' said Sam. 'Loretta's here, but he's not.'

'He had to work.' Barrett released Tubs, who sagged further.

'Work?' said Sam. 'At night?'

Barrett shrugged. 'What he told me.'

'So we can count on the four of you?' said Kerry. 'That's great. Thank you.'

Barrett smiled his killer smile, and Sidney wondered why he didn't have a girlfriend. How could any young woman resist?

'You don't get that many opportunities to clean the karmic slate,' he said. 'Speaking personally, I look forward to it.'

He raised his glass.

'To cleaning slates! Let's scrub away all our bad deeds along with the fish grime.'

'That Barrett's a good-looking lad, isn't he?'

Kerry sounded casual, which meant, judging by every time *she'd* tried it, that he felt anything but. She had two choices — wind him up, or reassure him that she haboured no desire to seduce a younger man. They were walking hand in hand, so it seemed churlish to pick the former.

'If you like that type,' she said.

He gave her a sidelong glance.

'The devastatingly handsome type is traditionally the most successful at attracting women,' he said. 'Followed closely, of course, by the ninety-year-old billionaire.'

'My gender thanks you for confirming that we're all shallow and avaricious,' said Sidney. 'For a moment there, we were worried that we might be building a reputation for being multi-dimensional individuals.'

After a beat, Kerry said, 'My seduction technique needs work, doesn't it?'

'More like your insecurities do,' Sidney said, with a smile. 'If it's any consolation, mine have been a lifelong project.'

'May I kiss you again?' he asked.

They were outside the gates of the primary school, a common gathering place for underage drinkers, petty vandals and teenagers who lacked cars to have sex in. It was eleven-thirty, and Gabriel's Bay street lighting was partial at best. Any number of eyes could be on them right now.

'Sure,' she replied. 'But if you hear applause, that's a hint we need to find somewhere more private.'

They kissed, and it was nicer than before, which was usually the case. First kisses were like exploring a dark cave — it took a few tries to find your footing and was always damper than you expected.

The kissing evolved into what teenagers of her mother's era — though never her mother — would have called heavy petting. But her body's keen desire to give in to the moment was derailed by her practical mother-brain planning ahead. She broke away.

'Sorry, but I think now's a good time to tell you that I will not do it up against a wall, in a doorway, on damp grass, wooden boards or any surface where I'm made aware of my hip bones. I detest the shower because bits of me get cold and if my face is under, it's like I'm being waterboarded. I'm not even that keen on carpet or rugs.'

'I'm not good with food,' he told her. 'To me, *Nine and a Half Weeks* was a horror movie.'

'Of course it was. It had Mickey Rourke in it.'

'Er,' said Kerry, 'I don't want to overstep the mark here — but now that all those other options have been, very fairly, eliminated, can I infer that you're keen on going to your place?'

The boys were at Mac's. She could bundle Kerry out the door before they got back. (Not because she didn't want to explain it to *them* — it was Mac who'd phone her up and give her the third degree.)

But should she rush in? Shouldn't she and Kerry get to know each other better?

Her body voted like a kid who'd been asked whether they wanted a puppy, a bicycle and a jumbo bag of free lollies. Her mind was more like a kid standing on the high-dive board, which had looked a lot less high from the ground.

Her body snuck up behind the second kid and pushed them off.

'My place it is,' she said. 'Let's go.'

Chapter 23

Bernard

Camaraderie. Was that the right word for what Bernard was witnessing, or was it too old-fashioned? 'Mucking in' was an ugly modern phrase, yet appropriate given the setting. Bernard had poked his head around the door of the old fish factory, expecting to see a few people attempting a task even Hercules might balk at — clearing out decades' worth of accumulated industrial residue. He'd been astonished to see at least thirty residents, young and old, shifting, scraping and cleaning, apparently all in willing good humour.

Although the Progressive Association had not yet given its stamp of approval to the project, Bernard found he did not mind seeing its team press on regardless. He had a duty to everyone in Gabriel's Bay to thoroughly assess the proposal, and so that is what he would do. But in his heart, he knew he wanted it to go ahead, and so this blatant disregard for due process and consultation bothered him less than it might. A second tempering factor was the knowledge that this activity would absolutely incense Elaine. Bernard liked to picture an outraged Elaine. He liked less that she was clearly plotting some kind of obstruction behind his back.

Oh well, until she revealed her plan (no doubt with triumphal fanfare), there was little point expending energy in worry.

Possibly having let thoughts of Elaine waft like miasma through his mind, Bernard's initial surprised pleasure at seeing so many hard at work began to slip sideways towards dejection. He was not part of this team, and even if he offered to help he suspected he'd be turned away. They'd be polite, but after he'd left they would grin at each other and probably deploy some vernacular phrase signalling their belief that he would be about as useful as udders on male cattle.

It took him back to times he would rather forget, but which, at moments like this, flared up like hotspots in a forest fire. At school, Bernard had never fitted in. Too small for the rugby team, too academically able, too rich, he'd spent the years between five and seventeen a daily target of suspicion and derision expressed (on good days) verbally and (on most days) physically. Bernard had been prescribed glasses at age ten, but after the third pair had been ground under someone's heel he dared wear them only indoors, meaning that when in the playground and travelling between school and home, he was effectively blind. So he stopped going outside. He stayed in his bedroom, or in a corner of the school library (guarded by the librarian, Mrs Philpott, whose ear tweak was legendary) and he read his way through Sir Walter Scott, H. Rider Haggard, Robert Louis Stevenson, Rudyard Kipling and all of Mallory's *Le Morte d'Arthur*. (There were more modern books, American ones also, but he didn't much care for those.)

Inside books, he lived adventurously, won hearts and vanquished enemies. He became a hero, capable, adored, muscular in body and intellect, with a tongue nearly as lethal as his first choice of weapon, a sleek, slim poignard, which, when the enemy was particularly dastardly, he augmented with a flanged mace. (In his dreams, Bernard's arch-nemesis, a thug named Kevin Nattriss, regularly felt the might of his mace. Kevin Nattriss's Datsun Violet went under the wheels of a logging truck on State Highway 30A back in 1976, but even now Bernard would often wake with fresh and satisfactory images of Kevin's skull after a single, well-placed mace blow.)

University had been a relief, but despite it being safe to wear glasses all day, he had still felt on the outer. No clubs to join: he neither skied nor drank beer and he'd rather stare at a page than a chessboard. He had hoped to bond with his fellow English Literature students, but none seemed to share his level of enthusiasm for the greats. They preferred modern writers, like Pynchon. Bernard hadn't got past page three of *The Crying of Lot 49*.

These days, he and Patricia had a respectable social circle, and invitations came at well-spaced intervals. But if Bernard were to summon one word to describe his relationships with others, that word would be 'formal'. The people he socialised with were well-mannered, with moderate voices and opinions, even if their political views did skew rather far right at times. They did not drink to excess, nor laugh raucously. And they certainly didn't rib each other, or hug, or put each other in affectionate headlocks like the group of young lads he was watching now.

Camaraderie. It was a good word. It would do.

'Bernard.'

His heart lurched, his pulse quickened, and silently he despaired. Forty-six years it had been. Forty-*six*! If nearly five decades could not act as a buffer to emotional turmoil, then there was no hope. He was doomed to a lurching heart and quickening pulse for the rest of his life.

'Meredith,' he said. 'I'm surprised to see you here.'

A raised eyebrow. 'Why? Am I too old for this kind of work?'

'No, no,' Bernard corrected hastily. 'I merely thought — well, that you are one of the patrons, I suppose. Surely your contribution has been made.'

'I'm not *quite* ready for that to be end of my involvement,' said Meredith, 'although I am less anxious about my little house now than I was at the start.'

She smiled, and Bernard realised that it was the first time in ages he'd not seen her look drawn and weary. There were still tired lines in evidence, but her eyes were clear again, warm brown and glinting with humour.

'Heikki the jeweller offered to replace the plastic chandelier in the dining room with one made of real quartz,' she said. 'I told him I couldn't possibly let him spend his own money, and so I brought out my grandmother's diamond tiara. Do you remember? I wore it at my wedding?'

Bernard remembered. Meredith had been an unbearably beautiful bride. He'd got quite drunk at the reception and fallen asleep face-down on a table. No one noticed.

'Heikki was horrified,' she continued. 'No, no, he protested. He couldn't possibly break up a family heirloom. Quartz it would be. I agreed but insisted on paying half, which he reluctantly accepted. But not two days later, he was back, pounding at my door, brandishing a drawing of his design for the chandelier. I must have the tiara!, he declared. That centre pear-shaped diamond is perfect for the drop!'

'And you gave it to him?' Bernard could not prevent his voice rising in dismay.

'Of course,' came her mild reply. 'What use do I have for a tiara?'

'But, but . . . the *insurance*. And the *security* — how on earth does the project team propose to protect' — he uttered the last in a whisper — 'a *diamond* chandelier?'

'No one but you, Heikki and I know it's made of real diamonds,' said Meredith. 'And Heikki won't tell. Finns are renowned for their love of silence.'

'That seems . . .' Bernard struggled to think of a word that would not sound insulting. 'Unwise.'

'In that case,' she said, amused, 'I'd better not let on that one of the drawings is a real Picasso. My parents were travelling in France, and in Vallauris, where he lived at the time, they spotted him in a café. My mother was pregnant with me, and he did a tiny doodle on a napkin, "pour le bébé". My mother put it in a silver locket. All I did was remove the cover. It's above the piano in the house's living room.'

'You delight in tormenting me.'

Bernard kept his tone jocular. She must never know how true those words were.

Meredith glanced around.

'Is Patricia with you?' she said. 'I can't see her.'

'She had an errand to run.' He'd forgotten what it was. 'Probably for the best, as I'm not sure what tasks she'd be keen to perform — it appears one can't avoid getting one's hands *very* dirty.'

'Oh, don't underestimate Patricia,' said Meredith. 'Your wife has a strong seam of resource and determination.'

Bernard received the compliment on his wife's behalf, despite being unconvinced of its veracity. Apart from that occasion when she'd asked him out, Patricia had never once been strong-willed or demanding. She'd expressed her opinions, of course, but any disagreements they had were quickly settled, due to his rational approach and her natural kindness. Patricia was a gentle soul, happy to be useful in the background. How odd that Meredith thought her determined.

'And are you here as an official observer, Bernard?' Meredith broke his train of thought. 'On behalf of the association?'

'I *have* publically expressed a personal interest.' He felt a need to make his presence seem more worthy in her eyes. 'Though I hope I have been clear that it will not bias my recommendation to the committee.'

'Very scrupulous of you,' said Meredith. 'And I'm being quite sincere. The association is fortunate to have someone of your calibre as chair.'

'Thank you.'

He, too, was being sincere, but Meredith's compliments were a mixed blessing. He felt like a knight receiving the beautiful queen's favour, while knowing she must remain by the side of her king.

'And, ah, how is Jonty?'

Bernard wasn't sure if he should raise the subject, but part of him craved to know how his rival fared.

Meredith hesitated, and Bernard's heart sank. He'd offended her.

'Jonty is . . . well, I suppose the best way to put it is that he needs his sense of self re-established. He needs to regain his personal power, rediscover the man he was.'

He must have looked perplexed, because she said, 'I'm not making any sense, am I?'

'You are,' he assured her. 'But I was wondering how one could go about effecting that aim?'

'Charles, Doctor Love, has finally persuaded him to take medication. He managed to convince him that antidepressants were not a crutch or a sign of weakness but a way to restore what was missing in the body, much as you'd do if you were vitamin-deficient, or needed hormone-replacement therapy.'

Bernard had a sudden vision of Patricia sobbing. Menopause, even though she had been well over fifty when it arrived, had destroyed her last faint hope of conceiving. He had felt inadequate then, and he felt inadequate now. He was no medical or psychological expert. How could he be of even the *slightest* help to Meredith?

But then Meredith said, 'However, what he needs most is a connection again to the outside world. He needs to feel that he is of value, that his knowledge and experience matter. I'd hoped being involved in *this* project might be a start, but it's not enough to truly motivate him. He needs more challenge, more intellectual stimulation.'

Bernard saw the opportunity — or, at least, what he might make of it.

'Would you like *me* to visit Jonty?' he said. 'Bring him up to date with association business, and any other civic business I am privy to? It might make him feel part of things again. And I always welcomed his contribution; it would be good to hear his views.'

This last statement was not scrupulously accurate, but Bernard hoped Meredith would let it pass.

'Why, Bernard.' Meredith looked both taken aback and genuinely touched. She took his hand, squeezed it. 'That is such a kind offer,' she said. 'How generous of you.'

He blushed, a look he knew did not become him. Fair-skinned and thinly haired, any blush infused Bernard's whole face and scalp so that he glowed bright as a freshly dipped toffee apple.

Of course, that was the moment Gene Collins chose to walk past.

'Greetings, Mrs B,' he said. 'In the pink I see, Bernardo.'

The man's smirk was intolerable.

'Gene, Kerry tells me that we have you to thank for this high turnout,' said Meredith. 'He said you put in a good word for him at the rugby club.'

'He's got the gift of the gab,' said Gene. 'But he's also a foreigner, English at that, who no one in the club knows from a bar of soap. So they sat around, stone-faced, and let him expel so much carbon dioxide that we were all in danger of asphyxiation. I *had* to step in.'

'That was kind of you,' said Meredith. 'Especially considering I gather you were unconvinced about the merit of the idea.'

Now it was Gene's turn to blush. Bernard's glee knew no bounds.

'Well, no, it wasn't the idea as such,' said Gene. 'I was concerned about your young bloke over-promising. Last thing this town needs is get-rich-quick schemes run by fly-by-night flakes who bail when the going gets tough.'

Bernard was surprised to find he wholeheartedly agreed with him. Had, in fact, to stifle a 'Hear, hear!'

'And do you believe Kerry to be a fly-by-nighter?' said Meredith.

Bernard saw Gene's gaze travel to where the young Englishman could be seen, like a milkmaid in overalls, carrying a plastic bucket of soapy water in each hand to where Sidney Gillespie and her two young sons scrubbed away at a wall with stiff brushes. The two adults appeared to swap a joke, and then Kerry left to advise the young lads Bernard had seen earlier engaging in a bit of rough-housing on where to shift a piece of lethal-looking machinery.

'Jury's out,' said Gene. 'Hard part's not yet begun.'

Again, Bernard was surprised to find his feelings in exact alignment with a man who, until this point, he had considered a professional mischief-maker.

'Yes, I'm not sure he is aware of quite what he's up against,' Bernard said.

'You mean you?' said Gene.

Gene was smirking once more, but this time Bernard felt in control. Felt able even to inject a little levity.

'Much worse,' he said. 'Elaine.'

'Jesus,' said Gene, and he sounded sincere.

'What could she do, Bernard?' said Meredith. 'Surely with this much support' — she indicated the busy room — 'she would find her objections fell on deaf ears?'

'I've no idea,' said Bernard, honestly. 'I imagine we will find out fairly soon.'

'Well, let's not stew about it,' said Gene. 'Let's crack on. Mrs B, Doc Love's out back in the old foreman's office drawing up plans for the space. Might pay to make sure your house isn't in the firing line of the 18th Panzer Division. Bernard, are you here to help or gawk?'

'Is there anything I *could* do?'

Bernard felt the tug of ambivalence. He did not want to look a fool by failing at some task another man might find simple. But the opportunity to be included, that had its appeal.

'How about supervising the rubbish disposal? Separate out all the stuff we shouldn't dump in the landfill? You don't have to get your hands dirty — there's a bunch of volunteers with trailers, and the club boys can do the heavy lifting.'

Gene was, most probably, enjoying offering him a job he felt Bernard would dislike. But supervision and attention to detail were his strengths, and besides, it might be amusing to see Gene's reaction when he said yes.

'I'd be more than happy to take that on,' said Bernard.

He'd been correct. For the rest of the afternoon, Gene's astonished expression gave Bernard almost as much pleasure as the memory of Meredith's hand on his.

Chapter 24

Sam

The problem with family get-togethers, thought Sam, was that he had no relatives his own age. The closest was his sister, Lea, but she was only fourteen. And she was a girl. They were *all* girls. His sisters, Lea and Toni. His cousins, Billie, Frankie and Jenna. And his mum had also invited Casey Marshall and her sister. Corinna and her husband had brought their two little daughters. It was girl power to the max.

Fortunately, he wasn't expected to babysit. Lea and Billie had the girls playing hide and seek with the littlies in and out of the apple trees, and they were all giggling like crazy. Sam watched them from his seat on the back porch, thought about joining in. Decided he was too big, might scare the babies. Besides, he was a bit knackered after yesterday's working bee, so it was good to sit in the sun, and the garden, with its big lawn, rough orchard at the rear, was pretty to look at, coming now at the start of summer into full leaf and flower. Sam kept getting a sweet whiff of rose, from the pink one sprawling up the trellis beside the porch. His parents weren't super into gardening, so they let plants go a bit wild. Sam liked that, always had. The back garden had been his adventure playground all his life, just like it was now for the girls playing amongst the trees.

Up it came, that feeling of fear, or sadness, or whatever; Sam always pushed it back down before it took hold long enough for him to inspect it closely. He knew what brought it on, though — the knowledge that his time here, in this family, in this place, was almost up. He was in the final year of his teens, and in a few short months he'd head to a new town and a bigger job. A lot of goodbyes to say, some of them he'd say only to himself.

He turned to watch the only blokes out in the back yard — his dad, Uncle Gene, and Corinna's husband, Tai. Casey's martial arts dude boyfriend was in Japan at some tournament. The men were in a knot together around the barbecue, holding beer bottles and checking the hotplate, waiting for the meat. He could go over to them, but Sam still felt unready to join in their conversation. Tai Te Wera (Corinna had kept her maiden name) was only twenty-eight, but he had confidence and life experience under his belt. Plus, he was a lawyer, too, like Corinna, university-educated, spent time with a big firm in Auckland before coming back to Hampton where he grew up. Uncle Gene and his dad were smart men, they could hold their own in conversation with Tai. Sam wasn't sure he'd be able to, and he didn't want to try and then look like a dick. Uncle Gene would show no mercy.

Sam wished Brownie were there. He'd been invited, but his dad had had a rough night with his breathing, so Brownie had driven him over the hill to hospital. He'd phoned Sam's mum early this morning to give his apologies. Sam had texted him an hour ago, but no answer. Probably weren't allowed mobiles in hospital wards.

'Sammo.'

Casey in the back doorway, holding a huge platter piled with marinated chops and chicken pieces, steaks and the fancy sausages his dad had bought at the farmers' market, plus the cheese-filled supermarket ones the little kids liked. They used to be his favourite, too, though Brownie always said the cheese tasted like spew.

Sam got up off the porch, and Casey held the laden dish out to him. She made it look like it was no effort but he could see the sinews in her forearms, so as he took it from her, he made sure he was ready for its weight. Wouldn't do to drop it, or be shown up by a woman half his size.

'Got it?' She was teasing him.

'Yup.' Just.

'Right, well, deliver that safely, and we might keep you on.'

'Sure.'

He didn't mind fetching and carrying. Did it a lot on the building site, being the junior and all.

'Whoa,' said Uncle Gene as Sam put the platter on the side shelf of the big steel barbecue his dad had got at staff price from the hardware store. 'Who else are we feeding? You got a busload of mates turning up?'

'Nah.' Sam shook his head.

'How's Ed?' said his dad.

'Haven't heard.'

His dad nodded. 'I'll pop round later. Take some leftovers.'

Sam wished he'd thought of that first. For half a second he resented his dad for being a more mature and thoughtful human being.

'Beer, Sam?'

His dad flicked the cap off a bottle with the metal fish slice, handed it to him, beaded with cold. Resentment gone.

'Kids today,' said Uncle Gene. '*We* had to wait until we were twenty-one.'

'Bet you didn't,' said Tai, with a grin. 'My guess — you were aged fourteen, you swiped two cans from your dad's stash of Lion Brown, and drank them in a bush fort that you biked to.

And then you sweated like crazy that your mum would smell it on your breath when you came home.'

'Incorrect,' said Uncle Gene. 'I was thirteen-and-a-half and it was Lion Red.'

'And Mum *did* smell it on your breath.'

Sam's mum, Talia, had brought clean platters for them to put the cooked meat on.

'And as I recall, she also kicked your arse.'

'Samoan-style, too,' said Uncle Gene. 'Equal parts physical pain and emotional blackmail.'

Sam's grandmother had died when he was five. He had only fuzzy memories, of loud, gleeful greetings, of being crushed into her soft bosom, and hauled onto her lap, where he fell asleep as she cooed over him. Of being fed sweet coconut cake until his mum intervened. His mum always said it was a shame his grandma had never known Sam's sisters and cousins. Grandpa Collins had died before any of them were born, hit by a car when he was walking home from the pub one night. Sam got the impression he'd been a bit hard to live with, a drinker, free with his fists.

He watched his own dad, checking the chicken was cooked, turning the sausages. He'd never once raised a hand to Sam or his sisters, even when he was clearly furious. Never raised a hand to anyone, despite being big and strong. Sam knew he should be grateful to have Wyatt as his dad, especially when he compared him to Tubs's and Deano's fathers. But sometimes he wondered if a tougher childhood would have made him less soft, less of a dreamer . . .

'Earth to Sam!'

His mum clicked her fingers in front of his face, made him blink.

'Sorry, yeah, what?' said Sam.

'Where *do* you go?' She sounded impatient but she was smiling.

'I said: can you get the plates and glasses? Lea's on placemats and cutlery, Toni on napkins. I expect seamless, polite co-ordination, OK?'

'Sure,' said Sam. 'Now?'

'No, mate,' said his Uncle Gene. 'Jesus's next appearance. When you hear trumpets and angelic voices, that's your cue.'

They all laughed at him, even his mum. Sam felt like stomping off, but that would only make them laugh more. So he smiled to show he'd taken it on the chin. Found everything he needed in the kitchen. Ignored his sisters's attempts to wind him up, and let his mother know the table was ready. Helped bring out the tomato sauce, bread and more bowls of salad than he felt strictly necessary, though he was glad to see his favourite potato salad, the one with crispy bacon bits and boiled egg in it. That was Brownie's favourite, too. Probably why his mum made it.

Sam checked his phone again. Nothing. Texted 'U OK?' Hoped that didn't sound too pathetic. Put the phone back in his pocket; his parents forbade the use of all electronic devices at meal times.

He had a moment of worry as his mother organised where everyone should sit. He didn't want to be stuck down the end with all the kids, including Corinna's two, who refused to be separated from the big girls, but he didn't want to be in the midst of the men, either. His mum sat him between Tai and Casey, opposite Corinna, Auntie Liz and his mum. Uncle Gene took the chair next to Sam's mum, and his dad sat beside Tai. Sam was relieved to be mainly among the women. He found their conversation easier because it was rarely directed at him. Tai, Uncle Gene and his dad could carry on with their barbecue discussion, which meant Sam could relax and focus on his food.

Or not.

'Sammo,' said Uncle Gene. 'What's your view on the proposed name change? You in the Onemanawa camp?'

Sam knew he looked like a stunned mullet whenever someone asked him a hard question. Brownie called him 'Bushbaby' because his eyes got so round, they covered half his face. Not only that, his mind would go totally blank and even if he'd *had* an answer, he'd struggle to get it out. Like now.

'Um, I dunno,' he began. 'I guess — if that's what the name was before . . . ?'

'So you'd support the change?' pressed Uncle Gene.

All the adults were waiting for his reply.

'Um — yeah?'

'There you go, Corinna,' said Uncle Gene. 'Another staunch convert. Who says the youth of today aren't politically informed and motivated?'

'Give the boy a break,' said Sam's Auntie Liz. 'It's not as if *you've* committed one way or the other. I can see the fence-post marks on the seat of your pants.'

'Harsh,' said Uncle Gene. 'I prefer to think that I take the time to make considered decisions, rather than leaping to emotional snap judgements.'

'What do your friends think, Sam? Have you discussed it?'

This from Tai, who was probably trying to give Sam a chance to redeem himself. Sam would prefer not to step back into the conversation, but he took a deep breath, got his head together before replying.

'Yeah, we did,' said Sam. 'Brownie's for it, Tubs is against it. No surprises there, I guess.'

The adults laughed. Sam had to make sure he didn't smile too widely. Keep cool. Keep cool.

'Have you seen your friend Dean lately?'

Casey sounded casual, but Sam was immediately on alert. Brownie had told them Deano had got some more hours at the vineyard. They'd had metal thieves or something, and the owner, that Auckland guy, was too cheap to hire a qualified guard, so they paid Deano to camp down overnight. He went home for a quick sleep in the morning, and then went back to do his daytime tasks. That's why they hadn't seen him, said Brownie. Their old mate, Deano, was working his scrawny butt off.

Sam had been pleased to hear it. Work would keep Deano out of trouble. Might even be a way for him to leave that world for good.

But if Constable Marshall was asking after him, it could only be cop business. Good thing Sam could give Deano an alibi.

'He's doing night watch at the vineyard,' he said. 'They had a break-in.'

'A break-in?' Casey nodded, slowly. 'Interesting.'

Sam saw his dad and Uncle Gene exchange a look.

'Bad luck,' said his Uncle Gene. 'Though, of course, Rick Jensen will be *fully* insured.'

'Did I tell you that Olivia Jensen has asked me to act as her divorce lawyer?' said Corinna.

'No, sis,' said Casey. 'You omitted to mention that little gem.'

'Can they afford to get divorced?' said Auntie Liz. 'I thought the money was all tied up?'

'It is,' said Corinna. 'But Olivia's had enough. Wants proceedings started.'

'And what does Rick want?' said Sam's mum.

Corinna shrugged. 'Guess I'll find out. If I say yes.'

'What about Madison?' Auntie Liz asked. 'Will Olivia sue for custody?'

'No idea,' said Corinna. 'As I say, Olivia's only just asked me to represent her.'

'And *will* you say yes?' said Casey.

'Mama!'

Corinna's littlest, two-year-old Hinemoana, was holding up hands covered in tomato sauce. Unnoticed, she'd got hold of the bottle and given it a good squeeze onto her plate and the tablecloth, and then she'd swirled her hands around in it like it was finger paint. Sam had a swift burst of envy at her sense of her own freedom.

'Mama, *mess*!'

'Lea,' reproved Sam's mum. 'I *did* ask you to keep an eye on them.'

'Oh, *what*?'

Sam was amused to see Lea's expression was textbook teenage rage-sulk. Strikes cold fear into the heart of every parent, his dad once said.

'No, no,' said Tai, peace-making. 'Our child, our responsibility. I'll get the wet wipes.'

'Will you say yes, sis? To Olivia?'

Even though her sister was struggling to hold a reluctant toddler's two slippery hands, Casey was still pushing for an answer. You wouldn't want her coming after *you*, thought Sam. She'd never give up.

'I think I will,' said Corinna. 'I'll do it for Madison.'

'You should talk to Sidney Gillespie,' said Auntie Liz. 'She's practically Maddie's official carer now.'

Tai had taken over from his wife, kneeling down on the grass, making a game out of wiping his daughter's hands and face clean. Corinna had to speak up over the giggles.

'Good tip,' she said, wiping her own hands. 'I shouldn't speak ill of a potential client, but in confidence, I'm not sure Olivia's grip on the reality of the situation is all that solid.'

'Like Rick's grip on money,' said Uncle Gene, with a smirk.

'OK, let's bring this to a close,' said Sam's mum. 'I don't think we need to traumatise the youngsters with any more glimpses into the bleak world of messed-up adults.'

'But that's life, isn't it?' said Uncle Gene. 'Can't spare them from harsh reality indefinitely.'

'We can spare them over lunch,' said Sam's mum, in her 'No arguing' tone.

'OK, but there's one lesson they *should* learn. Or this young man should, anyway.'

Uncle Gene pointed his fork at Sam.

'What's that?' said Sam, warily.

'Yes, what?' said Sam's dad. 'Speak up, fat Yoda.'

'Don't fight for anything you don't a hundred per cent believe in,' said Uncle Gene. 'But if you *do* believe, then don't fight for it with any *less* than a hundred per cent.'

'Did that make sense?' said Sam's mum. 'Or was it pure BS?'

'I think he's referring to me taking on Olivia Jensen,' said Corinna.

'Full guns, sis.' Casey raised a clenched fist. 'The Marshall way.'

'Of course, arbitration, mediation and other peaceful forms of dispute resolution could be an option also,' said Tai, amused.

Sam jumped as his phone vibrated. He slid it out of his pocket, held it under the table. Brownie: 'Sod of a day. Partake of fine ale @ club 2nght?'

Typed: 'C u @ 8!' Deleted the exclamation mark as being too naff. Hit send. Then he reached over and snatched up the last cheese-filled sausage, leaned back in his chair to relish this in-between limbo time of no demands. They'd come soon enough, but right now he was being asked for neither words nor action. He closed his eyes, and let the early summer breeze blow to him the faint, sweet scent of roses.

Chapter 25

Madison

'But when will we get to *play*?'

Madison could see Aidan was doing his best not to whine. Sidney hated whining.

'Understand your impatience, big fella,' said Kerry. 'But thing is, football season's over, and the only tournaments on right now we have to pay to be part of. Plus, you're a fine, talented lot, but there are only nine of you. Can you hold out until next year when the season starts again, and we can rustle up a few new players?'

'When *does* it start?'

'Erm, April, I think.'

'*April!*' Aidan kicked at a stone on the playground. 'That's like *years* away!'

'But think how much better we'll be by then.' Madison didn't want Aidan to be cross. 'We could win!'

Dylan gave a kind of snort. 'Yeah, right.'

'If you persist with that attitude,' said Kerry, 'then of course we won't win. Negative Nellies never do. Take José Mourinho. Ever see him smile? No! Were Chelsea, under his reign, big fat losers? Yes!'

'Madonna never smiles and she's super successful,' said Shari Booth.

'Madonna has never played football,' said Kerry. 'As far as I know.'

'She says her best exercise is sex—'

'OK!' Kerry clapped his hands together. 'Are we ready to train?'

'I want to *play*,' said Aidan. His ears were red, which Madison knew meant he was about to lose it. 'I'm *sick* of stupid training.'

'Yeah, training's dumb,' said Dylan. 'And this team's dumb. Too many spazzos.'

'*You're* a spazzo,' said Tanya Booth.

'Shut up, you fat moo,' said Dylan.

Tanya threw herself at him, hands out to grab his hair, but Kerry moved really quickly and caught her wrists.

'*Owww*!' Tanya yelled. 'You're *hurting-gg*!'

Kerry let her go and she began to cry, though Madison couldn't see any tears.

'Outta here,' said Dylan, and he walked off towards his bag.

Madison felt a sick thump in her stomach. He couldn't leave! The team might break up! Why wasn't Kerry stopping him!

But Kerry was looking worried, bent over Tanya, who was still bawling, and now Shari was crying, too, and all the other kids were staring at them. So Madison decided *she* had better run after Dylan.

'Don't go,' she said when she caught up. 'You're really good. We need you!'

Dylan grabbed his bag, hooked it onto his shoulder.

'Nah,' he said. 'Sick of it. Bunch of *retards*.'

He was usually nice, and fair, too, so why was he being so mean now? Maybe he was upset about something? But it wasn't polite to ask personal questions, her mum always said. Her mum couldn't understand why people like Ms Marshall the lawyer had to know about her private business. 'It has nothing to do with *anything*,' she told Madison, though Madison didn't really understand what she meant. Ms Marshall was really nice, and super pretty, like a model. She was kind and patient when she spoke to Madison. But Madison was careful about what she said to her.

Dylan was about to walk off.

'Please?' It was all she could think of.

He went a bit red, but his mouth was still set in a line.

'You're OK,' he said to her, 'but I don't like the others.'

'What about Aidan?'

Madison had thought the two boys were friends.

Dylan frowned, and his face got even redder.

'He's OK at school, but he's kind of a dick here. Competitive. Doesn't want anyone else to have the ball.'

She had to admit that was true. Aidan wanted to be the star. Sulked when Kerry praised anyone else. Sidney wouldn't like that if she knew, but Madison could never be a tattletale.

'Gotta go.' Dylan scrunched up his mouth, so she could barely hear him say, 'Sorry.'

As he walked away, Madison felt like someone was inside her, punching her stomach, making her gulp for air.

'Dylan!'

Kerry jogged up to her, but Dylan had disappeared around the back of the classrooms.

'Bugger,' she heard Kerry say quietly.

He squeezed her shoulder. 'Thank you for stepping into the breach. I know you will have done your very best. Who knows? We may still bring Dylan round.'

Madison nodded. Her throat was all thick.

'On the sunny side, said Kerry, 'I've managed to avert a Booth sisters-class-action lawsuit by bribing them — and everyone else — with ice cream. Our session today will now culminate with a trip to the Four Square.'

She followed him back to the others, and they did a bit of kicking around, but everyone was too half-hearted, so Kerry called time, got them to line up for their walk to the shop. He put the Booth sisters in front — 'Lead the way, Tanya' — and Madison and Reuben at the back, probably because Madison was the only one Reuben didn't fight with. Kerry jogged up and down beside the line, keeping an eye on everyone as they walked.

He made them all go into the shop, but only after they'd sworn not to touch anything. Mr McKee, the owner, didn't like children much, so he wasn't pleased, but Kerry promised they'd be in and out in a jiffy. Which didn't quite happen because Lincoln kept changing his mind and then went all sort of weird when Kerry asked him to give his final answer.

'Just buy him a sundae,' said Peter. 'He likes those. Likes finding the spoon in the lid.'

Madison chose a sundae, too, because they were small and so might not have so much sugar or fat in them. Her mum never ate ice cream or sweets or bread or pasta, though her dad had read the label on a bottle of wine out loud once and it had been a thousand calories, which for some reason had made him laugh.

Kerry wanted them to walk quickly back to the school because their parents might already be waiting, but Lincoln's mum had told him not to eat while walking because it made him sick, so they all had to wait outside the shop until he finished. Mr McKee came out to shoo them away and got quite cross when Kerry told them they had a right to be on a public street. Then when they were finally walking back, Tanya told Reuben that the red part of a Jellytip was frozen blood and Kerry had to hold Ruben's hand to stop him from hitting her, but he was still yelling swear words when they got to school, and Madison saw Lincoln's mum's mouth go all small. 'Lemon lips', Sidney called that look. It made Madison's throat feel tight again.

She wished Reuben wouldn't make it so hard for people to like him.

Madison looked around for her mum or dad, but they didn't seem to be there. Rory and Aidan had already started to walk home, and Peter was getting in Lincoln's mum's car. Mr Booth was standing by his muddy ute, and when Tanya and Shari ran up, the dogs in the cage on the back barked and snarled, like they were desperate to get out and bite someone. Madison saw Mr Booth say something that made Tanya and Shari look in her direction, and now her throat was so tight she couldn't breathe. She didn't want the Booths to take her home! She wanted to go to Sidney's! She wanted her *mum* . . .

'Oh, my.'

Kerry was peering into her face. He was still holding Reuben's hand. Reuben hung back, quiet, staring at Madison with big eyes.

'What's troubling you?' said Kerry. 'Can I help?'

She didn't say anything, but she couldn't help a quick look at the Booths, still waiting by their ute.

'Righty-ho,' said Kerry. 'Leave it with me.'

And he walked over, still holding Reuben's hand, though Madison saw Reuben start to drag his feet as they came up to the ute. Kerry had a quick talk with Mr Booth, who seemed cheerful, but Shari in the front seat poked her tongue out at Reuben. Luckily, he didn't see.

Kerry came back, Reuben skipping along faster now.

'Sorted,' said Kerry. 'I'll drive you both home.'

Madison's knees felt wobbly with relief, but she had to check that it really was OK. She knew her parents always had a lot on their plates, and couldn't easily find time to take her places. That's why she only asked them if there was no one else to drive her.

'Won't that be too far?' said Madison. Her mother always complained that their house was in the back of beyond.

'How very polite and grown-up of you,' Kerry said. 'Let me reassure you that it works for me, too. I've been meaning to drop in on the glass-blowers, who are between your place and Reuben's. Do either of you mind taking a little detour?'

Reuben just stared, but Madison said, 'My mum might be expecting me home.'

'Then I will call and explain. While you two' — he finally let go of Reuben's hand — 'pick up the gear. Last one to finish is a rotten banana.'

When Reuben raced off, Kerry bent down and whispered to Madison, 'Let him win.'

She nodded and smiled, but he hadn't needed to ask. She'd already decided that's what she'd do.

Madison had never been to the glass-blowing studio. She didn't think her parents even knew it was there, even though they had quite a few pieces in the house that her mum called 'art glass'. Oksana had nearly broken an Ann Robinson bowl, but it landed on the carpet and didn't even crack. Oksana seemed to think this meant it wasn't well made. 'Glass should be thin like leaf, not fat like log.'

The glass-blowers were called Nitro and Asphodel, but Madison was too shy to ask if those were their real names. Nitro had dusty brown dreadlocks piled on top of his head and lots of beaded leather thongs up his arms and around his neck. Asphodel had a shaven head but *heaps* of hair under her armpits, which Madison's mum would have *hated*. She wore dungarees with nothing underneath and every so often you could see her boobs.

Nitro had a black t-shirt printed with an A inside a red circle and rainbow baggy pants like a genie would wear.

They didn't mind kids being around, though Madison and Reuben had to stay behind the benches, away from the ovens and the blowing equipment. The studio was an old stable, Asphodel said. She could make them a little glass horse each later, if they had time? Madison was glad to hear Kerry say they had time.

Nitro told them there was a tyre swing under the macrocarpa, and Kerry let them go outside and swing on it. Madison pushed Reuben as high as she could, and twisted him around until he was so dizzy, he had to get off and lie on the ground on his back. Madison lay down next to him.

'That cloud looks like a dinosaur,' she said. 'And *that* one's a dog with pointy ears.'

Reuben scrinched up his eyes, trying to see the cloud shapes.

'This ground is hard, isn't it?' said Madison. 'I wouldn't want to sleep on it.'

Reuben turned his head, blinked at her as if she'd said something weird. Madison wondered what kind of bed he slept on. Maybe his *was* hard as this?

'Batman,' he said.

'Sorry?'

'The cloud.' Reuben pointed.

'Oh. Yes.'

Madison could see a cloud that looked a *bit* like Batman, if she used her imagination.

'Batman smashes the bad guys,' said Reuben. 'Smashes them *dead*.'

Kerry called from the studio door, and they both jumped up. Asphodel was going to make them horses!

She was so quick that Madison could hardly believe what she'd seen. Asphodel held a glowing blob on a stick — molten glass that wobbled like jelly — and then she got these metal tong things and just *pulled* the horse out of the blob! First its little head, and then its mane, and then two front legs at once! Then she twirled it round and pulled some more, and made the back legs and as she knocked it off the stick, she made the tail, which stuck up like a feather. All the time she worked at it, it glowed orange from the fire but as soon as she set it upright on the bench, it was clear.

'Still too hot to touch, though,' Asphodel warned, and placed it in what looked like another oven. 'It'll stay in there overnight and you can pick it up tomorrow, OK?'

Madison felt Kerry's hand on her shoulder. 'I'll pick it up,' he said. 'Don't you fret.'

Asphodel smiled at Reuben. 'And now I'll make *you* one.'

But he shook his head, fast, back and forth. No, no, no.

Asphodel was surprised, looked over at Kerry for help.

'What's the matter, Reuben?' said Kerry. 'Don't you want one?'

A firm shake of his head. No. Wouldn't look at anyone.

Madison put her hand on his back. 'You can share mine, if you like? I'll keep it at my place and you can come and visit it?'

His back was tense right across, his head bent. But he gave a quick nod. OK.

'Nice work,' said Kerry, softly. 'Now, time to get you both home.'

Chapter 26

Kerry

The dusting needed doing. Kerry was aware because Meredith had reminded him once already, and any time now would no doubt be donning the white gloves to run her finger over the mantelpiece. She'd reminded him, too, about the lightbulbs in the hallway, which he'd apparently been promising to replace for twelve days (he doubted it was that long, but she was his boss and so had the final word). Last shopping trip, he'd forgotten to buy milk and toilet paper, which, yes, fair call, were somewhat essential, and he'd cooked macaroni cheese for three lunches in a row, prompting complaints from Jonty, who, now that he was venturing downstairs and even out into the garden, should be perfectly able to cater for his own midday meal. If the man bothered to look, he'd find both an omelette pan and — all right, seemed eggs had also been forgotten on the shopping trip. Kerry made a mental note to make better mental notes. Proper notes on paper he invariably left behind.

Trouble was, his schedule — and hence his brain — was too full. There was so much to do, and *everyone* wanted a piece of his time. Doc Love had persuaded a draughtsman friend to work up his rough sketches for the fish factory space, and Kerry had made the mistake of saying they looked fine without consulting anyone else, which, verily, had brought the wrath of Mac down upon him.

'This is not a dictatorship, bucko,' she said. 'Everyone gets a vote.'

But, of course, finding a meeting date that suited everyone had been impossible, so Kerry had run around like the proverbial fly with the blue-hued rear, showing the drawings to them all individually, and (of course) coming away with seven completely different individual opinions. He decided that the opinions of Mac, Meredith and Doc Love were the ones to take heed of, and if Jacko, Gene and Bernard complained, he'd tell them it was Mac who'd overridden them. Kerry's worst feeling of disloyalty was to Sidney, but she wasn't precious, was she? She'd be happy to go with what she believed was the result of a genuinely collaborative effort.

Then there was old Mr Caracci, owner of the fish factory, who, after saying he had no wish to be involved, had been persuaded by his sons to change his mind. God knows why they'd become suddenly interested, but the Caracci Juniors now wanted a contract drawn up, giving the miniature displays a one-year lease. After that, they would revalue the fish factory and if the fortunes of Gabriel's Bay had improved enough to create a material rise in the property's market value then they reserved the right to boot their tenants out and advertise to potential buyers. The upside was that, for a year at least, they would not charge rent. Oh, and by the way, Mr Caracci Senior was to be ribbon-cutter at the opening, and receive a seat on the board of the charitable trust that had (obviously) been set up to manage the finances.

After a panicked phone call to Sidney for advice, Kerry made an appointment to grovel to Corinna Marshall, who laughed and suggested he make an appointment with her husband and grovel to him. Fortunately, Tai Te Wera proved to be a fine, upstanding human being who said he would donate his services and advise them on establishing a charitable trust, appointing a board and all the other legal hoo-ha that seemed fully unncessary but Tai assured him was Good Practice 101.

'Otherwise,' said Tai, 'you have no proper governance and no financial checks and balances. Someone could skim the profits and you'd be none the wiser.'

Privately, Kerry doubted there'd be any profits worth skimming, but he thanked Tai profusely and complimented him on the fine tailoring of his suit.

As Kerry was leaving, Tai said, 'I assume you've consulted with the local iwi? They're bound to feel they have a stake in this project.'

Kerry's hand tightened on the doorframe. 'I've talked to your wife,' he said. 'Does that qualify as consultation?'

Tai pursed his mouth. Kerry suspected him of trying to conceal a smile.

'It's certainly a good start,' said Tai. 'But you *might* need to go wider than that.'

'And, er, how would I go about it?' said Kerry. 'To date my only formal interaction with indigenous people has been with customs officials in Dar es Salaam. And that, so they claimed, was strictly routine.'

Tai was smiling openly now. 'Would you like me to make some calls?'

'That would be terrific,' said Kerry. 'And if you could come, too, and do all the talking, that'd top it off perfectly.'

Kerry couldn't say he'd understood much of what had been discussed in yet another extensive series of meetings, but according to Tai and Devon, who'd also helped out, the iwi had apparently agreed to support the project. A few conditions, of course. (Of course.) They, too, must have a representative on the board, and the war-game display must include a re-creation of the area's famous battle, in which the local tribe had, legend had it, given an invading tribe such a comprehensive drubbing that their enemies had been too cowed ever to return. Given the pre-European timing of the battle, Kerry doubted that tanks had been involved. But he was sure Doc Love would make an exception. Fairly sure, anyway.

At the last iwi consulation meeting, a terrifyingly competent woman in power-company management had asked, 'What's your marketing strategy?' Kerry hoped he'd sounded convincing when he'd replied that it was in development. That evening, at the Boat Shed after a well-earned beer, he'd asked, 'How does one go about developing a marketing strategy? What even *is* a marketing strategy?'

'It's how we advertise and promote our attraction to people,' said Sidney. 'Don't know how, but that's the idea.'

'And you've landed squarely on our first problem right there,' said Kerry. '"Our attraction" doesn't even have a name yet.'

'Tiny Town,' said Gene. 'Short, easy to remember.'

'Doesn't that sound a bit Enid Blyton-ish?' said Kerry.

'Better than Models Galore,' said Gene. 'That was Aggie Robotham's contribution.'

'You'd have to be careful Googling that one,' said Sidney. 'You might end up married to someone called Tatanya.'

'Smallville,' called Jacko from the kitchen.

'Think you'll find DC Comics owns that,' said Devon. 'You'll have to prise it out of Superman's cold, dead hands.'

'Littleville, then, for Pete's sake.'

'Wasn't that a kids' TV show in the seventies?' said Gene.

'Lidsville,' said Mac. 'Giant talking hats. Flying hippies.'

'No, the fools with wings were the Bugaloos,' said Gene. 'It's all coming back to me.'

Devon shook his head in disbelief. 'Was this, like, televised acid trips for kids?'

'Don't get us started on Pufinstuf,' said Mac. 'It's a wonder we stayed sober as long as we did.'

'I quite like Littleville,' said Sidney.

'It's a town in Alabama,' said Kerry, who'd searched on his phone. 'And an Indian preschool franchise. Doubt either of those will sue us. In saying that, it *is* Alabama.'

'What's Māori for "little", Dev?' said Gene.

'Iti.'

'Iti-ville?' said Gene. 'Iti Town? Iti Pā? Papaete? Come on, work with me here.'

'Littleville's still my frontrunner,' said Sidney.

'Little Town?' said Kerry.

'Want to pick a fight with Lyttelton?' said Mac.

'Depends,' said Kerry. 'Are they scarier than Alabama?'

'Littleville!' Jacko slapped a whole fish onto the kitchen bench. 'Stop messing about!'

'The mayor has spoken,' said Gene. 'All in favour?'

'Aye,' they all said.

'Step one towards a marketing strategy,' said Kerry. 'And I suppose we could use the Gabriel's Bay website to promote it.'

'What website?' said everyone.

He brought it up on his phone. Everyone clustered around to see. Everyone laughed.

'*Last updated 1998*,' Gene read from the bottom of the home page.

'Oh,' said Kerry. 'I missed that bit. Does Google not have quality control?'

'Google doesn't actually *own* the internet,' said Devon. 'OK, no, maybe they do. But they don't give a toss what's on it.'

'Models Galore,' said Gene, with a nod.

'The more the merrier.' Sidney raised her glass. 'To Littleville! And, as the Young Communists used to say with nary a hint of irony: To the success of the scheduled tasks!'

Fortunately, Littleville had been well received by the project's supporters, mainly, Kerry suspected, because it was Jacko's idea and he was scarier than Alabama and Lyttelton combined.

Still, it was a win, and Kerry needed those for morale in his struggle to complete his seemingly endless scheduled tasks. For every item he ticked off another two took its place, like a flow-chart Hydra. As well as consulting with every man and his dog about the layout for the space (yes, King did get a look), dealing with the Caraccis' offer he could not refuse, signing trust paperwork, attending meeting after meeting with iwi (which mostly consisted of sitting beside Tai and Devon and smiling a lot), there'd been a queue of artisans beating down his door. Word had got round that Gabriel's Bay was creating a showcase for their work, but the salient point about it being in miniature had been lost. Kerry had to disappoint a man who made sculptures from rusted cars, multiple crafters of sandstone garden statuary, a group who wrapped trees in knitting, and a travelling circus. Everyone else, he took names and contact details of those who were not off-grid and promised to get back to them.

And then there was Bernard, who had gone from being a 'supply me with evidence' sceptic to a fervent evangelist for the project. Kerry had no idea what had turned him, but every time Bernard came to see Jonty, he collared Kerry and grilled him about his progress. Bernard had his own list of tasks for Kerry, and became generally aggrieved when he discovered how much on that list Kerry had not yet done. Bernard's biggest bugbear was Elaine, and he insisted the only way to thwart her was for Kerry to suck up to the Hampton District Council.

'You must get in front of the mayor,' said Bernard, 'and the councillors who are likely to warm to our project — I can supply you with names. Build up a big enough base of support and any attempts to derail us will be themselves derailed.'

'And why can't *you* talk to them?' Kerry said.

'Because the Progressive Association has had cause in the past to take the council to task,' said Bernard. 'Perfectly justifiably, I might add. But grudges may have been formed. I think they'd be more amenable to an approach from a . . . a fresh face.'

Instead of your beardy, speccy old one. Kerry immediately retracted the thought as uncharitable. Bernard meant well, and it was good, yes, relatively, that they had him on side. But they'd not yet heard a dicky-bird from the dreaded Elaine, and in Kerry's opinion that meant she was stuck for ideas. Kerry was frantic enough right now. Until there was cause to worry, the council could wait.

He was doing his best, he really was, but things kept falling off, like green bottles from a wall. He'd had to cancel this week's football coaching, which caused Aidan to act up to the point where Sidney had to cut her tutoring session short, and waive her fee. Kerry offered to reimburse her, which had made her even more cross. She reminded him that these were kids he'd committed to, just in case, he supposed, he'd mistaken them for sentient plant-life with bad spatial awareness. He apologised, promised to do better, all the while wishing she would be more understanding. Sense encouraged him to refrain from telling her how much he had on his plate because, as sense pointed out, he'd been juggling multiple responsibilities for a matter of weeks and Sidney had been doing it for close to ten straight years.

And, to be fair, she hadn't been on his case about not spending enough time with her. Not that there was actually any chance of being in each other's pockets, thanks to a dearth of available evenings, and locations conducive to intimacy.

Mac babysat the boys when Sidney worked at the Boat Shed, but after being on her feet and smiling at people for hours, all Sidney wanted to do was crawl into bed — 'alone'. But then she'd been reluctant to do anything if the boys were in the house. 'It's not that I think they'll be traumatised,' she said. 'More that *we* will be if they point and laugh.' That left their respective vehicles — 'Ha, ha, no,' said Sidney, 'I hated it even when I *was* seventeen and desperate' — or his sleep-out on Meredith's property. But *that* meant sneaking past the main house, plus organising and paying babysitters and more sneaking to drop Sidney home by eleven. The result being that they'd had three nights together in two weeks, and now that she was miffed about the cancelled football session it seemed prudent to wait for her to arrange the next one.

Kerry checked his phone. No text from Sidney, but he saw one from his mother that he'd completely forgotten about. 'YOU DEAD???!!' it said. He'd been politely rebuffing the travelling circus when it arrived, so hadn't replied. That was two days ago. She may well now be weeping in an aeroplane seat, winging her way to reclaim her only son's body. He texted back: 'Am OK. V busy. Will call soon.'

Soon was probably overstating it, but at least she knew he wasn't laid out on a slab.

Jehoshaphat! It was nearly midday! He hadn't started lunch, and had, in fact, no idea what he intended to cook. Something that did not require eggs or milk, obviously, so on the plus side that put a fourth day of macaroni cheese out of the question. And he still hadn't done the dusting. Better hop to it.

The phone rang as he was running a damp cloth under the armpits of two cherubs atop an ormolu clock. Meredith had said she'd be in her study, doing an inventory on her doll's house contents, so Kerry waited for her to answer. The phone continued to ring. Jonty's voice floated mellifluously down from the upper floor.

'Will someone *pick up that infernal machine*?'

'Barton residence,' said Kerry, while his mind wafted curses upwards.

'Are you the only one there these days?'

Sophie.

'What did you do with the wrinklies?' she said. 'Bury them in the garden or brick them up behind a wall? The latter would be my preferred option. Especially if they were still alive beforehand.'

'Answering the telephone is my job,' said Kerry. 'Apparently.'

'I hear the old sod is up and about again,' said Sophie. 'Mother wrote me a letter. Thought I'd like to be *informed*.'

'Well, it will be a longish haul until he's back to his old self,' said Kerry, 'but there's been progress, yes.'

'Christ,' said Sophie. 'You say "his old self" as if that's a desirable goal.'

Did she vent only to him, Kerry wondered? Or was this her usual modus operandi? In which case, she must burn through friends like extra-spicy vindaloo.

'Anyway, I didn't call to talk to them,' she said.

'Oh?'

'Yeah, well, I'm sure you're *really* busy.' She'd retained that teenage ability to make a request sound like a declaration of war. 'But my show's opening is next week, so you know . . .'

The list Hydra grew yet another head. How could he say no, when she'd rung specially to invite a person she'd never even met? His theory that she burned through friends was gathering evidence. Was it possible he was the only person in the entire country with who she was still on speaking terms?

'Thank you,' said Kerry. 'I'd very much like to come. May I bring a plus one?'

'Girlfriend?'

'Not entirely sure at this juncture.'

'Anyone I know?'

If Sophie's views on his choice of romantic partner were negative — and what were the odds? — Kerry would rather not hear them.

'Discretion is my watchword,' he said. 'Early days and all.'

'OK, well, whatever. You can always keep me *informed*.'

Dear Lord, she was hard work. And while he could have empathy for her — Jonty was hardly his top pick for Father of the Year — he was a little tired of being a go-between. She needed to grow up and bridge the gap with her parents.

'Sophie, why don't you come and visit while your show's on?' he said. 'I'll provide lunch for us all. Or high tea. Or something.'

He could hear the doubt vibrating down the line.

'It's true that I lack several of Nigella Lawson's outstanding qualifications,' he said, 'but I can put tea and biscuits on a tray.'

Given his recent record, that wasn't entirely true. But his catering credentials weren't her problem.

'By "us all" you mean them, too?' she said.

'Why not?' Kerry said. 'I'll be there. Don't you think it's about time?'

'Who are you? Clarence the Christmas angel?'

'More Harvey the Invisible Rabbit, I'd say. Though not as tall.'

Pause. Kerry could hear the ormolu clock ticking away the minutes until the lunch that didn't yet exist.

'I'll think about it,' said Sophie, and hung up.

'And goodbye to you,' said Kerry to the air.

Twelve forty-five. Dusting would have to pause. What was there in the kitchen? One onion, a centimetre of hard cheese and two crusts.

And, right at the back of the cupboard, a packet of mushroom soup!

Sorted.

Chapter 27

Mac

Mac had three criteria that would rule young Doctor Ghadavi instantly out of contention. One: if he mentioned *Lord of the Rings*. Two: if he used the word 'wellness'. Three: if he seemed under the impression that Gabriel's Bay was populated by cheerful, humble folk who, gosh darn it, rubbed along together best they could.

She was self-aware enough to know that playing Elimination Bingo was a defensive strategy; a way of proving her heartfelt belief that no one could come close to Doc Love. She also knew any success would be a Pyrrhic victory that would set her right back to the next best contender, who was still, Lord love her, Mrs Joyce Zuma.

Maybe she'd allow him one black mark? All right, he could get away with a glancing reference to *Lord of the Rings*. But if he showed *any* familiarity with its plotlines, then she'd be doing him a service by keeping him away. New Zealand didn't need any more tourists who couldn't look at a spectacular mountain scene without feeling it would be improved by the addition of orcs.

The Skype interview was booked for one p.m., which, Mac calculated, was midnight UK time. Too bad. If he lacked stamina to pull all-nighters, he'd be useless as a GP.

Doc Love had declined to participate. 'No point,' he said. 'As you know, I have always ultimately deferred to your judgement.'

Besides, he was out this afternoon on emergency house calls. Evan Olsen claimed he'd broken his toe by accidentally kicking the refrigerator door, and was lying like a cast sheep on his couch. Mac fancied a cattle prod would get him up, but luckily for Evan she wasn't the one making the visit. She had more sympathy for Ed Tahana, who'd been in bad shape lately. Unlike chain-smoker Ngaire, Ed's lung disease was none of his doing, and the poor sod was so incapacitated now he couldn't do much more than sit at home in the living room. His poor lad, too — Ed could barely change his clothes, bathe or eat unless Barrett helped him. Mac knew that Doc Love had suggested respite care but that Barrett had refused. He said he wasn't going to make his father feel like a burden.

Barrett had come to fix the surgery security alarm last Friday afternoon. He seemed a bit distracted, dropped a screwdriver that skittered under Mac's desk. After bending to retrieve it, Mac had asked how he was doing.

'Fine,' he said. 'A lot to juggle right now. But I'm keeping on top of things.'

He'd pressed on the screwdriver's edge with a fingertip, hard enough to raise a red mark on his skin.

'You OK for money?' said Mac. 'Got enough for the bills, mortgage payments?'

Barrett had smiled at her. He was a handsome lad all right. Should be dating pretty girls and enjoying being young. But life wasn't fair, and there was no point railing against that. Life would only kick you in the arse even harder.

'I'm doing what needs to be done,' he told her.

'I'll assume that's a positive,' said Mac. 'Remember you've got support here whenever you need it.'

'Thank you.'

His face softened, and, for a moment, he'd looked about five years old. Then handsome, smiling Barrett was back, drumming the screwdriver against his palm with a jaunty beat.

'Better get on,' he said. 'That alarm won't fix itself.'

But as he was leaving, he'd paused in the doorway. 'Thank you for asking after me, Mrs Reid. Most people don't.'

No, they don't, thought Mac. Because ignorance is bliss. Don't look, don't listen and you won't be confronted by unpalatable truths. You won't feel obliged to step up.

Two minutes to one. Mac opened up Skype and waited. A burble, a pop, a face. Show-time.

'Mrs Reid?'

Ashwin Ghadavi was slim-faced and anxious-looking. Excellent bone structure and nice eyes, too, Mac noted. But no prizes for pretty.

'That's me.'

'Good day to you!'

Mac nodded. Silence, in her experience, was an effective tactic, as most people felt compelled to fill the space. What this young man chose to fill it with would determine his immediate future.

She saw his Adam's apple bob with a nervous swallow, and ratcheted her expectations down another notch.

'Thank you for considering my application,' said Ashwin. 'I know it might seem unusual for someone in my situation to make such a — let's say left-field — career move. But let me assure you that I have given it a great deal of thought. In Britain, I have had many wonderful opportunities, but I find my temporary home a country of strange repressions and circumlocutory modes of speech. No one ever says precisely what he or she means. I give you an example: "When you have a moment" does not mean, as it implies, "Please do this when convenient". It means, "Do it this instant". "Quite good" means exactly the opposite!'

He paused for a quick breath, carried right on.

'Now, I know that some consider my country's manner of communication in the English language to be equally long-winded, which one *could* blame on our prolonged period of British colonisation. But the difference is that we understand each other perfectly! There is no attempt to deceive! And that is what attracts me to your country — your directness, your open and plain manner. Australia, too, is known for its unvarnished speech, but having conducted research in several London pubs, I feel that it borders on harsh. New Zealanders, in my experience, are less free with the stinging rebarb.'

Mac had to press her lips together to prevent a smile. The young man was clearly a fruitcake, but he had an earnest appeal. And who wanted strait-laced, anyway? All the best people had quirks.

'Mrs Reid, I am sure you are thinking that this is a foolish complaint, childish even, and that would be a fair accusation.'

Ashwin may have taken her lack of reponse as disapproval. More likely, he hadn't noticed it at all, having, Mac suspected, prepared and rehearsed this speech for days.

'So may I emphasise,' he continued, 'that it is not my only reason for wanting to move to your country—'

The next one better not be anything to do with ringwraiths.

'I wish to make a difference to a small community,' said Ashwin. 'In India, I grew up in a large city, and I have completed my training in an even larger one. Here in London, it is hard to know your neighbour, or even your flatmate, who plays in some kind of trip-hop band that performs to an erractic schedule, and of whom sometimes the only trace is the lid left off the Horlicks Original Malt Drink and a ring around the bath.'

Mac had to look up at the ceiling and take a deep breath. She must not laugh. That'd be fatal.

'I know you are asking, Mrs Reid: what about the famed British countryside?'

On top of his many other skills, a mind-reader.

'It is true, there are many delightful villages, with historic churches and tea shops,' said Ashwin. 'But although, as I say, I do appreciate the opportunities this fine country has given me, I am almost ashamed to admit that I do not see the charm of these places. They are too safe. Established. Socially regimented. And there is, if you'll excuse my French, bugger all to do.'

He took Mac's raised eyebrows as encouragement to continue. Though she guessed he'd have pressed on even if a hooded assailant had crept up and started strangling her from behind.

'I very much enjoy rock climbing,' he informed her. 'Also kayaking and hiking, which I gather you call tramping. I am adept with a camp stove. Keen also on surfing, though I am not at all adept at that. I would like to learn to sail, and to hunt wild game. I have heard that there are deer, chamois and even moose in your woods, which I gather you call the bush.'

'You won't find moose,' said Mac. 'None spotted since the nineteen fifties.'

'Doesn't mean they are not there! Your bush, I gather, is very dense.'

A widening of eyes signalled he'd recollected his original point.

'And your town, while surrounded by natural wonder, is exactly the kind of small community in which I would like to work.'

OK, here it came: cheerful, humble folk time.

'Please don't mistake my enthusiasm for naïvety, Mrs Reid,' said Ashwin.

Maybe he *was* a mind-reader?

'I am not expecting some bucolic idyll, where everyone is rosy-cheeked and salt of the earth. Hoedowns in the barn and all that.'

Ashwin leaned in to the screen. Mac resisted a strong urge to mimic him, brought on by not knowing quite what he was going to say. Doc Love was like that, too. Kept you guessing.

'I know there will be drug addicts and alcoholics, and criminal behaviour. There will be difficult patients who refuse to heed advice, and patients who are abusive and ungrateful. I have seen and dealt with all of this — you may phone any of my references to check.'

There were references? Mac realised she'd been so thrilled to get a half-decent applicant, she'd forgotten to do her due diligence.

'I have taken up a lot of your time,' came the young man's voice across the miles. 'And spoken for too long, an unfortunate trait that comes to the fore when I am nervous, though I assure you I am never nervous on the job. Do you have anything to ask me? I am sure you must have.'

An almost plaintive tone. Questions meant she might still be interested. None meant she'd decided against him. He really did want this job, didn't he?

So — *was* she interested? Should she consider hiring Ashwin Ghadavi?

'It'd be your responsibility to get proper work status,' she said.

'Of course.'

'And find a place to live.'

'I'll make immediate enquiries.'

'Start date's not until next year. End of February.'

'That would give me ample time to get my affairs in order here.'

'I *will* check your references.'

'I'd expect nothing less.'

He was smiling. Mac felt like smiling, too. Why, for Pete's sake? He was too young, too inexperienced, and a garrulous fruitcake who wanted to hunt non-existent moose.

'I'll email you the draft employment agreement,' she said.

Doc Love was due back at five. Mac used the absence of appointments to do the usual tasks of bookkeeping, filing and magazine cull. Occasionally, she also disinfected the toys. Not often. It was good to build up children's immunity.

She sorted the mail. The usual bills, waste-of-time marketing bumf from drug companies, begging letters from charities, and fat envelopes congratulating her on the prize she'd already won ('Guaranteed!'). This month's free copies of a healthy-eating magazine that no one in the surgery even glanced at, let alone took home.

What was this one? An envelope in a particularly repellent shade of light purple and scented — Mac sniffed — with a hint of lavender. Had Sheila Swanson finally given in to her urges and sent Doc Love a proposal?

Oh well, if she wanted her communication to be private, she should have sent it to his house.

Mac read the letter. Read it again. Picked up the phone. Dialled Sidney's mobile.

'Elaine,' was all she said.

'Let me guess,' said Sidney. 'She's changed her mind about Littleville and intends to make a massive donation?'

'How about she's just given us a heads up, on her own personal stationery no less, that the district council is about to send us forty thousand consents that we'll need to apply for.'

'Such as?'

'Resource, building, health and safety, approval for use of sensitive land—'

'"Sensitive" as in easily hurt by an offhand remark?'

'Probably. In fact, I suspect they'll all be spurious, but that's beside the point,' said Mac. 'Officialdom is about to dump a giant steaming pile of bureaucracy on top of us, and even if we could find some poor sod to labour through endless applications, we can't afford the fees. Elaine's letter — a health hazard in itself with this amount of scent — helpfully lists them all. The total, underlined just in case we're blind imbeciles, is in the thousands.'

'But surely no one else has to jump through this many hoops?' said Sidney. 'Otherwise there'd be no tourist attractions at all.'

'No, I think we're the lucky targets of Elaine's special blend of vindictiveness and self-importance,' said Mac. 'I blame Bernard. He should have stayed mum about his allegiance and worked against her from the inside.'

'Does Kerry know?' said Sidney.

'No idea,' said Mac. 'But I wouldn't put it past Elaine to prolong her glee and write to all of us individually. Have you checked your letterbox today?'

'Not something I rush to do.'

Sidney's phone went ping.

'A text from Kerry,' she said. 'With many exclamation marks.' Another ping. 'Oh, and one from Gene, with — hmm, a *very* bad word and an emoji I suspect is not standard issue. Seems your instincts were spot on about the prolonged glee. Gosh, she's quite evil, isn't she?'

'Nothing a stake through the eyeball won't fix,' said Mac.

'Group meeting tonight at the Boat Shed?' said Sidney. 'I'll have to bring the boys.'

Mac sighed. 'I suppose we'd better get onto it,' she said. 'But everyone better appreciate the personal sacrifice I'm making.'

'Heavens, yes, how could I forget?' said Sidney. 'Don't worry, Gene has Sky. I'll make sure he records *Project Runway.*'

Chapter 28

Bernard

'That's the eternal dilemma with "I told you so",' said Patricia over the breakfast table. 'On the one hand, you're quite correct — you *did* tell them. But on the other, the damage is done, and crowing won't help fix it.'

'And at least young Macfarlane took full responsibility for not heeding my advice,' said Bernard. 'Though I find his explanation that he believed "all she'd do is harrumph" somewhat flimsy.'

'He doesn't know Elaine like you do,' said Patricia. 'My goodness, she certainly will be "Elated" now.'

She began to butter toast in her habitual slow, deliberate way. Normally, Bernard found it soothing. This morning, it irritated him. But then, to be fair, he had been irritable ever since Elaine had played her black hand, disguised as it was in a lavender-scented glove. The meeting yesterday evening at the Boat Shed had done nothing to alleviate his mood.

'Why does she want to cause us all this trouble?' young Macfarlane had asked.

'Because she feels personally affronted,' said Mac Reid. 'Which is, of course, all Bernard's fault.'

Bernard had tried not to huff indignantly, and failed. 'I *do* not see how—'

'You threw off the shackles,' said Mac Reid. 'The pink fluffy manacles of oppression.'

She patted him patronisingly on the arm.

'Elaine prefers her creatures completely docile. You went from neutered lap-dog to rat-catcher before her eyes.'

Back-handed as it was, Bernard decided to accept the compliment.

'Right, so now we've got the recriminations out of the way,' said Sidney Gillespie, who'd been struggling to find distractions for her surely abnormally active sons, 'how do we come up with a brilliant plan?'

But all the ideas put forward had been either impractical or imbecilic, leading to more recriminations and the meeting's early end. Bernard had returned home and lain awake for some hours, muttering.

'I'm driving into Hampton later this morning,' said Patricia. 'Would you like to come with me? We could have lunch at the Kozy Kettle. Or we could splash out at one of the vineyards?'

'You know I'm visiting Woodhall this afternoon,' said Bernard, more snappishly than he'd intended.

'Ah.' Patricia nodded. 'Yes, of course. And how is Jonty coming along? Is he improving?'

How to answer? Jonty was out of bed now during the day — he and Bernard met in his study — and had even begun to make calls to his former colleagues and clients, slowly reconnecting to the wider world. He had firm opinions on every subject Bernard raised, and did not care much to listen to Bernard's own, overriding and interrupting, sometimes giving Bernard only enough time to open his mouth. ('His Master's Voice', Patricia had once called him.) So in one sense of the word, yes, Jonty was improving. But he was also returning to form as an arrogant, patronising man with a streak of coldness and cruelty that most people mistakenly praised as astute ruthlessness. Every visit, Bernard remembered more about why he loathed him.

'Jonty is making great strides,' he replied shortly.

Patricia spooned the teabag out of her cup and dropped it onto the saucer. It was another of her habits that grated on Bernard. One, why use teabags at all when quality loose-leaf tea was readily available, and two, how could she tolerate it being that strong? The milk — put in after not before; Verity Weston would radiate scorn — barely altered the colour at all. It looked like a tanner was about to toss in a piece of raw hide.

Patricia took a sip. 'Meredith must be pleased.'

That seemingly innocuous comment stabbed Bernard's heart like an assassin's stiletto. Over these past weeks, he had become used to taking tea with Meredith after his visits with Jonty. They were always alone. Boosted by an hour of patronising Bernard, Jonty would be eager to pick up the phone and patronise others. And young Macfarlane was out, too. Meredith had generously given him time off each afternoon so he could do whatever it was he claimed he did. Waste time and energy, in Bernard's opinion.

Though their talk had initially been formal, courteous, about inconsequential matters, they'd lately begun to regain some of the easy intimacy they'd had when young. Meredith began to make confessions to him — she felt guilty for not seeking help earlier for her husband, and regretted deeply the rift with Sophie, while struggling to see how it could be mended. She'd looked so unhappy, Bernard had ached to reach out and take her hand. A fear that even that slight physical contact might be his undoing prevented him, and so he comforted and reassured her as best he could.

Last week, she'd told him that she suspected her grief over Nicola's death had been more intense than she'd realised at the time, and while her husband had retreated from the world in dramatic fashion, Meredith had more quietly, but perhaps as comprehensively, withdrawn.

'I locked myself away with my little house,' she said. 'Or lost myself in a far corner of the garden. Oh, yes, I still popped into town, still spoke to people, but I did all that on autopilot; I was never truly present. In fact, it's only now that I feel I'm beginning to reclaim who I was, as if Jonty's own recovery has given me permission.'

Then she'd smiled at him, reached out and placed her hand on his. 'And I — we — have you to thank for that, Bernard. Your generosity and thoughtfulness has brought us back to ourselves — and each other.'

Bernard had been pierced by the irony. His gallant offer to help, made rashly and only because it gave him a reason to be near Meredith, had been too effective. He had revived his rival — and returned him to his wife. The faint hope he'd harboured of proving his worth to Meredith, of making the case he should have made on that decades-ago Christmas Eve, was dashed like the infant prince from the walls of Troy. And now, he was caught. His visits to Jonty were expected, welcomed even, and he had no good reason to call a halt. Yet the pain of Meredith's presence would be worse than ever. It was no wonder he was irritable. Disappointment, regret, humiliation, not to mention visions of a preening Elaine, plagued him hourly. It was too much, it really was!

Of all this Patricia had reminded him — and right at that moment, he could not forgive her.

'How can you *possibly* know whether Meredith's pleased or not?' he accused her. 'When have you ever taken more than a superficial interest in her life?'

His wife's eyes brimmed with hurt, but Bernard's anger extinguished the small flicker of guilt. He threw his napkin onto the breakfast table, not caring if it landed on his toast and preserves.

'I am going out,' he informed her. 'I cannot say when I will be back.'

He took his car keys and jacket from the hallway, and shut the door firmly behind him. At the end of his driveway, he indicated to turn right, towards Gabriel's Bay. Changed his mind and turned left. Towards Woodhall.

It was time to be honest with Meredith. To tell her how he felt. He knew it would change nothing — she was Jonty's, always would be. But he could bear no longer the weight of this secret. He'd carried it for too many years.

The wash of relief that he was about to finally unburden himself doused his anger. And as that emotion subsided, conscience rose to fill the gap. Patricia. He'd treated her very badly, he knew that. There was no excuse for his outburst, and as soon as he'd talked with Meredith, he would return home to apologise. He hoped Patricia would remember that in all their years of marriage he'd never lost his temper with her to that extent. It was a one-off, the result of an unusually high level of provocation.

Yes, of course she would forgive him. She was generous and kind, and could never hold a grudge. He would stop off and buy her some flowers on his way home. Perhaps some chocolates also. He was *fairly* sure Patricia liked chocolate.

As he knocked on Woodhall's front door, he braced himself to be greeted by young Macfarlane. But it was Meredith who opened up. Her brown eyes widened briefly, but she was too well-bred to show surprise.

'Bernard,' she said. 'Did you arrange an earlier visit with Jonty?'

'No,' he replied, and girded himself. 'It's you I came to see.'

'Then come into the kitchen,' she said, 'and I'll make a pot of tea.'

Sitting at the table while Meredith prepared the tea, Bernard recalled how much he'd enjoyed his childhood time in Woodhall's kitchen. Unlike his own mother, Meredith's refused to hire a cook, and when she had people around for dinner, they more usually ate around this big rimu table than in the rarely used dining room. 'It's cosier,' Meredith's mother said, and it was. Warm, welcoming and redolent with the best smells, fresh-baked bread and biscuits, lemons, coffee and, later in the day, bubbling casseroles. The kitchen of his childhood home was a place his mother rarely frequented, but that was its only merit. The cook did not like young people — or any people for that matter. Or cooking, when it came down to it.

'Oh, *really*.'

Meredith shut the refrigerator with an irritated thud.

'I'm afraid there's no milk,' she said. 'Again.'

'I prefer my tea black,' said Bernard.

'And I do not,' said Meredith. 'But it seems I have no choice.'

'Master Macfarlane being a little derelict in his duties?'

'A little, yes.'

'He's not here?'

'No,' said Meredith, with a hint of heaviness. 'I gave him time off to consult with the project's lawyer, who could not, apparently, see him later in the day.'

Meredith assembled cups, sugar and teapot on the table, and took a seat at the head, so that Bernard was on her immediate left. He tried not to be aware of her physical presence. His hold on his nerve was shaky enough as it was.

She poured a cup for Bernard and then for herself.

'I'm too soft, that's my trouble,' she said. 'Too susceptible to enthusiasm and boyish charm.'

Bernard's disdain for young Macfarlane became a more complicated emotion. But he mustn't let that distract him, either. Meredith was eyeing him with calm expectancy. His moment had come.

'Meredith,' he began — and was immediately tongue-tied.

He could feel a blush rising, too, which only compounded matters. All he needed now was for Jonty to appear and demand to talk to him about the T20 cricket tournament, which Jonty considered an abomination and Bernard quite enjoyed.

'Bernard.' The voice of beauty spoke softly. 'I think I know what you wish to tell me.'

Please God let that not be true. That she'd known — and pitied him — all this time.

'You don't actually enjoy these visits with Jonty, do you?'

Insight of a different, and fortunately more manageable, kind.

'What makes you think that?' he said.

'Because I know him,' she replied. 'And I know you. You are not kindred spirits.'

'That doesn't mean we can't be civil to one another.'

'Of course not. But being civil is not the same as being friendly, is it?'

Bernard was unsure what response she intended him to make. Perhaps he should simply ignore the question, seize control of the conversation and say what he came to say?

Meredith was waiting. She wore her usual white shirt and tailored navy trousers, and for the millionth time, he marvelled at how she could invest even the plainest of attire with a matchless style. Patricia did her best, he knew, and always looked tidy and appropriate, but—

Guilt. And more than that. Shame. *Burning* shame.

How *could* he have treated Patricia like that? Kind, loving, gentle Patricia who had stood by him all these years — to have raised his voice in anger to her was unpardonable. And how *dare* he compare her unfavourably to Meredith, when she possessed so *many* fine qualities? Loyalty, generosity, compassion — his wife's character was outstanding. And here he was, about to commit the greatest act of treachery in his married life — confessing his adoration of another woman. He was a monster, a beast, an abject failure of a husband. He needed to leave here immediately, race home and beg Patricia to forgive him.

'Yes,' he said to Meredith. 'You're quite correct. I am not and never will be friendly with Jonty. I came to request that we call a halt to my visits. I trust that Jonty has other acquaintances who might be better suited to his company. Of course, I'm prepared to tell him directly—'

'No need. I'll inform Jonty.'

Meredith's manner was cool, formal, as if the previous week's growing intimacy had never happened. Bernard felt the loss of connection acutely but knew it had to be done. For the sake of his sanity — and his marriage.

'Thank you,' he said.

She rose. He was dismissed. He departed through the front door as swiftly as he could without actually breaking into a run. He exceeded the speed limit on the eighty-kilometres-an-hour stretch to home.

But Patricia's car was not in the driveway when he returned. He'd missed her — she'd gone to Hampton. He rang her mobile phone but it went through to voicemail. The urge to turn his car around immediately and drive to find her almost won, but having left his tea untouched, he was now expiring from thirst. He would have a glass of water, and then he would head over the hill.

On the hall table, he saw what must be the day's post, unopened. Usually, Patricia managed their household affairs with maximum efficiency, sorting the mail and placing any letters he needed to see on his library desk, topped with an explanatory Post-It note. On the Post-It accompanying Elaine's recent missive, Patricia had roughly drawn a poison bottle label complete with skull and crossbones, which had brought a smile to Bernard's face.

But as he looked closer, instead of a pile of mail, he saw a single plain white envelope with only his first name on it. Inside, he found a short letter that he would, over the long coming hours, re-read many times, as if the message within might have changed since he last looked.

Patricia had left him. She apologised for not letting him know in person, but had been too afraid that she'd lose her nerve.

'*I feel cowardly enough for doing this,*' she wrote. '*Working up to it, I changed my mind a thousand times. I interrogated and berated myself — I was overreacting, I could change how I felt if only I made more of an effort. I could change* us, *how we were. But this morning, I knew I had no hope of changing anything. I would forever more have to accept roses of shadow, accept that you reserved your true rose for someone else . . .*'

Bernard had no idea his wife had such a poetic soul.

The note went on to tell him that she had taken her car, a minimum amount of clothing and a credit card that she trusted he would not object to her using until she got on her feet financially.

He was not to worry about her safety, or to feel that she bore him any ill will. She had been letting herself live a half-life, and now it was time for her to take control.

She would be incommunicado for three weeks, and then she would telephone, and they could discuss the future.

She signed the letter '*Yours*'.

Bernard sat up in his library until after midnight. All his life, the presence of books had given him solace, reassurance. Their stories sang through wires, hummed all around him, alive, potent, transformative.

He sat among his books and heard nothing but silence, as if they, too, had departed. He did not, as he normally would, pick one out to read, but left them be. For he could not shake the strong conviction that if he opened a book now, any book, he'd find nothing inside but white, blank pages.

Chapter 29

Sidney

Mr Phipps told Sidney that the warm spring meant the bees might start producing honey any minute, instead of around Christmas as was usual for this part of the country. The honey was what some might call a paddock blend, the main floral source for the bees being clover, thistle and blackberry. But there was also a hint of the bush in there, mānuka, cabbage tree and the rewarewa from which it probably got its darker colour. Mr Phipps reckoned there was a bit of coastal kānuka, too, though Sidney could not for the life of her distinguish it in the taste.

Mr Phipps stirred honey into his mug of black tea, and added a squeeze of lemon. Sidney had tried it, but preferred to stick with a dash of milk. She was, however, entirely happy to melt a knob of butter with the honey in a saucepan and pour it liberally onto hot toasted crumpets. Terrible for her waistline, delicious beyond measure. It always amazed her how something so simple as tea, crumpets and honey could be so comforting and sustaining. You felt as if you ought to glow afterwards, like some kind of heavenly being.

'Crumpet?' She offered the warm stack to Mr Phipps.

He slid one onto his plate, let her pour a stream of gold on top.

Sidney sat down at Mr Phipps's battered old Formica table, once green with white speckles, now a kind of khaki. The chairs matched in that they and the table had once been a set, but were worn to shreds now, holes covered with stitched patches (Mary, probably) or duct tape (Mr Phipps, definitely). But no matter how old everything was in his kitchen — Sidney fancied the copper and brass coffee pot had seen service at the Battle of Fort Ticonderoga — it was scrupulously clean. The wooden floor was swept daily, the old wood-burning range kept blacked and polished, the tea towels laundered and pressed. It was also the sunniest room in the house, which had been built in the late 1800s and only marginally modernised. Victorians did not like sun fading their grimly vegetative upholstery and dour family portraits, so they angled their houses to ensure the sun cooked the servants instead. Sun streamed right now through the open back door and large windows, warming Sidney's back. She resisted the urge to lay her head on the table and snooze.

A solid morning's work around the hives followed by tea and crumpets, or sometimes her own fresh-baked scones, was one of Sidney's real pleasures. Beekeeping, to her, felt productive, planned and systematic — the polar opposite of mothering, with all its surprises and unplanned detours and on-the-spot problem-solving. She reminded herself that bees were creatures of habit, programmed by years of evolution to follow the same routine, whereas her sons were individuals, each one intent on forging his own path in his own way. And she did not love the bees, had no relationship with them whatsoever. If the bees saw her at all, it was as a large white shape that occasionally puffed smoke at them. Her sons she loved with a primal passion that surged up with terrifying force. She *would* die for them; that was beyond question. She also, at times, felt towards them a murderous rage. Being at ease with such contradictions, she decided, was the secret to good parenting. And, of course, maintaining sanity.

Across the table from her, Mr Phipps consumed his late-morning snack using the same method he'd employed since Sidney had first met him — one bite of crumpet followed by a mouthful of tea, until both were finished. Sidney never failed to marvel at the way he managed to make them come out even. It took foresight, patience and restraint, three traits she'd dearly love to possess in greater quantities. Seemed to Sidney that all she did these days was react, and not in a calm, controlled way. Her reactions were invariably accompanied by the words 'Oh, for God's *sake*', either spoken aloud or communicated via her expression. No wonder she was having trouble with Aidan. No wonder she and Kerry were making heavy weather of their — whatever it was. Felt too premature to call it a relationship. Correction, she was too wary to call it a relationship. That word implied a commitment to permanence she wasn't sure either of them had — she because of the aforementioned wariness, and Kerry because he'd never once brought up the subject of their future, unless you counted checking the calendar to see when they could next get together for sex.

And it was *good* sex, she had to admit, though a voice that sounded like her mother's piped up to suggest that any sex would feel magnificent after such a long period of drought. Plus, that initial thrill of lust would soon fade, the helpful voice reminded, and, stripped of that padding, the framework of the relationship would be laid bare. Sidney would see what it was made of — something solid and enduring? Or something that faded into the air like a smiling Cheshire cat?

'Have you heard of this new flow hive?' she said.

Sidney knew Mr Phipps to be an excellent listener, and a source of sensible, if pithy, advice. But you had to prepare the ground before seeding your questions. Bee talk, in her experience, was the most effective conversational hoe.

'Its frame comes partly constructed like honeycomb,' she explained. 'The bees complete the comb and cap it with beeswax, like they would normally. But it has this mechanism, like a spigot, that splits the comb when you turn it on and allows honey to flow down a tube and out the hive's base into sterile jars. When you turn it off, it sets the comb back into position. The bees are barely disturbed, and you get easy access to honey. Sounds pretty good, doesn't it?'

'How much?' Mr Phipps said.

'Not sure,' said Sidney. 'They were looking for investment last time I heard, to put the prototypes into production. Do you want me to find out?'

Mr Phipps shrugged. That meant: Yes, he would, because he was quite excited by what she'd told him. Despite all clues given by his appearances and surroundings, Mr Phipps was not against progress. It just had to be progress whose benefits were not offset by damage to people or the environment. If its manufacture required slave labour or the pillaging of natural resources and its use added to the world's waste and discontent, he wasn't interested. Hence why his house was powered by solar panels, his water supply came from filtered rainwater tanks and his outhouse was a composting toilet. Sidney had been sceptical of the latter, but it was surprisingly un-whiffy. The reason she held on until she got home was the spiders in the corners, huge ones the size of mice, though that might be her amygdala exaggerating.

Her source of primal fear wasn't too fond of the wētā in the woodpile, either, but Mr Phipps kindly did all the gathering. Sidney's own house had a fireplace, but the chimney was a wreck and she didn't know anyone who'd be willing to repair it in exchange for goods and not cash. Owing to being caught in the poor person's double-bind that put truly efficient heating out of her price range, she and the boys had no choice but to put up with ugly column-heaters that used too much electricity. The only upside was not having a woodpile full of wētā, an insect that, when he first spied one, had shocked Kerry into atypical silence. He'd contemplated its spiny legs, pointed mandibles and spiked rear for a solid minute before speaking.

'It's a grasshopper designed by Satan.'

'And yet entirely benign,' said Sidney. 'Though it can give you a good hard nip if you startle it. My advice is to check your shoes every morning before putting them on.'

'I haven't been doing that,' Kerry said, his face a little ashen.

'Trust me,' Sidney said, 'if you had a wētā in your shoe, you'd know all about it.'

'I thought New Zealand was free of creatures that bit and stung?'

'It's free of creatures that bite and sting *fatally*,' Sidney said. 'Well, mostly. Wild pigs can gore you to death. Cattle can trample you, horses kick you in the head, and I guess a charging stag might wreak some havoc with its antlers. Kea — one of our native parrots — have been known to eat sheep alive. And our magpies! Those buggers divebomb you and draw blood! Oh, and we have sharks. But you're more likely to die playing rugby than in a shark attack.'

'I'm never venturing outdoors again,' had been Kerry's response.

Sidney ran her finger around her plate to scoop up the last of the buttery honey. Manners, reprimanded the mother-voice. Sod off, she replied. When pleasure is in limited supply, you should grab it whenever you can.

Kerry. Was he a pleasure or not? Every time he came into her mind, which was frequently, her thoughts split into two teams: one side totting up his good points, the other his weaknesses and flaws.

And then both sides leapt into a good old tussle that was about as ordered as a game of shinty, that Scottish form of homicidal hockey, all shoving and stick-cracking, and swearing from the sidelines.

Trouble was, no matter how many times the match was contested, neither side came out a clear winner. Kerry was intelligent, funny, attractive, affectionate, skilled in bed (though, admittedly, her experience was limited), comfortable with the boys and generally adept at managing them, and he was enthusiastic, energetic and, at heart, a decent human being on the side of good.

He was also disorganised, in too much of a rush to tick off every important detail, and tended to gloss over his mistakes with flippant remarks, which gave the impression he didn't really care. He relied too much on charm and blarney, and he avoided all discussion of any future beyond the next few days. Not that Sidney wanted him to get down on one knee and pledge his troth for all eternity, but just a tiny glimpse into his plans would be nice. Did he intend to stay in Gabriel's Bay? She had no clue. For all she knew, he might see himself as a red-haired Mary Poppins, dropping in to fix everyone's lives, buggering off again when the wind turned.

So what was he? A boon or an alarm bell? Sidney wished she trusted her judgement more. Fergal's departure, which she had *not* seen coming, had destroyed any faith she had in her ability to read men, and to distinguish between rose-tinted wishful thinking and reality.

'Boys well?'

Contrary to Kerry's opinion, Mr Phipps was perfectly capable of conversation. His style matched how he lived — nothing unnecessary, nothing wasted.

'Fighting fit,' said Sidney. 'And acting up. Well, Aidan is. Rory won't push it past a certain point.'

'Energy.'

Sidney was well practised in deciphering Mr Phipps's shorthand.

'With inadequate outlet, correct. Used to be that I could send him outside to run around, work it off in play, but that's not enough now. My hunch is that he's at an age where goals start to be important. He needs to feel like he's achieving something, that his energy's being directed into meaningful activity, rather than aimless dashing about.'

'Growing up.'

'Oh, yes.'

Another thought that filled Sidney with ambivalence. Mothering was always presented as a series of developmental milestones that you guided your child towards and ticked off happily when they reached them. But no one warned you that for every milestone there was an accompanying loss. Your chubby, peach-skinned infant who craved your touch grew teeth and knobbly limbs and independence. When they learned to dress themselves, you no longer played the peekaboo game. Skill with a spoon meant no more giggles at swooping aeroplanes. When they learned to read, you went from narrator (doing all the voices) to lights-out monitor. No more piggybacks, no more falling asleep in your lap, no more make-it-better kisses. Hugs only when no one was looking. Teddy bears put away in cupboards. Clothes you'd made became outdated and outgrown. Every height mark chalked on the wall a countdown to them leaving home. Mothering was as much about grieving as loving. But no one ever mentioned that.

'Football coaching with Kerry was good while it lasted,' she told Mr Phipps, feeling a twinge of disloyalty as she did so. 'But Aidan needs competition, and there was no way he was going to get a proper match, so maybe it's better that . . .'

Why lie? It wasn't better that the coaching group had been — temporarily, Kerry insisted — disbanded. It left a void Sidney could not fill because Aidan refused all her suggestions. No other ball sports interested him; they were all dumb. No, he didn't like mountain biking or skateboarding — dumb, dumb, dumb. No, he didn't want to go fishing with Jacko; fishing was boring. He was too *young* to go hunting, how *dumb* was she not to know that?

Kerry was no help. He nodded and said soothing words, but he was no help. And his glib assurances when Sidney asked how the other kids were taking the end of coaching made her angry to the point of shrillness, never an attractive quality.

'What about Reuben?' she'd demanded. 'Are you going to cut him loose just like that? Who else do you think he has on his side?'

'I'll get Reuben to help me with Littleville,' Kerry had promised.

Dead silence so far on that front, but lately, she felt like she'd done nothing but nag — Kerry, the boys, people who'd eagerly volunteered for Littleville but then had apparently gone into witness protection. She didn't have to gnaw at every bone.

One bone she *did* need to get her teeth into was the situation with Madison, which was financially breaking her. The moment Olivia announced that she was suing for divorce, the Jensen household had gone into meltdown. Rick had checked into a cheap hotel in Hampton, and Olivia had checked out, apparently deciding it was OK to abdicate from all her responsibilities, including care of her own daughter. Sometimes, she'd pick Madison up from school, but more often these days she simply wouldn't appear, and three children would walk into Sidney's house at three-fifteen. Rick and Olivia's phones invariably went to sodding voicemail, and even her sharpest, testiest requests for one of them to pick up Madison before six were ignored. Madison ate dinner at Sidney's most nights, and if there was no response at all from either Rick or Olivia, Sidney had no choice but to let her stay overnight. Last week, she'd slept over three times, which was three whole days' worth of extra meals Sidney had to fund.

Checking her bank balance required nerves of steel these days, and deep breathing to quell the urge to hyperventilate. The urge had got the better of her when a sympathetic but adamant person from the power company had rung to say she had forty-eight hours to pay the (very) overdue bill before the electricity would be cut off. All she could do was ask Jacko to advance her a month's wages. She refused to tell Kerry because he'd just give her the money, whereas Jacko understood that intending to repay a loan meant you hung on to at least *one* shred of your pride, which seemed more important at the time than whether or not you could actually repay it. Mr Phipps had given her an extra ten dollars today because the hive work was entering its busy phase. Sidney had almost cried.

It *had* to stop. She *had* to put her foot down.

But, oh God, what would happen to Madison then? There was no way Rick or Olivia would part with a cent if Sidney demanded recompense, and how could she look into that angel face and tell Madison she wasn't welcome anymore because her parents were low-life, using cheapskates?

It was a mess. *She* was a mess — a seething stew of resentment, fear and guilt.

The person who bore the brunt of all this bottled-up stress was Kerry, and Sidney knew that was, for the most part, unfair. But it wasn't *completely* unfair. He could help himself by being more aware and more reliable. Was it really *that* hard to do what he said he was going to do?

Or was it *her* fault? Were her standards far too high? Was there such a thing as 'the right one'? Or were even the most successful relationships full of niggle, doubt and compromise?

Sidney suppressed a sigh and let her gaze travel around the kitchen. Mary Phipps had been dead five years and a fading framed photo on the kitchen window ledge was one of the few traces of her left in the house. Not that there'd been many in the first place, neither of the Phippses being much for interior décor or, for that matter, furniture. The photo was an accurate portrait of an unobtrusive woman, with the look of one who spent so much time outdoors that she'd taken on some of its aspects — slate-grey hair, limbs sinewy and supple as tree vines, eyes the grey-green of lichen. She didn't care about her appearance, and she and Mr Phipps often wore each other's chunky jumpers and flannel shirts. Only Mr Phipps wore short shorts, though, Mary preferring a pair of vintage woollen tramping trousers that must surely have chafed like the devil.

Sidney had met Mary only a few times, her friendship and beekeeping arrangement with Mr Phipps having begun after his wife's death. Her impression had been of a quietly contented but strong-minded woman, who knew what she liked and politely but firmly refused to engage with anything or anyone she didn't. Oh, to be that certain, thought Sidney. So clear about what did and didn't make you happy.

'Miss her.'

Mr Phipps had caught her looking.

'I bet you do,' said Sidney.

She longed to ask if they'd ever fought, or even occasionally bickered, but that would be untactful, selfish. Mr Phipps's eyes were damp around the edges at the best of times, but Sidney was sure she observed extra moisture.

'What do you miss most?' was all she dared to ask.

Mr Phipps's forehead creased, and he was silent a good, long while.

'She knew me,' he said.

Of course, thought Sidney. What else mattered but that?

Chapter 30

Madison

'I am not dog.'

Oksana held the cheque Madison's mum had given her by one corner. Madison had once seen her sweep a dead mouse out from behind the refrigerator and hold it up by the tail. Her expression then had not been as disgusted as it was now.

Madison knew she shouldn't be spying, but she hadn't meant to. She'd come in the back door and heard her mum and Oksana, but it was only because her boots were hard to get off that she'd had time to realise they didn't sound very happy. She'd peered around the laundry door into the kitchen, thinking they would notice her but they hadn't. She didn't feel brave enough to interrupt, so she just stayed half-hidden by the door and watched.

'Not dog. Not fool, either.'

'Oh, what does *that* mean?'

Madison's mum sounded cross, but Oksana was taller, and bigger, too, and when she took a step closer, Madison's mum shrunk back a bit.

'This is rubbish money.' Oksana waved the cheque in Madison's mum's face. 'Insult. It is play money, like in game.'

'You're saying the cheque will *bounce*? You bloody rude old cow.'

Oksana made a sound that was sort of a cross between a word and a spit. Then she took the cheque in both hands and ripped it up, let the little bits of paper fall like snowflakes onto the carpet.

'I tenk God I am fortunate woman,' she said. 'I haff life spirit and health and decent man, and I haff work with Mrs Barton and other *good* people. I do not need your work. You are terrible woman with terrible life, and I no more have to take your poison.'

Oksana made the spit sound again, as if there weren't any words in English for what she really wanted to say. She picked up her pink bag and jacket, ready to leave. The back door was through the laundry and boot room, and Madison looked about in a panic for a place to hide, convinced Oksana would tell her off, too. But Oksana walked through to the hall and out the front door instead, even though it meant she had to go right around the house to get to her car. Madison waited until she couldn't hear the car any more before leaving the boot room and walking quietly into the kitchen.

Her mum had sat down at the kitchen table, her hands propping up her head. Madison realised she'd been walking a bit too quietly, because her mum hadn't heard her, and now she might get a fright. It was like last Saturday, when Madison had taken her book and bag to the place in the trees but found the skinny man there already. He was sitting on the muddy ground, no blanket, wiping his eyes in a way that made Madison wonder if he'd been crying. Or maybe he was just tired; Sidney said she was tired when Madison saw her wiping her eyes the other day. Yes, tired was probably right. She knew the skinny man, Deano, had been working long hours at the vineyard, doing night shifts as well as day jobs. Rainer wasn't happy about it — he'd left a message on their home phone, which her mum had played on speaker. Madison didn't hear all of it, just something about Rainer refusing to have anything to do with what was going on and that Madison's dad might think he was the smartest man in the room, but in fact he was a stupid—

The last word was in German, her mum said, 'and no doubt one hundred per cent accurate'. Then she erased the message, so she must have memorised it well enough to tell Madison's dad.

Sitting in the secret tree spot, Deano didn't see Madison approach or slip away again, so he never got startled. She couldn't manage that with her mum, who spotted her out of the corner of her eye and jumped and let out a big huff of breath like someone had punched her.

'Jesus, *must* you?' said Madison's mum. 'Why do you have to creep around? It's not *normal*.'

But then she dragged her hands down her face and blew out a breath.

'Sorry, hon,' she said. 'Despite Doctor Love's best efforts, I'm still a wreck.'

Madison wanted to throw herself at her mum and hug her tight, but that wouldn't be nice and quiet, would it? So she patted her on the arm.

The doorbell rang. Her mum jumped again.

'Oh, fucking no,' she said. 'Seriously, I just can't . . .'

'I'll get it,' said Madison, and ran off.

'Madison.' Ms Marshall smiled down at her. 'I've got a meeting with your mother.'

The firm way she said it made Madison sure she couldn't make an excuse, pretend her mum was ill or something.

So she held the door open politely, and said, 'She's in the kitchen.'

'Thank you.'

Ms Marshall waited for her to shut the door and they walked to the kitchen together. Even though it was a Saturday, Ms Marshall was in a suit but one with a skirt not trousers. The suit fabric was pale pink, which looked really nice against her dark skin. Madison knew her mum thought Ms Marshall was pretty, too, because she never made comments about her appearance, only about how nosy and unreasonable she was.

'How are you, Olivia?'

Ms Marshall sat down at the table without being invited, and put her notebook and pen in front of her. Her phone, too, which her mum hated.

'Why does she need to record our meetings?' her mum had said. 'Is that her unsubtle way of calling me a liar?'

Madison began to walk to her room, but her mum said, 'Stay here!'

She pulled out the chair next to her, and said, in a voice that sounded as if Ms Marshall had objected, 'I'm entitled to *one* ally at least.'

'Are you all right about that, Madison?' said Ms Marshall.

'She's *my* daughter!'

Her mum grabbed Madison's waist, pulled her close so that Madison couldn't sit properly on her chair. It was uncomfortable but she didn't want her mum to stop holding her.

Ms Marshall gave her mum a steady look, but then she opened her notebook and said, 'Right. Let's get on with it.'

Madison *tried* to follow what they were saying, but she kept getting stuck on the big words and losing track. It didn't help that her mum was really upset and kept interrupting. In the end, because Ms Marshall had to repeat herself so many times, Madison understood that her dad was going to declare something called 'bankruptcy', which meant he wouldn't have any more debts. But it meant he wouldn't have any money either, and the banks would go ahead and sell everything he owned, like the resort and the vineyard, so Madison and her mum should start to look for somewhere else to live, and her mum should probably think about getting a job.

'That is *bullshit*!' said her mother. 'So he gets off scot-free and *I* have to suffer?'

'Hardly scot-free,' said Ms Marshall. 'He can't set up any limited liability companies for the term of bankruptcy, which is usually three years, and he won't be able to get a line of credit over one thousand dollars. So unless he wants to apply for the dole, he'll have to find a job, too.'

Madison's mum gave a laugh that wasn't really a laugh.

'Like hell,' she said. 'Rick's lying bullshit is the whole reason I decided to divorce him! He *has* got bloody money, I know he has! He may be dodgy, but he's not stupid. You can't tell *me* he hasn't been squirrelling away his own freaking private hoard!'

'He may well have,' said Ms Marshall, her words cut short as if she'd lost patience. 'He may have offshore trusts in Panama. Or a gem-filled cave guarded by a genie. But the *reality* is that even if he has all the money in the world, his declaration of bankruptcy shows he has no intention of sharing it — with his unsecured creditors *or* with you, Olivia.'

Her voice softened, as if she regretted being a bit mean.

'It's tough, I know. I'm sorry you're in this situation. But even if a financial settlement is likely to be meagre at best, we can still work out a positive custody arrangement.'

Madison was wondering about the custardy thing, when she noticed her mum had suddenly gone all still. It was weird, as if she'd been taken over by an icy ghost.

'That's Rick's problem,' she said. 'He made this mess — he needs to sort it. I want to make that perfectly clear.'

Ms Marshall gave Madison a quick look, then frowned at her mum as if she didn't quite understand.

'But you both—'

She stopped speaking, sat up in her chair and closed her notebook.

'Best if we discuss this another time,' she said. 'I'll call to set up a meeting.'

'At a time that suits *me*,' said Madison's mum.

'Of course.'

Ms Marshall stood, smoothed down her skirt, and picked up her things from the table. Madison's mum had stopped holding onto her a while back, but Madison had stayed put even though her leg was hurting from being pressed into the crack between their two chairs. But she'd better get up now, as it wasn't polite to stay sitting when guests were ready to leave.

'I'll show you to the door,' said Madison.

Ms Marshall touched her palm briefly to her own cheek, the way Madison had seen Sidney do when Rory brought her some buttercups he'd picked. Sidney acted like it was the best present ever, even though Rory had kind of crushed the flowers by holding them too tight.

'Thank you, sweetheart,' said Ms Marshall.

At the door, Ms Marshall hesitated, as if she wanted to say something but was worried it might come out wrong.

'It will be OK,' she said, after a bit. 'Don't you worry.'

Then she walked very quickly to her car, which Madison knew was a Suzuki Swift because her dad thought they were rubbish and couldn't pull the skin off a rice pudding.

Madison could hear her dad's voice, clear as if he was right next to her. She'd been trying not to think about him too often, which is how she'd managed not to miss him too much when he'd been living mainly in Auckland. But right now, as she watched Ms Marshall's little blue car drive off, she wanted him here so badly her heart felt like a big hand was squeezing it, crushing it like one of Rory's buttercups.

She ran back inside to see her mum, but the kitchen was empty and her mum's bedroom door was shut and Madison knew better than to disturb her.

It was sunny outside, and the skinny man probably wouldn't be in the secret tree place two Saturdays in a row, though she wouldn't mind if he was, because he liked reading. Her latest book was about a boy whose sister was a witch. She wasn't a nice person at *all*, but it seemed like there was nothing anyone could do to stop her being mean because she had such strong magic. She was getting away with it the way Tanya Booth got away with teasing Reuben who was this close, she heard the other kids say, to being expelled. Madison had tried to play with him one lunchtime, but he shouted a bad word at her and ran away. She wished they were still having football coaching because Reuben enjoyed that, but she knew that Kerry was busy with his project, which was really important to the town. There was no point talking to Tanya, because Tanya wouldn't listen to her. Madison couldn't control people with magic powers, like the girl in the book.

But it wouldn't be a good story if the bad sister weren't stopped, so Madison packed the book in her bag, and headed outside, being sure to close the front door quietly. She walked towards the trees, looking forward to sitting down and reading about a world where everything worked out right.

Chapter 31

Sam

'So, how about it?' said Tubs.

Brownie's smile was both amused and amazed. 'Wasn't the last trip enough of a debacle for you?'

'It was good fun!' protested Tubs.

'How do you know? You were shickered for most of it.'

'And we didn't shoot *any*thing,' said Sam.

He kept his voice down. Wouldn't want the old men of the club to overhear. They already had plenty to say about the youth of today.

'All the more reason to go back,' Tubs insisted. 'My dad'll lend us the gear again, and the truck.'

Brownie clapped his hand on Tubs's shoulder. 'Under a bit of pressure from the old man, are we?'

Tubs went bright red. 'Nah!' he said, too quickly.

Sam's eyes shifted to the prime spot in the clubroom, the big table, where only the important men sat. Sam hadn't been able to work out exactly what criteria defined them as important — some were wealthy, some had sod-all except loud opinions, some were former players, others' only exercise ever was lifting pints from the table to their mouths. Maybe the only thing they had in common was that they all *thought* they were important — and that conviction was enough to make everyone else believe it, too.

Tubs's dad, Rob, was one of them. He ticked more boxes than most, being wealthy, loud and opinionated *and* a former player, whose physical strength had not been totally buried under layers of lard. Honestly, some of these old guys looked like they'd been made out of the melted manky ends of old candles. Sam knew a youthful metabolism and a physical job were advantages he wouldn't always have, but you didn't *have* to go to seed, did you? His dad was heftier than he'd been when *he* was nineteen, sure, but he ate healthily and kept up the exercise, didn't smoke, or drink too much. Wyatt should live to a good old, age, shouldn't he . . . ?

'Earth to Sammo!'

Brownie had set down his beer so he could cup his hands around his mouth.

'Yeah, what?' said Sam.

'Seems Mr Hanrahan senior has been putting the hard word on his son and heir to come back with some proper trophies. Splashes of drunken vomit on boots don't count, apparently. Nor do blisters, itchy bites or tongue burns caused by inadequate blowing on gas-station pies.'

'So what does he want? Us to come back with an elephant?'

'Grizzly bear, probably,' said Brownie. 'Or a moose. There's rumours, you know.'

'A *deer*,' said Tubs. 'Just one fucken deer, OK?'

'And I assume you'll do the fucking?'

Brownie winked at Sam. He loved winding Tubs up, even though it was way too easy and he should, by rights, have got bored of it years back. Habit, Sam supposed. That's what kept them all in the same groove. Made even the old jokes still seem funny.

'Hardy ha,' said Tubs. 'Better a deer than that bush-pig you were chatting up in Hampton the other day. Man, she was as rough as guts!'

Brownie went still, no expression.

Then he said, 'You mean my long-lost sister?'

'What? Shit. *Really*?'

Brownie kept staring. Didn't blink or smile.

'No,' he said, and drained his beer. 'She's a customer of the firm. And she is, I will admit, not much of a looker.'

Tubs fair sagged with relief.

'But if she *had* been a relation,' Brownie set his glass down with deliberate care, 'I would have had to take you outside right now and smack you.'

'Yeah, yeah.'

Tubs's grin showed he felt he was on safe ground now. And he was, with Brownie. But Sam had seen him mis-read the situation time and again, his poor judgement made even ropier by drink. One day someone wouldn't know about Rob Hanrahan, or wouldn't care, and Tubs would get a whole lot worse than a smacking.

'So what about it?'

Brownie caught Sam's eye.

'What about it, Sammo? Care to go moose hunting?'

'*Deer*,' said Tubs.

Sam didn't. Not really. Once had been enough.

'Ah, c'mon,' said Tubs, seeing his face. 'Not like you've got anything else to do on weekends. Or are you too busy' — he put on an annoying singsong voice — '*baby*-sitting?'

It was Brownie's smirk that stung more than Tubs's comment.

'I do have stuff on!' Sam protested. 'I said I'd help out shifting the model train!'

'Oh, the *twain*,' said Tubs in same singsong voice. 'The widdle *twain* needs you.'

'Shut up.'

Sam glanced nervously about. The old men only pretended to be deaf when it suited them. And he knew from Uncle Gene that the vote to help out in the working bee had been carried by only a slim margin. Objectors still saw it as a waste of time, and even though they had none of their own, they seemed to be convinced a better idea to promote Gabriel's Bay was out there somewhere.

But, of course, Tubs was on a roll.

'Is Sammy gonna play with the widdle dollies, too? In their widdle dolly-house?'

'Shut *u*—'

'Tubs, give it a rest,' said Brownie.

And Tubs did. The fact he listened to Brownie and not him might have irked Sam more if he hadn't been so relieved Tubs had shut his trap.

'Dad says that whole thing's fucked anyway,' said Tubs.

'And why's that?' said Brownie.

'There's all these regulations and shit they have to meet. Won't have a hope, says Dad. Game over. Good riddance.'

'Mr Hanrahan senior not a supporter then?' said Brownie.

'Nah, he thinks it's a stupid use of the factory,' said Tubs. 'Thinks that old Eyetie bloke's been taken for a ride and he should just sell the place now.'

'Buyers queuing up, are they?' Brownie pushed on.

Sam watched Brownie for clues as to his intent, but his face matched his voice — bland and only casually interested.

'Been an offer in for a while,' said Tubs. 'But old Mr Crappy or whatever's a bit gaga, and his sons are useless, couldn't organise a shag in a whorehouse. Everything's like *mañana*, *mañana*.'

'Your father might have more success if he spoke to them in Italian, not Spanish,' said Brownie.

Like a cartoon, Tubs eyes bugged out in horror. 'Aw, nah, it's not *Dad*. Nah, it's — I didn't mean—'

Sam was suddenly grateful that Brownie was his friend. He'd be a shitter of an enemy.

Brownie clapped Tubs on the shoulder. 'Sure, sure. No sweat, pardner. How about you go buy us another round?'

'Yeah, yeah, I'll do that,' said Tubs, with the haste of a man who's just been offered an alibi by the police. 'Same again, yeah?'

He took off before they could confirm or deny.

'Sometimes,' said Sam, 'I'm really glad my dad's my dad, you know?'

'Yes, you certainly are the lucky one.'

The edge to Brownie's voice made Sam realise what he'd said.

'Shit, sorry, man. How *is* Ed?'

'He's dying, Sammo. And not quickly.'

'I know. I'm sorry.'

He knew his own dad, his mum, too, would have more words to say — *right* words. But Sam struggled. Could it be that he didn't really *want* to know? Come on, Brownie was his mate. He should make the effort.

'It's not fair,' he said. 'Your dad is a good guy. He doesn't deserve to be ill like this.'

'A good guy?'

Brownie's flat delivery flustered Sam.

'Well, yeah, you know,' he said. 'He was. Is . . .'

'Well, let's review that statement . . .' Brownie drew out the words, as if holding them up to the light. 'Has Ed ever smacked me around? No. Does he drink to excess, gamble or take hard drugs? No, again. Did he support me at school and on the sporting ground? Yes, as much as he was able. Sounds like a pretty good guy so far, don't you think, Sammo?'

'Um . . .'

There was a light in Brownie's eyes that made Sam want to duck for cover.

'Did Ed pull his weight around the house? Not really, but that's not unusual for our fathers's generation. Did Ed ever stretch himself to get a better job so his wife wouldn't have to work all the hours God gave? Now we're getting into trickier territory, but I'll press on. Did he pay the bills, do the banking or balance the household budget? That's a no. Did he take any responsibility for our financial situation after my mother, who *had* done all the above, died? Did he ever ask how we would manage without her income, even though she was the major breadwinner? Has he ever enquired as to how we're managing now that he has no income except a negligible sickness benefit? To all that a *resounding* no. But, you know, it's OK, because I got it sorted, because I *had* to. He tells me *I'm* a good boy, Sam, and I try to be, I really do. He's sick and it's bloody rough and I'm all he's got. But even if his body's buggered, his mind's OK. He can think, he can observe. So how hard would it be for him to pull his head out of the sand? How hard would it be for *him* to be the grown-up, just *one* fucking time?'

Sam felt accused of something, and part of him resented it. If Brownie's life was that shit, why didn't he ask for help? Or did he *want* to be the victim, did that make him feel special?

The other part of Sam knew he had no right to judge Brownie — how he felt, what he did — because he had *no* idea what it would feel like to be in his friend's shoes. Warmth, light, family and laughter — that was Sam's life. He hadn't known trouble at all, and probably had fuck-all of what it took to handle it.

'I'm sorry,' he said, again. 'I didn't know.'

Brownie seemed to be contemplating a choice of answers, shifting them along some internal slide rule.

'Well, what you don't know won't hurt you, will it?' he finally said.

Fair enough. And not as harsh as Sam had expected.

'Is there — can I help?' he asked.

'No,' said Brownie, firm and abrupt. 'As I said, I've got it sorted.'

Then he softened a fraction, and added, 'Thanks.'

Tubs was back, bringing with him two jugs and what Uncle Gene called 'the airspace of posturing aggression' that he felt compelled to create around him.

'So — one more hunting trip, right, girls?' He filled their glasses. 'Come on, you know you want to.'

'And abandon my gravely ill father?' said Brownie.

'Well, what'd you do last time?'

'Asked Doc Love to pop in.'

'There you go,' said Tubs. 'Sorted.'

'Indeed.'

Brownie grinned at Sam, as if their tense conversation had never happened.

'Come on, Sammo,' said Tubs. 'Lucky last. Or loser last, whatever.'

'What about Deano?' Sam said.

'What about him?' Tubs replied. 'Not like he's been anywhere near us lately.'

'We should at least ask him. He's our mate.'

'Yeah, he *was* . . .' Tubs screwed up his face. 'But he's kind of a loser now, don't you think? Bit fucken shabby on it.'

Sam knew this was true, but he didn't want to accept it. He wanted to keep Deano in his head as a cheerful, skinny, madly running boy. He wanted Brownie in there as his best mate, happy with two healthy parents and a good opinion of his father. He wanted Tubs before the drink and aggression and bad judgement. He couldn't bear to believe that any of them would suffer or fail or give up, even though those signs were already there. He had to believe that they'd succeed, that they *wouldn't* become old melted-candle men, marinating in beer and delusions that they had still some kind of value and purpose, some kind of small god power.

'Deano's the only one of us who actually knows how to hunt,' said Sam, too loudly. 'And you said at the start that this was about the four of us — our last summer together, and—'

'OK, OK!' Tubs held up his hand. 'Fucken go ask Deano!'

'I'll ask him,' said Brownie. 'I'm doing some work up at the vineyard next week.'

'He probably can't come, anyway,' said Tubs. 'Isn't he working, like, all day every day?'

'I'll have a chat to his boss,' said Brownie. 'Play the sympathy card.'

'He's German,' said Tubs. 'Thought they were hard as?'

'You forget I have a natural charm that transcends language.'

'Fuck off,' said Tubs. 'Natural charm, my hairy balls.'

'Now *there's* an oxymoron.'

'*You're* a moron!'

'Do you think you'll be able to talk the boss around?'

Sam needed to know. It felt wrong to take this trip without Deano. Worse, it felt — unlucky.

'Don't you trust me, Sam?'

Flustered again by that flat delivery. Or perhaps he just didn't know how to answer . . .

Brownie smiled. Sam let out a breath he didn't know he'd been holding.

'Leave it with me, Sammo,' said Brownie. 'I'll get the band back together for one more gig. I'll get it *all* sorted.'

Chapter 32

Mac

Mac rang all of Dr Ghadavi's references, and none of them had a bad word to say, so she rang Bronagh Macfarlane, whose advice to date had been a hundred per cent bang on the nail.

'He's earnest to the point of being borderline bananas,' Mac told her. 'And he talks even more than your son.'

'So the little fecker's still alive then?' said Bronagh.

'Kerry? Yes. Why do you ask?'

'Haven't heard a dicky-bird from him for yonks. I figured either he'd died, or had been caught up in some undercover police sting operation.'

'He's just been busy,' said Mac. 'Bitten off more than he can chew, I suspect, though he still insists he's waving not drowning. Excuse the mangled metaphor.'

'Irony is,' said Bronagh, 'I notice the absence of yak more because normally, as you yourself have observed, he never stops. We had none of the trouble other parents did when their teenagers became all cat's-bum-face and monosyllabic. Kerry-Francis said his first word at eight months and he's not, far as I can tell, drawn breath since. I appreciate that he communicates, though during his childhood, his father and I did fantasise more than once about becoming Trappist monks. I think we may have even sent away for the application form.'

'But is chattiness a good trait for a doctor?' said Mac. 'I'd have thought the main skill they require is an ability to listen.'

'The two are not mutually exclusive. I've often found chatter has a soothing quality for patients, like whale song in the background. And if they're relaxed, they're more willing to spill the beans about what's ailing them. As long as your man knows to shut up at that point, he'll be grand.'

Mac felt a spike of irritation, and realised it was because she'd been hoping Bronagh would give her a reason to change her mind, to halt the whole process and tell Doc Love that he could stay on until he dropped dead at his desk. Change was *hard*, for her, for the patients. It would alter the whole fabric of Gabriel's Bay, and tough cheddar for anyone who preferred it the way it was.

But then, if Littleville ever saw the light of day, *that* would bring change, too. New visitors, new expectations and demands on the town and its people. And in the words of whoever was in charge of developing annoying motivational sayings: 'If you don't move forwards, you start going backwards.' Mac had a moment like that going over the hill in the Love Bus last week; she really must get the gearbox sorted.

'So I should hire him?' Mac said, hoping, she knew, for one last out.

'His resumé is top-notch for a young fella,' said Bronagh. 'And he's keen, apparently clean living and unencumbered. Quite handsome, too, judging by his mugshot.'

'I'm terrified of making a wrong call,' said Mac.

'You can think of every contingency until you're blue in the face,' said Bronagh, 'and it still won't prevent things going arseways. Control is an illusion.'

'That so?'

'Kerry's father and I also considered entering a Buddhist monastery but the saffron robes made us look like we had kidney failure.'

Mac let out a long breath. She could prevaricate no longer, and no one else could make the decision. Now, it was all down to her.

'I'd better help him find a decent place to live,' she said. 'Strangely, most rental advertisements tend to leave "former meth lab" off their list of features.'

'You've a good soul,' said Bronagh. 'That should cut some ice with God or karma or the lucky leprechauns, I'd say.'

If only, Mac thought as she rang off. In her experience, Santa Claus might care whether you were naughty or nice, but in all other respects your moral orientation had zero impact on your fortunes. Bad deeds went unpunished daily, good deeds unrewarded. Fairness was a concept that humans could enforce amongst themselves, but when it came to fate, it was nothing but wishful thinking.

She wrote a brief official email to Ashwin Ghadavi, confirming his appointment. Hit send. Waited for a sign from the universe to acknowledge either the wisdom or stupidity of her act. Was irrationally annoyed that none came.

'Haven't you fixed that yet?' she snapped at the young electrician with his face in the security alarm control box.

He gazed at her wide-eyed. 'Uh, no — it's gone a bit — weird.'

Weird. Of course. That most excellent and specific of diagnoses.

Mac had decided her call to Bronagh was a justifiable business expense, so she'd come in to use the surgery phone, gone to deactivate the alarm and found it had beaten her to it. Having hastily confirmed that nothing was missing, it being Sunday morning, she'd phoned the electrician firm's twenty-four-hour service line and was sent to voicemail, so she left the kind of message that encourages a prompt response. She demanded Barrett come back and fix it properly, only to be told he wasn't on call that weekend. Her irritation was compounded by the fact that she'd trusted Barrett when he assured her confidently that the alarm was fixed, and right now she didn't want any hint that her ability to judge people was lacking.

'I think something in the circuit board's failed,' said the young man.

'And can you *fix* that something?'

'Nah, whole board'll probably need replacing.'

'So we will be alarm-less?'

'Uh, we could install a new one?'

'Today?'

'Uh, no, because we'd have to order it . . .'

Mac got up from behind her desk, causing the electrician to try to hide inside the control box.

'And how am I supposed to keep this place secure?' she said.

If the young man's eyes opened any wider, the top of his head would flip over backwards.

'Uh, have you got a dog?'

Mac tried to imagine King on guard duty. All the thieves would have to do is wave a sausage, and King would break the door down for them from the inside.

If King were around, of course. He'd been off on a wander that had lasted four days now, when the longest he'd ever been gone before was two. Even Jacko was starting to look worried.

The young electrician was waiting.

'No dog,' said Mac. 'All I have is this front-door key, and an old sign that says "No drugs or cash on the premises". I took it down because too many people decided it was some kind of reverse-psychology ruse. One person who broke in actually left an angry note of complaint that we hadn't lied to them.'

She flapped an impatient hand at the young man. 'Go on, bugger off and put in the order. And make sure you get back here the instant it arrives.'

He needed no more encouragement. Mac closed the front door, inserted the key in the inadequate lock. Her plan for the rest of the day had been to drive around King's usual haunts and see if she could spot him. But first, she had a message to deliver.

Doc Love lived in a modest villa with a rambling garden that rambled more every year because he spent all his spare time in the shed that housed his war-game dioramas. Mac didn't bother to knock on his front door, but let herself in the side gate and followed the mossy path, punching her way through hydrangeas and wisteria that hadn't been pruned since some Victorian had planted them over a century ago.

The shed looked as if it had been last painted about the same time, and had no windows whatsoever, but Mac knew the inside to be spotless, and with better ventilation and heating than the main house. When Doc Love first told her he'd agreed to contribute to the Littleville project, Mac had reacted with a snorting disbelief that masked a real concern. She'd seen too many people who'd worked hard and with robust energy all their lives enter retirement and immediately shrivel up like sprayed weeds. The warning about the devil was nonsense — Old Nick found *nothing* for idle hands to do, and that was a punishment worse than anything to be found in Hell.

'What will you do with yourself when the shed's empty?' she'd asked Doc Love.

'Fill it up again' was his simple and, in hindsight, obvious reply. Mac had been absurdly relieved.

She knocked on the shed door.

'Enter.'

'Why do you never ask who it is?' Mac said, as she pushed the door shut behind her. 'What if I was a crazed meth addict wielding a machete?'

'Then why bother to knock?' he replied, with unassailable if irksome logic.

He was seated at the workbench — an old chipboard door on a trestle — where he did all his painting. To give him more light and better vision for such close-up work, he'd attached a magnifying glass to a caver's helmet. When he looked up, he resembled one of those yellow cartoon bean creatures that had infested the internet. 'Mum memes,' her daughter, Emma, called them. 'Middle-aged women *love* Minions.'

Doc Love flipped the magnifying glass out of the way and carefully set the soldier he'd been painting upright on its metal boots. It had a pointed helmet, so Mac assumed it was German. How many war injuries the Kaiser's men had incurred by not looking before they sat down she could only speculate.

'To what do I owe the pleasure?' said Doc Love.

'I note you didn't add "on this fine Sunday morning",' she said. 'It could be raining frogs out of a boiling sky out there and you'd never know.'

'Artificial light is more easily controlled,' he said.

'Well, when your bones snap from rickets, don't come crawling to me.'

He smiled, as he always did at her cranky jokes, and Mac felt a stab of — what? Guilt, fear, both? She'd tried to imagine what it would be like not sharing an office, and the bulk of her weekdays, with Doc Love, and the abyss that opened in her mind was the kind that stares right back at you. One conversation and several emails with Ashwin Ghadavi were not enough to flesh him out as a comparable alternative. When she tried to picture him, he had the dimension of a notepad doodle. None of which helped one iota with her current mission . . .

Sod it. No point removing the Band-Aid slowly.

'I've hired your replacement,' she said. 'He starts the last week of February.'

The delay before Doc Love responded filled Mac with the anxious heebs. Had he thought she'd changed her mind?

But his reply, when it came, was 'Good.'

Mac wanted to grab his collar and shake him, yelling 'Is it? *Is it*??' into his face.

'Though I have to confess,' he went on, 'that I'm not as ready as I had convinced myself I was.'

'Look,' said Mac, in sudden panic. 'I can always email him back and—'

'No, no, no.' Doc Love smiled. 'I *am* ready. It *is* time. I should never have said that. I only did so, because — well, you and I, Mac. We understand each other, don't we?'

Hellfire, she was going to bawl. The last time Mac had cried in front of anyone was when her son Harry, aged seven, had been clipped by a car while riding his bike outside their house. He was fine, no bones broken, only concussed, but when she'd heard the crunch of metal and rushed outside, her first sight was of his little body lying on the road, pale and still, blood coming from his nose . . .

Doc Love was quick to make an accurate diagnosis.

'Whisky?' he said.

'It's barely noon,' said Mac.

'I could add it into a cup of tea?'

'God, no,' Mac shuddered. 'A dash of water will do fine.'

Doc Love removed his helmet, hung it on a special hook on the wall behind him. 'I also have a cake that Sheila Swanson baked for me.'

'Is it in the shape of a heart?'

Doc Love held the door open for her. 'It is, I believe, a seed cake.'

'Ah well,' said Mac, as they walked out, blinking into the sunlight. 'We don't need Freud to help us with *that* one, do we?'

The midday whisky put paid to any thought of driving around looking for King. Mac decided to leave her car at Doc Love's and walk the twenty minutes to home, where she intended to lie in a warm spot and read a book. Or snooze like an old nana, whatever.

On a clear, sunny early summer day, Gabriel's Bay was hard to beat. Even the shabbiest house looked welcoming, and the dandelions in the cracked pavement and buddleia that sprawled on untended verges flowered as if they'd been intentionally planted to add colour. The sea sparkled in glimpses, and the air carried whiffs of ozone and backyard barbecues along with the sounds of Sunday-afternoon industry, lawnmowers and hammers, radios providing tinny accompaniment to the washing of cars. Children wheeled free on bikes (helmeted these days, Mac was pleased to see) or shrieked under sprinklers, while parents who were done cooking or DIYing lounged in rickety deckchairs dragged out of the shed and dusted free of cobwebs. On a day like this, thought Mac, you could look through a bright filter and see only happiness, unity and productive endeavour. You could pretend there was no darkness, no cruelty or ignorant brutality, no addiction, destitution or despair.

Of course, whisky added a certain glow, too. Perhaps that was the secret to happiness? Stay permanently soused?

Her mobile rang. Jacko.

'Big Rog the DOC ranger says he saw King up by Carlton Peak.'

'What? All the way up there?'

'Probably chasing a wild pig.'

'What did the stupid mutt think he was going to do when he caught it? Roast it on a spit?'

'I'm heading up to look for him,' said Jacko. 'Might be gone a few days.'

'Can't Big Rog look for him?'

'Not his job.'

'Suppose not,' sighed Mac. 'Does that mean you're closing the Boat Shed?'

No one else could cook like Jacko. And his dedication to high standards meant he would refuse to risk serving food even fractionally below par.

'Won't hurt. Had a good last couple of months.'

'What about Dev and Sidney? I know Sid's been a bit short lately.'

'Can't be helped,' said Jacko. 'King won't know how to get home. If I don't find him soon, he'll die.'

Jacko's matter-of-fact tone didn't fool Mac. He loved that dog and would be worried sick. But his estimation of being gone 'a few days' was almost certainly understated. Carlton Peak was way up in the ranges, a full day's tramp. Mac knew Jacko would use the DOC hut as his base and search from there. She also knew he hadn't been on a serious tramp for years. The demands of the Boat Shed meant any hunting trips had to be less than a day, and that usually meant more driving than walking. There was no way she could persuade him not to go, so Mac tried not to think about the risks, or to calculate the distance between Carlton Peak and the nearest defibrillator.

'You off now?' she said.

'Yup,' said Jacko. 'Better not delay.'

He'd be offended if she asked him to take care. He always did — she should know that.

And they never ended phone calls with any twee endearments, either; that's just not how they rolled. But today had been a big day — she'd finally shut one door and opened another, and she still wasn't convinced it was a good move. Intellectually, she knew this was why Jacko's leaving felt more significant than it otherwise might. Rationally, she knew he was an experienced and sensible bushman. Emotionally, however . . .

'Love you,' she said.

There was a pause. She could picture his startled face.

'Yeahyoutoo,' he muttered.

Mac wasn't sure if that made her feel better or worse.

Chapter 33

Kerry

Last — and the only — time Kerry had been to the Coateses place was when he'd dropped Reuben off after visiting the glass-blowers. Reuben had jumped out of the car, run around the side of the house and disappeared. Kerry had considered knocking on the door, just to make sure there was someone home to supervise — Reuben *was* only eight, after all. But he had Madison in the car and he knew she was anxious to get home, so he waited a minute in case Reuben reappeared, then drove off, telling himself that generations before had grown up as latch-key kids and no harm had come to them. His own father used to let himself in after school, make a snack and supervise his own homework until whichever of his parents finished their factory shift first returned home. His father bore no ill effects except a taste for white bread spread with fat scraped from the bottom of the roasting tray, a foodstuff he was forbidden from consuming until Kerry and his mother had left the room.

Today, the Coateses' house looked just as empty as it had before. Possibly it was — surely any house in that state would be condemned? Decades ago, it had been painted white with green trim around the windows, but now more weatherboard was visible than paint. Even the undercoat had worn off. The corrugated-iron roof was lifting off, nails long rusted through, and it seemed the only thing keeping it in place was a solid crop of lichen. If there had ever been a garden, there wasn't one now, only weeds, foot-high grass and shrubs grown so wild and huge they covered one entire side of the house, blocking light from any windows that might be concealed beneath the dank greenery. In the windows that were visible, Kerry counted three broken panes, covered inadequately from the inside with taped-up cardboard. Surrounding the house on all sides was a decorative feature known as rubbish — piles of wood, rusted oil drums, an old smashed toilet, a rotting couch, lumps of concrete and other items whose identity Kerry was quite happy to leave unknown.

It was four-thirty. Reuben should be home from school — though Kerry realised he had no idea how the boy travelled between the two. There was no bus, so did he get a ride with the Booths, or someone else, perhaps? The house was a good five miles from the school, so he couldn't walk . . . could he?

Kerry sat in the car, well aware that he was putting off getting out. He had no desire to venture any closer to this ruin that passed for a house, let alone knock on its door and speak to whoever might answer. He hadn't grown up in the smartest part of London, and he'd seen plenty of rough, destructive and even criminal behaviour. But he hadn't personally been acquainted with any of the perpetrators or, indeed, their victims. He hadn't known any abused children, just read about them in the paper, and, as you did, shaken his head at such tragedies and moved on to the football results.

Then again, he didn't *know* that Reuben wasn't cared for. Judging by the house, and what Reuben wore, the Coateses were clearly not flush with cash. But poverty didn't automatically encompass domestic violence or neglect. The house's interior could be perfectly clean and tidy for all he knew, the pantry well stocked with homemade preserves. He shouldn't jump to conclusions.

Besides, this visit wasn't exactly his choice. He was only here because Sidney had — he should say 'reminded' rather than 'nagged' him about his promise to involve Reuben in Littleville.

'I don't have anything for him to do yet,' Kerry had protested. 'Unless he's capable, at eight, of negotiating with the Hampton District Council.'

'He doesn't have to *do* anything,' said Sidney. 'It will be enough that he feels involved. Take him with you when you go around enlisting support, like you did when you visited the glass-blowers.'

'That was hardly a success,' said Kerry. 'I still can't work out why he didn't want that horse. It was beautiful.'

'Is it possible he was afraid of owning anything he saw as precious?' said Sidney. 'Because the risk of it being destroyed was too great?'

Kerry had wanted to deny any such possibility. Mainly because it hadn't occurred to him first.

He stared hard at the Coateses' house, as if hoping to be suddenly endowed with X-ray vision. Sidney was convinced it was a terrible place for a child, though she hadn't been able to support her theory with any actual evidence. When he politely suggested that she had none because there was none, she got all defensive and declared that social services had no obligation to broadcast their work to the rest of the town, and nor did Casey Marshall. Interventions might already be in play.

When Kerry, again politely, pointed out that she'd contradicted herself — if the authorities were intervening then life for Reuben couldn't be terrible, could it? — Sidney lost her last grip on temper and accused him of being spineless.

'You're like a kid who covers his eyes and thinks because he can't see anyone, no one can see him! Out of sight, out of mind!'

He decided not to highlight the additional logic flaws in that argument because, even if it wasn't a hundred per cent coherent, its premise was correct. He *did* choose to relegate any tasks that weren't immediately pressing, giving priority instead to those that shouted loudest, sometimes literally. Bernard, who had thus far rebuked Kerry for his shortcomings in a moderate tone, had, at the last Littleville meeting at the Boat Shed, yelled at him, and for several minutes. Called him, among *many* other things, 'a shiftless charlatan'. The force-ten rant shocked even Gene into silence. Mac rose and fetched a bottle of single malt out from under the Boat Shed's bar. Poured Bernard alone a generous measure, even though it was Kerry who'd been under attack. The meeting dispersed soon after, and they had not held another since.

Shiftless, spineless — were those accusations fair? He'd tried so hard to be a better human being here, a man of integrity, dedication and commitment, and it seemed obvious to *him* that he was working every spare minute he had. Every day, he phoned the council and spoke, it seemed, to a different but identically intractable person. He was in constant communication with Tai Te Wera, who had no bright ideas about compliance but offered in return an endless supply of legal paperwork to read and sign. And he was pressing on with the plans for the space, orchestrating logistics and assuring the Caraccis that all was well, because — why not? Surely a solution to the compliance issues *would* be found? Bernard's belief — trenchantly and forcefully restated in the Boat Shed — was that the only person who could undo this regulatory knot was Elaine. Kerry needed to suck up to Elaine was the gist of Bernard's argument. Or find a way to turn the rest of the council against her.

Neither path glittered with golden promise to Kerry. If he sucked up to her, he'd have to keep at it for the rest of his natural life. The project would become hers and he her creature. But then he had no connections or influence with the council, and he'd never been good with conflict.

So to recap — he could confidently refute the accusation that he was shiftless, but the spineless charge? Perhaps not such a strong footing . . .

And getting weaker every minute he stayed in the car. He'd been outside the house of horror for nearly fifteen minutes now, which was unacceptable. Time to urinate or remove oneself from the latrine, to paraphrase and, indeed, bowdlerise, Jacko.

Kerry waded through grass, hoping not to stand on anything lethal, and knocked on the door. Stepped back a pace. But no sound came from inside — no snarling dogs, shotguns cocking, that sort of thing. No voices or footsteps, either.

He took a deep breath and knocked again, louder. Nothing. He peered cautiously through the front window but the interior was unlit and Kerry could glimpse only the sagging backs of two old armchairs and a side table on which sat a single saucer filled with cigarette butts. Either the house was empty or everyone inside was dead. Perhaps he should call Casey Marshall?

His other options were to shout out hello, see if that provoked a response. Or he could hack his way around the side through the shrubbery and rubbish and knock on the back door, if one existed.

But, frankly, this house gave him the creeps. And if anyone *was* inside, then answering the door was clearly the last thing they wanted to do. The first they wanted was for anyone knocking to go away.

Kerry went away, and felt worse for every mile he put between himself and young Reuben's home. By the time he drove into Gabriel's Bay, he felt so bad, he parked outside the police station — if an office with one desk, two chairs and a fern in a pot counted as a station — and went to see if Constable Marshall was in residence. Unusually, she was, so Kerry had no choice but to draw a picture that might not show his best side.

'I've never visited before, so I don't know if no response is typical,' he said.

'Depends.' Casey obviously didn't intend to elaborate.

'Is — is Reuben OK?' he asked.

She gave him an amused, assessing look, as if presuming, correctly as it happened, that his desire to hear the truth was minimal.

'His family situation is less than ideal,' she said. 'But not to the point where he should be taken into care.'

'Is there any way to communicate with his parents?' Kerry said.

'About what?'

'Er, whether I could take him along with me when I go and talk to people about Littleville.'

'Does Reuben want to come with you?'

She certainly had the knack for the pertinent question.

'I don't know,' Kerry had to admit. 'That's why I went to the house — to ask. It was Sidney's idea,' he added, immediately cringing at how petty it sounded.

But Casey only nodded. 'I can make some calls. Give me your mobile number and I'll let you know how I get on.'

'Thank you,' he said, though he wasn't entirely sure if he was being sincere.

Kerry returned to his car, rested his head back against the driver's seat and closed his eyes. There were approximately one million and twenty-three items clamouring for attention on his mental agenda, and he had lost all ability to work out which ones he should tackle first.

To be honest, all he wanted to do was lie on Sidney's sofa, head in her lap, while she stroked his hair and listened to his woes, but that was out of the question. For one, it was entirely wimpish and self-centered and he was disgusted enough by his behaviour this afternoon. Two, Sidney had woes of her own, both financial and emotional. Jacko going bush had left her short of a small but vital amount of income, Madison's parents were still using her as an unpaid childminder, and last week, Aidan had been escorted home by Constable Marshall, who'd found him in the company of marrow boy, Wade. There had been no sign of incipient anti-social activity, no spray cans, lighters or crowbars, but Casey felt Wade's aegis was one Aidan could happily forgo. She had spoken to both lads, and judging by Aidan's grey, tear-stained face, used words of unambiguous quality. Sidney was mortified and appalled, but wouldn't let Kerry comfort her. Wouldn't let Kerry lend her money, even just to tide her over. Didn't, truth be told, seem to want him around at all.

But did that mean he should do what she wanted? Or should he be fighting harder to break down her barriers, which, he could clearly see, were her first defence against fear and panic? Should he override her objections and gently but firmly compel her to let him in, let him help? Or would that simply make things worse?

Perhaps if they'd had more time together, they'd have had more of those deep, intimate conversations in which they revealed to each other all their vulnerabilities, regrets, hopes and dreams. He could finally tell her what had gone on for him, that morning of his wedding when all became clear and he'd resolved to transform, and she could release the last of the resentment she still held for her feckless ex. They'd made tentative forays into that emotional territory, but further progress had been cut short — by becoming frantically busy, in his case, and anxious and stressed in Sidney's. The result being that they did not feel as if they truly knew each other, and without that solid foundation, trust was hard to build. Well, *he* trusted Sidney because he was a naturally trusting person, but she had . . . issues. Fair enough, he supposed, her last man *had* been a chancer of the first water. But could she not see that Kerry would stand by her? That he had only her best interests at heart?

He should call her, tell her that he *had* been to Reuben's house and put steps in place with Casey to deliver on his promise. But he could almost hear Sidney's response: why hadn't he persisted at the house? Why hadn't he made *sure* Reuben was OK? He'd been right there, on the spot, whereas Casey might not get around there for days and ya, ya, ya . . .

Kerry started the engine, put the Fielder in gear without due care and winced at the graunching sound. The radio, the one bright constant during his recent endless to-ing and fro-ing, was in the middle of 'Hound Dog'. Mr Presley was advising the person of the title that he no longer considered him a friend due to an overestimation of his ability to catch rabbits. Kerry switched him off.

The Fielder's clock said five-forty. Sidney would be busy getting tea ready for the kids. He would demonstrate his thoughtfulness by not disturbing her. It was too late to call the council, and he'd had no text from Tai, so he may as well head back to Woodhall, stopping on the way at the Four Square to get milk and bread even though — he'd made a point of checking — they didn't need any. After Meredith had warned him that his job performance was sub-par, he'd vowed to pull his socks up. She hadn't used the words 'on borrowed time' but that was his distinct impression. And now that Jonty was up and about more, Kerry's job was at even greater risk. It still suited Meredith to have him there to help, but it might not be long before Jonty felt strong enough to call all the shots, and then it would be '*Sayonara*, Kerry' (or more likely '*Raus, raus*', in Jonty's case). Don't let the door hit you where the good Lord split you, to adapt another of Jacko's maxims.

He parked the car, and carried the shopping bag into the kitchen. Evening meals were outside his job description, though in the early days he had cooked a few to demonstrate his willingness to go above and beyond. An unexpected voice made him bang his head on the fridge door.

'Restocking the mushroom soup?'

Jonty in the doorway. He had ditched the tartan pyjamas and dressing gown a while back, and now looked every inch the picture of a country gentleman, with the emphasis, Kerry thought privately, on the first syllable of the first word. But he needed this job, so politeness was the way.

'Bread and milk.'

His smile was not returned.

'I trust my wife docked your wages for your failure to fulfil your duties?'

No, but she'd given him a stern telling-off did not seem a suitable reply. No reply at all seemed better still.

'What is the notice period of your contract?' said Jonty. 'For future reference.'

And that was it. The last straw, dressed up in tweed and moleskins. Kerry had nothing to lose, so why hold anything back?

'Look,' he said, 'I'm here solely for Mrs Barton and we both know it. You don't like me, and I'm certainly not fond of you. If you want me gone, be a man and do the deed. Don't slither about spitting like some toothless snake.'

Jonty stared at him, cold-eyed, much like the aforementioned serpent.

'Very well,' he said. 'You're dismissed.'

'Right.' Kerry resisted the urge to kick over a chair. 'Fine. The notice period you expressed such interest in is a week. I will be gone in three days.'

'What's this?'

Meredith had entered.

'I've fired him,' said Jonty, unperturbed.

'Why?'

'He's completely useless and an unnecessary drain on our finances.'

'Do I not get a say?' Meredith was bristling as much as someone with her cool demeanour could. 'They are, after all, mostly *my* finances.'

Now Jonty's composure began to slip. He hated being reminded of his dependency, despite it being predominantly of his own making.

'If you insist on having help, then we will advertise for a replacement. A *quality* replacement.'

'I dislike interviewing people,' said Meredith.

'So to avoid that, you're prepared to tolerate rudeness, lax time-keeping and meals an Algerian prisoner would reject?'

'That won't happen again.'

'No, it won't,' said Jonty. 'Because he is *dismissed*.'

The phrase 'and that's my final word' hung in the air like the miasma of Victorian nightsoil. But if Meredith intended to retort (for example with, 'We'll discuss this later when you've calmed down'), she was forestalled by the sound of the front door banging open, and a voice calling out 'Hello?' in a way that sounded more like a challenge than a greeting.

In the kitchen doorway appeared a young woman, chopped hair dyed black, every visible orifice pierced, a large upper arm tattoo of a woman wearing some kind of mediaeval gag. Her black singlet said *The Slits*, and her jeans (also black) must surely double as compression stockings. Her first impression distracted Kerry from noticing that she was exceptionally beautiful, and, when he did, he was so taken by surprise that his mind went completely blank.

Fortunately, Meredith said, 'Sophie.'

'Hello, Mother.'

Neither woman moved forward to embrace.

Sophie addressed her father. 'Hey, Pops.'

Without waiting for a response, she turned her — God, stunning, get a grip — gaze on Kerry.

'So you're him,' she said. 'Not what I pictured.'

And she grinned in a way that sent all coherent thoughts rushing once more from Kerry's mind like air escaping from a balloon, sound effects and all.

'Sophie, what are you doing here?'

Kerry had retained just enough mental capacity to pick up that Meredith's question was a tad lacking in maternal fondness.

'I was invited.'

Sophie's face may not be what Kerry had pictured either, but her expression was an exact match.

'By him.'

She pointed at Kerry, and, as both Meredith and Jonty turned their accusing gaze in his direction, it was all he could do not to back into the corner. He wanted to protest that he'd invited her to lunch — *lunch* — at a date yet to be determined! He hadn't thrown out some casual suggestion for her to drop in at any old time, unannounced.

'You didn't tell them, did you?'

Sophie's met three sets of accusing eyes.

'I, er—'

He'd *meant* to, he really had, but . . .

'Not that I'd expect any warmer welcome than this.' She was speaking to her parents now. 'But if you'd been warned, you'd probably make *some* effort to fucking pretend you were glad to see me.'

'I don't see why,' said her father. 'You're hardly thrilled to see us.'

'I'm your *daughter*,' she said. 'Parents are *supposed* to be glad to see their children. If I was Nic, you'd be all over me like a fucking *rash*—'

Jonty raised his hand, and Sophie flinched.

'Don't you *dare* use your sister as an excuse for your own poor behaviour,' said Jonty. And you're hardly a *child*. You're thirty years old, for God's sake.'

'Please.' Meredith stepped forward, between them. 'Can we—?'

But no, Sophie couldn't.

'See what I mean?' she said to Kerry, then closed her eyes and shook her head. 'Thirty years old. Thirty fucking years old . . .'

Her eyes flashed open. 'I'm thirty-*one*, you old cunt!'

'That's *enough*!' said Jonty, as Meredith said, '*Please!*'

But loudest of all was Kerry's phone. He'd programmed the ring tone to be the opening chords of AC/DC's 'Back in Black', and possibly had the volume set a little high.

He pulled it from his pocket. Sidney. Thank God. A reason to excuse himself from this pit of fire.

'Sorry, sorry.' He sidled past them all and jogged down to the entranceway, where he hit the green button.

'Hello. Thank God. Did you psychically receive my cry for help?'

'No.' Sidney sounded tense. 'No, I didn't.'

'OK, so, you'll never believe—'

'You need to shut up,' said Sidney. 'Shut up and listen.'

More than tense. Angry. He shut up.

'I've just got off the phone with your mother. Mac gave her my number because she hasn't heard from *you* for weeks.'

God, was something up with his mother? Or his father?

'We had a great old chat,' said Sidney.

Any relief that his parents were fine withered under the fury pulsing through the ether.

'She told me all about why you left England.'

Kerry couldn't work out why he was under attack. '*I* told you why.'

'You mentioned it, yes,' said Sidney. 'But you made it sound like *you* were the one who'd been left at the altar!'

'I did not! I *told* you what happened!'

But even as he protested, he sensed he was not on firm ground.

'You did no such thing,' said Sidney. 'You danced around like you always do, and you did *not* correct me, even though you *knew* I'd got the wrong end of the stick.'

'I *didn't* know you didn't know! You never said!'

'Did you tell me you'd jilted your fiancée? Did you come out with those exact words?'

'Well, I can't be—'

'What? Trusted?' Sidney's laugh was short and unamused. 'No, you can't. Sod off, Kerry. Don't call me. Don't come around. I don't want to see you.'

And she hung up.

The strength of Kerry's reaction surprised him. He'd not been this close to tears since childhood. All he wanted to do was crawl off into a warm, dark space and call his mother. Whose fault, of course, all this was in the first place . . .

No. It was his fault and his alone. He'd had an inkling Sidney thought he was the jiltee, and he'd *intended* to put her straight, he really had. What stopped him was shame, which was neither pure nor simple. Since leaving home, he'd worked hard to create that new, improved Kerry-Francis Macfarlane, and he'd enjoyed the reaction his upgraded self had received. Reflected in Sidney's eyes, he'd seen a man of substance and integrity, and he could not bring himself to shatter that mirror. Though, to be fair, he'd been giving it a few good hard knocks recently.

The thumping of blood in his ears meant he didn't hear Sophie's Doc Martens on the wooden floorboards until she was right beside him.

'Great idea,' she said. 'Really great. You should be proud of yourself. And thanks for coming to my fucking launch — not.'

She didn't wait for a response, yanked open the front door and slammed it shut.

Kerry stood there, feeling the phone cool in his hand. Then he walked back into the kitchen to formally accept his dismissal.

Chapter 34

Sidney

'I'm going to have to sell the car,' Sidney told Mac. 'It's either that or sell my soul to a loan shark. If I don't — well, it's not going to be a very merry Christmas.'

She tried to keep her tone light, but she knew Mac wasn't fooled. Her hands had trembled when she'd accepted the cup of tea, and Mac had pushed the sugar bowl across the table, watched without comment as Sidney added four spoonfuls. That kindness coupled with the realisation she could drink tea with sugar without mentally calculating the cost put Sidney close to tears. Oh, who was she kidding? *Everything* put Sidney close to tears right now.

How did other people cope? There were plenty worse off than she was, so how *did* they manage? Did they simply not think twice about using food banks or asking for help from charitable organisations? Sidney could no more do that than she could ask her parents for help. The *shame* of it! But perhaps that was her comfortable, middle-class upbringing talking? Chances were she didn't know what real poverty was actually like.

Because, let's face it, she'd avoided a real crisis until now. For nearly ten years, dammit, she'd teetered on the edge but not tipped over. And this failure was her own fault — she *knew* her budget was blowing out, but she'd let the situation with Madison go on, muttering but not acting, past the point of sense. And now she could barely afford to pay the bills, let alone buy Christmas presents for the boys.

She could explain it to them, she supposed, but they were still young enough to expect some magic around this time. They had never, fortunately, expected Game Boys or iPods, but they would be disappointed with stockings filled only with homemade fudge and crappy plastic toys from the dollar shop that broke by lunchtime. Right now, Sidney wasn't even sure she could afford the latter.

She'd been stupid — had crossed her fingers and hoped it would all turn out OK (obviously *she'd* never outgrown a belief in magic). But it hadn't, it *wasn't* OK. And it was all her fault.

A lone consolation was that she'd nipped her other stupidity in the bud. She'd given Kerry the boot, which was the right thing to do. Her sentiment hadn't got the better of her *that* time.

And she wasn't entirely devoid of solutions. She *could* sell the car, and she'd been thinking about how to manage without it.

'I wondered — could I come on the Love Bus with you on Mondays?' Sidney asked Mac. 'I can do the shopping and library run, and, you know, purchase clothes for the boys at the op shop. Then all I need to figure out is how to get to Mr Phipps's place. He might be able to pick me up, though, of course, I'll need to make sure he deducts part of my wages for his petrol expenses . . .'

Mac made a doubtful face, and Sidney's nerves twanged taut as garrotting wire.

'The Love Bus might be heading for the scrap heap,' said Mac. 'Keep this under your hat for now, but Doc Love is retiring, and I'm not sure his replacement will want to keep supporting that particular community service.'

'His replacement? You've already *found* someone?'

'Mm.'

Mac looked as close to embarrassed as she ever got, and Sidney was miffed. How many of her other friends were keeping secrets from her? Or was she just too dense to spot what was obvious to everyone else?

'I'm still sweating about it,' said Mac. 'It wasn't even my *job* to find a replacement, but it needed to be done, and once I'd started down the track . . .'

Mac wasn't embarrassed, she was anxious. Sidney knew how *that* felt.

'Well, go on, who is he? Or she?'

'He,' said Mac. 'His name's Ashwin Ghadavi, Indian-born, London-trained, young, presentable if you like them bony, and he and Kerry could form a doubles team in the Talking Olympics.' She caught herself. 'Oh. Sorry . . .'

'It's fine,' said Sidney. 'Really.'

'You know he lost his job at the Bartons?'

'Didn't know, don't care.'

'Guess that means he'll be leaving town.'

'Seriously — can we talk about something else?'

Mac pursed her mouth. 'Also means Littleville is scuppered. Are we happy with that?'

'Why should it be scuppered?' said Sidney, crossly. 'There's still you and me, and Bernard, and maybe Gene . . .'

'No one who's putting in the effort Kerry was, in other words.'

'Well, we could—'

'And no one who's able or prepared to put it in, either.'

It was the truth. Sidney could ignore a lot of harsh realities, it seemed, but not that one. Kerry, disorganised as he was, had been the lynchpin holding that project together. He'd had the vision, and had worked tirelessly to enrol supporters. Without his zeal and toil, Mac was right — Littleville would never see the light of day.

It didn't mean he could be trusted, however. No, she was right about *that* at least.

'He went to see Bernard,' Mac said. 'Finally got the Hampton District Council to agree to a meeting, and asked Bernard to deputise for him and plead our case. Bernard rang me to ask whether I thought it was worthwhile. Seems even Bernard's realised that Littleville doesn't really exist without Kerry.'

Sometimes Sidney wondered if Mac enjoyed twisting the knife. But no, she was simply a realist, a pragmatist, one who didn't see the point of gloss or euphemism. Mac delivered it straight, and if the recipient felt hurt or offended, that was their problem.

'And what did you tell him?' Sidney asked.

'That I'd talk to you and the others.'

Great. One more thorn thicket to bash through.

'There's been quite a bit of work put in already,' said Sidney. 'Certainly a lot of promises made . . .'

'And everything depends on getting the council off our backs,' said Mac. 'Kerry knew this meeting was our last shot. Thing is, even though Bernard has lately risen in my estimation, he's hardly Mr Charisma. And I suspect the council is well inured to being bored into agreement.'

'So we *are* scuppered?'

'Without Kerry we are.'

Sidney felt the thorn thicket closing in on her, much like a mediaeval iron maiden.

'I'm not talking to him,' she said. 'If you want him to stay on the project, fine. But I will *not* be the go-between!'

'Not asking you to be,' said Mac. 'Just wanted to know if you'd object to being in the same room as him. If that eventuality arose.'

'Oh, what does it matter what *I* want?'

Sidney knew she sounded childish, but really, it was all getting a bit much.

Mac stood up, patted Sidney on the shoulder.

'More tea? I might have a biscuit here somewhere, too. Jacko usually does the shopping, so who knows?'

'Have you heard from him?' Sidney felt guilty for not asking earlier.

'Yep.' Mac peered into a cupboard. 'Still no sign of the dog.'

Sidney felt both guilty *and* selfish for asking the next question. 'How long do you think he'll stay in the bush?'

Mac was squinting at the 'best before' date on a packet of Krispies.

'Big Rog the DOC ranger has dropped another week's supplies off to him at the hut.'

Sidney's heart sank. She'd been hoping for at least *one* evening's work next week. What was the best way to advertise a car for sale these days? She'd better find out pronto.

'Sammo might buy your car.' Mac the mind-reader dropped a teabag in each mug, and lifted the kettle. 'He'll need his own wheels when he moves to Christchurch. Can't take Daddy's Hilux.'

'I'll earn back all that babysitting money I paid him,' said Sidney, glumly. 'Probably.'

'Speaking of babysitting,' said Mac. 'Do you want a hand telling Olivia to shove it?'

Sidney had a sudden vision of entering the Jensens' with a Rottweiler, unclipping its lead and yelling 'Sick!'

'Thanks,' she said, 'but I got myself into this mess. Too soft, that's my problem. Too worried about someone else's child when I should have been thinking about my own two.'

Mac brought two steaming mugs back to the table, set one in front of Sidney.

'Don't fret about Madison,' she said. 'Corinna is keeping an eye on her, and if there's any hint of neglect, she'll have the authorities in there straight away.'

‘I’m not sure that makes me feel better,’ said Sidney. ‘How would that sweet child cope in care? Olivia and Rick might not win parents of the year, but they’re still her mum and dad. And she loves them — that’s heartbreakingly obvious.’

‘You know foster parents get paid?’

Mac was quite serious, but Sidney still wanted to laugh.

‘I’m pretty sure I wouldn’t qualify as suitable,’ she said. ‘I’m a single mother on the benefit, earning side-money waiting tables and tending bees.’

‘Worth investigating?’

Sidney appreciated the intent, but—

‘Let me haul myself out of this financial quagmire first,’ she said. ‘And then — well, we’ll see.’

By the time three o’clock came around, Sidney’s nerves were vibrating at such a high frequency she was amazed not to have attracted an entourage of dogs.

This was the plan: if Madison was not picked up, Sidney would grab one of the teachers, explain that she couldn’t take the child home, and leave the school to sort out Madison’s transport arrangements. The toughest part would be apologising to Madison. Last thing Sidney wanted was for her to feel she’d been an inconvenience, a burden. No part of this situation was Maddie’s fault. It was Olivia and Rick’s and, by taking this long to grow a spine, Sidney’s.

Waiting in the school grounds, trying to keep her breathing sub-hyperventilation level, Sidney barely noticed her own sons until they were under her nose, gabbling for her attention.

Achieving the physical feat only mothers can master, Sidney kept one eye on the boys and scanned for Madison with the other. Her brain being thus split, she only heard snatches of what they were telling her, but that didn't matter, because the part of the brain that *was* focused was specially programmed to pick out key words, such as 'trouble', 'principal's office' and 'fees', plus the names of illicit substances and inappropriate sexual references. Today, the boys' conversation seemed to be mercifully free of anything contentious, being mainly, as far as she could tell, about a new way to catch Pokémon.

'Hey, hey, that sounds great,' she interrupted, fairly certain she spoke the truth. 'Have you guys seen Madison?'

They shook their heads. Mind you, they were boys with Pokémon on the brain. Madison could be right in front of them sticking her fingers in their eyes and they wouldn't notice.

'She's with Mrs Dundy,' said Tanya Booth, in passing. That girl had the ears of a lynx and the psychological profile of a high-ranking member of the Stasi.

'Do you know why, Tanya?'

'Nah. Don't think she's in trouble, though.'

Sidney was sure she didn't imagine the look of disappointment.

'OK, guys,' she said to the boys. 'I have to check why Madison's with the principal. Can you hang here and be good for ten minutes?'

They nodded solemnly. God, they were sweet. Sidney headed off to Mrs Dundy's office, praying she would still hold that opinion when she returned in ten minutes' time.

Mrs Dundy sounded like she should be sixty with a matronly bust, but she was barely thirty and as rangy as a whippet. She competed in ultramarathons for fun. Sidney saw her door was ajar, so knocked and pushed it further open. The two were sitting on a small sofa, Maddie sitting straight, hands in her lap, Mrs Dundy angled in. As soon as Madison saw Sidney, she leapt up and ran towards her, smiling. For the nine-hundredth time that day, Sidney's heart lurched.

'Hi, sorry to barge in,' she said to Mrs Dundy.

'That's all right,' said the principal. 'Madison and I had just finished our chat.'

She moved to her desk, clearly expecting Sidney to take Madison home now. Madison's face said she expected the same. Sidney took a deep, deep breath.

'*I* need to have a chat with you now, I'm afraid.'

Why was wine so expensive? Sidney decided to rephrase: why was wine that didn't taste like the lees of a week-old salad bowl so expensive?

That was one of Kerry's good points — he was a source of decent wine. It could not, she reminded herself sternly, make up for his deal-breaking flaws. Besides, sorrows didn't really get drowned, did they? They only became temporarily submerged, like crabs at high tide, their ability to give you a nasty nip undiminished.

The boys were sound asleep in bed and she hoped Maddie was, too. Oh, God, her little face! So hurt, even though Sidney *stressed* to her it wasn't her fault. And she had to leave her there, in Mrs Dundy's office, feeling like she'd just abandoned a puppy in the pound. God knows how the principal got Madison home safely, but Sidney had to trust that she had.

Nothing on the two TV channels her dodgy aerial picked up, and she didn't have the strength to read a book. What she really wanted to do was drive up to the Jensens', bundle Madison up in her duvet and bring her back home, where she belonged.

Belonged — Sidney did a mental face-palm. She didn't belong anywhere but her *own* home, with her *own* parents. And she was *not* Sidney's responsibility.

And Kerry was *not* welcome in her mind! She was feeling vulnerable and sad and anxious and that's why she kept thinking about him. Because he'd been so adept at keeping gremlins at bay, for making the world seem sunnier and the impossible within reach—

Oh, for God's *sake*, get a grip! Kerry was gone and it was good riddance. It was *right* that he hadn't tried to contact her. Why would he? She'd made her position crystal-clear. He knew she'd only hang up on him . . .

Shame that his mother had been so nice. Funny as a fit, too; Kerry must get that from her. Sidney hoped she'd done a good job of covering up her shock when Bronagh spilled the beans about Kerry's wedding day. Bronagh wasn't to know her loose-with-the-truth son had fudged the key facts.

No, Sidney had kept her cool, or at least kept her boiling rage under a tight lid until she could politely end the call. Her only regret was that she'd not been *quite* cool enough to probe for more detail about Kerry's ex-fiancée, the bride left weeping at the altar. Was she pretty? How pretty? How long did she weep? How much had she loved him—?

A knock on the door — who at this hour? Not that it was late, not even eight-thirty, but Sidney never had visitors in the evening. Apart from Kerry, of cour—

Stop it!

At the door, Sidney wished she had a peephole. She couldn't shout 'Who is it?' because that would wake the boys. No choice. She opened up, hoping it wasn't anyone with bad news or ill intent.

'Olivia!'

She was about to add, 'What on earth?' but Olivia said, 'Yep, hi, can you get Madison?'

Sidney could have been offended by the abrupt — no, let's be real — *rude* tone. But any offence was swept away by a tsunami of panic. Sidney's heart hammered in her ears so loud, she could barely hear herself speak.

'Madison isn't *here*,' she said.

Olivia frowned, as much as Botox or whatever would allow.

'What do you mean? Is she at some school thing?'

'Jesus bloody hell.' Sidney fought dual urges to run in chicken circles, and to reach out and throttle the woman. 'Olivia, do you not know where your own *daughter* is?'

Olivia flinched, but then her face tightened with anger.

'She's not just *my* daughter. Her prick of a father has to take *some* fucking responsibility.'

Wow. A tiny, minuscule part of Sidney empathised with that frustration. But Olivia was a grown-up and a parent, and that came first.

'Well, let's bloody hope he's taken responsibility tonight.' Sidney was shaking, with anger now as well as fear. 'How about I call him — see if he has Madison? Because if he doesn't, we have a missing child. And while that may not bother *you* all that much, it freaks me out completely.'

Olivia gave her a look that Sidney had not seen since secondary school, and of which she had no fond memories. Sidney's parents — well, her mother — had insisted on sending her to a private school, the kind where a chubby, bookish, un-sporty girl from an only moderately well-off middle-class family attracts attention from shiny-haired, ski-tanned posh girls the way an injured deer attracts wolverines.

'That's right,' Olivia said. 'You go ahead and take that moral high ground. Kid yourself you're Miss Perfect Earth Mother because it makes you feel better about your crappy life in your crappy little house.'

Sidney had never slapped anyone. She'd never even smacked her boys despite being sorely tempted. But her hand twitched now, rose up with an instinct of its own. She was *so* close to acting on that impulse, she could feel the satisfying sting of impact, see the scarlet imprint of her fingers on Olivia's contemptuous cheek.

But what would that gain? How would that help Madison?

'I'm going inside now to call Rick,' Sidney informed Olivia. 'And if I get no joy, I'm calling the police. You can do whatever you like, I really don't care.'

And she shut the door in Olivia's face. Stood for a moment with her forehead pressed against it, to calm the trembling. Then she sprinted into the kitchen to find her phone.

Shit, her hands were still shaking. This was all her fault! She'd put money worries before a little girl's safety and now look what had happened.

Shit! *Double* shit! Rick's phone went through to voicemail. Should she do as she'd said and call the police? She didn't know for sure that Madison was missing . . .

Mac. That's who she'd call. Mac could think straight in a crisis.

Sidney scrolled through her contacts and saw 'Kerry' flash by. She had forgotten to delete his number, and for *just* a moment, an impulse took her to reverse back, find his name again and hit dial.

No. Bad choice, and she'd made enough of those today. Sidney found the 'M's, and dialled the ever-reliable Mac.

Chapter 35

Bernard

Bernard had until recently categorised his wife as one of those women, like Mac Reid, who had long been resigned to the physical changes aging wrought.

Now, he could distinguish the difference. Mac Reid's wayward hair, practical clothing and resolutely un-made-up face were the opposite of giving in. By not fighting the aging process, Mac Reid was making a statement, issuing a challenge. 'Take me as I am,' she declared to the world, 'or get lost!' Mac embraced aging, as if it allowed her to strip away artifice and reveal more of her true self.

Whereas Patricia, Bernard could see now, had surrended unhappily to the changes. She had despaired at her widening girth, sagging arms and jawline, her thinning, greying hair. She was a size twelve when he met her, with hair that bounced dark and glossy to her shoulders, and a curvy, fifties-style figure. The kind that he personally preferred, and that Patricia in those days dressed to enhance; Bernard had been both proud and jealous when she attracted wolf whistles. By the age of fifty, however, Patricia had expanded to a size eighteen and given away her pretty, feminine frocks, her red heels and colourful accessories.

To Bernard, she'd always been the same Patricia, unchanged in essentials. But that had not been true for her. For every part of her youthful exterior that faded, so too had a part of her sense of self. Every time she stared into the mirror, she became more unable to see a woman *worth* seeing. If she despised the way she looked, then why would the world feel any differently? Much better to become invisible.

He'd hardly helped, holding a candle for Meredith, one of those rare women whom aging suited. How anguished Patricia must have felt every time she and Meredith met. How greatly she must have felt the gap between them, though she would, he knew, have never shown any hint that Meredith's presence caused her pain.

No wonder she'd retreated into books. Here he'd been, criticising her choice of reading material, when he should have recognised that they were both driven by exactly the same impulse — to escape into another world. His world might have been more intellectually demanding, but his motives for entering it were not in any way superior. Why had it taken so long for him to see that? To read *all* the signs and understand how unhappy she was? Why had he been such a poor specimen of a husband?

She'd sent him a postcard from Queenstown, a destination Bernard rated only slightly higher than Las Vegas. A tourist trap packed with drunken, skiing yahoos — the tiny superstitious part of Bernard feared there was a circle being reserved for him in Hell that bore an uncanny resemblance. Not a place he'd ever thought Patricia would warm to, either. But there she was, or, at least, there she'd been — he'd have to wait for the next postcard to find out where she was now. True to her stated intent to be incommunicado for three weeks, the postcard gave no contact details. It gave barely any information at all, other than to reassure him that she was safe. He assumed he could also infer that she was enjoying herself, and he wondered if she'd taken steps to — what was the term? — make herself over? Had she dyed her hair and donned denim jeans and some kind of loose floral top? Bernard's lack of fashion knowledge prevented him envisaging anything more specific. Let's face it, he would not care if she decided to dress like Carmen Miranda. A hat made of tropical fruit would be a small price to pay for her return.

A hand clapped down on his shoulder, startling him. Hastily, he slipped the postcard into the folder on his knee.

Gene Collins sat down in the adjacent chair.

'All ready to kick some council butt, Bernardo?'

'I am prepared, yes.' He strove not to stiffen at the man's tone. 'Although more notice would have been appreciated.'

'Young Kerry dumped you in it, didn't he?' Gene sucked in his bottom lip. 'Always pegged him as a flake. Doubts about this project right from the start.'

'Then why are you here?' said Bernard.

Gene smirked in a positively wolf-like manner. 'And miss the fun? Hoo, boy, no. If they'd charged *admittance*, I would have paid.'

Bernard hoped no one else intended to join them. Lately, he'd been in an . . . unsatisfactory frame of mind. Normally of a moderate, equable temper, since Patricia's departure he'd been plagued by fits of both sadness and fury, culminating in his most uncharacteristic outburst at young Macfarlane. Perhaps it did not help that he had no outlet for his emotions. He had not told *anyone* about Patricia — partly from shame, and partly because if he spoke it aloud, the last faint hope that it might all be a dream would evaporate.

'Oh, looky — more of the gang.'

Gene whistled in a most uncouth fashion to gain the attention of Sidney Gillespie and Mac Reid, who had just entered. Charles Love must have given his office manager the afternoon off. Bernard was not inclined to thank him.

Fortunately, Sidney chose the chair on his other side, while Mac sat next to Gene. A little space where Mac Reid was concerned was always welcome. Though Bernard appreciated that she had not grilled him about the cause of his outburst that evening at the Boat Shed. And the single malt she'd offered him had been first class.

Sidney Gillespie's face was flushed, as if she'd been running. But she gave him a wide smile, and Bernard was surprised to realise that she was very attractive. Yet one more example of his failure to properly observe.

'Thanks so much for doing this, Bernard,' she said. 'We really appreciate it.'

'Sure do,' said Gene, with undoubtedly malevolent ambiguity.

'There's Meredith.'

Mac Reid said the one name guaranteed to make Bernard leap in his chair. He prayed Gene Collins had not noticed.

'Good grief,' Mac added, 'and his Lordship.'

Even Bernard could not help a glance over his shoulder. The pair were moving to seats at the rear of the room. Jonty's height, hawked features and cool stare, all enhanced by beautifully tailored clothes, made him an imposing presence, and Meredith, elegant in his wake, was the perfect match. Bernard felt the sick plunge of mortification. Why had he been *such* a fool as to harbour the slightest hope of any claim on her affections? Why had he not appreciated that the finest woman in his life was right beside him all along?

'Why is *Jonty* here?' said Sidney.

Her face, Bernard was surprised and gratified to see, showed a distinct lack of warmth.

'This used to be his stamping ground,' said Gene. 'Probably came to piss on the doorways, let everyone know he's back.'

The man was irredeemably vulgar. But almost certainly correct.

'Oh, here's Aggie, Chester and Peg!'

Sidney swivelled in her seat and waved cheerfully.

'Aggie's wearing a Victorian hat with a miniature train around the brim,' she informed them. 'And Peg's dress has little tin soldiers on it, and her hair's dyed like the Union Jack.'

Gene Collins guffawed. 'All we need now is that travelling circus. Oh, wait.'

'If you're not going to support us,' Mac Reid told him, 'you can shove off.'

'I'm here, aren't I!' he protested. 'I could have been enjoying a quiet coffee and a read of the paper, but instead, I trekked all the way here to sit in a stuffy room for an hour.'

'Do you *ever* do any work?' asked Sidney, echoing Bernard's thoughts exactly.

'Hush, children,' said Mac. 'The forces of darkness draw nigh.'

From a door at the rear of the room entered Elaine and three Hampton district councillors, who, in direct contrast to Elaine, didn't look overly happy to be there. Bernard guessed that they'd all committed the same mistake he had on past occasions, which was to agree in private to her badgering request, in the hope that she'd go away and get on with whatever it was, leaving you alone. Most often she did, but sometimes she expected you to come along with her. Of course, if you wanted to avoid more badgering, you had no choice but to follow.

Elaine took her seat and, like a headmistress out of some Victorian children's story where school is akin to a prison, waited until there was complete silence. Then she smiled and brought the meeting to order. Bernard had once enjoyed making that little tap on the table, but now it reeked of petty authority.

'We are here to listen to submissions from the group organising the—' Elaine paused to scan her notes, though she knew full well what the project was called '—Littleville children's attraction.'

Subtly demeaning it already.

'I gather the original spokesperson is no longer willing to attend, and at the eleventh hour has passed the baton to—'

More note-checking, then a terrible smile in his direction.

'Bernard! How generous of you to step in at the last minute.' Elaine's gimlet eye scoured the crowd. 'But how unusual not to see Patricia here also. Is she unwell?'

Damn the woman. That was not too strong a phrase. Although Bernard had told no one, Patricia was not a recluse. She had friends she met occasionally for coffee, and a library book group on Tuesday evenings. It was quite possible that others knew — or had guessed — and passed that piece of ammunition on to Elaine. It could only be a matter of minutes before Elaine asked after his mother, in the manner of a sadistic knight slowly scything off body parts with a blade.

'Don't rise,' Sidney Gillespie whispered to him. 'Imagine her in her underwear. Actually, sorry, that's terrible advice. Imagine her with a pillow over her face instead.'

Bernard, most atypically, released a snort of amusement. And suddenly, he relaxed. He no longer cared for Elaine's opinion of him, or her cronies', or even Jonty Barton's, who would no doubt enjoy seeing him stumble. He had nothing to lose and a worthy project had everything to gain. He stood up, and was gratified to be greeted by a scrappy but enthusiastic round of applause from the Littleville supporters.

The gist of his argument was that Littleville was no different to a school fair or other not-for-profit fund-raising event that was staffed by volunteers. Such an event required only standard civil-defence safety procedures to be in place. In fact, it could strongly be argued (Bernard was quite proud of this point) that the fish factory site should be considered private property, and as they had the property owner's consent and there were no adverse effects on safety or traffic, then the council had no jurisdiction over it at all.

'Ooh, *schmack*,' he thought he heard Gene mutter.

Bernard was pleased to see nodding among the heads of the three district councillors. Elaine's head, however, remained as immoveable as her smile. Never a good sign. Meant she had something up her polyester sleeve.

And so it proved.

'Thank you, Bernard, for a submission you've put *so* much thought into,' she said. 'But I must inform you that recent developments have most likely made this meeting an unfortunate waste of everyone's time.'

A wary, expectant stillness settled over the room. Bernard heard Sidney's hissed intake of breath, and Mac Reid mutter an indecipherable but short word. Gene Collins's shoulders appeared to be shaking. Bernard was glad *someone* was able to find amusement in the situation, though the temptation to clip the man around the ear was growing by the minute.

'Though not an *entire* waste,' Elaine continued, 'as we can take this opportunity to thank those few of your group who are present for putting these new wheels in motion.'

She smiled at her council colleagues, who smiled back in a way that suggested they feared she might lunge forward and bite them in the neck.

'I refer to the fact that the Littleville proposal has been instrumental in highlighting the potential of the factory site,' said Elaine. 'And it is with great pleasure that I announce that the Hampton District Council is placing its full support behind a consortium of local businessmen, who have just this morning completed the purchase of the former Caracci fish-processing factory, with the intention of developing it into an industrial park.'

'What the actual hell?'

Gene Collins wasn't amused now. He shot to his feet with more alacrity than Bernard had thought he was capable of.

'Where was the consultation process?' he demanded. 'You can't arbitrarily make decisions like that.'

'The council has no financial interest or role in the development, Mr Collins.' If Elaine's smile got any wider, it would surely cause lasting muscular damage. 'We have always been eager to encourage entrepreneurial investment in our region. The business consortium concerned has an excellent track record, and we have no doubt that they will make a success of this enterprise, one that can only be of lasting benefit to the region. And, of course, Gabriel's Bay.'

She picked up the folder in front of her — which was purely for show, as had been this entire meeting. Bernard found his hands clenching and made an enormous effort to breathe and relax. Letting fly a volley of abuse at Elaine might be cathartic but it would only enable her to climb still further up the ladder of victory. She was looking down on them from a great enough height as it was.

'I do apologise that you have all made a wasted journey.' Elaine did not even bother to sound sincere. 'As I say, the sale was completed just hours ago, so there was no time to inform anyone.'

Gene Collins, reluctantly back in his seat, emitted a cough that Bernard could have sworn sounded like the word 'Bullshit'.

'I have a question.'

The voice that came from the back was instantly recognisable. Bernard felt Sidney jump, just as he'd done when made aware of Meredith's presence.

Young Macfarlane was two rows behind, on his feet. His usual expression of slappable impishness was nowhere to be seen, his demeanour confident, unapologetic, that of a man who expected an answer.

Elaine's smile was tolerant. She'd already won; this was mere skirmishing around the edges.

'Mr Macfarlane,' she said. 'You've decided to join us, after all?'

'I have, Mrs Pardew, yes,' said the young man, briskly. 'And my question is this: was Mr Weston correct in his assertion that Littleville would not need council approval if it were on private property?'

Elaine arched an eyebrow. 'A little after the fact, don't you feel?'

Macfarlane checked his watch. 'We still have fifteen minutes of scheduled time,' he said. 'As you pointed out, we have come all this way, so why not do us the courtesy and allow us to use it?'

A palpable hit. There was nothing Elaine hated more than being thought of as ill-mannered.

'Very well,' she said, 'though I doubt that's a question that can be answered right at this—'

One of her colleagues piped up. 'I'll answer it.'

'Good Lord,' murmured Mac Reid. 'Spines growing all round.'

'I feel we should consult,' began Elaine.

'No, it's perfectly straightforward.'

Her colleague was an earnest man, with a knitted vest, black-rimmed square spectacles and possibly a death wish.

'If, as Mr Weston identified, you have the owner's permission to use the property, traffic is not impeded, and safety and risk-management procedures are in place, then, no, you do not need to obtain approval from the council.'

'Thank you,' said Kerry, and sat down.

Elaine seized her chance to wrap up the meeting. Bernard half expected her to lead her recalcitrant colleague from the room by his ear.

In the bustle of the room emptying, Mac Reid leaned across to address Sidney. 'What's he up to?'

'Why ask me?' she replied crossly.

'Yes, why not ask the man himself?' said Gene. 'He's right here.'

Macfarlane was indeed in the aisle beside them.

'Hello, everyone,' he said, though his eyes were on Sidney, who,

Bernard noted, was pretending to inspect the ceiling cornices.

'What are you up to?' said Mac Reid.

'Nope, don't answer that.' Gene Collins got to his feet. 'If I sit in this room any longer, I'll commit murder. And I won't be all that fussy about my victim.'

He pushed his way out into the aisle.

'Come on,' he said. 'The Kozy Kettle beckons us for the lukewarm beverage of our choice.'

Bernard had a moment of anxiety that he would be forced to converse with Meredith and Jonty — but the pair had gone. Jonty would be gleeful that the project had died a death, was probably crowing right now. Bernard tried not to speculate whether Meredith might be saying anything in their — his — defence. What did it matter? His humiliation was complete.

As if to keep that thought at the forefront of his mind, the Kozy Kettle insisted on reminding Bernard of Elaine. Its predominant decorative motif was the lacy frill, and it had shelves crammed with china figurines, cats mostly, and vases filled with plastic flowers. Where Elaine's house and the Kettle diverged was in the level of dust: not one speck in the former, so much in the latter that it brought to mind the truism about all cats being grey in the dark.

Sidney, presumably as an excuse to avoid young Macfarlane's company, went up to the counter to place orders.

'What are you up to?' Mac Reid pinned Macfarlane to the spot. One could grudgingly admire the woman's persistence.

'Mr Caracci phoned me,' Macfarlane replied. 'Wanted to warn me that his sons had done a deal for the factory. Apparently, the lads have lately got into a bit of strife with the restaurant, and the offer they'd considered beneath them became suddenly attractive. He apologised, but you know—' he attempted an appalling Italian accent '—eet's-a family.'

'Yes, but what are *you* up to?' said Mac Reid. 'We thought you'd skipped town.'

'Er, no,' said Macfarlane. 'Although my location *is* now more rural than urban. I've bought a barn.'

'*What*?' Collins's tone signified he was not in a mood for leg-pulling.

'Large agricultural outbuilding,' said Macfarlane. 'Often used for—'

'Yes, yes, stow it. *How* and *why* did you buy a barn?'

'And where?' added Mac Reid. 'And who from? Come on, hurry up.'

'Er, where: out by the glass-blowers. From who: a bank — mortgagee sale. How: with money from the sale of my own house in London. Why? Hmm . . .'

'Wait,' said Collins. 'You had a house in London?'

Sidney had returned with a tray, and began to place cups on the table. Bernard could see she was feigning indifference while straining every nerve to listen to young Macfarlane. It was a skill he himself had honed to a fine art, at every social gathering where Meredith was present.

'It wasn't *that* desirable a house,' said Macfarlane. 'I mean Dalston's no Stoke Newington. I bought it three years ago because — I don't know, that's what you did, between getting a job and getting . . .'

'Getting what?' demanded Collins. 'Mugged? Rabies?'

'Married,' said Mac Reid.

'You're *married*?' said Collins. 'Whoa, dark horse.'

'No, I'm not,' said Macfarlane. 'I, er, got cold feet. On the day . . .'

Collins laughed out loud, quite unashamed to be displaying an impolite, possibly prurient, level of amusement.

'Why?' he said. 'Was she a hairy-toed troll?'

'Indeed not, she was very pretty . . .'

Macfarlane was embarrassed, but clearly determined not to equivocate. Bernard had to give him credit for that.

'But she was someone I hadn't properly bothered to get to know,' he said. 'And because I'd been merrily skating along the surface of my whole life, I didn't realise that until the week before the big day. All I'd cared about up till then was that she was gorgeous, my friends thought her a catch, and she seemed very keen on me. And that it was high time I was married because most of my friends had already beaten me to it. I hadn't thought about the future at *all*, other than to form a fuzzy picture of the two of us smiling at each other across the breakfast table. I'd never talked to Julia about how we'd raise children, or even whether we would *have* children. I didn't know if she wanted to travel, if she considered herself a career woman or would prefer to stay at home. I didn't know if she had any spiritual inclinations or what her politics were. Until, as I say, a week before the wedding.'

'What happened?' said Mac Reid. 'Did you discover her collection of Nazi memorabilia?'

'Not a *million* miles from the truth,' said Macfarlane, with a slight grimace. 'We'd spent the night at my house in Dalston. We'd agreed it was our last one before we got hitched; Julia's parents were quite traditional. Plus they were paying for the whole wedding. Which is why I'd agreed to a grey morning suit that made me look as though I was going to a costume party as Sir Godfrey Tibbet from *A View to a Kill*—'

'Crank it along,' said Mac Reid. 'We haven't got all day.'

'All *right*,' said Macfarlane, not unfairly aggrieved. 'This is *difficult* for me, have a heart.'

'Wrong person to ask,' said Collins.

Bernard was quietly thrilled to see Gene quail a little under Mac Reid's stare.

'All right,' Macfarlane continued. 'So we were at my place, and it being a beautiful day, we decided to stroll around the neighbourhood. First time — usually Julia hopped straight in a taxi and went home to Highgate, or we taxied to Islington for brunch. Perhaps that should have been a clue right there. Anyway, we were passing a council estate that had been recently done up, and Julia said, "I'm surprised by how nice those gardens are. Not what I'd expect in public housing".'

'Uh oh,' said Collins.

'Indeed,' said Macfarlane. 'A little warning bell did sound, but, of course, I ignored it. I was walking with beautiful Julia, my fiancée. I was the squire, the big man about town. Then we came to the edge of the estate, and playing on a patch of grass were three small children making believe that an old plastic washing basket was a car. And Julia said . . .'

He screwed up his face as if uttering the words would pain him.

'Julia said: "Look how much they're loving that basket. Who says poor children need money for toys?"'

Not unexpectedly, Gene Collins and Mac Reid chuckled.

'Did she offer to give them tea in her gingerbread house?' Mac Reid enquired.

'Not that day,' said Macfarlane. 'The warning bell was now on full klaxon, so I couldn't ignore it. But I decided, as is my wont, to make light of it. "Did you not have a washing-basket car in your back garden?" I asked her. "That was all we had room for in mine because of my father's shed. I always craved a full-size football goal or, failing that, a trampoline."'

'And Julia said—?' asked Collins. 'I think I'm getting the hang of this now.'

'She said: "No". And then she added, "Mummy believed that a trampoline in the garden gave out entirely the wrong message."'

'Did you turn and run for the hills?' said Collins. 'I would have.'

'Of course not,' said Macfarlane. 'I completed our walk. During which she came out with other gems, such as "I do so loathe those oversize televisions. They simply cheapen a room" and "Have you ever noticed that neighbourhoods like this have a much higher proportion of fat children?" When we reached home, I put her in a taxi, and then I crawled into my bed and had a nervous breakdown.'

'Wait,' said Mac Reid. 'You said this was a week before the wedding? I thought you ditched her on the day?'

'Yes, well remembered,' said Macfarlane, with a sigh. He fiddled with the sugar dispenser, which had a most unhygienic crust around its aperture.

'I argued with myself right up until the wedding-day morning,' Macfarlane continued. 'I'd made a promise; I could work on her way of thinking; my father-in-law-to-be would murder me, etc. But I spent that last night in a cold sweat, not a wink of sleep, and when dawn broke, along with someone's car window, I knew I couldn't go through with it. I went around to Julia's parents', where she was staying, told her first and then them, and then I went home and told my own parents. I spent the next week tidying up my affairs — renting the house out, quitting my job. And then I legged it.'

'Hoo, boy.'

Collins shook his head, as if it were the funniest story he'd heard in years. Bernard would not have blamed young Macfarlane if he'd punched the man right in the smirk.

'OK, terrific,' said Mac Reid. 'Let's get back to the barn. What's the deal there?'

Was there anything that fazed the woman?

'Er, well, there's a cottage, too, and some land,' said Macfarlane. 'My plan is to do up the cottage and fit out the barn to accommodate Littleville. It has good access, room for parking. And it's on — ta da — my private property.'

'And you paid cash?'

'Mostly. As I say, it wasn't *that* great a house.'

'You're unemployed,' said Mac, as if she'd read Bernard's mind. 'Did you borrow from the local gang?'

'On the Monday after New Year, I start with an IT firm in Hampton. Database administration.'

'But you hated that work!'

Sidney went bright red, obviously regretting that she'd spoken.

'My hatred is undiminished. But it pays better than stacking shelves at the supermarket, which was the only other job I was qualified for.'

Macfarlane smiled at her, though she refused to meet his eye. Bernard felt a brief empathetic connection with the young man. He knew what it was to have his affections unrequited. Though with his new, if sadly hindsight-focused powers of observation, he could see that Patricia might have felt exactly the same way about her affections and him.

'So let's be clear — you're staying?'

It was hard to tell if Mac Reid supported or condemned the choice.

'Is it too much of a cliché to say I have unfinished business?' Macfarlane replied.

'You can say whatever you like,' said Mac. 'And as you're now a man of means, you can also go up and pay for our coffees.'

'I don't get paid till the end of January!'

'I'll get them,' said Collins, pushing back his chair. '*You* can lead the charge tackling problem number two: how we stop these grasping arseholes blighting our foreshore with a shitty industrial park.'

Chapter 36

Sam

Sam needed to focus on his driving — this was a bad road and he hadn't had much experience handling the big, black truck. But every few minutes, he would sneak glances at the other three: Tubs in the back, trying to be all casual and cool with his elbow out the rolled-down window, even though the truck was bouncing in the ruts like nobody's business. Deano next to him, staring out the opposite window, not said two words since they picked him up from the vineyard. Brownie, in the passenger seat, seemed the most content, smiled when he met Sam's eye, let out the occasional, quiet 'Yeeha' when they hit a particularly deep hole.

Why he felt a need to keep checking on all of them, Sam wasn't sure. There was no sign that Tubs or Brownie were any less than their usual selves. Deano wasn't looking great, but then he never did, and his quietness could be down to pulling some serious hours at work, for which, Sam hoped, he was finally getting paid a decent whack.

True to his word, Brownie had talked to the German boss guy, Rainer, and got Deano half of today plus the weekend off. Sam wished he had those same powers of persuasion. He couldn't even say no to his mum when she asked him to help out with the community Christmas dinner. Sam couldn't think of anything worse than spending Christmas Day dishing out food to a bunch of people he didn't know and who were probably a bit, well, manky. He wanted to spend it with his family, same as always. He'd long since been too old to get excited about Christmas stockings and all that kids' stuff, but he liked the rituals of the day — the rellies coming round mid-morning, someone being voted Father Christmas — usually his dad 'cos of the beard — and handing out the presents, and then the big lunch that everyone helped prepare, and after that the teasing about who needed an old person's nap and who drew the short straw for the presents that came unassembled and batteries not included, and the calls to play the same stupid board game that only got dragged out of the cupboard once a year.

Didn't his mum realise that this might be the last Christmas he could spend with them? But, no, his mum had decided needy people were more important, and that it would be 'a good experience' for him to help out. And he hadn't been quick-thinking enough to come up with a plausible excuse.

'How much further are we bloody driving?' said Tubs.

'He means: "Are we there yet, Dad?"' Brownie put on a kid's voice.

'To the end of the road.' Sam glanced in the rear-vision mirror. 'Right, Deano?'

Any answer Deano might have given was cut short by Tubs.

'So how much further is the end of the bloody *road*, moron?'

'Shouldn't have super-sized your lunch, my friend,' said Brownie. 'You wouldn't be carsick.'

'I'm not *car*sick,' said Tubs. 'I'm sick of being shaken around like a fucken Lotto ball!'

Brownie shook his head in mock despair. 'Youth of today,' he said. 'No stamina.'

'Well, don't sweat it,' said Sam. 'We're here.'

The road, such as it was, ended in a patch of grass and a low fence, beyond which was a scrubby, rough track that disappeared into denser bush. Sam pulled the truck as far onto the grass as he could, set the brake and killed the engine. The stillness was both a relief and slightly unsettling, as if they'd intruded on something private and caused offence.

'Thank fuck for that.'

Tubs banged open his door and jumped out.

'Woo hoo!' he yelled. 'Free at last!'

'I'm assuming he has no idea how ironic it is he's used that phrase,' said Brownie to Sam, as they unclipped their seatbelts.

Sam wasn't sure what he meant, but decided to laugh anyway.

Tubs went around the other side of the truck and banged on Deano's window.

'Rise and shine, cocksucker,' he said. 'We gotta get moving.'

It was true. They had a three-hour tramp to the spot where they'd planned to pitch their tent, and they needed to get there before dark. It was three o'clock now, so they should be OK, but this was country none of them knew. The route had been suggested by one of Tubs's dad's hunting mates, who said if they couldn't shoot at least one deer here, then they were all muppets. Sam had studied the map well, but as his dad always said: the map is not the territory. You don't know what you're dealing with until you're right amongst it.

Sam stood looking around at the back end of nowhere. They weren't skilled bushman, not even Deano, really, though he had more skills than any of them. Sam thought about Jacko Reid, who'd been living up on Carlton Peak for nearly two weeks now. Uncle Gene said that if he didn't find King by this Sunday, he'd give up. How did you live in the bush for two weeks? How did you go searching through all that dense, dark foliage, over hills and into gullies, and find your way back safe every time? Sam had already made his mates agree that they'd hunt together and not split up. He'd had nightmares of Tubs mistaking Deano for a deer. That kind of thing happened to *experienced* hunters, and it wasn't a mistake Sam ever wanted to witness.

Sam could see the tip of Carlton Peak over to his left, behind where they were heading. He found it strangely comforting to think that Jacko was, sort of, in sight. If they got into trouble, maybe it would be Jacko who rescued them, striding over the mountains like a legendary giant . . .

'Oy, Sammo!'

Sam turned only just in time to catch the pack Tubs chucked at him. Brownie and Deano had theirs on already, rifles too, slung over their shoulders. Tubs and Brownie had on the new clothing that Tubs's dad had given them all. Deano wore the old green Swanndri top of his father's, which came down almost to his knees. With his skinny face and unwashed, matted hair, he reminded Sam of photos he'd seen of Confederate soldiers in the American Civil War, near-dead from starvation and fatigue, their side the losers in more than just battle.

'You OK, Deano?' he said, shrugging on the pack.

Deano's eyes flashed wide, like he couldn't believe Sam had asked.

'Yeah,' he said, and made an effort to smile. 'Sure.'

'Well, let's not fuck about,' said Tubs. 'We got everything?'

'Everything but the moose-caller,' said Brownie. 'But if we see one, Tubs can do his usual imitation of a female.'

'*I'm* not the pretty one, Pretty Boy.'

'Come on,' said Sam. 'You can fight after we've made camp. Which is—' he pointed down the track '—thataway.'

It wasn't as tough as he'd expected, which made Sam feel more optimistic. The track wasn't well maintained or anything, but it was visible and the ground wasn't too rocky or overgrown. They had to cross one stream, but it was barely a trickle. Sam had worried their intended campground would be hard to spot, but at just before the three-hour mark, the trees and bush gave way to a grassy terrace with one side that dropped down to a river running shallow over stones. Ahead lay the hills where they'd go hunting. A much steeper, harder trek than the way in, that was for certain. Sam half hoped that might put them off — well, put Tubs off — going too far in. But Mr Hanrahan expected them to come back with a trophy, and Tubs wouldn't risk his dad's ridicule a second time.

'Should have brought a football,' Sam said to Brownie, who was surveying the grassy expanse. 'We could have had a game of touch.'

'Nah.' Tubs had overheard. 'But *drinking* games? That'd be a big yeah.'

'Bit hard with no alcohol,' Sam said, with a grin.

Given that their packs would be heavy enough, they'd decided to ditch anything that wasn't absolutely necessary. Which included, to Sam's relief, cans of beer. Tubs sober was a big enough risk as it was.

But out of his pack, with a flourish like a bad magician, Tubs pulled a bottle of bourbon.

'For fuck's sake, Tubs! We *agreed!*'

Sam was more panicked than angry, but it sounded the same.

Tubs frowned, confused. 'What are you on about?' he said. 'We agreed not to take anything we couldn't carry. I can carry this easy!'

Brownie spoke into Sam's ear. 'If it becomes a problem, we'll deal with it, OK?'

Sam felt better. It wasn't just him who had to figure out how to keep them all alive.

'OK,' he said. 'Come on, let's help Deano with the tent.'

After a patchy night's sleep, thanks to a shit-faced Tubs who wouldn't go to bed and who *then* snored the tent down, followed by a tasteless breakfast (*no one* had brought sugar), and two hours' solid uphill bush-whacking, Sam decided he was genuinely suffering from paranoia. He was convinced (a) that they would never, *ever* get out of the damn bush, (b) that any deer around were laughing at them, and (c) that Deano was trying to put as much distance between himself and Brownie as physically possible.

That last delusion, weirdly, was the most disturbing. Last night, he could almost have *sworn* that Deano flinched when Brownie reached over to take his plate. But maybe Deano was finally suffering the effects of too much weed? That made you jumpy, didn't it? Although the few times Sam had tried it, it made him stupid and sleepy. He hadn't touched it since he found himself making a balls-up of a simple nail-fastening job at work — just couldn't focus. If the boss had suspected, he'd have been fired, and then he'd have had to explain that to his parents. Wasn't worth it. He passed next time a joint came around at a party, and no one gave him too much grief.

Deano, he knew, smoked pretty much daily. And there was always the depressing possibility he'd moved on to harder stuff. Sam had hoped that these new work hours meant Deano had less time for petty dealing, that whoever he was doing it for would cut him loose as being of no further use to them. But maybe Deano was in deeper than ever?

'Oh, thank *fuck*.'

Tubs, uncharacteristically in the lead, could see what was up ahead, and they followed him out onto a tussocky, rocky plateau mercifully free of bush. On their left, it dropped steeply away, probably down into a river gully, and in front it carried on upwards in a series of slopes that drew the eye all the way to Carlton Peak, huge now, shadowed blue-black at the top where it hit the clouds.

'Right.' Brownie dumped his pack, and propped the rifle up against it. 'What now?'

'Check for deer, dickhead,' said Tubs, struggling to pull binoculars out of his own pack. 'It's called glassing.'

'Just like a standard night at the Crown,' said Brownie.

'Jeez, will you shut up,' said Tubs. 'I'm trying to concentrate.'

He turned in a slow half-circle, scanning for movement.

'Fuck,' he said in a whisper. 'I think I see some.'

'You *think*?' said Sam.

'It's hard to tell! Deer are brown! The whole hill is fucken brown!'

'Let me look,' said Brownie, and put his hand on the binoculars.

'Oh, right,' said Tubs, skewing out of reach. 'You got *native* vision or something?'

'Tubs, don't be a wanker.' Brownie sighed, beckoned for the binoculars.

'Fuck off. Get your own!'

'Better give them to him, Tubs.'

Sam hadn't heard Deano speak for so long, he wasn't even sure it sounded like him. Deano still had his pack on, thumbs hooked in the straps. He was standing a few feet away, Sam realised. Not with them. Apart.

'Deano.'

Brownie's face and voice were friendly, and it was only Sam's newly contracted condition of paranoia that detected a warning in the way he'd said the name.

Deano didn't look at Brownie, only at Tubs.

'Or else, you know?' he said. 'Yeah — or else.'

'What the fuck are you on about?' said Tubs.

But it was Brownie who Sam looked at, and as he did, the truth hit Sam like the clear slap of the plateau air after the earthy fug of the bush.

'You're in it, too,' he said. 'Whatever shit Deano's in, you're there as well.'

Brownie's smile was almost, but not quite, apologetic.

'Hardly the time,' Brownie said.

'What—?'

'Shut up, Tubs,' said Sam. 'Seriously, shut *right* the fuck up.'

And before Tubs could protest, Sam turned to Deano.

'What's happening? Tell me.'

'Deano.' No doubt this time. Even though it was pleasantly couched, Brownie had issued a warning.

Sam refused to be deterred.

'Is it drugs?' Sam kept on. 'Are you both in some kind of gang trouble?'

Deano swallowed, his Adam's apple bobbing like a cork in his scrawny neck. His eyes swivelled towards Brownie and away again. 'Not *both* of us, nah,' he said. 'Just . . . me.'

Sam, whose gaze had also been darting between the two, saw Brownie's shoulders fractionally relax. But it didn't feel right. It didn't *smell* right.

'You're lying,' he said to Deano. 'It's both of you, somehow. Isn't it?'

He turned to face Brownie. '*Isn't* it?' he yelled.

It was the smile that did it. Poor little Sam, it said, with your loving family and your nice, warm house and your comfy, *easy* life — what do *you* know about anything? You're soft and stupid, the smile said. *Far* too soft to handle the truth.

Sam launched himself at his friend, shoved him hard, and Brownie, taken by surprise, caught his heel on a rock and fell onto his back. Sam jumped on top of him, began laying his fists into every body part he could reach.

'You *fucker!*' he yelled. 'You lying fuck, what the *fuck* are you *doing*, what—'

Tears as well as punches were landing, and not just because Brownie had managed to smack Sam in the head a few times, trying to get him off. But Sam was as big and fit as Brownie was, and maddened by fear and rage, and Brownie hadn't a hope of dislodging him, just had to protect himself best he could.

But then Sam was grabbed under the arms, dragged up and off, who knows how, by slow, lardy Tubs.

'Jesus, stop, *stop*!' Tubs was saying. 'You'll *kill* him!'

Sam found himself on his knees, panting. Brownie was still lying on the ground, curled over, making no attempt to sit up. Sam was seized by an urge to go pummel him again, but he stifled it, took a few deep breaths instead.

Tubs was standing bent over, palms propped on his knees. He expelled a whoosh of air, straightened up.

'What the hell was that?' he said, plaintively. 'What the fuck just happened?'

A jolt shot through Sam. Deano!

But he was still there, didn't seem to have moved an inch. Was staring at Brownie on the ground. Then Deano seemed to become aware of Sam looking in his direction.

'It *is* just me who's in trouble,' he said. 'I'm in it and I can't get out. I was stupid. Thought I could do a bit of dealing on the side, and now they own me. Whatever they want me to do, I've gotta do, or they'll kill me. S'pose I should be grateful. They could have killed me already.'

Sam felt sick. Deano was right; the gang were bad bastards, and he was lucky to be alive. In truth, Sam didn't want to find out any more, but that would just prove how soft and gutless he was.

Time to step up. He jerked his head at Brownie.

'What about *him*? How is *he* involved?'

Deano gave him a sad, brief smile.

'Dunno,' he said, with a shrug. 'Dunno how it all works. Just know what happens to me if I don't do what I'm told.'

'You're saying Brownie beats you *up*?'

'Aw, nah, nah.' Deano's eyes did the swivel dance again. 'Not *him*. He's just, I dunno, like a messenger or something . . .'

'Essentially correct.'

Brownie was sitting up now. Shit, his face was a *mess*.

'I get paid to carry messages.' He winced, flexed his jaw. 'Among other things.'

'Drugs.'

'And money. Occasionally weapons. You know, all the things that make the world a better place.'

So now Sam knew. Now it was out. And maybe he should feel as sorry for Brownie as he did for Deano. But he couldn't, could he? Deano was a bit dumb and bit hopeless, whereas Brownie was *smart*. He was the smartest guy among them, and he'd probably thought it was funny to treat poor, dumb Sam like a mushroom — keep him in the dark and feed him shit. Probably thought the whole thing was just a big game, and he was taking all the losers for a ride. Losers like Sam, and—

'Deano,' Sam called out. 'Did you ever ask Brownie for help?'

God, Deano couldn't even answer. How could Sam not have seen how terrified he'd been all this time?

'*Did* you?' Sam insisted.

'Fuck . . .' Brownie sank his forehead down onto his knees.

'Yeah,' said Deano, in a small voice. 'I did.'

'Yeah,' echoed Sam softly. 'I thought so.'

'Oh, and how *could* I have helped Deano, Sam?' said Brownie, sharp, sarcastic. 'Do tell.'

'You got him time off work, didn't you?' Sam got to his feet. 'And I bet Rainer had nothing to do with *that* decision. You could've figured out how if you'd wanted to.'

'Well, you're wrong, Sammy boy.' Brownie was angry now. 'I am *not* that fucking clever. If I were, I would have found a *clever* way to solve my fucking money problems. But that's what happens when you're desperate — you grab onto the first lifeline that's offered to you, and you ignore the fact the dude on the other end has a gang patch and "Hate" tattooed on his knuckles. You persuade yourself that you only have to get out of *this* hole, and by the time you realise that you've just jumped into another one that's bottomless, it's too fucking late.'

So that was why. He needed money. Because of his dad.

Sam knew he should feel sympathy for his friend. But if Brownie was really his best mate, why didn't he ask for Sam's help? Why didn't he *tell* him what was going on?

Because he thought Sam was too soft to handle it, that's why. And deep down, Sam knew he was right, and he *knew* that was the real reason he was so angry. But, oh man, he wasn't ready to let it go. The shame *burned* and kept his anger hot and alive.

'You knew what you were getting into,' he said. 'You were probably laughing all along at how stupid I was, that I never guessed. Bet your hard gang mates thought it was a joke, too, eh? Laughing all the fucking way.'

'Sammo.'

Brownie sounded genuinely upset. But Sam could not forgive him. Not for the lies, or for making him feel like a fool. Not now.

'Why don't you just fuck off!' he yelled.

Brownie stared at him. A fat lip and swelling eyes made it hard to tell his expression.

'Good plan,' he said, quietly.

He got slowly to his feet, wincing as he dusted himself off.

Began to walk towards Deano, who backed away, firing anxious glances at Sam.

Sam started forward, ready to step between them and, if necessary, fight Brownie all over again, though the adrenaline from before was ebbing, and the pain in his hands was *way* worse than any time he'd hit his own fingers with a hammer.

But Brownie wasn't heading for Deano. He lifted the pack that he'd dumped on the ground. And the rifle—

'Don't even think about it!'

Tubs's voice came out all high and squeaky, and Sam fought back a surge of panicked nausea as he realised Tubs had his own rifle up to his shoulder, barrel shaking as he aimed it at Brownie.

Cautious but apparently unflustered, Brownie raised his hands.

'I need it, Tubs, mate,' he said. 'It's my only chance.'

'To fucking do *what*?'

'Survive,' he replied.

'Jesus,' Sam said to him. 'Are you really going bush?'

'Well, I can't say as I've thoroughly considered the alternatives,' said Brownie. 'But it seems like the best option right now.'

And they stared at each other, until Tubs's nerves gave way.

'Will someone fucken do *something*?'

'Sam?'

Brownie needed him to make the call. Him. Poor, ignorant, soft Sam.

'Give me the rifle, Tubs,' Sam said.

He didn't have to ask twice — Tubs practically threw it at him. Sam pointed it at his former best friend.

'Go on,' he said. 'Take the pack. Put the rifle over your shoulder and then keep your hands off it. Then start walking.' He nodded his head in the direction of the upper plateau.

Brownie did what he was told. Tubs and Deano had hustled back down to the bushline now, keeping their distance. Sam couldn't be entirely sure who they were most afraid of.

Pack and rifle hoisted, Brownie began to trudge up the slope. Sam intended to keep the rifle aimed until he was out of sight, no matter how long that took. He watched as Brownie took a curving path that led him up the left, to where the ground dropped away. He saw him pause, then turn, and Sam adjusted his hold on the gun, heart thumping.

'Sam?' Brownie called out.

'What?' Sam reluctantly responded.

'What you said. About me laughing at you.' Brownie took slow steps backwards as he spoke. 'It's not true.'

Sam felt tears sting, unbidden. It made him furious. '*Yeah*?'

'Yeah, mate. Not true at—'

And he was gone! A step, a startled yelp, and then all Sam had was an image imprinted in the negative, as if a camera had flashed right in his eyes.

Sam yelled in shock, heard echoes that might be him, might be Tubs and Deano. Dropped the rifle, not caring if the safety was on or off, sprinted to the edge fast as he could.

There was nothing to see. Below the edge was a rocky slope, steep and slippery, and not far below it bush through which Sam caught glimpses of river. No flash of movement or sound other than water, no tumbling blue pack, no Brownie . . .

Sam wanted to call out, but found he was gasping for breath, his mind a storm of whirling black panic.

'Shitshit*shit*!'

Tubs was beside him, eyes huge, face grey and sweaty, head craning over the edge far as he dared.

'Can you *see* him? I can't see him. *Shit* . . .'

Sam didn't realise he'd started down over the edge until Tubs grabbed his arm.

'You can't!' he said. 'It's too steep! You *can't*.'

And he held on tight, until Sam gave up struggling and slumped down onto his rear, head between his knees, gulping in big, shuddery breaths.

'Shit, Sammo . . .' Tubs knelt beside him, wrapped an arm round his shoulders and shook him. 'Sammo, we can't stay here. We've gotta get back, we've gotta *tell* someone!'

The sense, the logic of that finally calmed the tornado in his head. He wiped his eyes with hands that hurt like a bastard, and breathed in.

'Have we got coverage here?'

Tubs shook his head. 'Nup, already checked. Sorry, mate.' He put his hand on Sam's shoulder again, coaxing him up. 'We gotta go back.'

And go back they did — quicker back down the hill than up, but no mobile coverage at the camping spot either, so they kept on, not bothering to gather up the tent and campsite gear, walking as fast as they could, none of them speaking, Sam not looking at anything but the track, though every bit of him was aware of Tubs's vibrating anxiety and Deano's unnatural calm. They weren't his problem now, not even Deano. His priority was to find help.

They made it to the truck in two-and-a-half hours. Sam climbed into the driver's seat, pulled out his phone, dialled his father, who answered on the second ring and didn't bother to disguise the worry in his voice.

'Sam, you OK?'

He kept it together throughout the whole explanation, agreed that his dad would call the police, that they'd meet him and Uncle Gene at the Boat Shed, and that he'd not exceed the speed limit on the way back. But the second he hung up, all the pent-up emotion let loose, and he collapsed onto the steering wheel, body shuddering, face buried in his arms.

'You want me to drive?'

Tubs's offer brought him back.

Sam sat up, shook his head, wiped his face. 'Nah, I'm good.'

And he started the truck, did a u-turn that spun its wheels on the gravel and knew he was going to break the promise about the speed limit to his dad.

If the drive up had been bouncy, this was ridiculous. Tubs cracked his head on the window.

'Ow, *fuck*. Come on, Sammo,' he pleaded. 'Slow it down. We don't need *all* of us dea— *Shit!!*'

Sam saw it, too, the animal that ran out onto the road, barrel-like, brown and familiar. He shoved his foot hard down onto the brake, and the truck's ABS kicked in, making it judder and swerve but, mercifully, not roll. After a slow-motion lifetime, the truck slid to a complete halt.

Tubs was panting like he was giving birth. Sam glanced back at Deano, who gave him a weak smile while keeping hold of the grab handle with both hands. And out the back window, Sam spotted the animal, sitting in the road, pink tongue lolling. He *hadn't* been mistaken.

'Hang on,' he told the others, and jumped out.

Next minute, King was in the back seat next to Deano.

'You're shitting me,' said Tubs. 'I thought it was a fucken *pig*.'

'Close relation.'

Sam put the truck in gear. Finding the dog felt like a sign, and that tiny surge of optimism was enough to make him take his foot off the gas. Tubs was right — only one of them would be rescued today.

The Boat Shed was filled with people — official search co-ordinators and local volunteers. Sam saw Wyatt's tall, blond head and homed in, to be enveloped immediately in his father's big, crushing embrace. Today, he was grateful for his dad being OK with public displays of emotion.

Releasing him, his dad spotted the state of Sam's hands.

'What—?'

But he obviously decided an explanation could wait.

Casey came up to them, in full police mode — brisk, efficient, impersonal.

'Your mate Dean wants to have a chat with me,' she said to Sam. 'Should I make it a priority?'

Sam nodded.

'Anything you want to tell me first?'

'What's this about?' said Wyatt.

'I don't know any details,' Sam told the both of them. 'Brownie and Deano — it's drugs, I think. But I don't know the details.'

It was true. He'd accused his friend, and beaten the crap out of him — but he had no idea how deeply Brownie was involved, or what he'd actually done.

'OK,' said Casey, after a beat. 'I'll come back to you.'

'Sam?' said his father, gently, once she'd gone.

'I wasn't involved, Dad,' he said. 'Promise.'

No, he wasn't, was he? Because Brownie hadn't had enough faith in him to tell him what was going on. He'd known Sam wouldn't be able to help him.

'Jacko's on his way to the scene. He'll probably get there before the first search team.'

Uncle Gene. Dressed in outdoor gear that made him look like a cross between Action Man and a garden gnome.

'He says to pass on his thanks to you boys.'

King. Right. Sam had almost forgotten.

'Mac's taken the dumb mutt home and locked him up. Don't tell Jacko, but I suspect she gave him a swift boot up the arse as well.'

'He's OK, then?' Sam asked.

'Not even noticeably thinner,' said Uncle Gene. 'Some creatures are just better programmed for survival than most.'

Sam couldn't help a ragged intake of breath, and Uncle Gene's face filled with concern.

'Your mate could well be one of them.' He squeezed Sam's arm. 'Always hope.'

The trio became aware of a fourth, hovering. Tubs had both hands wrapped around a cup of tea. Not his usual beverage of choice, but probably better for the shock. He was still grey and sweaty around the edges, but his voice came out firm enough.

'Is there anything I can do?' he asked the men.

'That your flash truck out front?' said Uncle Gene.

'Um, it's Dad's . . .'

Uncle Gene's grin was the kind that made your primal survival instincts go 'Uh, oh.'

'Is it? Well, you tell Rob that we thank him for his kind donation to our rescue efforts.'

Sam, with an apologetic look at Tubs, drew the keys out of his pocket.

'Excellent.' Uncle Gene bounced them in his hand. 'Wyatt? Lads, if you're up for it?'

Of course they were. They had to be.

Uncle Gene closed his fist over the truck keys.

'Then let's see if we can beat Jacko.'

Chapter 37

Kerry

News came of the rescue mission via a text from Mac. Kerry was on the road, but he pulled over to phone Gene and offer help. Thanks, but they had enough volunteers, Gene told him. It was tough country; they needed people with experience in the bush. Kerry agreed that he was not one of those people. Evading an inquisitive bull mastiff in Clissold Park was the closest he'd come to requiring survival skills in a green space.

Briefly, he'd hoped Gene might offer him a reason to turn back, but now he had no excuse to put off his original plan for the day. He wasn't at all sure it was a *good* plan, but carrying it out seemed braver than ignoring it. And if it blew up in his face, then he'd have to be brave about that, too.

By mid-afternoon, Kerry was fifty kilometres from Hampton, parked outside an art gallery that looked surprisingly sleek and modern, given that he'd just had a late lunch in a café with slabby hand-carved furniture, mobiles made out of old cutlery, and lurid swirly paintings of whales and women with stars for hair.

He entered and was surprised again. On the white walls were portraits, close-ups of faces in monochrome, blue or black on white, painted in an almost Impressionistic style that made clever use of small light and dark blocks, like mosaic tesserae. The faces belonged to men and women, young and old, none beautiful but all with expressions that caught and held. If he knew anything about art, Kerry might have said that the paintings displayed rare psychological insight and sensitivity. In other words, everything he had not expected. He'd been girding himself for slashed canvases, scrawled, angry slogans, dismembered body parts and the like. Perhaps he was in the wrong gallery?

But no. There was her name on the wall, and a short explanation of the exhibition apparently written by a chimpanzee who'd been given long, pretentious and probably made-up words to assemble in any order. (If Kerry had 'dialectic flux', he'd be off down the chemist.)

And there was the door to the studio, the residence in which the artist was. Or might be; the door was closed.

He knocked, and it was immediately wrenched open from inside as if the occupant had had it up to here with kids ringing the bell and running away.

'What do *you* want?' said Sophie by way of greeting.

'To apologise,' said Kerry.

From the way she blinked, taken aback, he deduced that this was not the natural order of Sophie's life.

'I should have told your parents I'd invited you,' he said. 'I have no excuse. I took on too much and let it get out of hand. I should have been better organised.'

'Doubt it would have made a difference,' she said, fractionally mollified. 'Except that they would have pretended to be polite.'

'No offence, but you don't exactly give them the chance, do you?'

'No *offence*?' Sophie's eyebrow and the large metal stud stuck into it shot up. 'People who start a sentence with that are *always* offensive. It's like "I'm not a racist, but . . ."'

'Quite true,' said Kerry. 'Fair point.'

'And what do *you* know, anyway?'

'Not much,' he admitted. 'Only what I saw. Someone who'd already lit the fuse before they brought the dynamite into the house.'

Sophie folded her arms. Today's t-shirt had a picture of Johnny Rotten, bug-eyed and gurning. The tattoo below the gagged woman was of a skeleton giving the one-fingered salute.

'Thought you came here to apologise.'

This wasn't going so well.

Kerry gestured around the gallery.

'These are terrific,' he said. 'Really first-class.'

'And you'd know?'

Not well at all.

'Er, I know what I like,' he said. 'And I like these tremendously.'

He held her gaze, strove not to be distracted by the metal surrounding it.

She dropped her eyes first.

'I can't help it,' she said. 'I somehow convince myself that it will be different every time I go. That somehow we'll have been sprinkled by magic fairy dust that turns us into the perfect family. And then when it doesn't happen, I feel robbed, furious. Which I *know* is totally irrational, but it just . . . takes over. Stupid, huh?'

'No,' said Kerry. 'But not terribly useful.'

Sophie screwed up her face. It failed to diminish her astonishing good looks.

'I'm too old to change,' she said. 'If it hasn't happened by now, it ain't going to.'

'Not sure that's true. I surprised myself greatly about eighteen months ago.'

The metal on her eyebrow went up again, like a balloon caught in an elevator.

'Really? What happened?'

'I decided my life was going nowhere. So I took it somewhere.'

'What? To Gabriel's Bay?' she scoffed.

'Many, *many* places in between.'

'Did you ever go to St Petersburg?'

'I did not. Helsinki was the closest. You can wave to Russia across the Baltic.'

'Russia is absolutely bad-ass,' said Sophie. 'I *so* want to go.'

'Go then.'

'Right, yeah. With the five dollars I have to my name.'

Kerry glanced around. 'I see more than a few sold stickers.'

'I have to eat. And, after I get kicked out of here, pay rent.'

'OK.' Kerry shrugged. 'That's that, then.'

'Don't try any of that reverse-psychology shit on me!'

Kerry spread his hands. 'Wouldn't dare. I was merely agreeing with you that it was impossible.'

Sophie stared over his shoulder at her paintings, and then up at the ceiling, where there was nothing but those lights that hang on wires, like small square circus acrobats. And then back at him.

'I'm sorry I got you fired,' she said.

'You didn't,' he said, truthfully. 'My days of being a crap employee were numbered.'

'I think Mum liked you. It's hard to tell with her.'

'I apologised to her also. She was very gracious.'

'And Dad?'

'Not so much.'

'*God*, he's an arsehole,' said Sophie. 'How does she put *up* with him?'

'I'd suggest she has more power than you think.' Kerry hesitated, then added, 'As do you.'

'Who are you? The ginger Dr Phil?'

'I was hoping for someone more spiritual, but I'll take it. Dr Phil doesn't sugar-coat.'

Sophie smiled. A real smile. Wide and amused.

'Did you really come all this way to apologise?'

'I missed your launch. It was the least I could do.'

'Gallery's due to shut in ten, so do you want to get a drink? I'm not hitting on you,' she added, with a hint of the old belligerence. 'I know you've got a girlfriend.'

Kerry felt it wiser not to put her straight on that point. That was Sunday's mission. If he'd needed a dose of courage for today, he'd need an entire pharmacy for tomorrow.

He checked his watch. It was not quite four o'clock.

'A drink is exactly what I need,' he told her.

Chapter 38

Sidney

Sidney opened her front door, and saw a bunch of roses. The kind you buy in a service station, which had no smell and fell apart by the end of the day.

'I'm sorry,' said the person behind them. 'It's Sunday, so it was either these or dandelions and that purple stuff that grows like topsy in the wasteland.'

'Buddleia,' said Sidney. 'An invasive weed.'

'I've been called worse,' said Kerry.

He held the roses out to her. 'Can we talk?'

Her answer should have been simple, one word — no. But since the council meeting, Sidney had been doing some thinking. Oh, who was she kidding? She'd been thinking non-stop since she told him to bugger off.

'The boys are here,' she said. 'Can't guarantee privacy or uninterrupted conversation. Or a noise level below Russian MiG fighters doing a flyby.'

'If you don't mind, I don't.'

Sidney wasn't sure the presence of children was her main concern. But by agreeing, she wasn't committing to anything more than a chat, was she? And she had questions, all sorts of questions that zig-zagged around her brain like the cluster flies in the kitchen, persistent, irritating, resistant to all attempts to repel them.

'I've brought tea, and milk, too,' said Kerry, who indeed did have a plastic Four Square bag in his other hand.

She could take umbrage at the implication she was in such financial doo-doo that she couldn't even provide the makings for tea. Or she could accept it as a generous gesture, and enjoy saving five bucks this week on milk.

'Thanks.' Sidney opened up the door to let him in. 'I'll put the jug on.'

While it boiled, Kerry stepped out the back door to say hi to the boys, who greeted him cheerfully and openly, Sidney noticed. Any resentment they might have felt about their coaching being stopped had long gone. Children weren't programmed to hold grudges, she decided. They woke up fresh every morning assuming anything could happen. Whatever they wished for, today might be the day. If not, then tomorrow surely would be. How nice. How freeing. And who was to say they were wrong?

The conversation over cups of tea began on mutual safe ground — the possibility that Elaine had hexed the junior Caraccis' restaurant with, for example, a plague of flying monkeys; whether there was intentional irony in the Kozy Kettle calling black instant coffee 'espresso'; the good weather being a certain harbinger of the climate-change apocalypse. They talked about Littleville and agreed that Kerry's barn would be a great location. It didn't matter if the launch date was deferred. It would happen. Everyone who was anyone wanted it to. The industrial park — well, that might be hard to prevent, but if Gene was against it, who knows what unexpected delays might arise in the construction?

Sidney offered fresh-made scones and jam, and the sugar kick gave them confidence to move onto trickier, more emotionally charged subjects: the tragedy of young Barrett, of whom the search had found no trace; the situation with Madison, who *had* been with her father after all on the night her horrible mother came calling.

'Mac gave both Rick and Olivia separate earfuls for their useless communication,' said Sidney. 'Both of them, of course, blamed the other.'

'Is Madison all right?' said Kerry.

'Mac says Corinna Marshall is keeping an eye on her.' Sidney's face grew hot. 'I should be, too, but I just can't afford to. Which, every time I say it, sounds even more like a rubbish excuse.'

'And it doesn't help to tell yourself she's not your responsibility, does it?' said Kerry.

'Not a jot.'

'I visited Reuben's house.' Kerry's own face reddened. 'I knocked. No one answered. I bottled and left.'

'Casey said you came and saw her about him.'

'Did she? I haven't heard anything from her.'

'You may not,' said Sidney. 'She politely warned me off interfering, said it's complicated but under control. From the little she did tell me, I gather both parents are on the sickness benefit, mental rather than physical illness, and the kind that makes you hardly able to function, which must be unbelievably tough for the little guy. The older sister still at home looks after Reuben, and apparently does a good enough job for the authorities to feel they don't need to remove him.'

'And when the sister leaves?'

'I guess that's when they'll step in . . .'

Outside there began a high-pitched ululation. Tarzan, maybe? Or old-fashioned Injun warriors? Or maybe there was no reason, and they just wanted to run around and make noise for the sheer joy of it.

'God, I'm so lucky,' said Sidney. 'I really should be more grateful.'

Kerry's expression suggested a concern that he was prying.

'Mac said you sold the car.'

'I had no choice,' Sidney shrugged. 'Either that or give the boys lumps of coal for Christmas.'

His shoulders hunched, as if he expected a smack around the ears.

'You wouldn't accept a loan?'

Sidney gave him a sceptical look. 'Do you have any money *left* after your big property purchase?'

'I borrowed extra to do some renovations,' he said. 'But I can live with an outdoor toilet for a while longer. And a gas stove that I suspect is possessed by a witch finder. And wallpaper with mustard and dark green swirls that make me feel like I'm drowning in a stagnant pond.'

She'd missed his jokes. She'd missed *him*. But those questions — still circling like flies.

'Why didn't you tell me about Julia? I told you all about Fergal.'

He looked so miserable, Sidney's neat shot of gratification was annoyingly diluted by the tonic water of compassion.

'Possibly *because* you told me all about Fergal,' he said. 'I didn't want to be Fergal the Second.'

'Has she got over being jilted?' Sidney felt bad about twisting the knife, but not so bad that she wouldn't do it. 'Has she got over *you*?'

'Well, Ma told me she's getting married next April,' Kerry said. 'And though that doesn't necessarily reveal the inner workings of her psyche, I'd say it's a pretty fair indication she's moved on.'

'You finally spoke to your mother, then?'

Kerry grimaced. 'She told me I was an evil son. She made my father back her up from the breakfast table. He yelled that I was "a disgrrrace" through mouthfuls of Dundee chunky marmalade on toasted white Mother's Pride.'

Sidney had to smile. 'I liked your mother.'

'She liked you,' said Kerry. 'Mind, you, she likes everyone. Except me at the moment, of course. But that won't last.'

There was one of those pauses, where both of them felt a need to fiddle with their teaspoons, while inside, if Sidney's own brain was any guide, a maelstrom roared.

'*I* like you.'

Kerry broke first.

'In fact, I adore you,' he said. 'I've missed you like — I don't know, like a major *limb*. Or an organ. Or something nicer than that but just as vital—'

Before he drowned in bad metaphor, Sidney decided to throw him a lifebuoy.

'Me, too,' she said.

His face was a picture, one Picasso would paint, with multiple planes, all wearing a variant of expression — surprise, hope, joy, disbelief.

'Really?'

'No, I'm messing with you because I'm nasty and maladjusted.'

Slight pause.

'Well, it's good we're finally being honest with each other.'

Slam, crash, thump. The boys, entering with the same gentle touch of the comet that killed the dinosaurs.

'Kerry!' said Aidan. 'Can you play goalie?'

Kerry looked to Sidney. 'Can I?'

'*I'm* certainly not volunteering,' she said, with a smile.

'Right then, boys.' Kerry pushed back his chair. 'I'll channel my inner Grobbelaar.'

'Who?'

'*Who?* Dear Lord, what kind of sub-par education have you two been receiving . . . ?'

As the trio let the back door shut behind them, Sidney sat

for a moment, checking for residual qualms, unanswered flying questions. Of course, there were still some. If there weren't, she'd be delusional. Or she'd be a completely different person, one entirely serene and secure, like the Dalai Lama.

She took the dishes to the sink, and considered washing them. Instead, she grabbed her straw sunhat from its hook on the back door, and walked outside to sit in the sun and watch two people she definitely loved, and one she possibly did, having an enormous amount of energetic fun. And, for the first time, allowed herself to look forward to Christmas.

Chapter 39

Madison

Christmas morning! Madison woke early but stayed in bed until eight reading, because she knew her mum wouldn't like to be woken up before then. Her dad would come around that evening, so today it was just her and her mum, and Madison was really looking forward to what her mum called 'girl time'.

She found it hard to concentrate on her book because she kept looking at the clock, which took *ages* to come round to the right hour. As soon as it did, Madison was out from under the covers and running down to the living room to see what Father Christmas had brought her.

There was no tree because her mother didn't like the mess pine needles made, and she thought decorations were tacky. But the spot in front of the big gas heater that looked like a real coal fire was where the presents usually sat, and that's where Madison headed, trying to run softly and not thump her feet on the floor.

The spot in front of the heater was empty. Madison hunted around the living room, thinking her mum must have hidden the presents, like Easter eggs, but she couldn't find anything wrapped in Christmas paper.

Maybe her mum had hidden them somewhere else! Madison looked in the kitchen and dining room, her dad's study and her mum's reading room, the good living room, the sunroom, the spare bedrooms, the laundry and boot room — she even looked outside the back door. Nothing.

Madison thought hard, and then worked it out. The presents must be in the only place she hadn't looked — her mum's bedroom! Her mum wanted her to come in and open presents with her on the bed!

The door was closed, so Madison, little bubbles of excitement popping in her stomach, carefully opened it. If her mum was still asleep, she'd climb onto the bed and wait for her to wake up. She'd do her best not to look at the presents, otherwise she might be tempted to try to figure out what they were.

But the bed was empty. Madison checked the ensuite bathroom, but that was empty, too. Maybe her mum had got up when she was looking around the rest of the house?

She ran around, calling out for her mum, but no one answered. When Madison was absolutely sure the whole house was empty, she sat down in a chair in the sunroom and tried to think what she should do.

She couldn't phone anyone because the landline didn't work anymore, and she didn't have her own mobile phone because she wasn't old enough yet, according to her dad (her mum disagreed but hadn't got around to buying one yet).

And she couldn't go up to Rainer and Elke's because Elke had had a big argument with her mum a few days back. Madison wasn't sure what it was about, but her mum had told her to keep clear of 'that mad cow'. And Rainer was always grumpy, too; Madison didn't want him to shout at her.

Should she wait for her dad? He'd said he'd come around at about six, but that seemed a long time to wait. And she was starting to get worried about where her mum was and whether she was all right. She should really tell someone, in case her mum needed help, though Madison was *sure* she was OK. It was just a mistake that she wasn't here right now.

The more she thought, it seemed like the only thing she could do was walk to Sidney's. She'd better get dressed, and have some breakfast.

There was no milk, so Madison had toast, and then packed her backpack with a book, a bottle of water and a sandwich made from the last of the bread. Her mum never cooked Christmas lunch. They usually went out to eat, if they had Christmas lunch at all. 'So much effort,' her mum would say. 'Besides, what idiot decided it was a good idea to gorge on stodge in the middle of a scorching summer day?'

It was sunny outside, already warm. Madison had no idea how long it would take her to walk, and she hoped it wouldn't get *too* hot, otherwise her water might not last.

It was a long way to the main road, and no cars came past. Everyone must be inside, having Christmas. Madison suddenly felt like she wanted to cry and forced herself not to. It would be OK; she'd get Christmas later. That might have even been the plan, and somehow she got the wrong end of the stick? Sidney would help — she'd phone her mum and it would be all sorted.

After an even *longer* time, Madison realised she was at the entrance to the Booths' farm, the mossy old gate and the dirt driveway. She decided to run because she didn't want Tanya or Shari to spot her. It made her feel even hotter and sweatier, but she didn't stop until she was well past. She should probably have a drink of water, but she wanted to save it, just in case.

Up further ahead, she saw Reuben's house, which always looked to her like it was haunted. She thought about running past here, too, but then she saw someone sitting outside on a big pile of wood. Someone she recognised.

'Hi,' she said. 'Sorry, I didn't mean to make you jump.'

She'd startled him, and he'd leapt up, as if he was going to run away. But then Reuben saw it was her, and he was OK again.

'Are you having Christmas?' she asked him.

He stared at her with big eyes, like he didn't know what she meant, and then he dropped his head and shook it quickly.

Madison didn't feel so bad anymore. Now there were two of them!

'I'm going into town,' she told him. 'Do you want to come with me?'

Reuben looked around, like he was checking if anyone was watching.

'OK,' he said, and walked over to her.

Madison offered him half her sandwich and he wolfed it down like he was super-hungry. But then boys were always hungry, Sidney said. 'They're like Doctor Who's Tardis,' she told Madison. 'Bigger on the inside.' The thought of seeing Sidney lifted Madison's spirits even further. It couldn't be far now to town. They should be there by lunchtime.

They walked along for a bit side by side, and then Reuben reached out and took her hand. And even though his hand was hot and sweaty and holding it made walking more difficult, Madison did not let go.

Chapter 40

Bernard

When Patricia had, as she'd promised, telephoned Bernard at the three-week mark, he'd thrown dignity to the wind and begged her to come home.

'I'm touched, Bernard,' she'd said. 'And I *do* miss you, I really do. But I need more time. To think *properly* — about who I am, or, at least, what kind of person I want to be from now on. I should have thought about all that a long time ago, I realise, but I'm in good health so I should, fingers crossed, have another two decades in me. And I want to live those years on *my* terms. I want to make sure every one of them counts.'

'But what about Christmas?' Bernard had tried not to sound like a plaintive child.

'I know,' she said. 'It *will* be a bit miserable. I've no doubt I will get up on Christmas morning and feel so lonely that I'll want to rush back to you immediately. But,' she added, 'it's important I face those kinds of uncomfortable feelings head on. If I'm to take charge of my life, I need to become more resilient. So I suggest we raise a glass to each other, over our Christmas meal. And I will phone again, on Boxing Day.'

She'd said it kindly, but Bernard was still jarred by her toughness, her lack of compromise. Not even Christmas sentiment could sway her. All those years of giving each other thoughtful presents — book vouchers and the occasional scarf. It was as if there'd been a sudden run on the bank of mutual regard, and its coffers, built up over the decades, were now empty.

'Where *are* you?'

The plaintive child would not be suppressed, it seemed; his voice went all high and quavery.

'I'm in a small shack by a wild coast,' she said, with a laugh. 'Getting in touch with the elements. Literally — the place leaks like a sieve.'

He wanted to demand, 'What coast? Whose shack? Are you alone?' And, most pressingly, 'Do you still resemble my Patricia or have you transformed into someone I won't recognise?'

But Patricia had gently but firmly ended the call. And now here he was, at ten o'clock on Christmas morning, still in his dressing gown, not a decoration in sight, the radio silent because carols sickened him, his Christmas Day stretching out before him as dull and interminable as a long-haul aeroplane flight, in economy class.

Blow to this.

Bernard got up out his armchair.

At noon, the community hall's doors would open for a shared Christmas dinner. Bernard might not qualify as needy in the financial sense, but he'd be damned if he'd spend Christmas alone. Besides, he could always volunteer to dish soup, or whatever was on the menu. Probably not soup, now that he came to think of it. Roast goose á la the Cratchetts seemed also unlikely. Perhaps turkey?

And with thoughts of Dickens in his mind — of the 'God bless us, every one' ilk, as opposed to 'Darkness is cheap' — Bernard dressed in appropriate clothing, feeling marginally more cheerful with every minute.

Chapter 41

Sam

Sam no longer minded being made to help out at the community hall. His parents had been cheerful for the girls that morning, but he could see they were still worried about him, and still upset that Brownie hadn't been found.

The search team had located the site where he'd fallen, marked a trail of broken bushes and dislodged rocks, and found the rifle caught in a branch. But no sign of Brownie. After four days, the official search had been scaled back, and now only Sam's dad, Uncle Gene and Jacko were going in whenever they could, along with a few other locals, hunters and the like, who knew the area. They were even heading out again this afternoon, after lunch, and not even Sam's sisters had protested. Everyone knew how important it was to keep on looking.

But it'd been nine days now. Sam's dad had already sat him down and broken it to him that the chances of finding Brownie alive were pretty much nil. Falling from that height, he would have been badly hurt on the way down, and if he'd gone into the river, which everyone agreed he must have, he would have been too injured to swim. The search was now concentrating on the river because that's where they expected to find, well, his body. Trouble was, it was almost inaccessible in parts, so it might take a while. Sam's dad had hugged him, said he was sorry, and he knew how sad Sam must feel.

Sam couldn't tell him that the only emotion he felt was shame. He'd got so angry with Brownie for what he'd seen then as a betrayal. But wasn't Sam the one who'd let his best mate down? Brownie might have kept his problems from him, but in return Sam hadn't bothered to take a good, hard look, or ask questions that might lead to answers he didn't want to hear. He'd ignored everything that might ruffle the surface of his comfortable, easy life. And then he'd forced Brownie to run away, when what he *should* have done is said he'd support him. He should have promised to stick by his mate, stand up for him, rally help around him. It was Sam's fault that Brownie was probably dead.

Deano had talked to Casey Marshall, and hadn't been seen since, though apparently he was OK. Helping the police with their enquiries — that's what Casey had said. Thing is no one knew exactly what they were enquiring into. 'All very black ops,' as Uncle Gene put it. He also muttered about Devon's woo-wah or something, but Sam wasn't really listening. Because what did he care? What did it matter what Brownie had been into? He was out of it permanently now.

'Sam, can you carry these out to the serving tables?'

His mum, holding a huge dish of potatoes, looking hot and harassed. The community hall had no air-conditioning and it was twenty-five degrees already outside. People had started trickling in as early as ten-thirty and it'd been hard juggling the cooking with showing people to seats and getting them water and sparkling grape juice — Sam had to explain over and over that there was no alcohol, and Corinna even had to confiscate a Coke bottle filled with Jim Beam. Plus, there were quite a few families with kids, which surprised Sam, but his mum told him there were more people in Gabriel's Bay than he might expect who struggled at Christmas. Sam felt bad, like he should have known this, but he was a bit relieved, too. He'd been expecting a bunch of crusty old people, like Ngaire Bourke, who was one of the first to arrive but who kept getting up again and going outside to smoke. She looked like a raisin that had been rolled in grey ash. And her cough made him feel ill.

Sam ferried roast potatoes to the line of trestle tables, where Mr Weston stood guard. He'd turned up unexpectedly and asked to help, which had caused Sam's mum and Corinna to exchange a look. They had enough cooks, so they put him on serving duty. He had on a frilled apron like the kind Sam had seen Jacko Reid wearing. On Jacko, it didn't look ridiculous.

'Ah, potatoes!' said Mr Weston, like they were some magic vegetable.

'Yup,' said Sam.

'And what is the allocation for each person?'

Sam blinked, managed to decode. 'Dunno. I'll ask.'

'Good lad,' said Mr Weston.

Yeah, like Brownie's dad was a good guy, thought Sam.

More kids in the doorway. Two of them, holding hands. Wait, was that—?

'Madison?'

Sam squatted down. 'You OK?'

She looked knackered, her face, clothes and shoes all covered in dust and grime. And the little dude holding tight to her hand wasn't much cleaner.

'Reuben and I are going to see Sidney,' she announced. 'But we're very thirsty, so we decided to stop here first. Could we have some water?'

'Of course!'

Sam straightened up, took her hand, and the three of them became a small human chain. He led them to the water cooler, poured them a plastic cup each and then two more, as the first lot disappeared with hardly a glug.

'Madison, why aren't you at home?' he said.

'There's no one there,' she told him. 'I need Sidney to find my mum.'

Shit, really? Her mum was missing on *Christmas*?

'Corinna, Ms Marshall's in the kitchen,' said Sam. 'I should go get her.'

'No!'

Madison looked as if she was about to cry. 'I want Sidney,' she said. 'Sidney!'

'OK, OK.' Sam got out his mobile. 'I'll call her now.'

Chapter 42

Kerry

Sidney's mobile rang right when she was at a crucial moment with the gravy.

'I'll step in,' Kerry offered.

He took the wooden spoon, and set about beating lumps into submission.

'Mu-um, when's the food coming?' Aidan stuck his head around the door. 'We're *starving.*'

'Your mother's on the phone,' Kerry told him. 'Have another breadstick.'

Caught up in the mania of Christmas Eve food shopping, he'd thrown boxes of the things into his shopping trolley, along with some of that cheese with fruit bits that smelled and looked like a vomit terrine, and a dry panettone which would end up, he knew even at the time, being thrown out on the back lawn for the birds. On the plus side, he *had* managed to snaffle the last box of scorched almonds, and his credit card hadn't been declined. Roll on gainful employment and a salary.

Sidney re-entered the kitchen.

'I have to go.'

He saw her white face, dropped the wooden spoon in the roasting tray.

'My God, what's happened?'

She threw off his attempt to embrace her. 'No time to explain. I have to go!'

'Where?'

'Community hall.' She was heading for the front door. 'Feed the boys. And yourself. I'll be back.'

'No, no, no.' Kerry hurried after her.

'We'll come, too,' he said. 'The food will keep. I'll bring the breadsticks to keep the boys from expiring.'

Gratitude vied with doubt on Sidney's face.

'OK, but I can't wait. You walk down and meet me down there in ten.'

'Roger that,' said Kerry. 'I'll scramble the troops right away.'

Miraculously, his tactic of telling the boys they were on a top-secret rescue mission not only got them moving without protest, but also, as it transpired, wasn't an outright lie. When they arrived at the hall, Sidney was sitting with Madison and Reuben in a corner, while nearby stood Corinna Marshall, speaking in a terse manner to an unknown party on the phone.

'Madison woke up to find no one home,' Sidney explained.

'On Christmas *Day*?'

Sidney stroked the girl's hair. 'But it's all right. Ms Marshall has found mum. She'll be here shortly.'

'And?' Kerry slid his eyes to Reuben, busy with a plate of food balanced precariously in his lap.

'Corinna's sorted that, too.' She lowered her voice. 'Apparently *someone* didn't mention that they were going on a walk, and his poor sister has been beside herself. Corinna's organised a ride home for him.'

'Mum, can we have some of the food?'

Watching forty-odd people, including other children, tucking into turkey and all the trimmings had been too much for Aidan. Breadsticks were a poor substitute.

'Go and ask Sam.'

Sidney pointed at the line of tables where volunteers, including Sam and, to Kerry's astonishment, Bernard, were waiting for anyone who wanted seconds. Aidan and Rory sprinted over, and were duly given a plate each, piled with food.

'They'll still eat what we have at home,' said Sidney. 'And, yes, I do worm them.'

Then she said, 'Oh, God. Here she is.'

'Mum!'

Madison jumped up, ran to her mother, threw her arms around a waist no wider than an HB pencil. Dear Lord, there was more flesh on the turkey bones Aidan and Rory had already sucked clean. Kerry had never actually met Olivia, only Rick. However, he trusted Sidney's judgement that the woman did not eat actual food, but was preserving herself in a solution of alcohol and bile.

Kerry became aware that Sidney was on her feet, vibrating with fury.

'I'm going to kill her,' she said. 'I am going to punch her *clean* into next week.'

He could empathise fully with this sentiment, but he didn't want her arrested for inciting a fracas. He stood beside her, wondering how best to manage the situation. In her current mood, she might punch *him*.

'You don't know what happened,' he ventured, preparing to duck. 'There might be a very good reason.'

'For leaving a nine-year-old child alone? And on Christmas *morning*?'

'OK, no,' he agreed. 'No, there can never be a good reason for that.'

Corinna marched past them, and Sidney made to follow, but Kerry, having seen Corinna's expression, gently restrained her.

'Let Corinna deal with it,' he suggested. 'She looks in no mood to compromise.'

Sidney was still battling her fury, but seemed to accept that Corinna was better qualified to deal with Olivia. Besides, there was always the chance that *Corinna* might punch Olivia into next week.

From what they could see, Corinna's conversation with Olivia was brief, terse and primarily one-way. Olivia had her head bowed, but the angle of her body suggested a schoolgirl in the headmistress's office, who'd been caught bang to rights on an expulsion-level offence but was still attempting to preserve some semblance of 'up yours' defiance. Kerry thought of Sophie Barton. His drink with her had been enjoyable enough, but he'd been very aware that her hackles needed only the minutest excuse to rise. He hoped that Olivia and Sophie would never meet. The fabric of the universe would be but damp tissue in the face of their combined resentment.

At the conversation's end, Corinna bent and spoke to Madison, who shook her head and held tightly to her mother. Corinna hesitated before straightening up and making a motion with her hands as if she was wiping dirt from them. And then Olivia scuttled out of the hall, Madison still attached to her waist. Kerry heard Sidney gasp.

Corinna marched back. If she were in a children's cartoon, she'd be frying unwary bystanders with lasers from her eyes.

'Olivia was up at Rainer's cottage,' she told them. 'Christmas Eve drinks. Had a bit too much, slept there instead. Came back to the house, she swears at half-eight, to find Madison gone.'

Corinna puffed a breath in and out, to keep control. 'Thing is, I know she *wasn't* back at half-eight because that was Casey on the phone just before. Olivia and Rainer were both turfed out of bed at ten by the police.'

'What? Olivia and *Rainer*?' said Sidney.

'Not to mention the police,' said Kerry.

'Only recent,' said Corinna. 'Elke's left him; I bumped into her last week. She reckons they're both just doing it to get back at Rick. Not that he gives a shit, the slimy turd. He's too busy plotting his next money-making move — no doubt a Ponzi scheme targeting recently bereaved old people.'

'And — the police?' said Kerry. 'Apologies for finding that the most interesting part of this conversation.'

'Raided the vineyard,' said Corinna. 'It was being used as a drug-storage facility by the local gang, several members of which were caught with the goods.'

'Another dodgy Rick scheme?' said Sidney.

Corinna shrugged. 'Soon find out. Police picked him up in Hampton an hour ago.'

Kerry suddenly became aware of little pitchers in close proximity, eyes wide, big ears flapping.

'How about you take Reuben to get some of that meringue concoction?' he said to Aidan and Rory. They didn't need telling twice.

'What about Madison?' Sidney said urgently to Corinna. 'She can't stay with that *evil* woman. She *can't*.'

Kerry put his arm around her shoulder, but she remained rigid as a fence post.

'Madison only cares that she's with her mother.' Corinna clearly shared Sidney's view on the desirability of that arrangement. 'I can take steps, report Olivia for leaving a child unsupervised, but what will that serve? Madison is happier with her mother than without. That's the truth of it.'

'But she didn't even buy her any *presents*,' Sidney almost wailed.

'She says she did, that they're in a cupboard,' said Corinna.

'And, to be honest, even if she's lying, Maddie will find some way to forgive her.'

'I can't bear it,' said Sidney. 'If Rick ends up in the slammer, she'll *have* to get custody.'

'Yes, well, there are a few steps that still need to be taken.' Corinna held Sidney's eye. 'I'll advocate for Madison, you can be sure of that.'

A cough behind them. A man Kerry didn't know, but Corinna did, unless she greeted every stranger with a hug and a kiss on both cheeks.

'This is Niko,' she introduced him. 'He runs a buddy scheme in Hampton. I've asked him to take Reuben home.'

She pointed him towards Reuben, who was in a huddle at the end of the serving table with Aidan and Rory, clutching an empty paper plate and licking cream off his arm.

As Niko headed in that direction, Kerry squeezed Sidney's shoulder. This time she was more like a rag doll. All the fight had gone out of her.

It was bizarre — he should have been making soothing noises, but all he really wanted to do was yell out loud with joy. What a fantastic human being she was — a principled fighter, overflowing with care and love. How *blessed* was he?

Kerry raised his eyes to whatever deity was in session today, and offered up a quick prayer of thanks to him or her. Almost certainly her, which meant he would have to work harder than he ever had — no slacking or regressing — to be worthy.

'Come on,' he said, kissing his fighter's temple. 'Let's go home and feed the boys fourths. I'll organise it, all you need to do is relax with a nice glass of red. And then Aidan, Rory and I will do the washing up.'

His joy abounded anew when Sidney attempted a smile.

'My God,' she said. 'I think that's the most erotic thing a man's ever said to me.'

Aidan and Rory ran up at a speed Kerry considered inadvisable considering how much food they'd consumed.

'Ready, boys?'

'Yes!' They punched the air.

'Know what you're ready for?' Kerry enquired. 'Just checking.'

'Christmas dinner!'

'Good answer,' said Kerry. 'Let's get home and get stuck in.'

Chapter 43

Mac

Mac knew Jacko was going to be late. He'd contacted her four hours ago, on one of the portable radios they'd been using to compensate for, in Jacko's words, 'the craphouse mobile coverage' in the area. Said they'd found Barrett's pack and it looked like the food the lads had said they'd all packed had been eaten.

'Someone else?' she suggested. 'An animal?'

Someone else would have taken the whole pack; it was expensive and had good gear in it — brand-new sleeping bag and a bunch of stuff amateurs always feel compelled to buy at Kathmandu. And an animal wouldn't have peeled the wrapper off a protein bar and shoved it in the front pocket. Probably.

'Why'd he ditch the pack?' Mac had asked. 'If it had good gear in it.'

'Weight?' said Jacko. 'If he's injured, maybe he just couldn't carry it anymore.'

'Hell,' said Mac. 'Do you think he really could be alive?'

'We've got a much narrower search area now, so it won't be long until we know.'

'One way or the other' hung in the air, as Mac ended the call.

Jacko was exhausted — all the men were, but *they* hadn't been out in the bush for two weeks already. He came home and usually crashed right away, too tired to eat. Got up again the next day and headed out. Though she tried not to, Mac kept thinking of the story of folklore hero, John Henry, who with only a hammer beat a new drill machine to break through a mountain of rock, only to have his heart give out on the other side.

But what could she do? A young man they all knew was missing, and Jacko, Gene and Wyatt were determined to find him. Even if it meant going out on Christmas Day.

Jacko usually cooked the Christmas meal, but it had been Mac this year who'd butterflied the lamb, peeled the potatoes and trimmed the beans. She'd even made gravy, following Jacko's special recipe, which had a dash of applesauce. He'd originally aimed to be back by six — it *was* Christmas, after all — but now, she wouldn't expect him home before nine. Emma and Harry had both rung from overseas. They agreed their dad was a nutter, but he was a heroic nutter so more power to him. They both told Mac he'd be fine.

She checked her watch yet again. Eight-fifteen. Television would be dire — endlessly repeated movies or royal variety shows, most likely. She considered pouring a third glass of wine, rejected it as idiotic. She wanted to be awake when Jacko came home not sprawled on the couch, chin covered in drool.

An engine outside, rumbling. Thud as a car door closed. Footsteps pounded up the wooden steps onto the porch. The front door crashed open.

Gene, grim-faced, saying, 'They've got him. He's in the chopper, on his way to ICU.'

Mac burst into tears, sobbed into her hands.

'I knew it,' she said, not caring that she was wiping snot everywhere. 'His bloody heart, I *knew* it.'

'What are you on about?' said Gene. 'Whose heart?'

'Hey . . .'

Mac found herself being enveloped in arms that were entirely familiar.

'It's all right,' said her not-dead husband. 'He's going to be OK.'

'I thought he meant *you-ou*.' Mac's sobs made her hiccup. But she was past the point of trying to avoid embarrassment.

'Me?' Jacko held her by the shoulders, peered down into her face. 'You thought *I* was being carted off to hospital?'

'Oops,' said Gene, quietly.

Mac nodded.

'Dear, oh dear.' Jacko drew her back into a hug. 'Why didn't you bloody *say* you were that worried?'

Mac rested her head on his chest, listened to the beat of a big, strong heart, cursed herself for being a soft-headed moron.

'I was going to see the Doc next week, anyway,' said Jacko.

Mac tensed. 'What for?'

'Knee's been playing up.'

'I hate you,' said Mac.

Jacko laughed. 'Can we go sit down now?' he said. 'I am *completely* bloody rooted.'

Chapter 44

Sam

Going into Brownie's hospital room, Sam met Doc Love coming out. Had there been a setback? Why was he here?

'Sam,' the Doc nodded.

'Everything OK?'

'Remarkably so.'

Doc Love smiled and patted Sam's arm, a gesture that said the older man understood his concern but he had no need to worry. Mind you, Doc Love always made you feel like that. He was the human equivalent of a cup of hot Milo.

Brownie was sitting up, propped on pillows. His face still showed yellow-purple traces of Sam's fists, along with a bunch of new bruises and grazes, and one arm was in a cast. He'd broken it in the fall, and sustained multiple fractures to other bones, including his right foot and his ribs, which must still hurt like hell. Amazingly, he hadn't snapped a leg bone, or smacked his head. Brownie's recollections of the actual journey off the cliff were muzzy, being mainly, as he put it, a screaming blur. After stepping off the edge, he'd landed face-down but feet-first on the rocky slope like a failed base-jumper, and slid as if on a scree luge to the bush-line, where several conveniently placed trees slowed him down, while knocking what was left of the wind out of him and, for good measure, cracking a few more bones. Gravity, Brownie said, is a bitch.

The bush stopped him moving well before he landed in the river, and he'd lain on the ground for ages, trying to work out if he was dead or just wanted to be, to stop everything hurting. Then he crawled deeper into the bush, and kept on crawling, though he had no idea where he was headed.

'Why didn't you stay where you landed?' Sam had asked.

'Because my brain was addled,' said Brownie. 'Pain and panic are a really potent combination. I kept thinking I heard wolves coming after me, and my only thought was to get away, keep going, keep hiding. That's why I dumped the pack; I freaked out that it was slowing me down. I got this close to stripping naked, too, shedding the last of the excess weight, only it hurt too much to take my clothes off. And after a while, it hurt too much to do anything. So I stopped moving and just — waited for the wolves . . .'

That's how Jacko, Dad, Uncle Gene and two other hunters found him on Christmas Day, dehydrated, starving and incoherent with pain. They carried him for miles on a camp stretcher to the nearest clearing, where the rescue helicopter was waiting to pick him up and fly him to Hampton Hospital.

The peace provided by caring medical staff, a soft bed and strong painkillers had been temporary. Day after Boxing Day, according to Uncle Gene, the police had come, the big guns, drug squad, and interviewed him. Sam didn't know what that meant, and part of him wanted to stay ignorant. But that wouldn't cut it. Not anymore.

'Doc Love came to update me on Dad.'

It was as if Brownie knew what Sam was working up to ask, and wanted to forestall him, put off the bad news as long as possible. Why not? Sam had nowhere else to be. Not yet.

'He OK?'

'He'll stay in respite care for a couple more weeks. Then the Doc's organised some home help. If I'd had to thank him, I might have cried, but fortunately' — a trace of the old Brownie — 'he refused to let me, said it was his job.'

'You know he's retiring next year?' said Sam. 'There's a new bloke starting in February.'

'All change, eh, Sam?' Brownie managed half a smile. 'You must be off soon.'

'Next week. Driving my new wheels. Well, Ms Gillespie's old shitbox Nissan.'

Brownie's room had a tree outside it. An oak, Sam thought it was. Planted by people who believed they could control this new country, make it theirs. The need to feel connected — to family, roots, land — it was so strong, wasn't it? Made people do all kinds of things, good and not so much.

'What about you?' he said. 'What's going to happen?'

Brownie winced, as if the question was painful. Or he was embarrassed — hard to tell.

'Don't know,' he said. 'Powers that be are still deciding. There could be mitigating circumstances around my involvement — I acted under duress, I've given them helpful information, that kind of thing. But whether I go free or go to jail, I'm screwed. The people I worked for don't compose inspirational quotes about forgiveness.'

'What about Deano? Will they come after him, too?'

'Always looking out for us, aren't you, Sam?' said Brownie, with a half-smile. 'No one left behind.'

Sam's immediate reaction to that wrong-headed praise was anger — with himself, but it managed to come out like he was angry at Brownie.

'Don't take the piss!'

'I'm not.' Brownie's smile vanished. 'Believe me, I'm not. You've been a good mate, Sam. One of the best.'

'If I'd been a good mate, you would have trusted me enough to ask for my help.'

'Is that what you think?' Brownie said it softly. 'Is that why you were so worked up on the mountain?'

'Yeah.' Sam couldn't quite meet his eye. 'Kind of. Yeah.'

'Right . . .' Brownie nodded.

'Sammo,' he said. 'Has it ever occurred to you that I didn't tell you because I didn't want you involved?'

OK, so that seemed reasonable, and Sam's initial reaction was that he'd been stupid not to figure it out. But then he checked in with what the more grown-up part of his brain was telling him: that there'd been a time when Brownie wasn't involved in anything.

'Maybe,' said Sam. 'But you could have reached out before you got caught up with these arseholes. You *know* we would have helped — Mum and Dad love you. If you'd needed money, you only had to ask. Why didn't you?'

'Sammo, Sammo, Sammo . . .' Brownie was shaking his head, slowly. 'It sounds so obvious, doesn't it? Got money trouble? Hit up friends and family! Everyone will help because they care.'

'They *do* care!' Sam felt like Brownie was denying it.

'That's right, they do,' said Brownie. 'They'll give even when they can't afford to. Even when they're struggling to meet their own responsibilities. They'll give until it hurts because they care. Did you really think I could ask that of the people I love?'

Sam took the point. And Brownie and Ed had obviously needed more than a few bucks to tide them over.

'Besides, I have a stupid amount of pride,' Brownie went on. 'Mum's big thing was always for me to stand on my own two feet, take responsibility. If I made a mess, literally or figuratively, I had to clean it up. She hated excuses.'

Sam heard Millie's voice: 'Don't complain. Don't explain . . .'

'Yeah, but your mum wouldn't have wanted you to get in trouble like this,' he said.

The half-smile that wasn't really a smile at all.

'Stupid pride, Sam. I thought I could control things. I couldn't. I'm—' His voice began to crack, and he turned his head away. 'I'm sorry . . .'

Sam didn't know what to do. Brownie was crying? Maybe? It was hard to tell. He could hug him, but there was that pride thing. And the bloke thing, too, of course, couldn't forget that. He searched for something, anything, else to look at, locked onto the flowers on the bedside table, which were a *really* sickly marshmallow pink.

'It'll be OK,' he said, knowing it sounded like crap but *wanting* to believe it.

'It won't, Sam,' said Brownie, voice firm again. 'I fucked up too badly. But *your* life's going to be great.'

Sam forced himself to meet his friend's eye. It was the least he could do.

'We're all on your side,' were the only comforting words he could come up with. 'And we'll help in any way we can.'

'I know,' said Brownie. 'I'm grateful.'

It was time for Sam to go. They both knew it.

'Can you do me one favour, Sam?'

'Sure,' Sam said hastily, hoping he wouldn't regret it.

'Can you tell Mrs Reid I'm sorry about the alarm? Given everything, she probably thinks I did it on purpose. I didn't. Unlike the rest of my actions, that was an unintentional fuck-up. Just a common-or-garden regular mistake.'

'I'll tell her,' said Sam. 'But I think she probably knows.'

Brownie nodded. He held out the hand not in the cast. His left, which made shaking it kind of awkward.

'See ya,' said Sam.

'Of course,' said Brownie, with a solemn nod.

As Sam steered his new wheels out of the hospital car park, he realised they'd forgotten to wish each other Happy New Year. That was his next stop — the Boat Shed, where all his family and friends were getting ready for a New Year's Eve shindig, which they'd decided would double as his going-away party.

Lest auld acquaintance be forgot — was that the last he'd see of his friend?

No, bugger that, he told himself. If you want something bad enough, then you'll find ways to make it happen. And even if you're dreaming, and it's impossible, isn't it better that you at least gave it a go?

Epilogue

the dog

The dog loved parties. People spilled food on the floor, or left their paper plates too near the table edge, where they could be easily dislodged with a nudge of the nose. Many people were happy to feed the dog directly, particularly children, and also adults who'd had a few drinks. 'Aw, look at those big puppy eyes,' they'd say and toss it some steak fat or a roast potato.

It disliked raisins, but pretty much anything else qualified as food. It had even managed to hoover up the unclaimed sweets from the lolly scramble held earlier that day. The dog had observed that the children unwrapped their Fruit Bursts and Minties, but having consumed, on past occasions, milk cartons, birthday candles and plastic hose fittings, the dog was hardly going to be bothered by small squares of waxed paper.

There were no children to give it food at this party. They were all at the Master and Mistress's home, being looked after by two of Devon's cousins, who were old enough to babysit but too young to go out drinking. Devon had decided to spend his New Year's Eve with the Master and his friends. 'At my place, New Year's goes on for days,' he said. 'I won't miss out.'

The dog knew all the adults here. It knew them because of the way they smelled. In fact, everyone had multiple smells, which the dog mentally placed in order of appeal. It was now sitting beside the Master (roast meat and cigarette smoke, though he hadn't smelled of the latter for at least a week). The Master fondled the dog's ears, but no food was forthcoming from his other hand. The dog couldn't see the Mistress nearby, but that didn't mean she couldn't see it and the Master. The Mistress was ever vigilant. The dog wagged its tail and moved on.

'Here's trouble. In a hairy fat suit.'

The Master's best human friend, Gene (sausage rolls and black coffee), and Kerry, the cheerful man with red hair (jam toast and milky tea).

'Perhaps King should be the Gabriel's Bay tourist attraction?' Kerry said. 'The amazing bottomless dog. Like one of those Welsh caves, in canine form.'

'You backing out on Littleville?' said Gene. 'Realised it's going to be too much to handle with a full-time job?'

'I am not! Mainly because I've managed to recruit a new project leader. Well, in fact, *he* offered. I would never have thought of it otherwise.'

'Oh, yeah? Who?'

Kerry pointed to another part of the Boat Shed. The dog decided to head in that direction. It had noticed that both men had empty plates.

Here was a larger group. The bespectacled, bearded man (All Bran and old books), the grey-haired lady in Victorian dress (whisky and feathers), the young woman with rainbow hair (cupcakes and nail-polish remover), and her boyfriend who worked at the video store (identically cut carrot sticks and Spray'n'Wipe). They were gathered around Doc Love (shortbread and enamel paint), who immediately cemented his position as one of the dog's favourites by dropping it some shredded chicken.

'But will we still have our games?' the older lady was saying. 'I can't let Titus Phipps's last victory go unchallenged.'

'Of course,' said Doc Love. 'One of the perks of my new appointment will be a spare set of keys to the barn.'

'I'd better remember to give Tinker a lift,' said the older lady. 'He fell asleep at the wheel the other day. The car was still in his driveway, but nonetheless.'

'What can you tell us about the new doctor?' said the rainbow girl. 'Is he handsome? That's important, you know.'

'I'm flattered you think so, Peg,' said Doc Love, with a smile.

He turned and brought someone behind him into the group. It was the Mistress (Krispies and soap). She glared at the dog, still angry at something it had done. Or possibly many things.

'Here's Mac,' said Doc Love. 'She can tell you all about young Doctor Ghadavi . . .'

But the dog did not linger. Deeming it prudent to put a good distance between its rear and the Mistress's foot, it ran through the kitchen and out the back door.

On the steps were Devon (horse dung and horses), and Sam (Weetbix and sawdust).

'Hey, Kingy,' said Devon.

There was a half-eaten sausage-in-bread on Devon's plate, and a dollop of potato salad on Sam's. The dog lay down between the two of them, and waited. The beach and tussock stretched out in front, down to the glittery line of sea. If there were no leftovers, the dog might go down and hunt for rotten fish.

'Haven't you ever wanted to leave here?' Sam asked Devon. 'I mean, you know, it's pretty special on a day like today, but . . .'

'Gotta finish my study,' said Devon. 'No point until then.'

He kneaded the velvety spot behind the dog's ear.

'Sorry about your mate,' he said to Sam. 'I used to think . . .

I dunno. Sometimes the shadows in people are more sad than bad. If you know what I mean?'

'Yeah, kind of,' said Sam. 'Best not to let either get hold of you, eh?'

'Ain't that the truth.'

The two young men stared out towards the sea. The dog was just considering taking advantage of their inattention when Devon got to his feet, scooped up the two paper plates.

'Dessert?' he said to Sam. 'Jacko's made trifle with a shitload of alcohol. Might have to breathalyse the old folk on their way out.'

'Yeah, why not . . .'

Sam stepped over the dog, followed Devon back through the kitchen.

The dog had a choice: a chance of rotten fish on the beach or a certainty of trifle inside.

It had always liked custard. It went inside.

The dog fell in behind a queue of women at the dessert table: Sidney (honey and garden dirt), the woman police officer (avocado and Tiger Balm) and her sister (green tea and wet wipes), plus Sam's mother (fruit yoghurt and glitter glue) and his auntie (ditto).

'I'm sending my file, such as it is, to the new Auckland solicitor,' said the sister.

'Good riddance, eh?' said the policewoman.

'Maybe when it comes to Olivia,' said Sidney. 'But whenever I think of Maddie, I want to bawl.'

'She's OK,' said the sister. 'And I've lined up people to keep an eye on her. Any *hint* of an issue, they'll step in.'

'What's the story with Rick, Casey?' said Sam's mother.

'Can't say,' said the police officer.

Everyone accepted that without further comment. The dog was not surprised. The police officer was almost as fierce as the Mistress.

'Heard a rumour there's already a buyer for the vineyard,' said Sam's auntie.

'Better not be bloody Rob Hanrahan and his blight-the-foreshore-with-an-industrial park mates. I might have to actually kill him instead of just roughing him up.'

The Master's best human friend, Gene, had joined the women, along with Sam's dad (spicy sausage and woodsmoke), the sister's husband (also green tea and wet wipes), and cheerful Kerry.

'Getting seconds already?' said Sam's auntie, with a pointed look at Gene's belly, which was almost as round as the dog's.

'It's the holidays,' he said. 'Everyone's allowed a blow-out.'

'Well, as it's the holidays,' said Sam's dad, 'you can take a break from plotting vengeance against old Rob and his cronies. Or at least from harping on about it.'

'Not likely.' Gene slapped trifle into his bowl. 'Come next year, that bastard won't know what's hit him.'

'Is this a good time to remind you,' said the sister's husband, 'that neither Corinna nor I practise criminal law?'

'He's all talk,' said Sam's auntie. 'But if he *does* do anything stupid, you're all banned from standing him bail.'

The group moved off, leaving small splatters of cream and custard on the floor. The dog tidied them with its tongue. Then it trotted over to where the group were now seated around tables that had been pushed together. Sam and Devon had joined them. The Master and Mistress were at the other set of tables, with Doc Love and his friends. They were all chatting away, except for the bearded bespectacled man, who was staring off towards the front door.

'Poor old Bernard,' said Sidney, quietly, to her group. 'Do any of us buy his story that Patricia's gone off to nurse a sick relative?'

'No, but we won't let on, will we?' said Kerry. 'Every man deserves his dignity. Plus he fought for Littleville like a lion at evil Elaine's council meeting. We owe him.'

'He told me at the Christmas community lunch that he had no objection to the name change to Onemanawa,' said the police officer's sister.

'Wow,' said Sidney. 'He really *has* been cast low. I'm glad Mac and Jacko invited him,' she added. 'It'd be horrible to spend New Year's all alone.'

'Speaking of invitations, I'm surprised not to see Meredith and Jonty here,' said Gene. 'Or are we beneath them, now that he's better? Or worse, depending on how you look at it.'

'They're celebrating with their daughter,' said Kerry. 'And her new boyfriend. Who makes experimental video art.'

Gene chuckled. 'And who says God doesn't have a sense of humour?'

Kerry's phone began to play a tune. A loud tune.

'Begorrah, it's Ma,' he said, checking the screen. 'I'll take it outside, otherwise she'll insist on talking to everyone.'

'Say hi from me,' Sidney called after him.

As no one seemed to be interested in sending trifle its way, the dog had a short snooze. It awoke when Kerry returned.

'My parents are planning a trip out next year,' he announced. 'For all our sakes, let's pray that they're turned back at the border.'

'Hey, your phone plays "Back in Black",' said Devon. 'You like metal?'

'AC/DC are not strictly metal,' said Kerry. 'More hard rock.' He snapped his fingers. 'Which reminds me! Gad, I've been meaning to ask this for months now. Well, at least one-and-a-half. Who's the genius behind the Gabriel's Bay radio station?'

'No one knows,' said Sam's dad. 'It's a pirate frequency.'

'Most people reckon it's that recluse guy,' said Sam, 'who lives with Oksana.'

'Well, let's hope that *is* his hobby,' said Gene. 'If not, we should probably be checking the water supply more regularly.'

Second helping of trifle consumed, Gene leaned back and placed both hands on his belly, let out a satisfied 'Ahh'.

It was all right for him. The dog had been deprived of food now for a whole ten minutes.

'I'll make coffee.' Devon started to clear the paper plates and plastic cutlery. 'Then we should turn this place into a dance floor.'

'I'll give you a hand,' said Sam.

The dog saw Sam's mum and dad exchange a smile. But its interest in this group had waned. Sam and Devon were heading for the kitchen with plates laden with scraps. The dog followed and took up a position by the rubbish bin — close, but not too close, in case the Mistress should decide to pop her head in.

Through the back door, the dog saw the sky had darkened. Stars were out, and the moon, which provoked an instinct in the dog to bark. It chose not to. The Master might send it home for being a noisy dropkick.

Inside, the tables had been pushed back against the wall, and the music put on. As Devon had firmly secured the rubbish-bin lid, the dog decided to lie down beside the front door, out of the way, head on its paws, watching.

All were keen to dance but one. The bearded, bespectacled man sat alone on a chair, politely rebuffing every woman who invited him up onto the floor.

'I'm fine, really,' he told them.

But the dog could read human expressions — a necessary skill if you wanted to avoid a boot up the rear. The bearded man was not fine. He was miserable.

The dancing went on. The dog snoozed intermittently, dreaming of the moon and rotten fish, steak fat and roast potatoes. The Master's voice roused him.

'Right!' said the Master. Someone silenced the music. 'Before the witching hour's upon us, I'd like to raise a toast.'

He lifted his glass. 'To absent friends!'

'To absent friends,' everyone chorused.

'To you lot!'

'To us!'

Despite resistance from a blushing Mistress, the Master drew her into a hug.

'And to my wife! Ma Cherie Amour, the pretty one that I adore. Love of my life!'

'To Mac!' said everyone.

Kerry and Sidney were closest to the dog.

'My God, is *that* what Mac stands for?' said Kerry. 'Ma Cherie?'

'Why don't you ask her?' said Sidney.

'Ha ha, no,' said Kerry. 'Not even when she's slightly tiddly and cocooned in the rosy glow of love.'

The Master caught a nod from Devon.

'Ten!' he said.

And the countdown commenced.

At 'One! Happy New Year!', everyone began to hug and kiss. Even the bearded, bespectacled man, the dog noted, was doing his best to enter into the spirit of things, though his miserableness was still evident.

The dog detected a new smell, but a known one. Scones and library books. It was buried under another smell — Chanel No. 5, if the dog was not mistaken. The woman hesitated in the front doorway, as if unsure how to make her presence known.

But then the room went quiet.

The woman spoke.

She said, 'Bernard.'

Acknowledgements

Love and thanks to my writing group, who made this book much better: Whitney, Simon, Alisha, Meryl, Fiona, Ruby, Johnny, Libby, Redmer, Rijula and Stuart. And to my other MA in Creative Writing peeps and pub-goers, who continue to cheer me on: Pip Adam, my supervisor; Emily Perkins, my teacher; and my fellow writers, Helen C, Jackson, Justine, Nick, Helen H and Louise C, and poets Sarah, Louise W, Nina, Jane, Sam and Alex.

Huge thanks to Jasmyn Pearson of Pūmanawa Consultants, who reviewed my use of te reo Māori and gave me some excellent advice.

Thanks to Harriet and Margaret, and the team at Penguin Random House New Zealand, and my agent, Gaia Banks, who always makes me feel like I'm her favourite writer, even though she represents authors who are vastly more successful.

A shout-out to Matt at Lambanjo, Seatoun, and his dog, the late, much missed King, who ruled the neighbourhood.

And thanks to New Zealand for providing such great material.

Winner of the Nelson Public Libraries' Award for NZ Fiction 2015

Rich in myth, mystery, warmth and wit —
a touching novel about what it means to be alive.

When April Turner's small son is killed by a car, she decides she is no longer entitled to anything but the barest existence. Five years on, she has shed everything and everyone she loves, and expects to be this way for ever. Then a letter arrives from an English solicitor, informing April that she is the last surviving heir to Empyrean, a long-abandoned country house.

At first, April resists. But with the letter comes a map full of tiny mysteries, and she is drawn all the way from New Zealand to the English countryside, and into a small but intriguing circle of people: musician Oran, who remains loyal to his faithless wife; Jack, who lives wild in the woods with a dog; and Sunny, Lady Day, approaching ninety but more vital than others half her age.

Sunny knew Empyrean in its prime, and her stories bring the past to life. But will April be prepared to give up her principles and start coming alive again herself?

A romping chick-lit with heart-ache, misunderstandings, travel and love.

No one knows 'happy endings' like romance novelist Darrell Kincaid. She's delivered eight of them to her readers with pleasure. But it's not to be with book number nine. In the act of adding the final full stop, Darrell has a revelation: it's not the ending that really matters but what comes next. Darrell now sees that when her husband Tom died (twenty-one months and three days ago, but who's counting?), she lost more than the man she loved. She lost her own 'happy ever after'. The life she expected to live has gone, vanished forever in a puff of fickle, unfair smoke.

Darrell knows she has a choice. She can stay in New Zealand and live a half-life, or she can leave in search of something — perhaps someone — else. So Darrell decides upon London, the least romantic capital she knows (why set yourself up for disappointment?). Armed with Nancy Mitford's *Love In A Cold Climate* as her guide to proper Englishness and the ideal romantic hero, she sets out to live the sweet second life she deserves.

The entertaining companion novel to the best-selling The Sweet Second Life of Darrell Kincaid.

Michelle Lawrence's perfect life has been just as she's designed it. But then her husband, Chad, ruins everything by taking a job in San Francisco, about as far from their comfortable family home as it's possible to get without actually emigrating. Up until now, Chad's primary focus has been keeping her happy, and Michelle can see no good reason why this should change.

But change it has, and Michelle now has to deal with Chad's increasing detachment, while building a new life with her two small children in a place filled with cat-eating coyotes. On top of that, Michelle's oldest friend is turning against marriage while her newest is a little too obsessed with clean taps. And down the redwood-lined street, there's Aishe Herne, a woman who could pick a fight with a silent order of nuns. Aishe has designed her own kind of perfect life, in which there's room for her, her teenage son and no one else. But when cousin Patrick lands in town like a Cockney nemesis, both Aishe and Michelle must begin determined campaigns to regain their grip on the steering wheel of their lives.

Another entertaining novel from this internationally published writer, about tangled relationships, misunderstandings and truculent toddlers.

When Charlotte Fforbes inadvertently falls in love with her boss, her usually cool self-control is tested to its limit. Thus far, Charlotte has carefully avoided love's emotional tar pit, but suddenly she is in it up to her neck. Her first strategy is to ignore it — for one thing, boss Patrick is a husband and father.

Then Charlotte is given a clue that Patrick's marriage may not be as stable as believed, and that is enough to fan a spark of hope into an infatuation-fuelled inferno. Transformed from efficient PA into a woman whose reason has been muffled with duct-tape and locked in a cellar, she'll now do anything to find a way into Patrick's heart.

Anything includes arranging to be nanny-for-a-month to the small children of Patrick and his wife and two other families at a Lake Como villa. Charlotte's complete lack of child-minding experience daunts her the least. If she's to win Patrick, she must also prevent his cousin's wife being seduced by her charming, feckless ex, while fending off dogs, Gypsy gatecrashers and a large, vengeful ghost from Patrick's past.

But Charlotte's biggest test will come when she is forced to question whether her affections have been entirely misplaced — and, if so, was this her last ever chance to feel love like this again?